SKYSCRAPER

What Reviewers Say About Gun Brooke's Work

Ice Queen

"I'm a sucker for a story about a single mother and in this case, it really adds depth to Susanna's character. The conflict that threatens Susanna and Aislin's future isn't a convoluted series of events. It's the insecurities they each bring into the relationship that they're forced to acknowledge and deal with. To me this felt authentic. The book is a quick read with plenty of spice…"—*Lesbian Review*

Treason

"The adventure was edge-of-your-seat levels of gripping and exciting…I really enjoyed this final addition to the Exodus series and particularly liked the ending. As always it was a very well written book."—Melina Bickard, Librarian, Waterloo Library (UK)

Insult to Injury

"This novel tugged at my heart all the way, much the same way as *Coffee Sonata*. It's a story of new beginnings, of rediscovering oneself, of trusting again (both others and oneself)."—*Jude in the Stars*

"If you love a good, slow-burn romantic novel, then grab this book."—*Rainbow Reflections*

Wayworn Lovers

"*Wayworn Lovers* is a super dramatic, angsty read, very much in line with Brooke's other contemporary romances. …I'm definitely in the 'love them' camp."—*Lesbian Review*

Thorns of the Past

"I loved the romance between Darcy and Sabrina and the story really carried it well, with each of them learning that they have a safe haven with the other."—*Lesbian Review*

Escape: Exodus Book Three

"I've been a keen follower of the Exodus series for a while now and I was looking forward to the latest installment. It didn't disappoint. The action was edge-of-your-seat thrilling, especially towards the end, with several threats facing the Exodus mission. Some very intriguing subplots were introduced, and I look forward to reading more about these in the next book."—Melina Bickard, Librarian, Waterloo Library, London (UK)

Pathfinder

"I love Gun Brooke. She has successfully merged two of my reading loves: lesfic and sci-fi."—*Inked Rainbow Reads*

"I found the characters very likable and the plot compelling. I loved watching their relationship grow. From their first meeting, they're impressed and intrigued by each other. This matures into an easy friendship, and from there into dancing, kisses, and more. …I'm looking forward to seeing the rest of the series!"—*All Our Worlds: Diverse Fantastic Fiction*

Soul Unique

"Yet another success from Gun Brooke. The premise is interesting, the leads are likeable and the supporting characters are well-developed. The first person narrative works well, and I really enjoyed reading about a character with Asperger's."—Melina Bickard, Librarian, Waterloo Library (London)

Advance: Exodus Book One

"*Advance* is an exciting space adventure, hopeful even through times of darkness. The romance and action are balanced perfectly, interesting the audience as much in the fleet's mission as in Dael and Spinner's romance. I'm looking forward to the next book in the series!"—*All Our Worlds: Diverse Fantastic Fiction*

The Blush Factor

"Gun Brooke captures very well the two different 'worlds' the two main characters live in and folds this setting neatly into the story. So, if you are looking for a well-edited, multi-layered romance with engaging characters this is a great read and maybe a re-read for those days when comfort food is a must."—*Lesbians on the Loose*

The Supreme Constellations Series

"*Protector of the Realm* has it all; sabotage, corruption, erotic love and exhilarating space fights. Gun Brooke's second novel is forceful with a winning combination of solid characters and a brilliant plot. The book exemplifies her growth as inventive storyteller and is sure to garner multiple awards in the coming year."—*Just About Write*

"[*Protector of the Realm*] is first and foremost a romance, and whilst it has action and adventure, it is the romance that drives it. The book moves along at a cracking pace, and there is much happening throughout to make it a good page-turner. The action sequences are very well done, and make for an adrenaline rush."
—*Lesbian Review*

Fierce Overture

"Gun Brooke creates memorable characters, and Noelle and Helena are no exception. Each woman is 'more than meets the eye' as each exhibits depth, fears, and longings. And the sexual tension between them is real, hot, and raw."—*Just About Write*

September Canvas

"In this character-driven story, trust is earned and secrets are uncovered. Deanna and Faythe are fully fleshed out and prove to the reader each has much depth, talent, wit and problem-solving abilities. *September Canvas* is a good read with a thoroughly satisfying conclusion."—*Just About Write*

Sheridan's Fate—*Lambda Literary Award Finalist*

"Sheridan's fire and Lark's warm embers are enough to make this book sizzle. Brooke, however, has gone beyond the wonderful emotional explorations of these characters to tell the story of those who, for various reasons, become differently-abled. Whether it is a bullet, an illness, or a problem at birth, many women and men find themselves in Sheridan's situation. Her courage and Lark's gentleness and determination send this romance into a 'must read.'"—*Just About Write*

Coffee Sonata

"If you enjoy a good love story, a great setting, and wonderful characters, look for *Coffee Sonata* at your favorite gay and lesbian bookstore."—*MegaScene*

"Award-winning author Gun Brooke has given us another delightful romance with *Coffee Sonata*. I was so totally immersed in this story that I read it in one sitting."—*Just About Write*

"Each of these characters is intriguing, attractive and likeable, but they are heartbreaking, too, as the reader soon learns when their pasts and their deeply buried secrets are slowly and methodically revealed. Brooke does not give the reader predictable plot points, but builds a fascinating set of subplots and surprises around the romances."—*L-word.com Literature*

Course of Action

"Brooke's words capture the intensity of their growing relationship. Her prose throughout the book is breathtaking and heart-stopping. Where have you been hiding, Gun Brooke? I, for one, would like to see more romances from this author."—*Independent Gay Writer*

"When we first picked up this book we glanced at the author's profile and upon finding that Gun Brooke lives in Sweden wondered how on earth she could write a believable story centered around something as American as Hollywood. But, she did it, and did it big. …You can't put this book down. Brooke's ability to weave a story through her characters has us anxiously waiting for her next effort."—*Family and Friends Magazine*

"Brooke gets to the core of her characters' emotions and vulnerabilities and points out their strengths and weaknesses in very human terms."—*Just About Write*

"The setting created by Brooke is a glimpse into that fantasy world of celebrity and high rollers, escapist to be sure, but witnessing the relationship develop between Carolyn and Annelie is well worth the trip. As the reader progresses, the trappings become secondary to the characters' desire to reach goals both professional and personal."—*Midwest Book Review*

"The characters are the strength of *Course Of Action* and are the reason why I keep coming back to it again and again. Carolyn and Annelie are smart, strong, successful women who have come up from difficult pasts. Their chemistry builds slowly as they get to know each other, and the book satisfyingly leaves them in an established relationship, each having grown and been enriched by the other. I love every second that the two spend together."
—*Lesbian Review*

Visit us at www.boldstrokesbooks.com

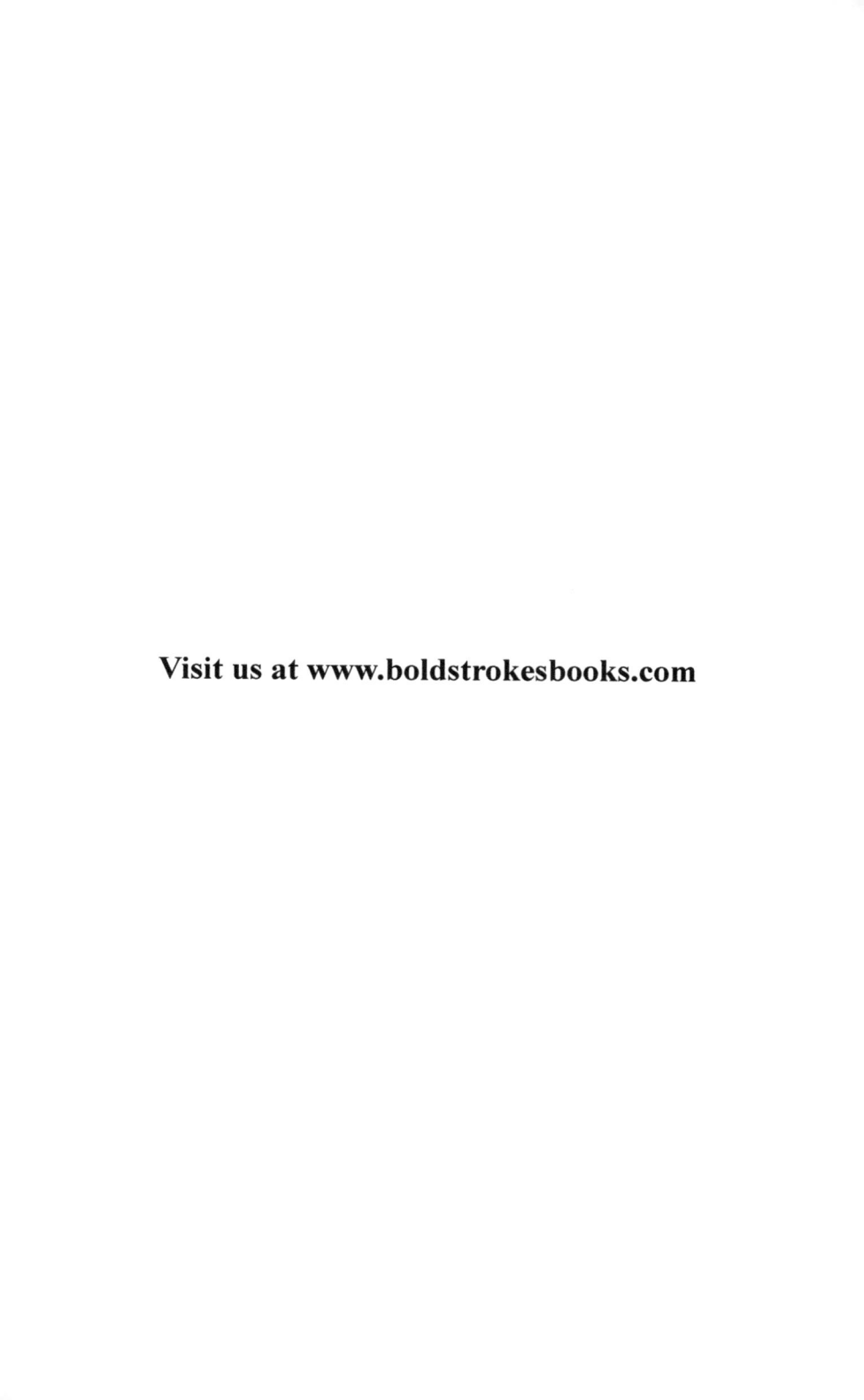

By the Author

Romances:
Course of Action
Coffee Sonata
Sheridan's Fate
September Canvas
Fierce Overture
Speed Demons
The Blush Factor
Soul Unique
A Reluctant Enterprise
Piece of Cake
Thorns of the Past
Wayworn Lovers
Insult to Injury
Ice Queen
Limelight

Science Fiction

Supreme Constellations series:
Protector of the Realm
Rebel's Quest
Warrior's Valor
Pirate's Fortune

Exodus series:
Advance
Pathfinder
Escape
Arrival
Treason

The Dennamore Scrolls
Yearning
Velocity
Homeworld

Lunar Eclipse
Renegade's War
The Amaranthine Law
Skyscraper

Novella Anthology:
Change Horizons

SKYSCRAPER

by
Gun Brooke

2024

SKYSCRAPER
© 2024 By Gun Brooke. All Rights Reserved.

ISBN 13: 978-1-63679-657-4

This Trade Paperback Original Is Published By
Bold Strokes Books, Inc.
P.O. Box 249
Valley Falls, NY 12185

First Edition: August 2024

This is a work of fiction. Names, characters, places, and incidents are the product of the author's imagination or are used fictitiously. Any resemblance to actual persons, living or dead, business establishments, events, or locales is entirely coincidental.

This book, or parts thereof, may not be reproduced in any form without permission.

Credits
Editor: Shelley Thrasher
Production Design: Susan Ramundo
Cover Design By Gun Brooke

Acknowledgments

First of all, I want to show my endless appreciation and gratitude to you, yes YOU, my reader, who bought this book, or any of my other books. Thank you for giving me yet another chance to hopefully entertain you. I hope you will like the story.

I want to thank Len Barot, aka Radclyffe, for her continued faith in me for twenty years. I take nothing for granted so please know that I am so glad to belong to the BSB family.

Thank you also to Dr. Shelley Thrasher, my editor, who I can't imagine not having in my corner. We work so well together, and I really love editing the books with you.

For the others at BSB who help us authors look good and help make the book the best it can be, I want to acknowledge Sandy, Stacia, Toni, Ruth, Cindy, Susan, and those of you whose names I don't know, including the valiant proofreaders.

My first readers, Sam, Gin, and Mayra—you are my first line of defense, in a manner of speaking. I deeply appreciate your thoughts and beta reading. You certainly help me catch a lot of things and nip mistakes in the bud.

I want to thank William, my oldest grandson, who kindly shared opinions about the concept of this story last summer. The same goes for my son, Henrik, who patiently listened to my musings and gave his opinion when I asked.

Then there are the people around me without whom my writing wouldn't be the same, even if they don't have anything directly to do with the actual process. Malin, my daughter, who thinks I'm the best. How can I go wrong when you keep saying such things? My six grandchildren who I love and adore, and my brother Ove and Monica, always encourage me.

My friend Birgitta, who reads everything I write, even the sci-fi, is a constant source of love and support. for a long time now, thanks for being there. Soli, Rosemarie, and my group of painter friends, I treasure you!

And—as always—I owe my dogs for their unconditional love and for keeping me safe.

Dedication

For Malin and Henrik—my children.

For Elon—you would have loved this!

Chapter One

Dr. Rayne Garcia stepped off the lift and into what could best be described as controlled pandemonium.

"Perfect timing, Doc!" An orderly, whom Rayne recognized, pushing one gurney with one hand and pulling the other behind him, called out as he expertly maneuvered among the throngs of soldiers lining the halls.

"Another attack?" Rayne snatched an apron off a cart and ducked into it, feeling how it formed itself around her, then snapped into place. She moved alongside the orderly, quickly using her scanner to assess the two soldiers: one male, one female. "He's stable enough to go to an open station." She pointed at the man, who was starting to come around. "She, on the other hand, needs a full-body scan. I'll take her. Can you let the matron know I'm here?"

"Will do, Doc," the orderly said, sticking his thumb in the air.

Rayne pushed the gurney with the woman around the corner and into the area that held scanning booths for injured law enforcement. She frowned as she discovered signs of respiratory distress. "I need a hand here!" she called out.

Two technicians approached. One attached a breathing apparatus meant to be used in the field, but which was often the only available option at the level of this clinic. It infused the required oxygen, but not even near the way the state-of-the-art equipment Rayne was used to in the hospital on the 2810th floor. Here, on the third floor, barely above ground level, resources were scarce, and a lot had to do with the insurrectionists in the tunnels. Scavengers by nature, and they stole everything they could get their hands on, which made it impossible to outfit clinics like these throughout the Eastern Coastal City adequately.

"O2 at eighty-two percent," one tech said as she started to remove the soldier's uniform.

"I'll take it." Rayne followed with her scanner, one that was her own property, which she always brought to the lower-level clinic. "Diminished breath sounds on the left. Pneumothorax." Not about to wait for the tech to remove the uniform completely, Rayne pulled up a tray. She found the obviously crude auto-thorax and pushed it in place between the ribs. As low-tech as it was, the device did its job and released the trapped air outside the lung, making it possible for it to expand.

"Hey. O2 on eighty-nine and climbing," The tech gave a tired smile. "This is great. I needed a win before my shift ends."

"I heard it's been an intense day." Rayne kept scanning the woman. "This, wait, do we have a name for this patient?"

"You never learn, eh, sir?" The tech tapped the dog tag around the still-unconscious woman's neck. "Just a code. 93delta33."

The soldiers were anonymous. Rayne had been donating her time as a physician for more than ten years, but she had a problem with what she considered the dehumanization of the ones who helped guard the skyscrapers against the enemy. This nameless woman would live unless Rayne found something else amiss with her. She always tried to alert the authorities about the vitamin and mineral deficiencies among the ranks. That problem provided some challenging recuperations for the soldiers who survived.

"All right. Send her through the body scan, but keep an eye on that breather." Rayne motioned at the mask that was too big for the woman's narrow features.

"Will do." The tech nodded and began pushing the gurney into one of the stalls. "Once she's settled, I'll be clocking out for today. Then I'm on a long weekend vacation with my partner."

"Really? That sounds like fun." Rayne knew how many hours the medical staff at the Soldiers' Clinics had to work to get time off and be able to afford anything but the bare necessities. Where are you going?"

"Hal won a trip to the Skyqueen Four resort. It's only on the 1203rd floor, but it's supposed to be nice." The tech shrugged. "It'll be a change of pace, for sure. Don't think Hal's been higher than the 800s."

"I hear it's good too." Rayne hoped she didn't come off as condescending. She had never been to any of the lower level's resorts, that was for damn sure.

"Thanks. All right, Doc. I've got this girl. You'll see the results of the scans in a few." Grinning now, perhaps at the idea of finally ending her shift soon, the tech shut the lining behind her as she entered the scan booth.

Rayne hurried back to the pit, where the influx had slowed down, but she still had a lot to do. Here, nurses and techs moved in patterns a person not used to this type of clinic would find chaotic. These days, their movements automatically directed Rayne where she was needed the most.

❖

The child in Kaelyn's arms seemed to weigh three times as much as before. His head lolled against her shoulder as she ran with him tightly pressed against her. She had known Wes since he was born, and now his blood was seeping through his clothes onto hers.

"Are you sure, Kae?" Foster, her next in command, was running beside her. Behind them, eight armed members of the resistance kept up the pace, two of them half-carrying a third. "They'll deport us all. You'll never see the boy again."

"Hence the guards. If we convince these cloudheads that not even they can let a child die on their watch, not like this, they'll have our backs." Kaelyn shifted her grip as she felt Wes's body begin to slip. *Please, God, let the boy be all right.* The eight-year-old was the only family member his older sister had. If they lost him…it just couldn't happen.

They were just below the ground, making their way through the more treacherous tunnel system that could be crawling with cloudhead soldiers on any given day. It was past midnight, and the raids against their outposts had been relentless all day until a few hours ago. When Kaelyn had made her rounds, Wes had snuck out of his dwelling, followed her, as he idolized her, and ended up in the ambush orchestrated by the Celestial soldiers. Clearly a covert group, they were highly trained, as they managed to get the drop on Kaelyn and her team. They had managed to push the cloudheads back, but then, as they intended to fall back with their wounded, Foster had spotted the small body lying by a column.

Kaelyn had struggled to breathe as she examined Wes. When she saw the extent of his injuries, she wanted to howl, but instead she field-dressed his wounds and grabbed him.

"We're taking him to their soldiers' clinic on the third floor. The closest one. He's not going to make it otherwise. He'll bleed out if we attempt to make it down the tunnels to Doc Boro."

She heard grumbling in the ranks, but one of her men turned to display a horrific injury where a nova-blaster had nearly severed his arm at the elbow. He too was hemorrhaging far too fast for them to be able to take him home.

They turned a corner, with Foster and another of her fighters taking lead. The air gushing from the vents above them was cold yet oddly stale. The tunnel would become wider and the ground more even. Kaelyn prepared to run faster with her precious burden.

Foster made an all-clear gesture with his left hand, flagging them forward.

"How do you plan to get us past the checkpoint and onto the lift?" Foster asked over his shoulder, his voice hushed.

"Brute force, if need be," Kaelyn said harshly. "They may not have known it, but they shot yet another child. Wes is going to make it and return to his sister below. We're not going to lose another one. Not tonight."

"All right. Brute force it is, then." Foster was the best lieutenant Kaelyn had ever known. When she rose through the resistance ranks as she grew older, she soon realized that surrounding herself with people she could trust implicitly, and who put their faith in her, was absolutely key. When you were trying to defend the home of your people and their right to survive, you didn't have time to grandstand or play the hero.

"Just remember," Foster added, "the kids at the checkpoints, some of them are just a bit over sixteen. We may have to try to keep them alive as well. They must have siblings or parents too."

It wasn't as if Kaelyn didn't realize this point. Naturally, she did. The Celestials ran a corrupt society that allowed children to be their first line of defense. Her own people, the Subterraneans, at least kept the junior fighters at the far back of the forces. No kids would be cannon fodder on Kaelyn's watch.

Foster made a fist and raised it sharply. "Checkpoint. Just one boy and one girl." He held out his binoculars, and she pressed her face into the viewfinder.

"I think it's a trap. See the girl? She's not a day over sixteen. Why would they place her, and that guy next to her, to guard the checkpoint? We can easily walk straight over them." Kaelyn hoisted Wes closer on her shoulder. "That said, trap or not, we're going in." She could feel Wes's life force seep out of him.

"Got it." Foster raised his hand and gave a series of non-verbal commands. Four of Kaelyn's fighters moved up next to him and spread out.

The columns under the skyscraper were massive and provided good protection for Kaelyn and her team. But they would obscure the enemy just as effectively. She slipped around the circumference of the nearest column, making her way just behind her advancing fighters. To her far left, someone raised their fist, and everyone halted. The woman elevated her gleamer, a stub-nosed rifle able to send a modified laser beam as well as throw fire.

Kaelyn watched Foster repeat the woman's gesture.

Then someone fired. Kaelyn was confident it wasn't one of hers. They were all well trained and seasoned resistance fighters. Peering around a column, she saw it was the young female sentry.

"Fuck. She's going to get herself killed!" Kaelyn hissed at Foster.

"On it." Foster moved so fast, nobody had time to react. He circled two columns and then fired a green beam, set to stun. The thud of a body hitting the floor, followed by yet another one, a second later, was all Kaelyn needed to hear. She moved into position behind two of her fighters as they advanced toward the checkpoint. There, Foster and three of her team held the rest of the cloudhead soldiers at gunpoint, ready to disarm them. The tension between them felt sliceable, but eventually the rest of the young sentries lowered their weapons and stepped back.

"Nova blasters. On the floor!" Foster said, and he didn't have to raise his voice. His six-foot, five-inch frame, sinewy and muscular, appeared to be enough.

The weapons ended up in a pile, as did their communicators and hand-to-hand combat equipment. Obviously, the Celestial government didn't issue any of the newer tech to their first line of defense. Scuffed, repaired multiple times, and perhaps even poorly maintained, the sentries' weapons didn't look much better than her own.

"Secure them. We're moving up." Kaelyn shifted her grip of the unconscious Wes, praying they weren't too late. She managed to hold him in place with her left arm, pulling her sidearm with her right hand.

Together with Foster, they found the narrow tube lift that would take them to the clinic. Foster had ripped a passkey from the lapel of one of the cloudhead soldiers and now used it to open the door. Only six of them fit into the tube, including the injured man, who was now conscious but clinging to his teammate. Though bleary-eyed and in pain, he still had a weapon in his good arm. She wasn't surprised.

The tube began its ascent to the third floor. Bracing herself for what was to come, Kaelyn twisted her torso to protect Wes, keeping her gun raised. Next to her, Foster raised his modified gleamer. As the door slid open and delivered them straight into the midst of the clinic, Kaelyn let Foster go first, then immediately followed, scanning for a proper physician to help Wes.

Chapter Two

Rayne dipped behind the circular counter in the center of the nurses' pit. She knew they kept energy nuts there and managed to snag the last small package. Opening it, she rose to her feet, but just as she popped the first nut into her mouth, already anticipating the rush of new energy, something caught her attention.

Over by the tube lifts, people not wearing scrubs or Celestial uniforms milled in. Within moments, the second lift opened and more followed. Rayne took in their raised weapons.

"Hit the alarm!" the head nurse, a middle-aged woman who had spent her career at this clinic, called out. "Insurgents!"

Rayne stood still, staring at the rough-looking men and women. The woman standing in front of the others, holding her sidearm trained on the closest orderly, was also holding a small person against her. A child. Rayne spat the nut into the closest bin and took two steps forward.

"Stop where you are. We need a doctor for this boy and this man," the woman said. Her short brown hair framed sharp features and hard, dark-brown eyes. She was tall and looked like she could break just about anyone in the pit in half with her sinewy arms.

"I'm a doctor," Rayne said calmly. Inside, she was trembling, but she refused to let her fear show. Having worked as a physician for more than twenty-five years, she knew how to fake both calm and patience. "The boy looks like he needs urgent treatment." She nodded over to a man being held upright by another insurgent. "And he'll lose his arm if you don't let us treat him."

The woman blinked, perhaps surprised by Rayne's matter-of-fact tone. "Where do I put him? I'm staying with him, and he's coming back down with me."

"Very well." They would have to see about that. From what Rayne knew of the cavers, they probably didn't have the means to treat severe wounds like this. Or attach nearly severed arms. "Come this way."

The woman glanced over at an impressive-looking man who towered over them all. "You good here?"

"We've got all the exits covered. Nobody's getting in until after we leave." The man ruffled the boy's hair. "Come on, Wes. You'll be fine." His eyes were mere black marbles as he looked around the room. "As long as you just keep doing your job, and don't consider any foolish action, we'll be out of your hair soon. We mean no harm." But it was obvious from his tone that he could dole out harm if he, or the woman, deemed it necessary. Rayne clung to the fact that, so far, they hadn't even touched anyone at the clinic. What they had done with the kids at the checkpoints was anybody's guess. Rayne hoped they weren't seriously injured—or worse.

Rayne and a nurse showed the woman carrying the child into a cubicle. As soon as the woman had placed him on the gurney, she stepped back a few inches and kept her weapon lowered but readily available.

The nurse was already cutting off the boy's clothes.

"What's his name?" Rayne said as she began to assess his injuries.

"Wes." The woman spoke through tense lips. Her clothes, a uniform of sorts, looked like a mismatch of regular clothes and stolen Celestial uniforms. Rayne recognized the protective vest as a Celestial-soldier issue.

"My name's Dr. Rayne Garcia. And you are?"

"Kae," the woman answered curtly. Apparently, this was all she was going to share.

"Well, Kae, you brought him here with little time to spare. Wes is going to need a set of infusions to boost his blood volume. Then we need to patch up whatever is making him bleed out like this." Rayne gently rolled Wes onto his side. "It looks like the beam went straight through him. He's far too young to be part of the conflict. Why was he there?" Did they really use children in the insurrection movement? Rayne had heard that, and worse, ever since she was a young girl. The cavers were ready to steal anything from you and take any advantage, given half the chance. Only the fact that the Celestial military cracked down on them often kept them from advancing up the skyscrapers. Thieves, scavengers, and foragers, the people living underground were of a completely different kind.

Still, Rayne had assisted the nurse in removing the last stitch of clothes from the boy. He was thin, but not painfully so, not emaciated. His hair was shiny, and apart from all the smeared blood, he looked clean. A quick glance at Kae suggested that the same went for her.

"Of course he isn't part of this unit. He's a child!" Kae's dark eyes took on an amber glow. "He was curious. And he's not the first Subterranean child to be injured by Celestial forces. Covert strikes at habitats are all too common." She pressed her lips together and stopped talking.

Rayne had no idea what Kae was going on about. Covert strikes? The Celestial soldiers were ordered only to keep the cavers away from the skyscrapers.

"Run a scan over his chest and abdomen." Rayne turned to the nurse. "I want to make sure that beam didn't bounce off any of his organs and hide any bleeders from me." She had already given Wes some of the medication he would need to survive. In the back of her mind, she listed what she would have to put in a bag for him later.

The scans showed no internal bleeders other than the small artery branching off from beneath Wes's right collarbone. "I'm going to try to heal the artery with this," she said and held up a medical instrument that she in fact had helped invent. It knitted patches of tissue around the damaged blood vessels and fused them together. She had used them on a child very rarely, but the principle was the same. Slide it along the vein, allow for it to touch it, and then fuse them onto his own tissue. She stood back and let the nurse sedate the boy.

Kae stood to Rayne's left as she worked on Wes. Keenly, her gaze followed Rayne's every move. When Rayne eventually glued the skin back in place over the wound, the boy's color was already improving.

"Will he live?" Kae asked.

"Unless his wound gets infected or if something else ruptures, I'd say so." Pulling off her gloves, Rayne folded her arms over her chest. "He would be better off at one of the Celestial rescue camps."

Kae's glance was tinged with lava. "One of their reformation camps? Which is just a fancy word for death camps. No way. Nobody ever comes back from there."

"Lots of children and grownups have been repatriated after a successful period of nourishment and schooling." Rayne was stunned at how Kae spat the words. "I don't know where you get the information, but I assure you, this boy will have a much better chance of recovering if he is installed at one of the government-run places."

The nurse had bandaged young Wes and was now administering a drug that would counter the effect of the sedatives. She came to stand next to Rayne, her stance clearly defiant.

"You are misinformed," Kae said, glancing at her crew before she replaced the sidearm in her holster. Her makeshift-looking uniform was blood-soaked and dirty, but she appeared well equipped regarding weapons. The woman carried enough extra ammo to take out half the building. "I'm carrying him with me now, back to our own doctor."

Rayne huffed. "Doctor. May I ask at which university they obtained their diplomas?"

Kae didn't answer. She carefully lifted Wes from the gurney and tucked him into her shoulder. He whimpered, but his arms came around her neck.

"I got you, kid," Kae murmured and quickly stroked his back. "You'll be back with Tania soon."

A loud boom rattled the medical cubicle.

"I can't keep you from moving the child," Rayne said, nodding in the direction of the nurses' pit area. "But they will."

"Only if you tell them." Kae stared at Rayne. "You can let us leave."

"Me? I'm just a volunteer physician. I have no pull with the military—let alone the authorities." Rayne shifted and peered out into the open area. She didn't like what she saw.

Rayne counted eight heavily armed men and women, and these appeared to be seasoned soldiers, not the young kids normally sent to guard the front line. This unit looked like what you sent if something was truly wrong, like an invasion of Subterranean insurgents. Rayne groaned. She should have seen this coming.

Unlike what she had just told Kae, she did have some pull with the ones sitting on the power. Merely because she was one of the Tower One Garcias, she stood out in a crowd of wannabe posh people. It was practically impossible to climb socially at her level. You were born into your social position, depending on which floor your family resided on. Her family lived above the 2800th floor. Tower One was legendary as the first of its kind, ready in 2401. The Garcias were the first and only tenants of their apartments in the 3000-story skyscraper.

"You can't let them take him." Kae was whispering now, but she managed to infuse enough authority into her voice to make Rayne hesitate. Didn't everything this woman implied about the camps tie into her own suspicions that had escalated the last few years? Hadn't Rayne recently discovered odd patterns of methods that just didn't make sense?

The tall man returned to the cubicle, his lips pressed together. "They've cut off the lifts. I have no doubt that they're sending forces to ground level. I have warned our team waiting there."

"Good." Kae turned her focus back on Rayne. "Listen. You worked hard to save this boy, and I owe you for that, but we also need to leave. We haven't harmed anyone here. We pose no threat, unless you attack us. That's not our way. Let us out some other way, and let us go."

"And they'll be back to continue killing our soldiers all over again," the nurse spat. "The boy too, when he's old enough. He won't bother with the fact that you saved him. These people just want to spread terror and steal from us. Call the commander out there into the cubicle and force them to surrender."

"I'm not going to argue." Kae's voice sank an octave. "If you don't order the soldiers to retreat, people will die. It's not a threat—it's a fact. Just let us be on our way, and you can continue patching up young men and women who have no business being on the front line in the first place."

This was another undeniable truth. The Celestial soldiers showing up on Rayne's gurney were sometimes barely seventeen. The words cannon fodder flickered through Rayne's mind.

"Nurse," she said calmly. "We all feel strongly about this conflict, no matter which side we're on. But I do know that this boy is not part of it. If he has a family to look after him—"

"He does. His sister. And he also has me and our entire community. We look after our own." Kae inched toward the door. Someone fired a nova blaster, and the high-pitched sound made Rayne flinch. She'd heard it in the distance, while working at the bottom of the skyscraper, but never this close. Kae didn't so much as blink.

"It's now or risk being caught," the tall man muttered. "We need an exit strategy, fast."

Rayne regarded the way Kae wrapped a towel around herself and the boy, effectively tying him close to her, thus freeing her hands.

"Doctor? Help us get out of here and avoid complete mayhem. My team is under orders to leave peacefully, but there's no way they won't return fire if cornered. The choice is yours."

Rayne glanced at the furious nurse. "We can't risk the other patients and the staff. I'm going to take them to the garbage shoot."

"That's treason!" The nurse wasn't going to back down. Rayne could feel it. "You'll be charged at the next tribunal."

Rayne knew this might have been the case if her status had been humbler. She might get a slap on the wrist, and perhaps even lose some of her VIP patients, but she doubted that too. She was too good at her job. "I'll risk it. You should check your moral compass. We're talking about a child, in fact several, as a lot of the soldiers on those gurneys out there are barely seventeen." Rayne moved to the opening toward the nurses' pit and peered outside. "Right now, there's more shouting than firing." She turned to Kae. "Can you get your team to follow us—and very fast? I can't guarantee that they won't be under fire while retreating."

"I can." Kae held weapons in both hands, one trained on the glowering nurse. "And you, just back down," she told the nurse with a dark growl in her voice. "I know very little about nursing, but something tells me you skipped the class where you vowed to save lives."

The nurse stared at the weapon and took a step back. "My father will have your head," she said.

Rayne groaned inwardly, remembering that this nurse had volunteered as well and that she resided almost as high up in this skyscraper as she herself did.

"Well, he can try," Kae said and moved to stand behind Rayne. "Let me go first, and tell me where to go as we leave."

"All right." Rayne would rather have stayed in the cubicle until the matter resolved itself, but she needed to get the child somewhere reasonably safe, and this medical unit wasn't it.

Trailing Kae, she heard the woman murmur into a communicator for her team to follow and "take up the rear," whatever that meant. She directed Kae through a set of corridors until they reach the utility area. Here was the large chute where they disposed of used scrubs and other pieces of laundry. "There." She pointed at two square hatches. Large enough to accommodate mattresses, each one would easily fit an adult male.

"The drop will be hard. It goes straight down."

"Will there be laundry at the bottom?" Kae placed one of her sidearms into its holster and held the boy closer with her now-free hand.

"They empty it in the mornings, so yes, there should. Be careful with the boy. You don't want the glue and fusing matter to rupture, or he'll be back in the same dangerous situation." Rayne always responded in a more personal way when it came to sick or injured children. She figured it was the same for most health-care workers. Well, perhaps except for the nurse that had just assisted her.

"I'll go first, Kae," the tall man said. "That way I'll be able to help you land without hurting Wes." Not waiting for permission, he pulled the hatch open and sat on the edge. Flipping his legs into the dark chute, he simply disappeared.

"Damn it, Foster," Kae murmured. "The last of my team are running this way. Can you close the hatch behind them?"

"Yes. Just go." Rayne ushered Kae toward the hatch. Heavy footfalls told her that the approaching insurgents had company.

"Thanks." Kae locked her gaze firmly on Rayne's. "Honestly. Thank you."

Nodding, Rayne watched Kae shift her legs over the edge of the chute, and then she, and Wes, were gone.

The soldiers didn't waste any time. One by one the men and women threw themselves into the chute, possibly landing on top of each other. As the last one disappeared over the edge, Rayne moved to close the hatch, but a shrill voice made her freeze with her hand on the rim.

"That's her. That's Doctor Garcia! She has colluded with the enemy and now helped them all escape." The nurse stood next to the gruff-looking soldier who was leading his team in pursuit of the insurgents. "She's a traitor!"

Rayne saw hesitation in the eyes of some of the troops. She had no doubt worked on quite a few of them. But the major in the front raised his nova blaster and took aim. Rayne acted from sheer self-preservation. Gripping the rim harder with both hands, she pushed off the floor and jumped into the laundry chute.

Chapter Three

The sound of something, or someone, landing among the sacks of laundry in the crate beneath the chute behind them made the Subterraneans raise their weapon in that direction. After Foster's second-in-command had landed, nearly kicking the one before him in the chin, they didn't expect anyone else.

At first, the flash of white made Kaelyn think it could be a laundry bag, but this bag turned out to have arms, legs, and easily recognizable dark-blond hair. It was loose now, falling around Doctor Rayne Garcia's shoulders, when she climbed out of the crate.

"It's the doc," Beth, the youngest of their team, said. She still had her weapon trained on Garcia.

"What the hell are you doing?" Kaelyn stared at the rumpled woman. They had to get out of there before new guards started flooding the basement. Surmising they were on the minus-fourth floor, Kaelyn kept looking for exits to the ground.

"When the team sent to deal with you aimed at me, I jumped." Garcia looked shell-shocked and was awkwardly trying to control her hair. After finding a clasp in a pocket, she placed her hands on her hips. "We need to move."

"Obviously." Kaelyn bit back a growl. She motioned with her chin. "Don't lose sight of Foster if you intend to stay alive. Once we're at the surface, we'll blindfold you." Kaelyn ignored the side-eye glances from some of her crew. "Let's move out. Foster, you heard me. Keep the doc alive."

Foster nodded, his expression not giving away his true feelings at being put on a babysitting detail.

Kaelyn adjusted the towel around Wes and checked his breathing. He was pale, but his chest moved effortlessly. Wrapping her free arm around him, she kept her sidearm pointing downward.

"How is he?" Garcia stepped closer and peered behind the towel. "His color's not too bad."

Kaelyn merely nodded, then took the lead by following the wall heading north. If they didn't find an exit before the soldiers began showing up in the crates beneath the chutes, they would be captured, at best. Most likely, they would be shot on the spot, perhaps even the doctor, unless she was a spy.

After several hundred meters, the corridor broadened and ended in a vast cave-like area full of columns. Attached deeply into bedrock, these were part of the structural integrity of the skyscraper.

"This way," Foster said and motioned for Garcia to follow him. Kaelyn walked behind them, making sure nobody approached from the flanks. The columns created a dizzying pattern of black against light gray, and she squinted. If a team of raiders was waiting behind the columns, they'd be hard to spot until it was too late.

The air smelled of mud and mold, and moisture seeped down the columns in rivulets. Over time, they'd become slippery, and only the fact that they were covered by something that didn't allow water to permeate them kept them from eroding. Kaelyn had heard that some skyscrapers in the southern part of the Eastern Coastal City had problems with an increasing tilt. So far, this wasn't the case in the northern parts.

After another ten minutes of dodging behind columns and nearly slipping on the algae-covered parts of the floor, Foster stopped by a ladder attached to the wall.

"This is our only way out for miles," he said. "My scanner says we're right above section five." He glanced at Garcia, but she merely looked quizzically at him.

"That's all right. We can ride the line back." Kaelyn turned to Garcia. "Once we've climbed to ground level, and if you intend to remain with us, the blindfold goes on."

"I really don't see why—" Garcia frowned, her green eyes glowing as if backlit by something yellow.

"It's that or be left here to face the raiders." Kaelyn motioned back at the forest of columns. "Can you even find your way back?"

Pursing her lips briefly, Garcia then tossed her makeshift ponytail back over her shoulder. "Very well." She got in line at the ladder, right behind Foster.

"Thought as much." Kaelyn watched as Garcia began to ascend after Foster.

Kaelyn tucked her weapon back into its holster and made sure Wes was secured, as she would have to use both her hands to climb the ladder safely. She looked at who was beneath her and saw Beth wink up at her.

"Don't worry. I won't let either of you slip past me." She crinkled her nose, and she reminded Kaelyn so much of Wes's sister, she couldn't think of anything except taking the boy safely back to their own doctor.

The ascent normally wouldn't have fazed Kaelyn, but the added weight of the boy, along with her fear of dropping him to his death, took a toll on her. Looking up, she could tell that Foster and Garcia had made good time and were halfway to ground level. Beneath her, the last of her team, one of her seasoned officers had just begun his climb.

"Hurry up!" he called loud enough for her to hear. "Company."

"Fuck." Kaelyn gripped the next bar and pushed up. The muscles in her arms trembled as she kept going. She lost count of how many steps she'd managed so far. She knew only that she had to keep climbing so her crew could reach the next level and be out of sight of the pursuing raiders. The taste of iron in her mouth didn't surprise her. She had been on her feet, fighting off the attack against the Subterraneans, for more than twelve hours. Taking Wes to the clinic had been a long shot, but now that they had almost reached what went for safety as far as they were concerned, she refused to be the one slowing everyone down.

"Let me take him," a voice said from above.

Kaelyn gasped for air as she blinked sweat out of her eyes so she could see Garcia. Hanging halfway out of a small opening in the wall next to the ladder, she reached for Wes with both hands.

"No. I'm almost there." No way Kaelyn would hand over Wes to someone she didn't trust completely. "Back off." She pushed off another step on the ladder. When she moved her left foot to join the right, she could barely budge it. Cramps and lactic acid didn't allow her to move, let alone speed up.

"Please. Take my hand, then. Foster's anchoring me." Garcia's hair had come undone again and framed her flushed face as she hung down, bent at the hips. "Let me help pull you up."

Or push her, and the rest of her team, down, Kaelyn thought bitterly. Yet what chance did she have, barely able to move? She pressed her forehead against the bar she clung to.

"Kae, you have to let her help you. We need to get out of here," Beth said from below. "We're all exhausted."

Hissing, Kaelyn pushed up one more step, using sheer willpower, then reached for Garcia's right hand. "I don't dare dislodge Wes. Just pull me." It would hurt her already-sore shoulders, but it was the only way. She still didn't trust the physician, but Beth was right.

Garcia locked her hands around Kaelyn's wrist and pulled. She grimaced, and Kaelyn realized that having Foster push her from behind hurt as well. Step by step, Garcia tugged at her arm, and Kaelyn used the last of her strength to reach the opening. When her shoulders were aligned with it, more hands reached out, and she found herself yanked through to what had to be the outdoor ground level. Rain hit her in the face as Foster pulled her to her feet and pressed her against the wall.

"You okay, Garcia?" he asked, even if he didn't take his eyes off Kaelyn.

"Reasonably." Garcia joined them and pushed her hands into the towel. "And this little guy slept through it all." Garcia's voice was strained, but when Kaelyn managed to draw enough breath to get her bearings, she watched the cloudhead doctor stubbornly give the entire team a quick examination as they emerged one by one. When the last one was outside, she and Foster pushed a heavy piece of metal over the opening. They pulled a pipe out from beneath some debris and slid it through two hooks, thus efficiently jamming it against being opened from inside.

"We'll have to remove the pipe later, in case we need to use that space again," Kaelyn murmured. "Foster? We need to get to one of our chutes. Blindfold her." She motioned toward Garcia with her chin.

Foster didn't hesitate. He pulled the black bandana from around his neck and tied it around Garcia's head. He shone a light around it and then shrugged. "That's as good as it gets." He took the doctor by her shoulders and spun her several times in several directions.

"Hey. I'm getting dizzy." Garcia appeared as if she was truly in pain. "I have no idea where we are or where we're going. Don't make me throw up on top of everything else."

"That'll do. Now help me." Kaelyn waved Foster over. "I need you to carry Wes. I'll head up the team. Chute six."

"That's right." Foster took Wes in his arms and tucked the little boy against his shoulder. He nodded briskly at Kaelyn. "Don't worry. I've got him."

Kaelyn hesitated for a fraction of a moment but then made sure her sidearm was set. She grabbed Garcia by the arm. "Keep up if you don't want us to leave you behind."

"Charming." Garcia sounded more affronted than afraid. "Are you going to drag me along blindfolded the entire way?"

"Only until we're inside," Kaelyn said. "If you slow us down, we won't hesitate to ditch you in some worm alley." She tugged at Garcia's arm as she began to walk.

"Worm alley?" Garcia stumbled to keep up but remained upright.

"You can't expect a cloudhead to know what a worm alley is, Kae," Beth said from behind them.

"True." Kaelyn stopped at the corner before one of the larger junctions between vast bases of the structurers towering above them. She shoved Garcia in behind her. "A worm alley is a narrow pathway between two skyscrapers, where barely two people can fit next to each other. If you get caught in one of those, there's no escape if you run into the wrong people."

"I see." Garcia's voice gave nothing away, but her breath tickled the back of Kaelyn's neck. "And what the hell's a cloudhead?"

"That'd be you, Doc," Beth answered merrily. "Head in the clouds. Literally."

"Not right now," Garcia muttered. "The opposite in fact."

Kaelyn stretched her lips into a smirk. Yes, this was the opposite of the luxury the doctor and her peers enjoyed in the sky. This must seem like utter hell to a pampered woman like Rayne Garcia. She glanced up into the rainy darkness. But who could really blame her?

Kaelyn turned to look at Garcia. "Now that you know how dangerous it can be here, grab hold of my belt and don't let go. Once we're inside, you can remove the blindfold."

"All right." Garcia shifted, and Kaelyn felt a hand against the small of her back as it gripped the bottom of her harness. "Let's go." She made sure the narrow pathway was clear and then rushed down along it. Garcia breathed hard behind her but didn't let go.

The worm alley became increasingly narrow as they pressed on. The pathway wound through the unevenly shaped foundation that marked the perimeter of the vast feet holding up the structures looming above them. An acid smell tinged the air around them, and Kaelyn knew it came from the material used farther up the gigantic skyscrapers. She knew it was bad for their health to inhale, which was one of the reasons they moved as fast as they could.

"Please. I can't keep up." Garcia's words came in staccato gasps.

"Not much farther," Kaelyn said. She knew she sounded harsh, but it was vital that they reach chute six. "Remember what I said. Keep up."

Garcia didn't reply but stumbled along in a run behind Kaelyn, her hand still on her harness.

After they rounded the structure, its base the standard 2600 feet, Kaelyn called out "Left" and turned into a wider alley. Here they had to look out for narrow vehicles carrying anything from soldiers to maintenance personnel. If they were spotted, they had nowhere to hide.

Moving even faster than before, Kaelyn felt the tug on her harness become stronger. She realized that running blindfolded and not being used to the outdoors beneath the skyscrapers, Garcia was fading fast. "Hey, just another three hundred feet!"

"I can't…" Whether it was fury or desperation in Garcia's voice was anyone's guess.

Kaelyn checked ahead, squinting against the rain now splashing down on them rather than pouring. Not seeing anything that posed a threat, she slowed her pace marginally and reached back. She grabbed at Garcia's shirt, only now realizing that the woman was wearing nothing but scrubs. She must be completely drenched. It was late fall, and the temperatures hovered around forty-five degrees Fahrenheit. If they didn't provide shelter and dry clothes to this woman, she could suffer severe hypothermia. The sheltered cloudheads weren't used to roughing it.

They reached the last worm alley, one of the worst ones, which was why Kaelyn and her team favored it. It was hazardous for them but also for the raiders sent to hunt them down. It led straight between two skyscrapers but took a ninety-degree turn about five hundred feet in—a perfect spot for an ambush.

Kaelyn raised her sidearm and made sure it was set to rapid-fire. "Don't let go. Keep up, and we'll be out of this rain soon." Behind her, Garcia was bouncing off the walls of the narrow path, barely twenty inches wide at some places. The walls were rough and coated with something resembling damp soot.

Fifty-some feet from where the alley veered to the right, Kaelyn stopped. She peered over her shoulder, not surprised that her team was right behind her.

"Better get the chute open before the doc faints on us." Beth managed to squeeze past the team members between them and sling her free arm around Garcia's waist. "Fear not, Doc. We're almost home."

"Ah. Home." Garcia pressed her lips together, perhaps to keep them from trembling. "Can't wait."

After another few steps, Kaelyn removed a rusty plate and pushed her hand inside. Finding the lever, she pulled at it hard. After she checked her wristband, hoping she hadn't broken it again, she used the thumbprints of both hands to identify herself. Just to her left, a small, jagged opening appeared, and she nodded at Beth. "Take her down and keep her safe." Kaelyn realized Garcia couldn't possibly identify their location. She removed the blindfold.

Garcia blinked against the rain now hitting her fully in the face. "Where are we?"

"About to go on a ride—sort of." Beth maneuvered Garcia toward the opening. "This slide will be much more fun than the one before. I promise."

"What slide?" Flinching, Garcia took a step back, her eyes narrowing as she looked at the hole in the wall.

Beth kept her grip of Garcia's waist and pulled her along. "On the count of three, you jump and keep your hands tight to your chest, okay? I'll help you."

Garcia appeared to give in, as the two of them teetered on the edge of the chute that would take them into the depths beneath the structure.

Chapter Four

Rayne knew for a fact she was going to die. This wasn't a slide. She was freefalling toward certain death. She hugged herself tightly, knowing that if she didn't protect her hands and survived this, she would damage them irreparably. If she couldn't perform surgery ever again, she might as well be dead.

"Not long now, Doc!" the younger woman who had pushed her into this death spiral called out. "Bend your knees!"

Rayne felt as if she'd fallen forever, which was just as disconcerting as the idea of slamming into the ground at full force. She bent her knees and found she had to keep her feet up so she wouldn't start to spin if her soles touched the chute. A faint light appeared below her, and then she heard the other woman laugh. "And roll out of the way, or the next person will land right on top of you."

Jump. Bend. Roll. This day had to be the worst in her life. If she lived to tell the story and wasn't indicted for treason, she doubted anyone would believe her.

One second, cold, slippery walls surrounded her, and then, nothing did. She whimpered as she fell but then landed on her feet on top of something, but not hard enough to break her bones. Remembering the insurgent's last order, she rolled to the side and blinked against the light as she struggled to stand upright. The young woman assisted her, and, for once, Rayne was glad for the support. "I'm all right."

"And I'm Beth, by the way." Beth grinned as she tugged Rayne farther to the side. "And here they come."

Behind them, Foster performed a perfect roll, keeping Wes from touching the ground.

Rayne clenched her teeth to block the pain in her arms and stumbled over to him. "Let me check on the boy." She didn't wait for permission but rubbed her stinging hands on the side of her scrubs to remove the worst of the dirt before she placed two fingers against Wes's carotid. The child had a fluttering, thin pulse and appeared warm to her cold touch. He didn't stir, but his color was all right. "He needs fluids as soon as possible."

"We're not far from transportation." Kae appeared next to them. She looked over Rayne at someone else. "Hatch secured?"

"Like an old safety box," one of the young men said.

"Excellent. Move on to the station." Kae had tucked her weapon away, and so had most of the others. "Garcia, you okay to walk just a little longer?"

"Call me Rayne. I'm not one of your team." Rayne straightened her back and ignored the dots that filled her field of vision. She'd never fainted and didn't intend to in front of the enemy. "I can walk."

"Hm. Just tell me if you're about to go down. We don't want another injured person to stretch our resources." Kae motioned for Rayne to walk next to her. "You're all kinds of stubborn, which I can relate to, but keep close."

Rayne started to huff at the presumptuous comments, but she was too exhausted. She just wanted to find somewhere to sit and wrap something warm around her screaming muscles.

"Here. You're shaking." Kae tugged a thin, foil-looking sheet from one of her pockets, which she unfolded and wrapped around Rayne's shoulders, then tied two corners to keep it in place. "Better?"

The foil began conserving what body warmth Rayne still possessed and radiating it back to her. "It works." Falling into step with Kae, Rayne was so relieved, she had to fight back unwelcome tears.

"Good. It's saved me so many times, it's ridiculous." Kae led them through a large hall filled with more of the now-familiar columns. The ceiling was low here, perhaps ten feet high. As they wove in and out among the posts, the light became brighter until Rayne saw tighter rows of lanterns showing the way. The walls had changed from the slippery, disgusting surface to something resembling tiles. Though now dirty and gritty, they had probably once been white.

"How far down are we?" Rayne asked quietly.

Kae studied her briefly. "Anywhere between eighty to a hundred and ninety feet, depending on location. Unlike you lot, we don't have unlimited space vertically. Obviously."

Rayne swallowed against the bile that stirred just below her esophagus. "Ever get claustrophobic?" she murmured, trying not to think of the vast masses of rock, dirt, and damn skyscrapers above her head. She imagined the thunderous sound of everything crashing down on her and shuddered.

"This is the safest place for me and any other Subterraneans as far as I'm concerned. What the people aboveground launch at us causes our problem. Sure, we have cave-ins, but they're rare these days. Our own engineers are good at coming up with ways to reinforce our dwellings."

Engineers? Kae had mentioned that they had their own doctor, but what kind of makeshift education could the cavers possibly offer? "I see."

"No, you don't." Kae snorted, not an entirely happy sound "But how could you?"

Just as Rayne was about to let Kae know she couldn't walk one more step, she spotted something even brighter than the area of columns ahead. As they approached, she gaped at the sight of the oddest piece of apparatus imaginable. Some sort of track ran along the ground, consisting of several rows of metal bars, and on top of it, a flat-looking surface rested on wheels that hugged the bars. She turned her head from side to side, and the bars seemed to reach as far as she could see, in both directions. The one to her right appeared to curve and run out of sight.

"What's this?" Rayne barely got the words out. She wasn't sure if she was swaying or if the ground had become unstable.

"Transportation." Kae grabbed Rayne's shoulder. "And you're about to collapse. I thought I told you to let me know."

"I'm fine." Rayne lied. She was barely able to focus on Kae and was only vaguely aware of being lifted onto the flat surface in front of her. Someone pushed something under her head.

"Just lie still. Here's Wes." Kae's voice was oddly reassuring, and then someone placed a small body half on top of Rayne. Automatically, she raised her free arm and steadied the child against her. Though she wasn't at her best, her oath as a physician still applied, and she had a duty to keep this child alive.

"Would you look at that?" a gruff male voice said, and Rayne recognized it as Foster's. "She can't be among the worst of them, Kae. She saved the kid and risked a lot, perhaps everything, to help us—and helped save your life."

"Yeah. But not among the worst isn't something I would bet any Subterranean's life on," Kae said. "Still, we're supposed to be better than them, right? More humane? Less murderous? I say we keep her safe until we can ditch her in a place where her own kind can pick her up."

Ditch her? Rayne wanted to open her eyes, object to the broad characterization of her people. Set the record straight. After all, Kae and her team had forced themselves into the clinic at gunpoint. Granted, to save a child, but still. The thought of the boy curled up against her, still unconscious, still needing her expertise in this backward part of the world that she knew nothing about, made her keep her eyes and mouth shut. Perhaps they hadn't realized she was still conscious and heard their callous plans? Rayne knew she wasn't well enough to get away from this unit of insurgents yet, but one day she would be, or they might just dump her before then, and she could return to her own people with the intel they so badly needed to keep the cavers at bay.

The strange vehicle on wheels gave a jolt, making her wrap her arm more firmly around Wes, and then began to move. It had to be the shakiest ride Rayne had ever been on, including the space coaster in the Southern-Border skyscraper her parents had taken her on as a child. She kept her eyes closed and found it impossible to judge their speed or how long they would be on this contraption.

"Tania must be frantic, not knowing if her little brother is dead or alive," Beth said, and Rayne felt the young woman sit down somewhere around her feet. "I don't envy you having to explain how none of us noticed him sneaking out after us."

"Me either," Kae muttered. "She's scary for being seventeen. They're each other's whole family."

"Nonsense. They have you, most important of all, and they have all of us, not to mention the people Tania works with." Beth spoke sternly, and Rayne managed to open her eyes, mere slits, observing that the woman had removed her headgear. Short, choppy, blond hair framed the pale, freckled face. She was clearly very young, but her eyes weren't. Gone was the mirth and bravado, and Rayne could tell Beth was exhausted. Of course. They all had to be.

The repetitive rocking and clacking of the vehicle as it was propelled along the tracks by an unknown power source nearly made Rayne fall asleep. Only the deep worry for where she would end up, and if they planned to throw her in a cage, or worse, shackle her, kept her awake. She tried to convince herself that they had much more use for her as a doctor than a prisoner, but pain and fatigue made it impossible to think straight. At some point, she even contemplated rolling off the flat bed of the vehicle and trying to get away.

A long, whining sound and the sensation of a violent deceleration made Rayne fully open her eyes. The ceiling above her was lit by small sconces placed far apart, which they passed at an increasingly slower pace.

"Good. You're awake." Kae bent over Rayne. "And you don't look any worse, at least."

"Wes?" Rayne sat up, bringing the child with her, holding him gently as she checked what vital signs she could without instruments. "He's colder. We need to hurry to whatever you call a clinic."

"Your faculties are clearly as strong as ever." Kae took the boy and placed him against her shoulder. "Foster, help her."

Rayne waved dismissively at the tall man. "I'm fine." She struggled but got onto her feet, barely able to feel them through the wet socks and shoes. Telling herself that she could make her way to wherever they were going without falling over, she raised her chin and hid her trembling hands inside the foil still tied around her.

"All right, then," Kae said, looking exasperated, but perhaps also a little impressed. "The welcoming committee is here. Time to face the music."

Rayne turned around and flinched so hard, she nearly did fall after all. Righting herself, she saw a vast platform along the track. At least a hundred people stood there, and when all eyes seemed to land on her, soft murmurs grew in intensity. As the vehicle came to a stop, something apparently everyone but her had anticipated would happen with a formidable jolt, Rayne reached to steady herself against the closest person, which happened to be Beth.

"Don't worry. You'll be, as you love to put it, fine."

Rayne wasn't so sure. A lot of the people on the platform stared at her with unmistakable hatred. How could they know she wasn't one of them? She was dirty and roughed up enough to look the part. Glancing down at herself, she felt foolish. Of course. The scrubs.

"Move on, people. We have casualties." Kae's strong voice magically parted the crowd immediately in front of the vehicle. When Foster helped Rayne down, the murmur rose in volume again, but nobody approached her. Apparently, Kae and Foster, and their team enjoyed the respect of their fellow Subterraneans enough to keep them from attacking her on sight. Rayne had learned since she was a child that the cavers were outlaws without honor. The latter part didn't seem to be true for all of them, or Kae would never have risked her team's life to save the boy, but it applied to the rest. She'd heard too much evidence of how the insurgents fostered below-ground committed atrocities against the Celestials.

"She your prisoner, Dark?" a young man called out. He was sitting in a recess high up on the tiled wall. "She looks like you dragged her along by her hair."

"Shut up!" Kae sounded stern. "Run ahead to the clinic and make yourself useful. Tell Tania that we have Wes, and he's alive."

"Fuck! That's him?" The gangly young man, who looked as if he was about twenty, stared wide-eyed at the bundle in Kae's arms. "On it!" He jumped down and weaved in and out through the crowd with impressive speed.

"Come on. We better hurry." Kae lengthened her stride. "Keep up."

Rayne planned to. No way would she risk being lynched by the mob on the platform. When she felt an arm around her shoulders, she winced but then saw it was Foster. He carried, more than ushered, her along. Grateful enough to have to blink away a few tears, Rayne allowed him to help.

Chapter Five

It was formidable, and not a little intimidating, to see Tania's wrath as she rushed through the clinic. Kaelyn could hear her long before she was within sight and mentally braced for impact as the diminutive teenager barged through the doors.

"Where is he? Where's Wes? Don't even *try*." She snarled the last of her words at a medic who made the mistake of attempting to get in her way.

"Kae!" Tania pushed forward and shoved a cart aside and abruptly stopped at the foot of Wes's gurney. "He...is he...?" She flipped her long, black braid back over her shoulder, and as fierce as this girl was, her eyes shone from emerging tears as they pleaded with Kae.

"He's alive," Rayne said before Kae had a chance.

Rayne clung to Wes's gurney. "He's going to need antibiotics, fluids, and warm blankets. I'll have to see what I can do to his wound now that I have more time, even if I have less...equipment." She looked over at Tania. "You're his sister, right?"

Rayne was pale and shivering. Kaelyn let go of Tania and moved to stand next to her.

"Who the hell's she?" Tania hissed. "And where's Boro?"

"No idea who that is, but I'm Dr. Rayne Garcia, and if you don't get in the way, you can stay while we try to save your brother." Rayne was already sterilizing her unsteady hands, using a few of the tissues Kaelyn's people had stolen from a medical storage unit when it was in transit on the ground level.

"She's a cloudhead doc?" Tania moved closer to Kaelyn and looked accusingly at her. "First you let him go on a damn mission—"

"Stop right there." Kaelyn spoke gently but placed a firm hand on Tania's shoulder. It was time to reel her in. Tania was all plasma fire, and if you didn't help her set boundaries, she could spiral. "I didn't let him do anything. He snuck out because he's curious. You know him better than anyone. He wanted to see what we were up to, and of course, he's too young to realize the true danger. When I found him, we couldn't waste any time. I took him to a skyscraper facility. Dr. Garcia works there. Someone said Dr. Boro is at the other clinic, performing surgery."

Tania stood rigid within Kaelyn's grip. "Are you trying to tell me that those monsters helped him out of the goodness of their hearts and then let you all go?"

"*Dr. Garcia* helped him. Our team made sure we got out of there." Glancing over at Wes, Kae studied Rayne as she uncovered Wes's wound, assisted by two medics. She was pale, nearly transparent, and looked like she might collapse any minute. The woman should be on another gurney, but apparently Rayne took her medical oath seriously. She had refused to let anyone tend to her when they arrived at the clinic. "Get the doc a stool and adjust the gurney so she can work." Kae gently maneuvered the now-trembling Tania over to Foster, who had taken up sentry duty by the door. "Stay with Foster, okay?"

"Mm-hm." Tania kept looking at her brother as if hypnotized.

Kae moved to Rayne's left side and sterilized her hands. A medic tied a clean apron around her, just as someone had done to Rayne. "Tell me how I can help."

An orderly showed up with a metal stool and shoved it against Rayne, but a glare from Kae made him help Rayne onto it.

"Can you find anything for me to use to permanently close this wound? The mending of the small artery is holding, despite what we put him through getting back here." The trauma room was probably poorly equipped, by Celestial standards, but it was the best the Subterraneans had in the area.

"Here you go. Careful. It's our only one. If we break this, we're back at stitching up people the old-fashioned way." Rayne handed over a derma rod. She didn't say that two people had sacrificed their lives for the rod and some other vital equipment.

"Can you apply an infulizer with saline?" Rayne asked after accepting the obviously stolen piece of equipment.

Kaelyn shook her head. Something as high-tech as an infulizer was far beyond their experience. "No, but I can attach an IV bag." She reached for a cart holding bags and cannulas. "I'm no medic, but I've done that more times than I care to recount."

"Via venal tubes?" Rayne sounded dismayed but appeared to accept what she had to work with. "Very well."

Kaelyn worked by Rayne's side until they had stabilized Wes enough for him to be tucked into a medical bed. Made from iron bars sourced from the vast net of tunnels, they were crude, but at least the mattresses were good, though of course products from yet another heist in a storage facility.

Tania never let Wes out of her sight. She was by the bed, thin as a wraith, making sure he was breathing, checking the old-fashioned monitors that showed his vital signs on flickering screens.

"Hey, she's going down!" Foster called out as they turned to leave Wes with his sister and in the medic's care.

Kaelyn whipped her head around and saw what was left of Rayne's color drain from her cheeks. Her legs folded beneath her, and only Foster's quick reaction kept her from falling headlong into the cabinets to her left.

"She needs to get warm." Foster frowned. "She's like ice."

"She refused to change before we tended to Wes. When she heard Boro wasn't here, she just pushed through it." Kaelyn helped Foster hoist the unconscious Rayne in his arms. Looking over at the far end of the clinic, where she had spotted an empty bed earlier, she motioned with her chin. "There."

Foster placed Rayne on the bed and stood back. "I'll fetch Neely. I saw her start her shift just as you finished with the boy."

"Yes. Good. And put up a screen, okay? It's enough that people stare at her when she's conscious." Kaelyn had removed her harness and jacket earlier and now shivered as she began unfastening the top of Rayne's scrubs. "And if you could find me something warmer to wear, that would be great."

"Yeah. You need to change too. That damn rain washed right through our gear." Foster scowled. "I'm going to put in credits for a hot shower later."

"Fancy." Kaelyn thought it sounded like a great idea. She might even splurge for a bath. The people running the bath facilities in Subterra would make some extra credits tonight.

Neely, the head medic, came around the screen, and Kaelyn was pleased that her childhood friend didn't so much as flinch at the sight of Rayne. She placed a thermometer patch behind one of Rayne's ears. "92.2. She's going into hypothermic shock. Undress her, and I'll fetch the heating blankets." She turned and hurried back into the open area.

Kaelyn pulled Rayne's clothes as gently as possible. When she uncovered her arms and saw the swelling and bruises, she gasped and touched them carefully. Helping pull Kaelyn and Wes to safety must have caused these wounds and, no doubt, being banged around while blindfolded and going down the chute.

Returning with the blanket, Neely quickly examined Rayne. She had more bruises, mainly on her legs, but the medic focused on her arms.

"What on earth happened to her? Aren't they pampered like royalty up there?" She glanced at Kaelyn sharply. "Or are you responsible for this?"

"In a manner of speaking." Kaelyn rolled her stiff shoulder and held back a grimace of pain. "She helped us get away after saving Wes the first time. Then she saved his and my life again, helping pull us from danger." When she listed the undeniable proof of Rayne's courage, Kaelyn discovered an unexpected sense of guilt and remorse.

"You owe her, then." Neely quickly pushed a cleansing wipe over the exposed scratches on Rayne's extremities and then covered her with a hot blanket. They wrapped it firmly around Rayne, who was naked. Kaelyn pressed the sensor that would monitor Rayne's temperature and adjust accordingly.

Neely rounded the table and put another heated blanket around Kaelyn's shoulders. "Change your clothes."

"Foster's bringing me some. The rain came down in buckets." Kaelyn pulled up a metal stool and sat down next to Rayne's bed. "How's she doing?"

"I'm going to start a saline-glucose. I've given her some pain relief already, as those bruises must hurt like hell. She'll need monitoring, obviously." Neely studied Rayne's face. "She has a good constitution. I don't have to say that she's probably the healthiest below-ground right now. That said, she's been through trauma."

"Has the hypothermia caused her diminished consciousness?" Even Rayne's lips looked pale.

"I'd say so, unless you know for certain that she's sustained a head injury. Boro took the portable body-scanner with him to use during the complex surgery he's performing in the Main Hole."

"The Main Hole? I had no idea he was that far away." Kaelyn frowned. The Main Hole served as the Subterranean capital. The hub of a set of tunnels on what had once been the Upper West part of Manhattan was the densest area in the Subterranean infrastructure. It was also crime-infested and run by gangs that took turns ruling. Right now, a gang of far-too-young people calling themselves The Martians were in control. They weren't as bad as some of their predecessors, but bad enough for Kaelyn to worry about Boro traveling there. A cold tremor traveled along her neck. "The surgery. One of the Martians?"

Neely was busy placing medical supplies into a re-sterilizer, which she had to slap twice before the reluctant old piece of technology began running its cycle. "Exactly. They didn't give him a choice. Boro's curse for being the best."

Kaelyn nodded. "As long as we get him back. Those young fools are damn entitled for being Subterrans." She saw Foster approach carrying a knitted tote for her. "Thanks."

Foster handed the tote over, and a quick glance showed Kaelyn that he'd fetched more than just a cardigan. It was her own clothes, mended and re-mended many times over, but there were too many items. Then it dawned on her. "For her." She motioned toward Rayne with her chin.

"She has no other clothes but scrubs, and they make her stand out too much. Unless we want someone with less restraint to pick her off as soon as she's well enough to leave the clinic, she has to look like one of us." Foster squinted at Kaelyn. "Are you planning to keep watch?"

"I am. She's my responsibility until I can send her packing up among the clouds. Which can't happen soon enough." Kaelyn was about to get up to change, when someone unexpectedly interrupted her.

"Now that's harsh. Without me, the kid would be dead, several times over. And you too, I seem to recall," Rayne said as she curled up on her left side and tugged at the hot blanket. Her bloodshot eyes didn't waver. "As for getting out of here, just point me to the closest skyscraper."

Shaking his head, Foster obviously tried not to smile. "Not that easy, even if I admire your fortitude. For us to get you back to your world, we would have to sneak in much like we snuck out."

Rayne didn't take her eyes off Kaelyn. "Is that true?"

"It is. Nobody just walks into one of the structures from ground level. Not even from the level where they have the raider clinics. You have to enter the right way, move through the bowels of those giants. Considering that you look less like a cloudhead and more like a caver right now, I'm not sure you'd survive the attempt."

Rayne blinked slowly. "I see. I suppose you have no way of contacting any of the authorities, or even private individuals."

It was Kaelyn's turn to smile. Her expression turned into a snort, and then she couldn't keep herself from laughing. "That's an understatement! No. We've never had a communication session with a clou—with a Celestial, because signals from down here to the surface fail nine times out of ten. You didn't notice that we never tried to contact our people below while we were topside?"

Rayne appeared to consider Kaelyn's words. "I see," she said again, this time with less force. "Who the hell would volunteer to take me home?" She paled and tugged the hot blanket closer. "No. Don't tell me. Not a single person would risk their life for someone like me." She clung to the blanket as if it were the only solid thing in this new world.

"That's premature reasoning," Neely said, checking the patch behind one of Rayne's ears for her temperature. "Blanket's helping. 96.4."

Rayne nodded but seemed uninterested in continuing any conversation as she rolled over on her other side and brought the blanket up, almost covering her head.

"I'm going to change clothes. Will you stay here until I'm back?" Kaelyn asked, looking at Foster.

"That's okay. I'll sit with her until then." Neely pushed her black, curly hair out of the way and secured it with a snap-on ribbon. "Foster, go take care of yourself."

"Yes, ma'am," Foster said and saluted. He glanced at Kaelyn, who nodded.

"You heard her. Take that shower you talked about and get some sleep. We'll talk later." She grabbed her clothes and changed quickly behind a screen, her scrapes and bruises not bad enough for her to waste the clinic's resources. She could easily clean them later with her medical kit.

Returning to the bed, she wore tight black trousers and a faded, beige linen shirt. No button was the same as the one next to it, having been hers for more than fifteen years. Scavenging just outside the borders of the Eastern Coastal City had been dangerous back then, and even worse now. Back in the day, they used to find old storage units filled with clothes from another era, but now, most of what Subterraneans wore had been mended many times over. The black market for second-hand clothes and items profited from people's needs. When clothes were beyond repair, they were made into diapers for the children born into their perilous world.

Returning to Rayne, Kaelyn raised a questioning eyebrow at Neely. "Asleep?"

"Yes. As tough as she appears, she's exhausted." Without warning, Neely pinched the left side of Kaelyn's waist.

"Ow, fuck! Why did you—"

"Just checking how your latest injury is doing. You need to rest too. I can bring in a cot—"

"No cot. I'll be fine in that one." Kaelyn pointed at an office chair that had seen better decades. "If I can persuade you to lend me a pillow." No way was she going to let Rayne out of her sight. The woman might try to return home by herself. That was a surefire way to get yourself killed, either by an incensed Subterran or the raiders looming in the alleys on ground level.

"One pillow coming up." Neely looked bemused before ducking out behind the screen. She returned with the pillow and remained until Kaelyn had settled into the creaking chair. "All right. I'll keep checking in on you. You look just about exhausted enough to be able to sleep in that excuse for a chair. "

Kaelyn didn't plan to sleep, but she agreed to being tired. "Catch you in a few hours, then."

"Sleep tight." Neely disappeared.

Kaelyn wriggled into a semi-comfortable position and tried to not give in to the whirling thoughts that ran like sewer rats through her brain. Wes's still body when she had found him nearly bleeding out. How they had pushed past the baby-raiders guarding the entrance to the clinic. When she stood eye-to-eye with the only physician that offered to help a stranger, a little caver boy. The escape through the chutes. Saving lives—and being saved.

She gazed over at the bruised woman next to her. Rayne seemed to have settled into a fitful sleep. Still trembling, and with her long, dark-blond hair spread across the pillow, Rayne moved her lips as if talking with someone. Kaelyn yawned. Rayne was brave, no doubt about that. She was also adamant about her job. But what the hell was Kaelyn going to do with her?

Yawning again, Kaelyn began to drift off, no matter how hard she fought sleep. Eventually, it was too much of a temptation to not give in.

Chapter Six

Something was wrong with how Rayne's surroundings smelled. Had she fallen asleep on a gurney at the soldiers' clinic? A certain dampness combined with an old-fashioned antiseptic scent. Carefully, she opened her eyes and squinted as she saw a sharp light from a naked light source just above her. The ceiling appeared strangely close.

Her short-term memories returned with a painful twitch of her brain. Turning her head, she saw an empty chair to her left and a tattered screen to her right. In front of her, medical equipment—a mix between the latest technology and the obsolete.

The sound of approaching footfalls made Rayne take stock of her current condition. She wore some sort of shirt, the gray fabric thin and soft. She pushed the blanket off and slipped from the bed, keeping it between her and whoever was walking toward her.

Trembling, but steady on her feet, Rayne looked around for anything she could use as a weapon. A metal bar with hooks was attached to the bed, and she pulled it free with little effort. Gripping it with both hands, she made sure she was in control of her balance.

A dark figure rounded the screen and halted at the sight of Rayne.

"You planning to knock me out with that thing and steal the food? No need. It's for you."

Kae stood there, holding a small tray. She looked different from the rain-drenched, dirty woman from—yesterday? Her dark brown hair framed an angular face. Eyes of almost the same color studied her with interest. A fresh uniform, clearly worn; no harness, but a shoulder holster holding her side arm. A handheld, modified gleamer, if Rayne wasn't mistaken. Her father was a weapons buff and had taken her to a shooting range at the local military facility. Rayne was a decent shooter. Her father was an exceptional marksman, of course. It was his nature to always be the best. At everything.

"Rayne?" Kae placed the tray on the foot of the bed.

"How long was I out?" Rayne had to clear her throat to be able to speak.

"About eight hours, I think. It's 1400 hours." Kae motioned to a chair where a blanket was neatly folded over the backrest. "Why don't you have a seat and eat something? It's obviously not near what you're used to, but it's from a reliable source."

"Really." Feeling ridiculous now, holding what had to be a rudimentary infusion bag hanger, Rayne reattached it to the bedframe. "Can't be too careful," she murmured, eyeing the content on the tray. Instead of using the chair, which looked ready to collapse, she crawled back onto the bed and pulled the blanket over her naked legs. The damn shirt barely reached mid-thigh, and she'd been exposed to Kaelyn enough as it was.

Kae surprised her by not using the chair either. Without asking for permission, she sat down on the foot of the bed. "That chair made all our running around last night seem like child's play. I'm too old to spend a night like that." She motioned toward the offending piece of furniture. "See that back leg to the right? It's half loose."

"*You're* too old?" Rayne shook her head and then decided to be brave and try one of the thin sandwiches. She didn't want to know what the spread was made of, so she didn't ask.

"I'm thirty-nine. Old enough." Kae shrugged and then seemed to regret the movement. Apparently, Rayne wasn't the only one sore.

"Well, I'll be fifty in two months." Rayne closed her eyes as if in supplication when she bit into the sandwich. To her surprise, the thin bread was like a cracker, and the spread, despite its lack of appealing color, tasted of fresh vegetables and spices. "Mm." She was starving and ate the remaining two quickly. A steaming mug of an undefinable tea sat next to the plate, and she tasted it with less concern. It was a little more bitter than she normally took her tea, but it was hot and oddly rejuvenating.

"I'm impressed." Kae had raised both eyebrows in a way that looked entirely deliberate and appeared to try to hide a smile.

"Excuse me?"

"I was sure you'd balk at the idea of Subterranean food. Not that I would have blamed you. It's not exactly Celestial standard." Kae pulled a bag closer. "Foster brought us both clothes. I'll return the tray to the orderly, and you can change. We've got to get out of here."

Rayne stared at the bag. "Whose clothes are those?"

"Mine. My dwelling's not far from here, and Foster went over there and retrieved some for us to wear. It's important, Rayne. You can't walk the tunnels looking like a cloudhead. You simply won't last very long." Kae took the tray and stood. "I'm not sure you noticed the animosity last night, as you were about to go down at any moment, but Subterraneans don't take kindly to visiting Celestials."

"Are you taking me home?" Rayne reluctantly accepted the bag and peered into it. Fabrics in muted colors, mainly gray and rust. Also a flat pair of shoes.

Kae shook her head and didn't appear concerned. "Not yet. We have to let everything die down. The best thing we can do right now is to make you appear local."

Rayne chuckled, a thoroughly ironic sound. "And that's where you're wrong. My father may be eighty years old, but he has a lot of influence, and he has connections. No way is he taking my disappearance, or the potential accusations of treason on my part, lightly. He's on a mission right now. That's a given." Rayne could picture Rocque Garcia plowing his way up the chain of power to retrieve her. Her mother would do the same from her position as a high-ranking socialite. Her mother's eccentricity, which was a nice word for someone who drove Rayne to the brink of despair on a regular basis, was nearly enough to deter her from wanting to return to her normal life. Nearly.

"Fuck." Kae shoved her fingers through her hair. "Of course, you had to be a daddy's girl. As if the pressure from the raiders isn't enough as it is." She motioned at the bag again. "This proves my point. Get dressed. I hope you can wear the shoes. At least they're not too small. I'll be right back."

When Kae left, Rayne was still bristling over the "daddy's girl" comment but pushed her annoyance away. She removed the hospital shirt and quietly gasped at the sight of her arms. They were so bruised and swollen around the wrists, she wasn't surprised they hurt so badly. Rayne knew better than to ask for pain relief. The cavers must have a very limited supply.

She was just closing the buckles on the shoes as tightly as possible when Kae returned. And she wasn't alone. Next to her, Foster and a medic both studied her intently.

"Not bad. Put your hair up in a ponytail, and you can pass for a Subterranean woman." Neely came over and handed her a ribbon. "Need help?"

"I can manage." Rayne cursed inwardly as she tied the ribbon around her hair at the nape of her neck. "There."

"We've got to get out of here." Kae began walking, clearly expecting Rayne to follow.

"Hold on," Rayne called out and watched Kae pivot. "I have to check on Wes before we leave."

"No time," Kae said. "We better hurry before some hothead decides he needs to come find you. Most people around here realize you had nothing to do with Wes getting injured, but that you saved him. Yet some make up their own truth, and nothing will penetrate their hatred for all things Celestial."

"I don't care. He was my patient first. I need to make sure everything that can be done, *is* being done." Certain that Neely would take offense to the implied criticism against this clinic, Rayne was taken aback at the polite nod the woman gave her.

Kae said, "It's too dangerous—"

"It's my job to make sure I have handed him over to your own doctor in the best shape possible. Unless you mean to physically drag me out of here by my hair, I suggest you let me take a few more minutes." Rayne was prepared to argue further but saw something dart over Kae's face, something soft. What was it?

Kae raised her hands in a "by all means, risk own damn life, you fool" kind of gesture.

"Let me show you where he is." Neely motioned in the opposite direction. "We have only four intensive-care beds, and he's occupying one of them. We have a strict triage system, and only the ones that have a reasonable chance of making it are eligible for one of those beds—unless the patient is a child. When he was brought in, he was a whisper away from going to the beyond. You, together with our medics, and Kae, brought him back."

Rayne nearly uttered her usual "all in a day's work" comment, but she caught herself. Here, below-ground, where people had to be counted out to save resources for those that stood a better chance, her platitudes and false modesty weren't appropriate. At her hospital, among her wealthy patients, nobody had to give up their bed, or their medication, for someone else. It was unheard of by most of Rayne's peers. At least among those who never volunteered on the third-floor clinic for the soldiers and law enforcement. There, resources were, if not scarce, then limited. Here, among the Subterrans, it was a thousand times worse. Rayne felt so angry, she could howl. How could the insurgents, like Kae, justify their attacks on the Celestial soldiers and not put all their efforts into providing for their people? How, and why, had it come to this? "I'm glad it was at all possible."

As they approached the large bed holding a very small boy, Rayne saw the young woman called Tania, the boy's sister, stand up so fast, the chair wavered on two legs and threatened to topple over.

"Is it true?" Tania placed her hands on her hips. "The medics told me that you saved Wes twice." Tania looked oddly angered by this fact.

"I did my job, yes. Your brother was very badly wounded, and if I hadn't, he definitely wouldn't have made it." Rayne knew she sounded apologetic, which was of course ridiculous.

"You have no idea what you've done." Her voice thickening, Tania kicked with the toe of her shoe against the concrete floor. "He's—he's everything to me."

"And how's he doing?" Rayne pulled up Wes's chart on the computer that sat clamped at the foot of the bed. It was slow, almost antique, but she found some of his labs and vital signs. She browsed them and then turned to the medic sitting on the other side of Wes's bed. "I don't see the latest readings on this chart."

"I haven't entered them yet. Here you go." The medic handed over a piece of paper attached to a metal plate, an old-style pen clamped at the top. They were writing by hand. Rayne couldn't count how many times she'd had to do that, because it had never happened. Celestials didn't use such crude equipment. Everything was computerized, even on the lower floors. She tried to make out the handwriting, and fortunately the medic had used print letters.

His fever has been down the last four hours. This is good. His vital signs are improving every hour. He might need a few passes with a hemo-stimulator if his hemoglobin doesn't come up enough.

"That's not a product readily available down here," Kae said from behind. "He'll get a direct transfusion from Tania or someone else who matches his blood type. We have a small storage of O-neg blood, for extreme emergencies, but that's it."

"I see." Rayne was shocked. Storing human blood for transfusion hadn't been done since they started constructing the skyscrapers more than a century ago. She knew of the technique, and the history of it, but it felt…barbaric. "Let's hope he manages without it."

She talked some more with the medic and was informed that Dr. Boro was in transit and would take over Wes's care once he was back.

Rayne still found it hard to leave the little boy's side until Kae finally lost her patience and took her by her waist, effectively dragging her toward what turned out to be a side exit into a less-populated tunnel. Here, moisture dripped along the walls, and the damp, thick smell was unmistakable.

"All right. You can let go." Rayne pulled free of Kae's grip, relieved that she hadn't grabbed her by either arm. They were both throbbing, and Rayne found they hurt less if she kept them from hanging straight down. She folded them over her chest, though she probably looked angry and defensive, which wasn't far from the truth.

"Listen. I'm not fond of repeating myself," Kae said through clenched teeth. "You had to get out of the clinic before someone came looking. I told you that. Or do you have a death wish?"

"Of course, I don't." Rayne knew her lowered tone made her sound menacing, but unlike most other people she normally used this tone on, Kae didn't even flinch. "Why would you think that?"

"Because you threw yourself into a chute after us, and I know you think we're terrorists. Nobody would consider that a healthy decision. Now, keep walking." Pointing to the narrowing end of the tunnel, Kae sounded exasperated.

"It was that or be incarcerated by that big oaf," Rayne muttered, but she began walking, making sure she kept up with Kae. She lasted for only a few minutes, and then her back started to spasm so badly, she had to stop. "Damn. I'm sorry. I'm not trying to be difficult—"

"I can tell. Damn it. I should have realized you couldn't keep up." Again, Kae pushed her fingers through her hair. "What's wrong?"

"I'm in pain, and my back is in knots. I probably am reinforcing your idea of me as some hothouse flower, but physical pain is rather alien to me. I'm not doing well at all." Disgusted with herself, Rayne began walking again, now much slower, but at least she was moving.

"Are you saying that you've never experienced pain until yesterday?" Kae sounded astonished.

"Don't be ridiculous. I've had my share. I just haven't had to succumb to sustained pain." *Or complete agony, like now.* "Where I live, pain medication is readily available."

"Sounds great." Kae's words should have sounded scornful, but her tone was remarkably gentle. "This must be a shock to your entire system. You did get some pain meds last night, but they must've worn off by now."

"I'd say a few hours ago. I was doing well until we started walking." Rayne focused on breathing. If she kept counting each new breath, perhaps she could tell herself that this second of pain was over and done with and wouldn't return. After a minute, she knew this plan wasn't working as well as she'd hoped.

"When I'm really sore, I use some of my credits in one of the bath facilities," Kae said. She walked close to Rayne, looking ready to catch her if she stumbled.

Rayne wondered why. Why wasn't this woman ready to just throw her to the wolves and be rid of her? Was it because of Wes? There couldn't be any other reason, as the cavers hated the Celestials as much as the other way around.

"Bath facilities? What is that?"

"I'm sure you'll be shocked to hear that private bathrooms are rare down here. Clean water is also a treasured commodity and thus expensive. We have small faucets and keep ourselves clean using sponges, but on occasion a hot shower or bath is just what a person needs. After I fell down a shaft, hot baths were the only things that helped. I had only enough credits for a few sessions, but my team pitched in." Kae's voice caught.

"They're very loyal to you." A warm shower or bath. Something Rayne could have as many times as she wanted in her apartment. She pictured her white and golden bathroom that held every luxury. She had taken so much for granted all her life.

"They are. And now I can pay it forward. Here. Turn left." Kae placed a gentle hand against Rayne's shoulder blades and guided her into a wider, better-lit tunnel. It opened in all directions, and bright signs helped light it up.

"Are these shops? Restaurants?" Rayne knew she was gaping and closed her mouth.

"Sure are. And if we take the second tunnel to the right, we'll come across one of the smaller, but best, bath facilities. It's run by a friend, and I get a discount since I bring him…things."

Stolen goods, most likely. Rayne made sure she kept close to Kae, as the crowd around them was becoming denser with each step. Nobody looked at either of them. In fact, most seemed to just go about their day as if everything was normal. And she supposed it was, for them. She felt she was in a foreign country, even more alien than Europe or Africa. She'd even visited skyscrapers in Antarctica, and yet, comparatively, this place made her feel she was on another planet.

About ten doors down the new tunnel, Kae stopped in front of an oval doorframe. The door inside it was bright red, but nothing suggested it was a public facility. Kae knocked three times, and in only a few seconds, a voice sounded via a speaker.

"Yes?"

"Harlow? It's Kae. And a—friend," Kae said.

"A friend? This I've got to see." Several locks clicked, and the door swung open. Inside, a small man dressed in a long, green-tinted jacket over black pants stood, looking up at them. "Dearest Kaelyn. Did you have to hunt down a woman and beat her up to make her come with you, or did she come voluntarily? My sweet lady, you look positively exhausted."

Harlow, because Rayne surmised it was the same person Kae had spoken to just moments ago, took her hand and pulled her inside. When she couldn't hold back a moan of pain, he let go, and his eyes grew enormous in his triangular face.

"I was just joking, Kae. What's happened to this beauty?" He pulled up a stool and motioned for Rayne to take a seat.

"Just some trouble topside." Kae waved her hand dismissively. "Nothing that one of your tubs can't fix."

"Damn straight." Harlow grinned. "Rooms Alpha and Epsilon are available. I recommend the one with a double bath as it looks like this beauty will need a bit of assistance." He winked so overtly, Kae looked torn between grinning and being angry.

"Mind your own business. That said, I think the Alpha room will do nicely. A full hour. Subtract it from my credits." Kae held her wrist above a sensor on Harlow's counter and raised what looked like rusty old spectacles to her eyes. A green light ran along both her eyes, obviously scanning her identity. It hadn't dawned on Rayne that cavers would need a payment system of some kind. Perhaps, if she had given it any thought, she would have surmised that they used a barter system. Clearly not.

"Towels are on the rack next to the tub." Harlow peered curiously at Rayne. "No such things as auto-dryers here, Countess."

Being in the medical profession, Rayne was well acquainted with the concept of towels. Granted, she had several types of auto-dryers in her apartment and at the hospital where she normally worked. Down at the soldiers' clinic, the staff used towels, as they also helped administer pressure when their patients were hemorrhaging.

Rayne followed Kae to a narrow door just around the corner of a barely lit corridor. After they stepped inside, Rayne blinked at the soft, indirect light from an unknown source. The walls were painted a muted golden hue, but the main item in the room was the square tub sitting in the center of the floor.

"Perfect," Kae said and began unfastening her jacket. Once she had freed herself from it and her holster, she began to push down her pants. Rayne held up a hand.

"What are you doing?" Rayne's cheeks warmed.

"That bath isn't staying hot forever. I'm not about to waste a second of my credits. I suggest you hurry as well. I had a quick cold shower earlier, but you've seen better days." Kae pushed her pants and boots off completely.

The bluntness made it obvious that Kae truly did mean for them to bathe together. Not a prude by any means, Rayne was torn between her deep desire to finally get clean and her urge to refuse. She could count the number of times she had shared a bath with anyone. Zero.

Chapter Seven

Kaelyn wasn't entirely obtuse. She could tell that Rayne wasn't comfortable with the idea of sharing a tub. It should have been more obvious to her, but growing up below-ground, where having personal space was a luxury nobody could afford, it simply hadn't until now.

"Come on. You'll thank me later." She tried to sound casual, light-hearted even, to reassure Rayne, who seemed cemented to the floor.

Hesitantly, Rayne took a step back, as if adding to their distance would help. She unfastened her pants and pushed them down after kicking off her shoes. When she raised her arms to pull off the top, she winced and lowered them quickly. "I don't think I'm up for this. I'm too sore."

Kaelyn frowned. "That's why you need a bath. Trust me. Harlow's got the best equipment. Not only will it soothe you, but he has filters that clean the water repeatedly. You'll feel much better. When we get to my place, we'll have something to eat." She stepped closer. "I can help you get the shirt off."

Rayne looked up at Kaelyn, and since it was the first time they were both barefooted, Kaelyn realized she had a good four inches on Rayne. "I know you don't have a ton of reasons to trust me, but you can do so now. I promise." She waited a beat, while debating how honest she meant to be. "I trust you, at least."

Rayne blinked. "You do." The tension around her eyes lessened, which in turn made the green in her irises go from dark forest to almost sage. "All right. Thank you."

Kaelyn eased the top off Rayne and forced herself not to wince at the now even-darker bruises. Some of them had already taken on a purplish-yellow hue at the edges. Of course, if Rayne had had access to cloudhead medical equipment, those bruises marring her otherwise perfect skin would have already been gone.

"I look like I've been put through a garbage compacter." Rayne sighed. "Honestly, I'm amazed we're alive. Most of all, I'm relieved that Wes is."

"Yeah. I love the little guy, and if he'd died on us, we might as well have been dead too, knowing how Tania would have reacted." Kaelyn huffed. "I've known her from the day she was born, and it was easy to see even then that she was going to terrify other people."

"Are you related to her and Wes?" Rayne averted her gaze as Kaelyn began to undress.

"No. At least not by blood. But in many other ways." Kaelyn removed her clothes quickly as she saw how Rayne had begun to shiver where she stood in just a pair of briefs. "Her mother was Dorie's sister, and as such, she was my sister-in-law." She wasn't keen on telling her entire life story, but it seemed it gave Rayne something other than her pain and awkwardness about nudity to focus on.

"Dorie?" Rayne walked over to the tub, where she quickly dropped her briefs. She climbed inside so fast, she nearly slipped.

"Hey. Careful." Kaelyn offered a hand, but Rayne sat down quickly, gasping as the water engulfed her.

"It's hot!" She breathed deeply in and out. "I rarely shower this hot."

"It's one of Harlow's ways of keeping the tubs from becoming petri dishes." Kae dropped the last of her clothes and climbed into the other half of the tub, causing them to sit head to toe in reversed positions.

"So, who is Dorie?" Rayne reached for a miniscule piece of soap and smelled it cautiously.

"She was my wife." Kaelyn kept her voice noncommittal.

"Was?" Rayne lowered the piece of soap from her face and accepted a sponge from Kaelyn. "Is this…?" She looked at the sponge with something between suspicion and disgust.

"Don't worry. Harlow both boils and sterilizes them. It's as good as a single-use sponge."

"Hm." Rayne didn't look convinced. "You're not with your wife anymore?" Rayne kept probing, and normally Kaelyn would have blown off the questions with humor or sarcasm, but obviously Rayne needed the distraction. Yet why did that matter at all?

"She died ten years ago. And before you ask, no, it wasn't from an attack by the cloudhead raiders. I've lost enough people to them. In Dorie's case it was a case of septicemia. She cut her hand on a burst pipe, and we didn't have any antibiotics."

Rayne's lips parted, and she lowered her hands into the water. "I'm so sorry. I shouldn't have pried."

"It's all right. I don't mind talking about her. Tania was seven years old then, and her mother, Dorie's older sister, gave birth to Wes two years later. When Tania was fourteen, and Wes about to turn five, their mother was caught in the crossfire when raiders came through the market where she was buying food. They shot her in the head." Now Kaelyn could hear the darkness in her own voice and stopped talking. "Well. You asked."

"I did." Rayne had begun to slowly scrub her arms, moving lightly over the bruised areas. "You call them raiders. Back home, they're revered soldiers." She tilted her head. "And we call teams like yours insurgents, even terrorists. I'm sure there's another term you prefer."

"Some say freedom fighters. Me, I think we're just soldiers."

"And you're a leader." Rayne held up a finger as if to forestall the answer. She dunked under the water and stayed below the surface so long, Kaelyn began to think something was wrong. She came up, sleek like a sea creature, resembling the ones in the old pictures Kaelyn had seen as a child. Rubbing the soap against her scalp, Rayne nodded to her. "Do you have a rank?"

"I'm a team leader. They call me boss, or by my name. Some of the younger soldiers call me 'sir,' which I prefer to 'ma'am.'" Kaelyn shrugged and began scrubbing vigorously. She had washed her hair less than twelve hours ago and was more interested in the soothing effects of the water. Harlow sometimes put a few salt pills into the tub for her, and she could tell he'd done so this time as well.

"If you had seen what I witness every week at the soldiers' clinic, you might understand how young and vulnerable our units are. We struggle to keep them alive, as even our resources are scarce." Rayne was done scrubbing and now leaned back against the side of the tub. The water was cloudy from the soap they'd used, but Kaelyn could still glimpse the outline of this aloof or cool woman's full breasts. Clearly dedicated to her job, she seemed to be more comfortable if she was in charge. Besides that, she was also softly and distractingly feminine, a quality her clothes didn't reveal.

"Kae?" Rayne said, her voice matter-of-fact. "You're staring."

Kaelyn did her best to mask her reaction. "I apologize. Just lost in thought." For some unfathomable reason, Rayne's poise and level gaze made her breathless.

Kaelyn knew she was being ridiculous, but she truly wanted to close her eyes and just finish this bath. Normally, she would have stayed in the heated bath until the last second, but now, with Rayne's smooth legs occasionally rubbing along hers, she was ready to bolt.

Kaelyn continued scrubbing her skin, which felt raw after her vigorous use of the coarse soap, and focused so hard on the task that it freed her mind to wander along paths she normally kept well in check. Exposing her affection for Tania, Wes, and her friends in her team was not good, because it made her lose focus and dulled her when she needed to stay sharp. Friendship with her team, caring for Tania and Wes, helped her remain sane on those days when everything went to hell. She snorted. Much like last night. Her duties were never-ending. She supervised all the different teams in her area of the tunnel system. Keeping the raiders out, as well as dealing with local fools indulging in crime—and sometimes even causing more trouble with the cloudheads topside—normally took all her time. Was that why Wes had managed to sneak out? Was she slipping?

Kaelyn squirmed under the milky water, torn between needing the soothing heat and wanting to put some distance between herself and Rayne. Whether because of the hot water, or mere fatigue, Rayne, on the other hand, looked entirely Zen. She let the soap glide along her legs in slow, dreamy movements.

Her stomach clenching at the sight that shouldn't be remotely sensuous, Kaelyn tore her gaze from Rayne's milky, bruised skin. She absolutely didn't want to be caught staring again.

"I should get up before I fall asleep and drown." Rayne shifted and got onto her knees. She appeared unsteady and gripped the edge of the tub hard.

"I'll get out first." Feeling back in charge now, Kaelyn rose hastily and reached for one of the sadly threadbare towels, quickly wrapping it around her. Harlow used his profits to keep the tubs in perfect condition, not on the peripherals. She grabbed another towel and put it around Rayne. "Hold on to me." She guided Rayne over the tub's rim. "There." She let go and stepped back.

"Thanks." Rayne tugged the towel around her, patting herself dry. "This is one way of exfoliating, I suppose." She gave a broad smile, and Kaelyn realized that she had barely witnessed Rayne smile before. And what did the woman have to smile about, after all? Held at gunpoint, pushed through chutes, blindfolded, and utterly bruised.

Kaelyn knew it was important to establish some kind of trust, camaraderie, which was a strange idea, as her response to Rayne took it a smidge too far to be considered pal-like. She returned the smile. "This is very true."

After putting her briefs back on, Rayne looked, bemused, at her top. "I'm afraid I need to solicit your help again." She held it up but made no gesture to cover her naked breasts.

Kaelyn did her best not to stare. "Of course." She gently maneuvered the most badly injured arm into its sleeve. When she helped Rayne with her other one, her own arm brushed against not just one of Rayne's hard nipples, but both. Rayne shivered, and Kaelyn could taste iron in her mouth, as she had painfully bitten the tip of her tongue while attempting to seem casual. She stepped back and suspected that her own smile was just as stiff as Rayne's.

Breaking out of a brief reverie, they dressed and began making their way back to the reception area. A jovial Harlow kept winking at them, which made Rayne look annoyed, and Kaelyn was sure she must be blushing, as her face and neck burned. When had *that* happened last?

Devoid of makeup and with her hair in a tight ponytail, Rayne could easily pass for a middle-class Subterranean. She doubted that any Celestial citizen knew that classes existed even among the disenfranchised. Now, dressed in some of Kaelyn's better-looking clothes, Rayne looked the part. A glance in the mirror proved that Kaelyn appeared to be her normal, unapproachable, tough self. Just like she preferred it.

They made their way through the busy lanes where bikes, scooters, and carts, powered by human effort, or, in case the person in question was well enough off, by battery-operated propulsion systems. Kaelyn noticed how Rayne's stamina dwindled after only a few blocks and hailed a small cart. She recognized the young woman maneuvering it, who had gone to school with Tania, but didn't remember her name.

"Homeward bound, sir?" the girl called out as she wove in and out between the people milling along what passed for a sidewalk. The tunnel was at its widest along this part, about forty feet. Vendors, pedestrians, and vehicles fought for space.

"Yes. Thank you. How many credits?"

"None!" The girl driving the cart grinned. "That lady there saved young Wes, unless I'm mistaken?"

The rumor mill was intact. Kaelyn merely nodded. "What's your name? I know you know Tania, but—"

"Zoe." Zoe jumped off and adjusted the thin padding on the seat. "No offense, but your lady friend looks close to dozing off."

"I'm fine. Thank you, Zoe," Rayne said, sounding stronger than her demeanor suggested. She appeared to use her last bit of strength to climb into the cart and then slumped on the seat. "That said, I'm glad you stopped for us."

"No problem." Zoe was back on the pedals, and as soon as Kaelyn had sat down next to Rayne, she made a one-eighty turn and took off toward Kaelyn's dwelling. In only a couple of additional seconds, Rayne was asleep against her shoulder. When an especially risky maneuver by Zoe nearly threw Rayne off, Kaelyn wrapped an arm around her and pulled her close. For the few minutes it took for Zoe to whisk them to Kaelyn's dwelling, she allowed herself to experience the softness of Rayne's body pressed against her own. When Rayne murmured something unintelligible and pressed her face into Kaelyn's neck, she could care less if anyone among the crowd parting before them saw the gesture.

Chapter Eight

Kae's dwelling was not at all what Rayne expected, which was a ridiculous thought, as she hadn't pictured any Subterranean quarters at all. Until last night, she had lived in comfort, and the only time she considered the existence of Kae's people was when she cursed them for hurting the soldiers she kept trying to patch.

Now she sat on a well-used, but very comfortable, couch, studying the space that Kae called home. Rayne estimated it to be about 300 square feet, which was less than her own living room area on the 2823rd floor. The wall in the back held Kae's bed, and shelving units flanked it on both sides. She squinted to make out what the box-looking items around it were.

"Before you ask, those are books, most of them from the twentieth and twenty-first century." Kae was putting away her protective gear and clothing, locking them in a metal cabinet. "I like to be able to read even when I can't charge my usual device because of energy restrictions."

As if on cue, the lights flickered for a few seconds and then went out. Kae had already lit candles on the table in front of Rayne and then fetched a lamp of sorts. Rusty, with a blackened glass surrounding a wide wick, it effectively lit up half the room once Kae put another match to it.

Rayne sniffed the air. "It has a certain scent."

"Tallow." Kae tapped the foot of the lamp after adjusting the flame.

"Excuse me?" Rayne looked between the old lamp and Kae.

"Tallow, animal fat, in the lamp. It used to be run on kerosene before the petroleum-based products were depleted in the late 2400s." Kae shrugged. "Whatever works, right?"

"How can you get animal fat down here?" The conversation was ridiculous, but discussing just about anything, preferably mundane, kept Rayne from thinking of how she was supposed to get home. *If* she could ever go home.

"Uh…in former subway and sewage tunnels? Trust me, we still have all kinds of rodents. Rats and mice procreate fast enough to keep us from having to live in the dark when we can't siphon electricity from the skyscrapers. Your engineers keep finding new ways to stop us, but our people aren't half-bad at coming up with new methods either."

Kae opened a small, metal cabinet. "I have some vegetables and fruit. Hungry?"

Another set of questions, about how they could get their hands on fruit and vegetables, whirled through Rayne's mind, but she refused to go there right now. She still hoped she wouldn't have to learn the ways of the Subterraneans just yet. Surely she could find a way home and resume her career—her life.

"I'd love some fruit. Thank you."

"It's not as lush as I'm sure you're used to, but it's all right." Kae placed what looked like two miniature apples and a pear on a plate and put it on one of the wide armrests. "It's vital that you keep your strength up. You're still recuperating."

"And I need to go home." There. Her words, which she planned to use with more caution this time, were out in the open.

"I know, but I haven't figured out a suitable way that doesn't endanger any of my people. It's one thing to ask them to protect Wes, but to risk their lives for a Celestial? That's entirely different." Kae took a seat next to Rayne. "And before you state the obvious, I'm not oblivious to the fact that I owe you Wes's life."

Rayne hadn't even thought of it that way, but she wasn't surprised that Kae had. She was starting to realize that this woman was about as honorable as a person could be, Celestial or Subterranean. Kae also had a violent streak when she led her team against Celestial interests.

"You don't owe me anything," Rayne said quietly, not wanting to talk Kae out of helping her return home. "I'm a doctor. I took the oath that doctors have sworn for centuries. To do no harm and to save lives. Nobody has to thank me, or feel they owe me, least of all a child, no matter which society he stems from." She bit into one of the apples, surprised at how flavorful it was. She continued after swallowing. "We need to address the crux of the problem. A paradox, you could say."

"Go on," Kae said guardedly.

"Two different scenarios are playing out among my people as we speak. One involves my father. He's undoubtably using all his contacts to rally any effort to retrieve me. However, the authorities most likely believe I facilitated your escape, which is true. They won't care that I did it to save a child, and the patients in the soldiers' clinic, from being further injured in the crossfire."

Kae's complete devotion to saving the child had played a part, but Rayne refused to admit to that here. Seeing Kae risk bringing a wounded child into a lion's den had been her first step in realizing the people below-ground were something more than what the media, and most of the people she knew, had fed her all her life. And still, as they'd passed the people in the tunnels on their way to Kae's dwelling, even if she had been half asleep for most of the ride, she had registered how easily her surroundings could have been a scene from one of the busy plazas on the commercial floors of the skyscrapers, if you disregarded their difference in social status. People were simply going about their business, trying to live their lives the best way they could.

Rayne thought about the nurse who had assisted her last evening, who had been so excited about going on vacation to one of the humbler resorts. From a Subterranean point of view, her vacation would have seemed to be pure luxury, while Rayne had fought back her damn entitled thoughts about the resort being too commonplace for someone of her background. Feeling flustered, she stealthily pinched her thigh to steer her mind back on track.

"You have a point. Several, in fact." Kae pulled up one leg and rested her chin on her knee. She had already wolfed down her small portion. "If we just send you back, as in leave you outside the proverbial Celestial gate, the raiders will get their hands on you. No matter how well-connected your family is, this situation can still be disastrous for you." She tilted her head and looked at Rayne through slitted eyes. "Can you think of any way to safely contact your father and have him collect you before you're taken into custody?"

"You're forgetting that I know very little about the world outside the skyscrapers. Until last night, I had never set foot on ground level, let alone ventured into the tunnel system. I've been on the ocean a few times, but that was in a professional capacity. So, no, I have no idea."

"You're kidding?"

"About which part?" Rayne recapped what she'd just said. "Oh, the ocean?"

"Yeah. That one." Kae raised her head, and it was obvious the topic intrigued her.

"I was airlifted to a dragnet-craft outside the coast around the sixtieth latitude. Some Celestials go on those working adventure trips during vacation, and while on one, the son of a minister sustained a possible spinal fracture."

"You were on a ship on the ocean..." Kae fell back against the backrest. "I've never been jealous about your lifestyle in the towers, with the exception of having unlimited access to food and medication, but this...the ocean." She gave a half smile. "Makes me sound like a kid, I know. Guess we all have some impossible dreams."

"I guess." A sharp, painful sensation erupted in Rayne's stomach at the thought of a very young Kaelyn Dark dreaming about the ocean while she went to bed hungry or was sick without any soothing remedies.

"So, to get back on topic," Kae said, and resumed her position with her chin resting on her bent knee. "We have to find a way to reach—wait, what's your father's name?"

"Rocque Garcia. My mother is Madelon." Rayne wondered what her mother was doing. As influential as Rocque was, Madelon had her own circle, where a lot was decided behind the scenes. "It might be easier to reach her. She's heavily into fund-raising and charities, which, in her case, means sending already rich kids to even more expensive schools."

"We'll keep both options open when we brainstorm with the team." Kae pursed her lips. "At first, I meant to run every angle by my commander, but in retrospect, I think we need to know more about your situation. Command is less flexible and sometimes proceeds with its gut-reaction ideas without fully understanding the consequences for regular people. That's one reason I work my unit rather independently. Not just Celestials have various levels. We do here too."

"Yes. I'm beginning to understand that fact." Rayne shifted in her corner of the couch, wanting to study Kae's expression carefully. "I get the feeling they might not be above using me as a bargaining chip. That's what the authorities would do at my end. Have done, on many occasions."

"Yes. They have—and so have we." Kae looked uncomfortable. "I should say—so have I."

Rayne wrapped her arms around herself. It was important to be honest with each other if they were going to resolve their situation, but it still stung to envision Kae using a person as a pawn in the conflict between cavers and cloudheads.

"Did it work?"

Kae's eyes darkened, and she appeared to grow distant. "No."

Chapter Nine

Kaelyn looked at the people who had gathered in her dwelling, amazed yet again how twenty-five or so people managed to fit in her home. She was aware that most Subterraneans lived in far smaller quarters, and a lot of them didn't have running water or the ability to keep their food cool. Others profited yet again from that fact, charging for storage, water, and electricity. Thankfully, most people had a personal waste feature, even if it was just a bucket hooked up to the sewage. At least they had one perk for living underground, close to the pipes that carried their waste to an unknown location. They didn't have to compete with the skyscrapers. The cloudheads had other ways to deal with their waste.

Foster sat on the couch next to Rayne and Beth. The rest sat on Kaelyn's bed and on the floor. She kept thin cushions around for that exact purpose, as nobody below-ground ever sat directly on the floor for an extended period if they could help it.

"As I see it, we have a paradoxical problem," Harlow said. He had been part of the armed teams longer than any of them. He didn't want to be in charge, he'd made that fact obvious, but he always had an opinion, and it was often astute. "The doc goes back, and we end up thanking her by getting her incarcerated, at best. We keep her, we invite the wrath of her well-connected family and the raiders."

"I say we send her packing," one of the younger team members said flippantly. Kaelyn groaned inwardly. Most young men seemed to go through this phase. Quick to judge, hasty to act, they rarely slowed down enough to consider potential consequences.

"Thank you." Kaelyn waved her hand dismissively. "The situation's even more complex. Who's to say that the Celestial authorities still won't use this as a reason to invade, as they've been planning for years?"

The room went quiet, and Kaelyn glanced over at Rayne, who had lost some of her restored color. "Doctor Garcia? What is your opinion on this matter? After all, this is your life we're shuffling around the board here. Your good name."

"My good name is most likely a lost cause among the Celestial authorities right now. Rayne stood. "I want you to listen to me now. In this whole discussion you're having, you forget one thing. I wasn't kidnapped. I jumped into the laundry chute voluntarily. Those of you who were there know this is true. This means you don't owe me anything. I, on the other hand, am a liability for you. That's another fact."

More voices made themselves heard after Rayne spoke, ranging from the earlier statement all the way to Beth's opposite view.

"The doc is valuable to them. She tends to the raiders when we've made them bleed. I bet a lot of doctors don't care a smidge about how hard that is, and all the hours she puts in every week. I'm no fool. She could stay on the umpteenth-whatever floor and wear her crisp, tailored lab coat and let the raiders fend for themselves. And when we came in with Wes…" Beth's voice broke, and she sat down quickly.

"Yeah, yeah, she's a damn cloudhead angel. We get it. That doesn't mean it's safe for us to keep her around." Another one of the young men slammed his palm against the floor where he sat. "I second the idea of taking her topside. I'm sure she can make up a story to blame us for everything. The way the raiders have been attacking lately, it can't get much worse."

Kaelyn raised her hand. "Trust me, it can get a lot worse. I know from experience. And unless we want to take a page from the cloudhead playbook, we're not going to have an innocent life on our conscience." She wouldn't hesitate firing at the raiders if they crossed the border between their world and hers, but no way would she risk Rayne's life. It wasn't just the raiders. Topside, you could run into the gangs, often referred to as dopers, who lived in the border zone, ready to do anything for food, drink, and drugs. They attacked raiders and Subterraneans alike. Anything for the next fix. Subterraneans lost young people to the dopers all the time. She wondered if any Celestial kid had ever risked ending up on the surface level, running with the dopers. It was hard to picture.

"Calm down," Foster said without raising his voice, visually nailing the young men who had begun exchanging their volatile ideas. We must—"

A thunderous banging on Kaylyn's metal door made most of them jump. Kaelyn rose and went over to peer through her peephole. When she saw a young girl who worked at the clinic, wiping her tears and getting ready to bang again, Kaelyn flung the door open.

"What's going on?" Kaelyn tugged the girl inside, but as she moved to close the door again, she heard faint roars in the tunnels, growing in intensity.

The girl hiccupped and wiped at her tears. "It's…it's terrible. He's dead. He's dead, along with everyone in his cart." New tears ran down the girl's cheeks and dropped from her soft, round jawline.

"First of all, take a deep breath," Kaelyn said and held the young woman by the shoulders. "Then tell me your name."

"Poppy. I'm a medic…and…Neely sent me." Still gasping for air between the words, Poppy appeared to be calming down.

"All right. Who is dead?" Dreading the answer, thinking of Wes, his frail little body clinging stubbornly to life, Kaelyn fought to not shake Poppy by her narrow shoulders.

"Doctor Boro! Raiders ambushed the tracks just outside of the Main Hole. That's what his chief medic said before he died.

Nobody in Doctor Boro's cart survived." Shaking now, Poppy sank onto one of the floor cushions and seemed to withdraw into herself.

Around them, pandemonium erupted. Only Rayne remained calm, which Kaelyn could tell from the tense expression around her eyes and lips. When the noise died down and Poppy had had some water, Rayne walked over to stand next to Kaelyn.

"If this is true," she asked in a somber tone, "I suppose that takes the guessing out of the equation regarding my status." She glanced at Kaelyn. "Did I understand this correctly? Doctor Boro is—was—your only physician worth the name around these parts?"

"He was the best," Beth whispered. "The absolute best."

"All right." Kaelyn pushed back against the shock and grief that was simmering just below her ribcage. "We must confirm Poppy's and Neely's information. Also, what did you mean by this taking the guessing out of the equation?" She turned to face Rayne head-on.

"If your only true physician is gone, and obviously I hope this is not the case, but if it is, you'll need my services until you can find a replacement." The even expression in Rayne's eyes didn't give her emotions away.

"If things are as bad as they appear, we'll discuss that possibility." Kaelyn drew a quick, trembling breath. If Boro was gone, along with the medic who was also his life partner, they were screwed. Yes, Boro had been training his staff, but there was no one like him in their parts of the vast tunnel system that was their home.

"Let's adjourn this meeting. We didn't get much done, but we need to hustle." Kaelyn began issuing orders. She sent one team to check out the site where the raiders had gained access to their tracks. Needing to keep panic to a minimum, two teams intended to head out and exercise crowd control. They couldn't afford to add more injured to the mess since they currently might be without a doctor. "Rayne, Foster, Beth, you're with me. We're going back to the clinic." Kaelyn studied Rayne closely. "Are you fit enough to come with us? We need your expertise, even if you can manage only to tell us what to do if we get wounded."

"I can manage," Rayne answered calmly. "I'm all right."

Of course. This woman would claim she was okay as she drew her last breath. "Then let's go. Foster, you take up the rear. We're in for a lot of concerned people wanting answers."

"Agreed. Good thing this version of Doc looks like one of us now. Makes it easier." Beth nodded solemnly.

Kaelyn wasn't sure she agreed, as Rayne's affluent background seemed to ooze out of her pores, but at least she wasn't wearing the damn telltale scrubs. Nobody that gave her only a passing glance would guess. "All right. Everyone knows where to bring their teams and what to do?"

A chorus of affirmative answers echoed her question. Kaelyn remembered to grab two canisters of double-filtered water for her and Rayne and then opened the door. "If you need to pick something up from your dwellings, then do it quickly. We don't know when we'll get a handle on this situation, or if we're facing additional attacks."

The pathway outside was full of people standing in groups, talking in increasingly louder voices, as others hurried in the direction of either the clinic or the tracks. Kaelyn made sure Rayne was close by. "You have to keep up, Doc. If I lose you in this crowd, you'll get turned around fast."

"Got it." Rayne accepted her water canister. She was pale and moved a little stiffly, but her eyes betrayed her adrenaline surge, something Kaelyn recognized in herself.

Checking that Beth and Foster were ready, Kaelyn rotated her index finger in the air. "Let's move!"

Chapter Ten

It was twice as crowded in the tunnels as it had been when they made their way to Kae's earlier. Rayne focused on keeping pace with her. Every now and then she heard the name Boro being chanted around them. This man, whom she had never met, was obviously revered. Perhaps he had been the only decent doctor in this part of the Subterranean world, or maybe he was simply a well-liked human being.

Every now and then, someone bumped into her, a few times nearly knocking her over, but for the most part, as they were all moving in the same direction, she had no problem keeping her balance. It was something of a culture shock, as nobody would ever dream of stepping within anyone else's personal space where she lived. The only crowded location she had ever visited before was the Soldiers' Clinic.

"Kae! This isn't fast enough," Foster called out from behind. "I can't see any available carts. Can you manage the wire, Doctor?"

Surprised that Foster addressed her directly, Rayne frowned. "The wire? I have no idea what that is."

"One of the more antiquated, but still functioning, ways to travel fast if you have a permit." Kae stopped and pulled Rayne toward the wall. She pointed to the ceiling about thirty or forty feet at its highest point. "There. See the wires with grips attached to them?"

"You mean we have to dangle from those?" Rayne cringed. "I'm not sure—"

"It's perfectly safe, unless you let go," Kae said, an unexpected grin forming as she spoke. "I'll lower them to our position, and when we're secure, I'll flip the lever that runs the power to the engine. We'll be hoisted up and propelled all the way to the clinic."

"I enjoy it, actually." Beth grinned.

But Rayne was sure she would hate it. "I don't have your stamina for such things."

"That's why you'll ride with me. I won't let you fall." Kae opened a metal box on the wall and pressed in a code on an old-fashioned-looking console. The wires jerked, and then the contraption began to move. When it reached their location by the tunnel wall, it lowered semicircle handles of sorts. The grips were wrapped with what looked like silicon, which would help with their grip.

"I promise that I can't dangle all the way over to the clinic." Rayne pressed her back against the wall.

"I'll help you. You'll be fine."

Kae pulled at a set of four semicircular handles and tucked her feet into the lower two. She held out her hand to Rayne. "Place your feet just beside mine." She wrapped an arm around Rayne's waist and pulled her tight. "Come on."

Rayne had never felt so clumsy. She stepped onto what she realized were footrests and took two fistfuls of Kae's jacket to keep from falling over backward.

"I've got you," Kae murmured, her lips nearly touching Rayne's ear. "Put your arms around me, and I'll keep us secure with these." She took both hand supports in her free hand as she shifted to glance over Rayne's shoulder. "Foster. Start us up."

A jerk, then a loud whirr, accompanied by a distinct tremor in the wire, made Rayne cling to Kae. It was ridiculous to be afraid of heights in a tunnel when she normally had no issue with any type of vertigo as she moved about on the 2800th floor. The difference in perspective caused the problem. In the skyscrapers, very rarely did someone plummet to the ground through the fool-proof windows. Here in the tunnels, where makeshift gadgets and refurbishments ruled, it was distinctly possible to fall and break your neck. And that was just one of many ways you could die down here, Rayne was certain.

They moved above the crowd with impressive speed, attracting attention as they passed above people's heads. The shouts and cheers startled Rayne, but as they sounded mostly benevolent, she focused on holding onto Kae. Standing face-to-face, pressed hard against each other, she managed to block the idea of them falling to their deaths among the people below. Instead, she inhaled Kae's clean scent, which she shared after their visit to the bath facility.

Her left arm like a band of steel around Rayne's waist, Kae kept a firm grip of her pant lining. Rayne clung to, rather than gripped, Kae's shoulders.

"You're doing fine. Next time, you'll be able to ride alone," Kae said with her cheek against Rayne's temple.

Rayne pressed her forehead against Kae to avoid watching the crowd below become a blur as they whirred along the wire. Who knew if this thing had some corroded spots that would break and send them neck-first onto some innocent soul below? She could barely breathe. Her heart drummed so fast, she grew dizzy as the percussion echoed throughout her. A tingling sensation in her hands made her realize she might be close to panicking or, worse, fainting. A normally well-buried memory of being stuck in a rapid-lift as a child, certain the car would fall the 2800 some floors, surfaced, making it impossible to remain calm. She clung harder to Kae, pressing her face to her neck.

"You're fine. I won't let you fall!" Kae shouted the words. "You have to ease up and let me breathe, however."

How could she possibly risk loosening her grip? Reluctantly, Rayne pulled her arms down toward Kae's shoulders, freeing her neck.

"Better!" Kae called out. "Not long now."

It still seemed like an eternity before the whirring sound from the wires went from whining to growling as they slowed down. As they abruptly halted, which made them swing violently, Kae's strong arms were the only things that kept Rayne from slipping off.

"Sorry. Should have warned you. Now, climb down fast, or the others will collide with us."

Her body didn't feel like her own, but Rayne made sure the space below was empty and not too far away, and then she jumped. Moving aside, she watched Kae move with that lethal grace she had come to associate with her, getting their wires out of the way as Foster and Beth arrived.

"You did good, Doc," Beth said, smiling. "Not bad for a first try."

"That's because of Kae. I would have fallen and broken my neck if she hadn't held on to me." Rayne rolled her shoulders and tried to disregard the pain in her arms.

"We need to keep moving. The crowd's not as bad here—yet." Kae motioned for them to follow her.

"I'm going to stop by the armory. We'll need more than sidearms if an attack takes place." Foster motioned to a small tunnel to their left. "Or an uproar."

"Get a small sidearm for Rayne," Kae said, then held up her hand, her palm toward Foster. "And I don't need a lecture about trusting a cloudhead."

"The furthest thing from my mind." Foster gave a crooked smile, then took off with an impressive speed, considering his size.

"Know how to use a weapon, Doc?" Beth asked as they made their way down the last block before the clinic. She appeared to have her own little arsenal—two sidearms, one glimmer rifle, and an assortment of intricately patterned vials and balls attached to her battle harness.

"Yes. Weapons' training is mandatory when you work at the Soldiers' Clinic. I'm a decent shot when it comes to the shooting range." How she would fare when aiming at a live target and trying to combine that with her oath to save lives was another matter.

"Good." Kae motioned left with her hand. "Almost there. Crowd's getting denser. Ready, Beth?"

A hissing sound as Beth removed the safety off her glimmer answered that question. "A gun is enough in a crowd," Kae said calmly as she kept her weapon pointed down along her leg. "Easier to maneuver."

"Spoilsport." Beth attached the glimmer to her back and pulled out the larger of her guns. "This still gets the job done, I suppose. I'd rather not shoot at one of our own, though."

Rayne was getting used to shadowing Kae as they weaved through the crowd. Most of the people stepped aside when they recognized Kae, but some began shouting questions.

"Is it true, Dark? Is Boro gone?"

"What about my son? He needs his surgery!"

"Hey, Dark! Are we going to finally hit the bastards where it really hurts?"

Kae only shook her head and kept pressing on. Rayne was grateful nobody had identified her as a Celestial, or the furious man uttering the last question would have attacked, she was sure. Looking around was a mistake, as the blend of hatred, sorrow, and anguish pouring from the crowd seemed to engulf her completely. She had never met anything harsher than occasional jealousy from male peers, mostly because they coveted her position and social rank. This massive wave of frightening negativity felt almost physical as it washed over her, creating goose bumps.

"That's a relief. The guards are already handling crowd control." Kae nodded at the four guards keeping watch, weapons drawn, at the entrance to the clinic.

Just inside the door, ambulatory patients and next of kin flocked around Neely. Rayne had just begun to regain her equilibrium, when Neely saw her.

"Doctor Garcia!" Neely excused herself to the group around her and hurried toward them. "You're an answer to my prayer. We need you in the OR, and we need more guards on the other entrance."

"Help's coming. Foster's bringing more arms, and the troops are organizing crowd control." Kae shot Rayne a glance. "Think you can help?"

"I'm better in the OR than on the barricades." Rayne used the familiar setting of a clinic, as humble as this was from her point of view, to calm herself, before turning to Neely. "What have we got?"

"Several injured from the attack. They rode in the last car. I can manage all but one with the help of my staff, but there's a woman with shrapnel in her lower abdomen and thigh. I know it's unlikely that we can save her—"

"Let me be the judge of that," Rayne said and followed Neely into a narrow tunnel to their right. She soon found herself in the same area where they had taken Wes only a day ago. What Neely referred to as an OR wouldn't even have been considered appropriate as a storage unit at Rayne's hospital. She eyed the trays holding the instruments, and her heart skipped a few beats. She would have to be extra inventive and dig deep into her knowledge of old-fashioned medical procedures.

The patient, a middle-aged woman, lay on the table where medics had prepared her, probably not knowing if anyone with a decent set of skills would come through the door.

"This is Doctor Garcia. If any of you has a problem with her performing the surgery, step outside. The patient deserves our best." Neely looked at the medics, one at a time. "Understood?"

"Sure." The medic closest to Rayne nodded, but his expression wasn't exactly warm. She didn't have time to worry about their feelings. Pulling on sterile garments after using the strong-smelling liquid that Neely provided to wash her hands, Rayne bent over the woman. She had shrapnel buried in several places on her right side, but the long, narrow piece of wood lodged just below her sternum worried Rayne the most.

"We're going to roll her very gently," she said, back into a role she knew well. She could see out of the corners of her eyes that the medics unanimously straightened and began to work as a unit. They rolled the woman, and Rayne was relieved to see that no shrapnel had gone straight through her. "What do you have that I can use to scan her abdomen?"

"Just this, I'm afraid," a female medic said and held up a flat wand, about twenty-five inches long. A small screen was attached to one end, while the other boasted a set of sensors. Thinking back to her old mentor's collection of antique medical instruments, Rayne realized that it was an ultrasound wand from the 2200s. It looked modified, or perhaps just repaired.

"Just hold down the largest sensor and run it over the area you need scanned. It gives a decent image." The woman to Rayne's left looked somewhat less tense.

"Thanks." Rayne pressed her thumb against the sensor as instructed and ran it around the enormous wood splinter. The screen lit up, and a blue-tinted image emerged. Rayne squinted but found the image resolution wasn't bad, just very blue. The splinter had perforated the woman just below her diaphragm but missed her liver by a hair. Rayne would have used a laparoscopic robot at her hospital, and a proper cutting tool at the Soldiers' Clinic, but here, she would have to wing it. "I'm going to extract this, very slowly. Be prepared with something to soak up blood. Anything will do, if it's sterile, and if you have a cauterizer, that'd be great."

"We have a modified soldering iron." The male medic pointed to his side, where an actual soldering iron was plugged into a portable energy bar, the latter clearly stolen from a skyscraper.

"All right." Rayne slowly pulled on the splinter, trying not to wiggle it, as she wasn't sure where the tip was located, or the condition of it. If she lost a piece of it inside this woman, she would have no choice but to open her up.

"Is it her?" A young man entered the room, halting at the foot of the table. Neely was right behind him.

"Roddy. Let the doctor do her job. She'll inform you—"

"Mom!"

"Stay away from the sterile field!" Rayne spoke harshly, as she was palpating the wound while using the ultrasound.

"It's my mother," Roddy, who was more a teenage boy than a man, roared. "They killed Dad, and now I'm losing her too."

"We don't know that. Dr. Garcia is very skilled—" Roddy shoved Neely aside and moved toward Rayne.

"And this happened only because they let a fucking cloudhead into our tunnels!"

"Stop right there," a serene, strong voice said.

Rayne sighed in relief. Kae. Thank the creator. "Listen," she said, not taking her eyes off her task but wanting to reassure the traumatized boy. "Your mother has a good chance of making it if you let me work. After I've tended to her wounds, we're going to monitor her, and you can be at her side. She'll know you're there even if she's not awake."

"You a bigshot cloudhead doctor, like they say?" Roddy sobbed between every other word.

"Not sure about the bigshot part, but yes, I'm a Celestial physician." Rayne didn't look at him, just kept working, palpating the wound as far in as she could. A small vessel pumped blood up over her fingers. "I need the cauter—the soldering tool. Is the handle sterile?" Rayne didn't care about that as much as she normally would. She needed to cauterize the bleeder.

"As good as it's going to get," the male medic said, sounding less hostile.

Rayne burned the offending little artery and made sure no other blood vessels had the same idea. Then she scanned the wound several times before she decided to close. When she looked up, Roddy had left the theater, and so had Neely and Kae.

"Doctor Boro's son?" Rayne asked, although she was quite certain.

"Yes. And this is his wife, Zara." The female medic drew a trembling breath. "Staples or sutures?"

"Sutures. They're easier to remove using just a clean pair of scissors, or a small knife, rather than trying to take out staples without a proper tool." Something told Rayne that the situation in the tunnels would only escalate, and who knew if anyone had access to proper medical equipment.

They spent a good ninety minutes cleaning out the rest of Zara's wounds. Only when they were done did Rayne fully exhale and straighten her back. She was used to performing surgery for hours on end, but today, after everything she had been through the last two days, she felt close to crumbling.

Rayne accompanied Zara on her gurney to an area that she recognized from earlier. They passed Wes's bed, where he was half sitting up, able to sip something from a mug. Tania was sitting next to him on the bed, her arm around him as she appeared to read. She looked up as they passed, and her eyes grew wide at the sight of Zara. Getting up, she padded over to where the medics lifted Zara onto a bed. She was still intubated, and it would be at least twenty-four hours before they could attempt to wake her.

"What's happening? No one's telling us anything." Tania took Rayne by the arm and looked at her as if she had all the answers.

"There was an explosion." Rayne wasn't about to lie to the girl. "Zara was injured."

"And Boro?" Tania whispered, going white.

Now this was another matter. It was one thing to offer information that was common knowledge, but Rayne didn't know who Boro might be to Tania on a personal level.

"He's dead, sweetheart." Neely appeared on the other side of Zara's bed. "I'm sorry."

Tania stood rigid for a moment, then swiveled and returned to Wes's bed, where she pulled the curtain closed. The whimpers, barely audible, tore at Rayne's heart.

"Were they close?" she asked Neely. She adjusted Zara's pillow to provide support to the ventilator equipment.

"In a way. Tania, like so many others down here, suffered from childhood asthma and allergies. She spent quite a few nights in intensive care. Zara is the head medic here, and she was very good friends with Tanya and Wes's mother. When they lost her, Kae became their protector, and Zara was already like a favorite aunt. Boro was their hero, like he was to many people here. He rarely left this area. Why he had to be summoned to the Main Hole, I have no idea—it rarely happened." Neely looked exasperated. "And he took our portable scanner, which I can only assume may be lost. We have only our ultrasound wands for the foreseeable future."

Remembering this shortage from before the surgery, Rayne realized that these people truly scraped by with old, reconfigured equipment that was nearly impossible to replace. At her hospital, all she had to do was make a nurse call maintenance to replace anything. Not even at the Soldiers' Clinic did they have to settle for anything like this.

The sound of running feet startled everyone still standing around Zara's bed. Voices called out, but with so many, Rayne couldn't make out what they were shouting.

Neely quickly pulled the curtain around Zara's bed and motioned for a medic to remain by the unconscious woman's side before pulling Rayne with her. "We have to hide you."

Rayne's heart began to race again. She could barely breathe. What was going on? Was someone coming for her?

Neely pulled the covers off an empty bed. "Quickly! Get in!"

Rayne blinked. "What?"

"Do as I say." Neely shoved Rayne, making her stumble and fall onto the bed. She understood what Neely was trying to do and kicked off her shoes. Neely tucked the sheets and blankets around her, all the way up to her chin. Then she attached an oxygen mask to Rayne's face. "Don't move. No matter what you hear. Keep your eyes closed."

Rayne was trembling and could only hope her shaking wasn't visible on top of the covers. She closed her eyes. Now the loud footfalls were closer, and just as she felt something click onto the frame at the foot of the bed, people entered Intensive Care.

"Boro, Boro, Boro!" Voices chanted the dead doctor's name, and the sound bounced off the walls.

"What the hell do you think you're doing? We have seriously sick people here." Neely's sharp voice cut through the angry cries of whatever crowd had broken through and entered the clinic. Her question seemed to have no effect. The crowd howled words of hatred against the raiders responsible for Boro's death. Then they resumed calling out his name.

"What the fuck?" a young, furious voice shouted. Tania. It had to be. And now Rayne could hear a young child crying as well. Wes? "You idiots are scaring my brother, and he had surgery yesterday." Tania appeared to move across the floor. "Get out of here. All of you."

"Hey, that's Dark's foster kid," a young, male voice called out. "We should move on."

"I'm no one's foster kid. But Boro's wife is here, badly injured. You trying to kill her by being assholes?" Tania asked.

"Uh!" Another male voice, or maybe the same, gave a loud groan. "No need to push, girl!"

"I'll do more than push if you don't take your grimy, sorry asses out of here." Tania moved back toward Wes's bed. "Just fuck off."

"Is that Boro's old lady?" a young woman asked.

"No," Neely said quickly. "This is another patient."

Rayne forced herself to be still and breathe evenly into the mask. She was sweating beneath the covers, as she was still fully dressed.

"What's wrong with her? Do we know her?" the woman asked.

"You know any medical condition is confidential." Neely spoke harshly. "Leave."

"I just want to take a look." The woman was clearly not about to give up. "A lot of strange things going on today. You might have an injured raider there for all we know. You lot have saved some of them before so they can come back and kill us all."

"Stay. Away. Ow!" Neely cried out, and something slammed into Rayne's bed, jostling her. She wanted to open her eyes and find out what was going on, but if she did, it could be all over.

The sound of a safety being removed from a rifle turned the room dead quiet. "Get out of here. If I find any of you here, or stirring up trouble somewhere else, I will come after you. And don't think I don't recognize each and every one of you." Kae's husky voice was low but still reached every corner of Intensive Care. "This is your one chance. Move!"

A few among the crowd objected, but Rayne could tell from the way a certain calm blanketed the room that all the intruders had left.

"I apologize, Dark," an unknown man said. "There were too many, and I couldn't fire at them. They're kids."

"Kids with murder in their eyes." Kae's tone was harsh. "Next time, stun them."

"I will." The man sighed.

Rayne decided it was time to get out of bed. She tore off the mask and wiped her face as she sat up.

"Damn. That was a quick recovery." A young man standing with his side to Rayne turned around and stared at her.

Kae had even raised her rifle but lowered it immediately. "Why are you—oh. That was smart." She looked relieved.

"Neely's idea." Rayne took off the formerly sterile garments and placed them on the bed. She drew a deep breath. "We need to check on Zara—and Wes." She removed the curtain and found the medic checking Zara's blood pressure. "How is she?"

"The same. Stable. BP 110/60. Pulse 88."

Rayne would have liked to see all the bloodwork she was used to getting in her own hospital, but here, you didn't run bloodwork unless something was truly wrong. "Thank you." She turned and walked over to Tania and Wes. Kae was already there. The rest of her team was guarding the entrance to the room.

"Hello, Wes. Tania." Kae studied the boy carefully. His tearstained cheeks were flushed. She placed the back of her hand against his forehead. He was hot. She turned to Neely, who was right behind her. "Take his temperature, please."

Tania raised her chin. "What's wrong?"

"Wes is a little warm. Could be all the excitement, but we need to see just how warm he is." Rayne waited while Neely measured Wes's temperature.

"102.2," Neely said. "I'll get some fever-reducing medication."

"Does he have an infection?" Kae murmured after joining Rayne at the foot of Wes's bed.

"I don't know yet." Placing her fingertips on one of Wes's thin wrists, she could tell his pulse was rapid but strong. She turned to Tania. "We need to make sure we can lower his fever. If he has an infection brewing, he'll need medication."

"I see." Tania had Wes on her lap, where they both sat on the bed. She looked pale and worried. She glowered up at Kae. "You need to find Mama Doe."

"I will." Kae rubbed the back of her neck. "Getting there in this upheaval might take too long though."

"Who's this Mama Doe?" Rayne asked.

"Our herbal apothecary, who works in one of the hydroponic areas. She grows what we can't scavenge from the tower storage units." Kae ran her hand over her cheek, and Rayne could see her own exhaustion mirrored on her face. They had been on their feet for so long, minus the few hours of sleep they managed to get last night, and even if she was used to long shifts at the Soldiers' Clinic, this was far beyond that.

Neely returned, looking relieved. "I found some actual antibiotics in storage. They're for adults, but we can dilute them." She held up a vial. "We're very low on fever-reducing medication, but I found some." Placing two small pills next to a glass of water, Neely reached for the IV bag attached to Wes's bed.

"Let me see." Rayne took it from her before the medic had time to object. She read the label and then frowned. "This expired more than six months ago."

"Most of our traditional meds are." Kae nodded at Neely.

"Don't give it to him unless we know he truly has an infection." Rayne's mind whirled as she discarded one option after another. "Surely you have simple test strips?"

Kae's eyes grew cold, which reminded Rayne that she hadn't seen this version of Kae since she stormed into the Soldiers' Clinic carrying Wes and demanding treatment. "You still don't get it. We don't have anything of what you take for granted in your palace in the clouds. We have no medication and no way to manufacture it. We have no test strips. And what we do have, we have to risk our fucking lives to steal, and we run out of that very fast because the need keeps building—and we're never able to catch up."

Rayne stood silent, unsure how to respond.

"And if this kid dies, that's on me, for not noticing he followed me topside." Kae moved into Rayne's personal space, her lips tense as she continued. "So, we're going to give him the antibiotics to be sure we've done everything we can. We have no margins for the sit-and-wait approach. Tell me, what would you do if a child came into your hospital on the umpteenth floor with the same symptoms?"

Rayne gazed at the people flocking around her. Hard eyes in hard faces. She set her jaw and clenched her fists. "I would do a complete workup with non-invasive bloodwork, as we are talking about a small child, and get the answers in less than fifteen minutes. Then I would put the child through a scan to find out where the infection originated. When I'd established that fact, I would treat that area with an antibiotic wand and then put him in a bed that would monitor every change. Usually, that child would be released in a day or two."

"An antibiotic wand?" Neely gaped. "Haven't even heard about that."

"They're not used at the Soldiers' Clinics. The stuff you can get your hands on is mainly what's used there. The hospital I usually work in is on the 2810th floor."

"Of course, it is." Kae was visibly trying to calm down but still snarled the words while staring at the floor. "And how many of those wands do you have access to?"

Rayne didn't want to answer. Not because she was ashamed of the resources she was used to accessing, but because she loathed to rub their excess into the faces of the people around her. "As many as I need. They're a staple in modern medicine."

"Then go get a couple of boxes for us." Tania's voice trembled, from fury or fear, or both. She was cradling Wes and pushed the hair from his face. "Go up there to the 2810th floor and grab a few boxes for the kids down here that die from simple cuts."

Rayne looked down at the girl who had lost so much, and who risked losing her little brother if they couldn't turn his condition around. "All right," she said. "Start what antibiotics you have, and I'll get you whatever supplies I can."

If the small crowd of soldiers and medics had stared at Rayne before, they were gawking now. Kae snapped her head up. "That's not remotely funny."

"Not meant to be. Show me where I can get topside and the closest access point. I have my subdermal identification chip. They'll let me in." Rayne hoped they would.

"Or incarcerate you for treason for helping us." Kae's voice grew softer. She placed a hand on Rayne's shoulder and shook her gently. "You know I'm right."

"I know nothing of the sort." Rayne didn't want to sound so haughty, but if Kae was going to let her go, she couldn't give in to the touch the way her body ached to. It would be so easy to just let Kae, the ever-resilient and brave resistance fighter, do all the hard work. This was, however, Rayne's area of expertise, and if she could somehow persuade the contacts she had to let her bring supplies down to the lower floors—perhaps under the guise of using them on the soldiers—it was worth the risk. "Unless *you* intend to incarcerate me, I'm going."

"Are you for real?" Tania looked up at Rayne. "Or are you simply taking the chance to get home to your cushy existence?"

Rayne had to steady herself against the foot of Wes's bed. "I mean what I say. I know people. I can't guarantee anything, but I'm currently your best bet of getting the supplies you need."

"We need to talk about this. Alone." Kae wrapped her arm around Rayne's shoulders. "We both need to put our feet up for a while, and while we do that, you're going to tell me just how you plan to perform this heist." She turned to one of her team. "Hold the fort. And by that, I mean, keep those not in need of medical attention out."

"Will do." The man nodded briskly and took the rest of the team out into the corridor.

Kae ushered Rayne toward a narrow, metal door. Behind it was a tiny restroom for staff, boasting a couch, a small table, and what could be a food cooler. "Sit."

Rayne wanted to object to being ordered around, but she had run out of steam and slumped down onto the couch, moaning as she seemed to melt into the fabric.

"We're going to rest, and when we've done that, you'll tell me just how you plan to make something so crazy work." Kae sat down next to Rayne. She took a folded towel and placed it on her thighs as she put her feet up on the small table. "Lie down." She patted the towel.

"What?" Rayne looked at the towel and then up at Kae. Did she really intend for Rayne to sleep with her head on her lap?

"You are pale, bordering on gray. If you're going to pull off a major stunt, you need your rest. Come on."

Rayne didn't have the strength to argue. "Damn it." She leaned sideways until her head was on Kae's lap, then put her legs up on the couch. Through the towel, she could feel the strong, wiry muscles in Kae's thighs move as she shifted.

"Now rest." Kae moved her left arm around on the backrest, until she gave up and placed it around Rayne in an almost protective position.

Rayne closed her eyes. Her heart was pounding as she felt the warmth from Kae's body permeate the towel. Kae shifted again, which made Rayne slide backward until the back of her head rested against her belly. Now she felt every single breath Kae took, and was it her imagination, or did it sound labored? Kae's arm slid farther down along Rayne's side and ended up on her hip. She didn't dare move or comment, as the situation was already completely strange. Having been in forced proximity with this woman several times now didn't make it any easier. Instead, Rayne realized that no matter what dire circumstances a person found themselves in, the body did its own thing.

Stealthily drawing a deep breath, her thoughts whirling incessantly, Rayne fully expected to relive every single thing that had happened since she woke up in the clinic today. As it turned out, surrounded by the warmth of Kae's body, it didn't take very long for her to fall asleep.

Chapter Eleven

Kaelyn stirred, then jerked as her neck smarted more than usual. Realizing she was staring at the ceiling, she suppressed a moan while raising her head. She didn't recognize the room at first but then remembered the break room at the intensive care at the clinic. Glancing down, she saw Rayne was still asleep with her head on Kaelyn's thighs. Rayne's left hand appeared to be steadying her where it cradled one of Kaelyn's knees.

"Hey. We need to talk. I need to know that resting a bit has made you see reason." Kaelyn shook Rayne's hip gently, then more firmly, as she appeared fast asleep. "Rayne?"

"Mm." Rayne didn't even open her eyes. Her long, dark blond hair ran like a river flooding Kaelyn's entire lap. She pushed it aside and found that it still smelled of the soap from the bath facility. Kaelyn had never felt such silky hair and couldn't help taking a handful and squeezing it gently.

"Mm. Kae?" Rayne opened her eyes, and Kaelyn quickly let go of her hair, annoyed at how flustered she'd become.

"We need to rehydrate and eat something. We're running on fumes, and even if I'm used to that at times, you're not." Kae tried to inch away from Rayne, but she turned onto her back and squinted up at Kaelyn. Her dazed expression and the way she slowly blinked made Kae grip the edge of the cushion she was sitting on. Those large, green eyes, framed by light-brown lashes, and the band of bronzed freckles that created a ribbon across Rayne's high cheekbones and her nose, made her the most enticing woman she had ever seen. A woman of her poise and proficiency shouldn't have to be down in the tunnels, where the most you could hope for was work that didn't get you dirty and didn't wear you out in every way possible. Then again, perhaps being a doctor on the 2810th floor could be just as hard. Kaelyn had no way of knowing, as she had never been above the third floor.

"Yes. Water." Rayne ran the tip of her tongue over her lips. "And a toothbrush?"

"Those we have plenty of, since we make them ourselves." Kae attempted a light tone but inhaled sharply when Rayne turned to sit up and managed to place a hand far too high up on her thighs. It was ridiculous how the accidental touch made Kaelyn's stomach clench. Steadying Rayne with both hands, she tried not to let her reaction show.

As soon as Rayne had moved off her, Kaelyn got up and opened the door. "I'll be right back." She took her time finding toothbrushes, made from spun acrylic straws attached to handles made of the same material. A couple of small pouches of menthol cream and a hairbrush found its way into her pockets. She nodded to Neely, who hurried past her, looking exhausted. Kae made a detour to the storage room, where she had stashed four nutribars, all made from produce from the hydroponic bay, with added mushrooms and algae.

Kaelyn returned to the break room, where she stopped just outside the door, her hand on the doorframe for a moment before she opened it and stepped back inside. "Here you go." She handed Rayne the food, the brushes, and the paste. "Even if we had access to your teeth cleaner, we couldn't plug it in here, as it's apparently supposed to go into a special socket."

"I'm not fussy, as long as I can do something after not having cleaned my teeth in days." She turned over the small packages in an oiled paper. "And what's this?"

"A nutribar. Lots of good stuff in it, but the most important part is the berries, which make it taste pretty good." Sitting down on the couch again, Kaelyn opened one of her bars and bit into it. It tasted sweet and salty, and the mushrooms made it chewy in a pleasant way.

Rayne took a proper bite, clearly not afraid to taste something different, and nodded after swallowing. "Not bad."

They finished their bars, and then Kae threw the empty wrappers into a bucket sitting by the door before she turned to face Rayne. "Unless you have to use the latrine immediately, we have to talk about your so-called plan."

"What do you mean, 'so-called'?" Rayne folded her arms across her chest.

"It's a damn risky plan to just waltz back into your skyscraper and act as if nothing has happened. You haven't thought it through." Kaelyn kept her eyes locked on Rayne's. "They won't buy it."

"They have to buy it only long enough for me to reach my floor and, thus, my parents. We don't see eye-to-eye on a lot of things, but they're loyal—and they love me. If I get a chance to explain to them, they'll be able to help."

"Now that's even more farfetched. Why would your parents—who sound like they're enjoying the sweet life among their fellow cloudheads, if you ask me—do anything for a bunch of terrorists?"

"Wes." Rayne met her gaze calmly.

"Excuse me?"

"I thought about it some more when I was awake for a bit in the middle of our nap. I have to take Wes back with me." Rayne slid closer to Kaelyn and placed a pleading hand on her knee. "To be frank, it's his best chance."

"I must be hallucinating. I thought you just told me you want to take Wes back there. After we nearly lost our lives returning him to his sister and, also, after your people attacked us and killed at least fifteen of us and injured more than twenty? You think taking Wes to them, only to have them send him to one of their 'rescue camps,' which is kidnapping at best, and certain death at worst, is a possibility? No way would Tania ever let him go, so this is a moot point anyway."

"Have you asked her? Have you looked at her where she sits and keeps vigil? She's worse off than you and I are. Pale, frightened, and ready to strike out at anyone who dares to come close. She's terrified of losing him, and trust me, that can still happen—will happen, if the medication you have available doesn't do the trick. If I put the truth to Tania, I believe she will let him come with us." Rayne grew quiet, and Kaelyn could tell she was thinking fast. "And it might even be better if she came too."

"Insanity!" Kaelyn threw her hands up. "You'd be walking them into a trap, yourself too."

"I know my parents. I believe they would help because they never had more children after I was born." Rayne looked uncomfortable. "My mother desperately wanted a son. If I play my cards right, she could be persuaded to make sure no harm came to Wes—or Tania, even. As much as they try to run my life, and they're no doubt as entitled as many of their generation of Celestials are, I still think there's a chance."

"I can't risk Wes's life because you say there's a chance." It was hard for Kaelyn to get the words out without snarling.

"You're risking Wes's life right now!" Rayne's temper flared, and she squeezed Kaelyn's knee harder. "I should have been clearer yesterday about him having an infection. I was hoping it was too soon to tell, but in my heart, I know he's in trouble."

"Damn." Kaelyn looked down at Rayne's hand touching her knee. What if this was a made-up excuse for Rayne to get her way? But why would she want to take the same child she had helped, at great risk, bring back to the tunnels, back to her people, knowing how dangerous it was? It didn't make sense either way.

"Please, Kae. Let's give Wes a chance. And let's try to get my parents, and also their entire social circle, and their friends and acquaintances, who all live in the major skyscrapers in the Eastern Coastal Seaboard, to see the truth. Some even reside in the mansions against the Inner Border."

Kaelyn grew rigid. "What?"

"All the main skyscrapers—"

"No. What you said after that. About the Inner Border."

Rayne opened her mouth to speak but closed it again. She took the hairbrush and began to pull it through her hair. Kaelyn gave her time, but it wasn't easy. She wanted to scoot closer and shake Rayne until she told her everything she wanted to know. She had never discussed the Inner Border with Rayne, as it was one of their most highly confidential topics. Only the high-ranking freedom fighters knew why.

"The Inner Border." Rayne had taken back her hand and now fiddled with the hem of her shirt. "It's not a place anyone goes, as it's a border along the state farms. Beyond them is just wasteland."

"And your family has connections among the ones running the farms. Patrolling the border?" Kaelyn knew she didn't sound casual, as there was nothing casual about this topic. She couldn't let on how astonishing Rayne's information could turn out to be. If word got out about this secret topic, rescuing one boy, no matter how much she loved him, would look like nothing compared to the grim future they could all face.

"They do." Rayne looked far too certain to convince Kaelyn.

"And you think you could change their minds about something they've been indoctrinated with all their lives?"

Rayne took Kaelyn's hand. "I can do it. Wes and I can do it. Even Tania's presence would help tip the scale. My parents aren't easy to deal with, but they value family loyalty. That's one reason they weren't too happy I became a physician—but that was before I became sort of famous." Rayne looked uncomfortable, and Kaelyn, who reluctantly enjoyed both fame and infamy among her people, understood. Having any sort of notoriety glued to you was rarely a positive thing. If Rayne thought she could pull off this insane plan, the Celestials would have to regard her as something more than famous. They would have to revere her, to see her as someone beyond reproach. And that would probably still not be enough for the authorities who had their own agenda and reasons for keeping the status quo intact.

"You're sure this is the only way to save Wes?" Setting her jaw, Kaelyn studied Rayne closely. She didn't think this woman would ever exaggerate her own importance, but that didn't mean she wasn't inexperienced in the ways of the Celestial authorities from a Subterranean point of view.

"No. There is a small chance that what medication you have on hand down here might be enough to save his life. And if that's the case, he might stand a certain chance of recuperating. What I can guarantee, though, is that even if he lives through a potential sepsis, he'll need better treatment than you could ever hope to provide. He'll need therapies that we can offer topside. Please, at least let me examine him again and see how fast the medication is working?"

"Of course." Watching Rayne walk back toward the intensive-care area, Kaelyn had to admit she hadn't considered Wes's long-term convalescence. That was usually a moot point in the tunnels, with their cold, damp environment and lack of daylight, and where viruses could spread far too fast and complicate even the simplest recuperation. Too many of her people had lost their lives to small cuts or simple viruses that the Celestials would deem barely worth a second glance.

"Kae?" A hand on her shoulder made her jump. Foster stood next to her, looking down at her with concern.

"Report," Kaelyn said and stood.

"We have pushed back the herds of youngsters, some of them barely twelve. Twelve! The anger-filled youth become younger and younger. We're going to lose generations of our young to hatred and quests for revenge if we don't act soon."

Kaelyn knew he was right. It wasn't the first time they'd had this discussion. Among her team, only her core people knew of the plans set in motion a decade ago. Every time the Subterranean leadership thought the time had come, the attacks from the raiders intensified, eating up too much of their resources.

"Where's the doc?" Foster rolled his shoulders and adjusted the two weapons attached to his harness.

"Checking on Wes. He's showing signs of infection." Kaelyn slapped her hand against the wall. "And she wants to take him up to her hospital. She's crazy."

"She's brave. She risked everything to let us escape and save Wes the first time around. I wouldn't be surprised if she pulled it off again." Foster gave one of his crooked smiles. "And if pure determination can make something happen, you two would be unstoppable."

"She'd be arrested on the spot. I'd be arrested and, at best, sent to one of their reformation camps," Kaelyn muttered as she tried get her mind to focus on one thing at a time.

"Does she have any leverage that can ensure her plan to take Wes into her skyscraper? I'm sure she realizes that she burned her bridges by her actions when she left the Soldiers' Clinic. She must have something else up her sleeve." Foster pulled out a small box and opened it, offering her one of the leaves rolled up in small, square packages. About to decline, but thinking she might need the buzz to stay sharp, she accepted it.

"Thanks." The leaf was filled with a caffeine-filled herb, and the bitter taste wasn't Kaelyn's favorite, but it would do the trick in a few moments. "I'm sure her plan to just step through the doors and throw herself at the mercy of her parents won't work. They might not be as benevolent to her, no matter how much they love her, after the stunt she pulled. She's banking on her own rep as a famous physician, plus their influence with the higher-echelon Celestials. I'm afraid she might not even have a chance to get a word out."

"But…" Foster leaned his right shoulder against the wall, his gaze intent.

"But something she said makes me think there is something we can use, if I can figure out how. She says her parents know people who live in mansions along the Inner Border."

Foster nearly dropped the box of leaves. He tucked it into his breast pocket and then drew a deep breath. "What? I'm sure I didn't hear you right."

"That's what she said. And considering she would have no idea how important that information potentially is to us, I think it might just be true."

"We've never even gotten close to anyone with connections in that part of the continent. These people she's talking about…are they border guards, or farmers, or—"

"No clue. I'm not sure how to ask for more detail without sounding suspicious."

Foster nodded. "Unless you do as she asks, let her take Wes topside and save him again. We can sit down with her and go over a plan that will give her, and you, a fighting chance."

"Are you serious?" Kaelyn gaped at Foster. "What the hell was in your leaf?"

"Think about it. If you gain her trust, she'll be more likely to discuss these matters with you. This situation can save Wes and, ultimately, give our people a fighting chance."

"What if they keep him? She wants Tania to come join us. She thinks Wes and Tania being a family unit will make the more soft-hearted Celestials see them as worth saving. I'm not so sure her parents fall into that category. From what I understand, they're hard-nosed and ambitious. They only started to see her as an equal with self-worth once her fame in the medical field rose."

"She told you that?" Foster walked over to a garbage bin and spit what was left of his leaf package into it. Then he pulled a canister of water from his harness and drank.

"Not in so many words, but yes, she did." Not sure why her cheeks warmed, Kaelyn did the same, glad to be rid of the taste of the herbs. She too drank some water and took her time as she willed her facial capillaries to behave. Why did she react to his question that way? Redirecting her thoughts, she returned to the important part of their talk. "What matters most is how invaluable firsthand intel about the Inner Border would be to our plans. It could make it possible for us to commence the Departure within the foreseeable future."

Foster tipped his head back and appeared to be studying the ceiling. After he returned his gaze to Kaelyn, his dark eyes were shiny from lingering tears. The sight almost sent her to her knees, as she couldn't remember her friend and second-in-command ever crying.

"Is that what you truly think?" he asked, his voice raspier than normal.

"Honestly, I have no idea if she can deliver such information, but if she can, then yes, I know we could be underway soon."

"That says a lot, coming from you. You never exaggerate the positive nature of any mission." Foster placed a gentle hand on Kaelyn's shoulder. "Are you certain you can create a plan that will keep her in the dark?"

"Why wouldn't I?" Kaelyn raised her chin and stared up at his stark face. Kind, worried eyes looked back at her without blinking.

"You admire her. You're protective of her."

Fuck. Her cheeks were growing hot again. What the hell was that about? She never blushed, hadn't even as a kid. "Someone has to make sure our people don't kill her."

"True. But this is me, Kae. I know you better than most. I see the way you look at her." He didn't appear offended when she shook his hand from her shoulder.

"Yes, you do, but you're exaggerating. I just don't want her to have to pay with her life for saving Wes. And us." Shrugging, Kaelyn changed direction again. "You agree that we should prioritize this opportunity?"

"If you can do it with a reasonably good chance of surviving. If you can't make it back and deliver the intel, your sacrifice will have been for nothing, and we will all be worse off. You're important here, in more ways than one." He nudged her gently with his fist. "You're important to me."

Nothing else would have pierced Kaelyn's heart the way his last words did. "Damn." She closed her eyes briefly. "We better get over to Wes and Tania and see how he's doing. If he's not improving, we might have to come up with the plan fast."

She began to walk toward the intensive-care area. The moment she saw Neely approaching from the other direction, carrying a tall, slender bundle of fabric, metal pipes sticking out at both ends of it, Kaelyn began lengthening her stride. Behind her, she heard Foster curse under his breath.

Something was up.

Chapter Twelve

Rayne checked Wes's pulse. Neely had placed damp, cool towels over him, as his temperature was spiking again. Fast and fluttering under her fingertips, Wes's heart rate concerned her. His body was doing its best to fight whatever bacteria had found its way into his system. She wished for the readily available equipment at her hospital, but wishing wouldn't help this boy recover.

"Tania, listen to me." Rayne cupped Tania's shoulder and shook her gently. The girl was fully focused on her brother, and who could blame her? He had seemed to be on the mend yesterday, and now he showed signs of sepsis. Tania looked up at Rayne from where she sat on a chair by Wes's bed, having had to move off the bed when they placed the cooling towels on him.

Her brown eyes burned a dark amber. "What?" Her voice contained embers as well.

"Wes is in trouble. We have only a very brief window of opportunity before his condition becomes irreparable. This clinic doesn't have the medication or equipment required to keep him alive." Rayne loathed being so blunt and talking to such a young girl like this, but then she realized she was comparing this streetwise, hardened-by-life teenager to the pampered children she came across back home.

Tania gave her brother a long glance and took his hand. "His fever's still up." Her voice was husky, but she remained composed. Rayne suspected Tania deep down wanted to throttle her for bringing such horrible news. "What can be done about it? I can tell you have more to say. Spit it out."

Rayne reached for a stool and sat down close enough to Tania for their knees to brush. "I want you and Wes to come topside with me. I want to take him to my hospital—not the Soldiers' Clinic. There, he will have a chance to fully recover, unless something else unforeseen happens."

"Topside? Are you crazy? They'll send us to a reformation camp. I'll never go underground again. We'll never see Kae, or Foster, or Neely..." No matter how tough Tania was, here was a cornered teenager who couldn't see a path beyond her panic. Rayne felt for her. An only child, she'd sometimes wished for a sibling, but that was never to be.

"Nobody's going to any camp." Rayne infused her usual authority into her voice. "You will stay with Wes until he's well enough to be discharged. By then, we will have plans in place about how to proceed."

"And how are you going to sneak a dirty caver kid into your fancy hospital? I bet it's on the millionth floor." Hands curled into tight fists, Tania glowered at Rayne. "It sounds like an idiotic plan that some naive, cloudhead do-gooder thought up."

"You have a point." Rayne wanted to place a reassuring hand on Tania but figured she might lose a finger if she tried. "That said, your little brother deserves this chance. I've saved him once, almost twice, and with the right resources, I'll do my best to help him once and for all."

Tania shrank back into the old wooden chair. "He can't die." She glanced back and forth between Wes and Rayne. "So, you're saying that if I do nothing, and hope for our own remedies to work, he'll die. And then there's the risk that he and I'll be shot by raiders, point-blank. Come to think of it, the way you're dressed and look now, so will you." She snorted, a thoroughly unhappy sound.

"Tania...please..." Rayne wasn't above begging, if it meant a new chance to save Wes.

Pressing Wes's hand to her lips, Tania drew a deep breath before looking at Rayne again. "Can you promise to save him?"

"I never make promises unless I'm a hundred percent certain. In this case, I'm ninety percent sure when it comes to his injuries and the sepsis. Considering that there is probably a warrant for me or, best-case scenario, a search-and-rescue team trying to locate me, that brings down the percentage a tad."

"Tania." Neely spoke softly as she appeared at the young girl's side. "Not even herbal remedies will be able to help Wes now. The question is, is going topside toward an unknown fate worth it for you? You have no way of knowing what will happen to you once you get there. But if Wes is the only one that matters, and I suspect that's the case, you need to take the chance."

"There's no time to waste. We need to arrange to go right away." Rayne stood and turned to Neely. "Do you have any fever-reducing remedies or medication that you can spare for us to take on the road?"

"We have some, mostly herbal. I'll fetch it." Neely hurried out of the room.

Tania was already putting some small things from a bedside table into a tattered backpack. "I suppose we have to carry him?"

Rayne hoped her sore arm wouldn't fail her, but she'd do her damndest. "Perhaps we can use a stretcher, at least part of the way." She had seen a few of the patients arrive at this clinic, carried on stretchers consisting of two metal poles and coarse fabric. Knowing how futile it was to compare them to the technologically advanced beds and gurneys topside, she shut the image of such luxury from her mind. She had to deal with what was available at any given time—not what she wished for or knew existed somewhere else.

Turning to Neely, who looked at her with a startled expression, Rayne infused her usual command into her voice. After sliding down the laundry tube two days ago, she had nearly forgotten how it felt to completely take charge. Now she deliberately lowered her voice half an octave. "Fetch a stretcher, and what intravenous fluids you can spare. We have to get ready to save this child."

• 123 •

"Doctor Garcia…" Neely wasn't the type to wring her hands, but now she looked as if she wanted to. "Kae—"

"Knows of my plan. Just do as I ask, please. And hurry. Every minute counts." Rayne turned and pulled another blanket from a shelf. "Help me wrap him up," she said to Tania. Wes was hot now, but once they got outside the clinic, the cold dampness of the tunnels, not to mention the unforgiving weather topside, would be too cold for him. Together, they swaddled him like an infant.

"What's going on here?"

Rayne flinched inwardly at Kae's stern tone but refused to let her hesitation show. She turned around and saw Kae and Foster standing there. Neely stood just behind them, clutching the stretcher. Rayne gestured at Wes. "He doesn't have long before this condition becomes irreversible. Tania has given her permission for me to take Wes to my hospital, like we discussed." She didn't take her eyes off Kae's.

"Yes. We discussed it but haven't decided anything yet. We don't have a plan, not even a consensus." Kae stepped closer, eyeing Wes. "You're serious? You intend to carry Wes out of here on a stretcher, through the throngs of infuriated and upset people, and just walk into your skyscraper with him and Tania?"

"That's the plan. I—I had hoped you understood. And that you would provide protection until we're safely inside the entrance to the skyscraper." Rayne didn't care to be addressed as a naive child, but perhaps Kae had a point.

"Oh, you're not moving an inch without me and some of my team. Going alone would be a death wish. If the Subterraneans didn't kill you, then the topside gangs would carry out atrocities I refuse to even describe."

"Kae, please." Tania stood between Rayne and Kae. "Wes is really bad off…and I can't lose him. I truly can't." Her dark eyes glimmered with tears, and her small, heart-shaped face showed equal parts fear and fury.

"I know." Kae sighed between tense lips. "Foster? You in?"

"Going somewhere dangerous without a plan and too few hands? Sure. Why not?" Foster shouldered his gleamer rifle and studied the stretcher in Neely's hands. "That contraption's only going to slow us down. Strap young Wes to me, and I'll wrap an anti-energy sheet around us. That won't stop a full-on projectile, but at least fusion weapons and pulsators won't kill us."

Neely looked relieved and placed her burden on the floor behind the beds.

"And no matter how fast we need to act, we need a plan." Kae cupped Tania's chin. "As you'll be going too, I need you to check your temper and promise me you'll do as I say, no arguing."

"I'll be good. I promise. I just need someone to fix him." Tania hiccupped. "How long before we can go?"

"Rayne? How long before—" Kae stopped talking just in time, but Rayne understood the unspoken part of the sentence anyway. Before it was too late for Wes.

"I have no idea how long it'll take us to gain access to sufficient care, but we shouldn't wait. Can't you plan on the way? Surely you're used to getting to the exit topside?"

Kae's dark eyes narrowed. "Plan while in transit? You do have a high opinion of us."

"I do. I've seen you in action. You think fast." Rayne ran a temperature gauge across Wes's forehead and felt for his carotid. "And that's what we need now. To act fast."

"I'm fetching Beth. If we're going to be stealthy, we can't take the entire team," Foster said.

"Agreed. She's good at bringing up the rear. The best. Get weapons for Tania and Rayne as well. Handhelds," Kae said. "Let's hope they won't have to use them." The way Kae sounded, Rayne knew she fully expected them to have to shoot their way past all kinds of hostiles.

It took Foster less than ten minutes before he returned with Beth and a tall, burly man Rayne hadn't seen before. Foster carried a rucksack that Kae attached to her harness and another large bag that contained clothes for Tania and Rayne, belts for their sidearms, and the weapons themselves.

"These are fusionblades," Foster said and showed the handheld to Rayne. "You can't go wrong with one as long as you release the safety by pressing these two sensors at the same time." He pointed at either side of the small weapon, where two touch sensors sat slightly recessed. "Use your thumb and index finger for those. Flip the handle in your hand to reverse it, and press your fingertips into this groove."

Cautiously, Rayne moved the weapon around in her hand, so it followed the outline of her little finger. Pressing her other fingers into the long indentation on the back of the grip, she felt a hum, and a blue-tinted humming blade appeared at the top of the barrel. "Fusionblades, huh? Makes sense."

"Use it in a close, hand-to-hand combat situation only. If the enemy isn't within reach, just fire on them. I heard you've had some training."

"Some, yes." Rayne glanced at Kae.

Beth put an arm around Tania as the others readied themselves. She looked amazingly fresh-faced and eager to go. "We'll do our best to get Wes the help he needs, T."

"I know," Tania whispered. "I hate being this afraid."

"Let's get this little guy tucked in properly. Neely? Is his IV running properly?" Rayne checked Wes's vital signs again. He wasn't worse than a few minutes before, but with sepsis, things went fast once they started to decline.

They all helped attach yet another harness to Foster's massive form. They placed Wes, wrapped and unconscious, into it, tucking him close to Foster's chest. After Rayne fastened Wes's IV fluid bag to Foster's shoulder, Kae and Beth wrapped the anti-energy sheet around Wes and also around Foster's back. Thanks to the extra harness around Wes, Foster's hands were free to hold his gleamer, but he wouldn't be as agile or quick when carrying the extra burden.

"All right. We do it like this to start with." Kae gazed at each of them, one after another. "I take the front. Foster, you're next. After you are Tania and Rayne. Beth, you do what you do best. Take up the rear."

"Affirmative." Beth held her gleamer against her shoulder, but her otherwise glittering eyes looked focused and cold.

"We leave through the other side tunnel. Some people will be there, but you know, it's mostly firechems and shroomers."

"Firechems? Shroomers?" Rayne had no idea what Kae was talking about. She looked at herself in the reflection of the door of an old stainless-steel cabinet. The distorted image showed a woman who appeared to fully belong to Kae's team. Her well-worn clothes along with the weapon on her hip sent part of the message. A completely new look in her eyes sent the rest.

"Addicts. Some favor mushrooms they grow themselves, while others find different kinds of residual chemicals and burn them to inhale the fumes." Kae shook her head. "Normally anyone who isn't into these things avoids those tunnels, which makes them a good choice for us to bypass the crowds." She turned to the man Foster had brought with him. "You're in charge until I return. And if I don't—well, you know our objectives as well as I do."

He nodded. "Sure do. But you'll be back, Kae. You always return." He looked confident in his words.

"Thanks. From your lips to the ears of the creator." Kae bumped her fist into his shoulder. "Hold the fort. Make sure the youngsters stay in line."

"Will do." He nodded to Kae and then left the intensive-care unit.

"All right. Better get going." Kae hoisted her gleamer and raised her hand to Neely. "Be safe."

"You as well," Neely said, setting her jaw. Her eyes shone, and a single tear fell down her cheek. "Keep the kids safe." She changed her focus to Rayne. "And save him."

Rayne could only nod as they left the room in the order Kae had determined. Other medics stood lining each side of the corridor, and for the first time, Rayne couldn't see any hatred or disdain in the eyes of the people she passed. Perhaps they realized they were all ready to risk their lives to save Wes's.

When they reached the far end of the other side of the clinic, they came to a round metal hatch. Foster kept his weapon ready as Kae and Tania rotated four small wheels to unlock it. As it swung away from them, a faint scent of soil and something else, faintly chemical, wafted against Rayne. Shroomers and firechems indeed. The odors weren't too bad now, but she guessed they would truly assault her sense of smell when they neared the unfortunate souls addicted to them. She thought of how she might one day be able to help those people but filed her idea away in the back of her mind.

Stepping through the hatch after Foster and Tania, Rayne turned as she heard Beth shut it, a metallic sound reverberating around them. Only when she then heard someone, probably one of the medics, roll the locking wheels on the other side did she truly realize that the small team was truly alone in their quest to save Wes now.

They had no way back.

CHAPTER THIRTEEN

Kaelyn felt as if her brain was split in two. One side kept her sharp while she navigated the narrow tunnel, which she knew had a multitude of shallow niches along the way. The other part of her mind kept trying to think of a scenario that wouldn't get them all killed. After passing a couple of clusters of shroomers and noticing that nobody seemed to care about their presence, she called out to Rayne to join her. She needed more information.

Rayne passed Foster and took the time to check Wes's vitals. "His condition is unchanged, which right now is the best we can hope for."

Relief was too strong a word, but at least Rayne's words made Kaelyn able to dial her nerves back a notch. She normally found it easy to block personal emotions when on a mission, as slipping into her resistance-fighter persona was second nature to her. Now, with Wes's life on the line, and risking everyone's freedom—and yes, their lives too—it was hard to focus.

"I need information," Kaelyn said without preamble when Rayne caught up with her. "The main entrance to the Skyscraper is heavily guarded. How are we supposed to get past the guards?"

"I thought about that and have an idea." Rayne lengthened her stride to keep up with Kaelyn. "We can't approach the entrance carrying weapons. Somehow, we have to safely ditch them somewhere we can retrieve them if we need to. Is that possible?"

Surprised at how Rayne had begun to think tactically, Kaelyn nodded. "It'll leave us exposed, which means we can't do it too far from the entrance. What about the guards? The ones at the Soldiers' Clinic were barely in their twenties. Won't the force at the main entrance be more seasoned?"

"I've heard it's like a fortress. And after you invaded the Soldiers' Clinic, I'm sure security has been elevated at all entrances." Rayne stepped closer to Kaelyn. "These poor people."

Looking at two young men sitting with rags in their hands, glassy-eyed and with a sickeningly gray pallor, Kaelyn agreed. "It's a hard life down here. A lot of kids are orphaned early in life, and if they don't have someone to look out for them, they risk ending up here to ease the anxiety, hunger, or pain."

"And thanks to you, Wes and Tania aren't here," Rayne said softly.

"Thanks to me, Wes is in mortal danger." Kaelyn didn't mean to sound so harsh, but her statement didn't seem to faze Rayne. She patted Kaelyn's shoulder twice, very gently.

"Nobody blames you, except you." Rayne cleared her throat. "I think our safest bet is still my subcutaneous ID chip, my rank in the medical community, and my parents' influence. Even if I am initially incarcerated, they'll let me go when my parents start making enough noise."

"You think they'll grab you?" Kaelyn didn't like this idea.

"I'm not sure, of course, but they might, depending on what the reports from the Soldiers' Clinic said. If that damn nurse played it up good and proper, I might be wanted for treason. Even so, I'm sure my father especially has started with sincere damage control. He can be quite formidable, and my mother can outdo him."

"What are their names again? I know you told me, but I didn't retain them. Can be useful if we get separated and one or more of us needs to name-drop." This was a cringe-worthy thing to say, but to save Wes, Kaelyn would leave her ego behind and grovel if necessary.

"Madelon and Rocque Garcia, 3001st floor, apartment 000008. Their connection via link is easy to remember—3001000008. Floor and apartment number."

Kaelyn raised her wrist and spoke into her recorder, repeating the information. "Foster, remember these names and numbers." She motioned to Rayne with her chin to repeat the intel to him.

While Rayne relayed the information to him and, on her own account, to Tania and Beth as well, Kaelyn scrutinized the area where the tunnel would turn in a ninety-degree angle to the left. Every junction or bend was potentially dangerous, and she gripped her gleamer rifle harder and pressed the safety release. When Rayne returned to her side, Kaelyn spoke fast.

"Pull your fusionblade and keep the safety on for now. If you see me use my weapon in any way, release your safety and prepare to fire if Foster and I do. Understood?"

"What's wrong?" Rayne asked but produced her weapon with steady hands.

"Tunnel turns left up there. We have no way of knowing what's behind the bend. It's just a precaution."

"Got it." Rayne gripped her weapon with both hands.

The bend grew closer, and Kaelyn deliberately slowed down and moved to the right side of Rayne, making sure she was the first to spot any trouble.

As it turned out, they came upon more shroomers, though none of them moved at all when they carefully stepped over arms and legs. Rayne crouched momentarily, pressing her fingertips to the carotid on several of the people. "They're all dead, I'm afraid."

The expression in her eyes appeared darker and flatter than Kaelyn had ever seen it. "I see charred mushrooms in pouches made of cloth."

"Someone could have sold them a bad batch. Or they mixed the mushrooms with firechems. Usually, shroomers that stick to their drug of choice don't overdose this way unless someone manipulated their stuff." Kaelyn shook her head. "We have to move on."

Raine pushed escaped tresses of hair from her face with jerky movements. "What kind of law enforcement do you have access to down here? I mean to handle situations like this. Alerting next of kin, if nothing else."

Kaelyn grew rigid and motioned for Rayne to keep walking, knowing any answer she could give wouldn't go down well. As it turned out, Foster beat her to it. He walked behind her and Rayne, his step providing a steady percussion to his words.

"You're looking at three of them. We provide what security we can, but the raider attacks constantly undermine us. And the consequences of those attacks, long term, are some of the reasons for what you just saw. You speak of next of kin. Schroomers and firechems usually don't have any. They find camaraderie of sorts among each other, but that's it. The community either shuns or disregards them. They don't contribute to anything, though the Subterraneans value participation highly. You have to somehow make yourself useful. As long as you create, or provide, something others require, people will count you as one of their own. When these souls veered off that path, for whatever reason, they became non-members of the community."

"That's inhumane," Rayne muttered. "They need help with their addiction. If they're orphaned, they need to be reintegrated!"

Kae couldn't stay quiet. "You mean they need a psych doc? A psychologist that places them on a soft couch and listens to their problems. That's the help they need? How many Subterranean shrinks do you think have clinics in the tunnels?" She knew her scorn was as evident as it was misplaced, when directed toward Rayne. Rayne was only reacting from her own reality, not theirs.

"I realize that." Rayne's lips were tight as she obviously attempted to harness her annoyance. "I'm not an idiot. I meant, on an amateur level, a lot can still be done. It can't be good for anyone to know that addicts are roaming the tunnels, ready to commit misdeeds so they can feed their hunger for mushrooms and chemical drugs. I'm willing to bet that some of them have raided your medical storages on occasion. Putting a stop to such things should be in everyone's interest. Helping addicts heal is a huge step toward that goal."

"Anyone caught stealing medical supplies has forfeited his or her life," Kaelyn said darkly. She would have preferred not to have this discussion right now, but Rayne was incensed and clearly not ready to drop the subject.

"Excuse me?" Rayne stopped walking for a fraction of a moment but then took a few extra-long strides to catch up with Kaelyn again. "What the hell, Kae? You execute people? Just like that?"

"If they're caught red-handed by, well, a civilian, their lives aren't worth much. You should know by now how pressed we are for resources, especially medical equipment. When I was a kid, we had a steadier supply from someone topside. You've already used some of our older technology. It was old when we got it. Some things had expired. So, we fixed everything, over and over. These days, we don't have a contact like that, and neither do any of the southern Subterraneans, which means that we scavenge for everything we need. We die trying sometimes. Wes, in his own, naive way, thought he was helping since Tania has brought him up right—to help his people at all costs. If someone the community regards as weak, an addict, gets their grubby hands on the supplies someone else sacrificed their lives for—you can bet their life is in danger." Kaelyn inhaled sharply through the nose and exhaled between clenched teeth. She deliberately counted slowly to five and back down to one. "Now, that said, I agree with you in principle. It's just that down here, nobody can afford to stand on principle."

Rayne didn't speak as they made their way farther into the tunnel. She kept pace with Kaelyn and seemed unwilling to talk anymore, and Kaelyn stealthily sighed. She wasn't keen on the topic either.

Behind them, Wes whimpered softly. Rayne pivoted midstep and placed a hand on one of Foster's impressive biceps. "Let me check on him." She pulled out the stethoscope Neely had given her and pushed the sensor in under the blankets. Kaelyn placed her arm around Tania's shoulders, but the girl shook it off, like she usually did.

Rayne turned her head toward Tania after checking more vitals. "His fever's back up to 102.1 degrees. I have to give him more of the fever-reducer." Rayne produced a powder mixed with Mama Doe's herbs. "This is supposedly the best we have access to right now." She didn't look discouraged but appeared far from confident. "Here, Wes. There's a good boy. That's it. I know it must taste horrible." Rayne glanced at Tania again. "It's a good sign that he can swallow on command, and that he shows signs of disliking the taste."

"He hates taking medication. Probably because I hate it too." Tania shuddered but then raised her chin. "Keep him alive. Please."

Kaelyn had rarely heard Tania say please to anyone. The fact that she did so now showed just how afraid she was for Wes's sake. She was no fool. She knew the odds weren't on their side."

"So, we keep moving, and we move faster," Beth said from behind Foster. "We're not far from our exit point."

Kaelyn had kept an absentminded eye on the discreet markings on the dripping walls and knew Beth was tracking their progress too. "She's right. You okay, big guy? Should I carry Wes for a bit?"

"This little bird?" Foster's chiseled features softened for a second. "I can barely feel he's there. We can't waste the time."

They began walking faster now, and Rayne moved closer to Kaelyn. She kept up, obviously not about to slow anyone down, despite her lack of training. "I was too harsh in my judgment. There's a lot I don't know." Rayne didn't offer an apology, and Kaelyn wasn't looking for one. Just these words, showing that she had understood some of Foster's explanation, were enough right now.

"Okay. Thank you." Not sure why she came off sounding so awkward, Kaelyn pushed that feeling away and focused on the path before them as the tunnel widened. "We'll reach the stairs soon. That area can be more densely packed with people. I need you all to keep your weapons ready. Some of the firechems could be coming off their stuff and ready to risk anything to score some more."

"I'm ready, Kae," Beth said from behind.

"Good." Kaelyn could see that Rayne held her fusionblade pointing to the floor, as did Tania. Both their weapons had their safety off. Kaelyn nodded as she double-checked her gleamer and made sure the strap securing her own fusionblade was open. "All right. Keep your focus and obey my commands." Kaelyn took the lead, with Rayne only half a step behind her. Behind them, she knew Foster was ready to guard Wes with his life. Tania resumed her position behind him and in front of Beth.

Kaelyn put every other thought than their mission out of her head. So many dangerous moments loomed ahead, some she even doubted they'd all survive, but this first hurdle was not that moment. Wes was going to get the best treatment possible.

Chapter Fourteen

Rayne's heart rate nearly doubled at the sight of the groups of people slumped along the walls or ambling about the wider parts of the tunnel they had just entered. The smell of dirt, damp mold, and chemical substances filled her nostrils, and she pulled up her collar to avoid it. Thankful that her hand was steady where she gripped her fusionblade, she kept glancing back and forth, trying to judge the movements of the crowd near them. She was used to sizing up people, though it was her more civilized Celestial patients, but loose cannons existed among them too.

Ahead, to Rayne's right, an emaciated woman rose from kneeling next to a bundle that she surmised was an equally afflicted individual.

"What the fuck are you doing down here?" a male voice called out. He was stick thin, approaching from behind the first woman.

"Just passing through. We're not here for any of you." Kae spoke firmly.

"I know him." The woman in front of him pointed to Foster. "He's that big-ass fighter. He took down Fleischmann."

Rayne didn't turn to look at Foster but knew the situation had just gone from precarious to dangerous.

"Let us through and we won't bother you again." Kae didn't make any movements with any of her weapons, but her voice alone seemed to have the same effect. "Move aside, please."

"She says please." The woman snarled. "I recognize her too. Neither of them said please when they gunned down Fleishmann!"

"Please," Rayne heard herself say, trying to not be too obvious with her posh Celestial accent. "We have a sick child."

"What?" The man now stood only standing eight feet from Kae. "Is that what that big oaf is carrying? A kid?"

"It is," Foster said, sounding calm. "I remember Fleishmann. He stole the medicine meant for the open clinic. It was meant to tend to everyone, all of you as well, but it failed before it started, because of Fleishmann's action. If you think he meant to share his stash with you, you know better. He managed to sell more than half of it to another Subterranean community and kept the firechems he got for it for himself. That's what we found when we caught up with him just east of the tracks."

The woman didn't appear to believe Foster. "So you say."

"Honey. So say I, as well," a weak voice said, making Rayne jump, as she had forgotten about the small bundle on the floor. A bearded man raised on his elbow, waving a weak hand. "Fl-Fleishman was scum. He stole from us."

"But—" The woman fell to her knees next to him.

"No. It's true. I knew him all his sorry life. He was scum from the day the raiders shot his parents to pieces in front of him and his sister."

"Hell, yeah," a slightly stronger voice called out from the darker depths of the area. "Fleishman stole food from us."

"That doesn't mean he deserved to die," the woman said, all the anger seeping out of her voice with every word.

"No, ma'am, it doesn't," Foster said. "It is a sad affair from the beginning, thanks to the people sending the raiders. Let us use the stairs in peace, and we'll be gone in less than a minute."

"Now there's a true word," the man still standing close to Kae said darkly. "Our so-called fellow Subterranean brothers and sisters. Gone. Poof." He moved his hand in a trembly arch at the last word.

Rayne spoke before thinking. "If I can, if we make it on this mission of mercy for this child, I will return with what help I can provide."

"You don't sound like your everyday Subterranean." The man eyed her suspiciously.

"She isn't. She's a medic from the Main Hole." Kae sent Rayne a warning glance. "And she has a good heart, so don't make her regret what she said."

"Ha. We'll see how long that lasts when she's staying with you lot here." The man stepped aside and held onto the wall as he waved them by. "Go ahead. No one will ever say that Mikey B endangered a kid."

Gripping her sidearm tighter, keeping her fingers off the trigger, Rayne was still ready to use it in self-defense if Mikey B changed his mind. Fortunately, he didn't, and soon they were ascending the precariously narrow, winding staircase. Rayne wanted to make sure Foster had enough space to maneuver but didn't dare turn her head, as the metal steps were slippery. She gripped the handrail, which helped propel her upward. She wanted to keep up with Kae's pace, but it was inevitable that she would fall behind.

"If you intend to perform more medical procedures among us, you can't break your neck on these stairs." Foster was right behind her. "And as much as I appreciate your empathy toward some of our most vulnerable, I urge you to keep your focus. If you give in too much to whatever oath the cloudheads have their doctors swear, you'll lose sight of your immediate objective, which is Wes."

Rayne knew it was pointless to try to discuss the ethics a physician undertook as part of their job with Foster—or perhaps any of the Subterraneans. Here, ethics and morals were a luxury. Survival and, in many cases, survival of the fittest, had become the creed they lived by. She wasn't even sure if they had laws here. Rayne smirked at herself for having begun using some of the caver vocabulary. All these intricacies of this society were as alien to her as if it were located in another solar system. "I hear you," she answered Foster. "Today is not the time to discuss the finer points in triage."

The higher they climbed, the more the lactic acid burned in Rayne's thighs. Her death grip on the handrail made her left hand start to feel like a lump of ice. The gloves that had been part of her outfit were threadbare and had a few holes. She considered pulling the sleeve of her jacket over her frozen knuckles, but she didn't dare let go of the handrail. If she fell, she would land on Foster and Wes, and if they fell…Shuddering, Rayne kept climbing.

After what seemed like hours, but was probably twenty-some minutes, she reached a plateau, where Kae waited. They had passed at least ten other plateaus like this, but this was their first rest since they started climbing.

"Why are we stopping?" Foster asked as he joined them. A few dim lights were attached next to a hatch. Rayne looked up, still clinging to the metal bar on the wall. It looked as if it wound its way up in a shrinking spiral as far as she could see. A bout of dizziness made her return her focus to Kae.

"We could climb longer here, but as you know, that'll take us only to the maintenance structure, and that won't get Wes any closer to where he needs to go." Kae leaned over and peered into the blanket surrounding Wes. "How is he?"

"Let me." Still holding the bar firmly, Rayne moved closer to Foster and examined what she could reach of the boy with her free hand. "Temperature holding where it was last time, which is only marginally encouraging. No matter which direction we need to go, we have to find the entrance to my skyscraper." She didn't have to say that Wes was barely hanging on. They already knew that fact.

"All right." Kae turned and used a flat metal tool to unlock the hatch. She cracked it open, and a hard gush of cold, damp air wafted over them. "We're at ground level."

"Glad you kept tabs on the floors. I lost count halfway." Foster nodded. "To be honest, I was afraid of slipping and missing a step with this little guy strapped to my chest."

It was small comfort that she wasn't the only one with the same fear. Rayne pulled the jacket tighter at the gale outside the door. Peering through the small opening, she saw outside for the first time. Without a blindfold, she was surprised at how dark it was. Stepping through the hatch after Kae, she gasped as the wind took her breath away. Not counting the other day when Kae had pulled her through the alleys and she could use only her confused senses, this was the first time she had been outdoors in years. At the 2800th floor, people had no way of experiencing anything but the perfectly tempered, filtered, and sometimes scented air unless they ventured to the park areas, where trees, grass, and plants provided a sense of fresh air.

Her times on the sea vessels in a professional capacity had been just as overwhelming as this. Being out on the water, even if it was on one of the vast dragnet-crafts, had momentarily given her a sense of familiarity. Standing by the railing in one of the few small spots where a person could go outside, watching the vessel's bow crash into the waves, was a treasured memory. Being here with Kae and the team, on another lifesaving mission, nearly knocked over by the gale tearing through the alleys, might become one too.

"Line up, everyone," Kae called out. "Stay close to the walls. Beth, keep your head on a swivel back there."

Rayne quickly made sure Wes was covered up once Tania had managed to press her lips to his hot forehead, and then she assumed her position in front of Foster. She was supposed to walk behind him, but this way, it was easier to tend to Wes. Nobody objected.

"I'll take us to a position near the main entrance," Kae said, having lowered her voice. "After that, it's all on you, Doc." She glanced at Rayne earnestly. "All right?"

"Affirmative." Rayne adjusted the straps of the bag she carried on her back.

"Well, then. Keep your fusionblades or gleamers directed to the ground, safeties off. This is not friendly territory." Kae waited until they all exited into the narrow alley and then secured the hatch with her metal tool. From the outside it was impossible to detect unless you knew where it was. "Keep close together, and stay sharp."

Rayne rechecked her fusionblade and tried to mentally prepare for her role in saving Wes. If she could just get inside and somehow reach her parents, they had a chance. Anything else would be disastrous.

Chapter Fifteen

Kaelyn sent out her mirror on a stick and checked the next alley. It was wider than the one they were leaving and posed a bigger risk. She scanned both directions, barely able to see anything, as the damp walls of the skyscrapers created a thick mist. At least potential raiders or elements roaming the alleys ready to do anything to steal their belongings couldn't easily detect Kaelyn and her team. Of course they could be only a few feet away, completely obscured.

She couldn't hear any voices or footfalls, and as they had to keep moving, Kaelyn gestured for everyone to raise their weapons. Slipping out from the temporary shelter, she led the others along the left side of the alley, mindful of debris and protruding parts of the wall. Just kicking something by mistake would make enough noise to attract anyone within earshot. Sound bounced and traveled a long distance among the skyscrapers' gigantic bases.

After rounding two more bases and not running into anyone, Kaelyn, knowing they were only two skyscrapers away from their goal, raised her right hand in a fist. Everyone stopped.

"Two blocks." Kae spoke just above a whisper but still winced at how her voice seemed to float in all directions.

Rayne was pale under her knitted hat. She nodded and turned her upper body to peer down at Wes. Her frown bothered Kaelyn, and then a soft whimper from the bundle made them all go rigid. Foster immediately began rocking Wes.

"Shh," he murmured, his face only inches from the boy as he lifted him closer. "Just shh."

"We better hurry," Rayne mouthed, motioning with her hand.

Her chest constricting, Kaelyn merely nodded and turned around. She performed her mirror scan, squinting at some unknown shadows moving in the mist. Raising her hand, she showed first two fingers, but when the mist dissipated some, she changed it to four. The figures appeared lumpy and moved slowly, almost erratically. These weren't raiders, nor were they part of the gangs that roamed the alleys to pounce on anyone they could corner. This didn't make sense.

Kaelyn debated taking a detour, but it might be too late for Wes if they did. And for all she knew, they could run into a larger group of hostiles if she altered the plan.

Making sure everyone had their weapons ready, Kaelyn guided them along the wall. As they approached the figures in the mist, she slowed. Something was off. Sure, she and the team took great care to move with stealth, but they weren't soundless. These forms didn't appear to notice them. One was pushing at the lid of a container farther up, but the effort appeared futile.

As the closest figure came into clear view, Kaelyn had to stop herself from gasping. She couldn't tell if it was a man or a woman, although she guessed the latter. They all wore what looked like coarse fabric, perhaps burlap, some of it tied over their eyes, and another strip covering their mouth.

"Damn," Foster said, his voice like a soft breath behind her. "Wraiths."

Kaelyn had received reports about wraiths the past year but hadn't put stock in it, as she knew how figures in the alley mist appeared in the distance. Yet, she had never personally come across anyone that looked like this.

"Ngh…" The closest figure flinched. "Ngh…an-ge…"

Kaelyn sensed fear rather than wrath or hostility. The other three figures extended wrapped arms toward the one in front of her, making similar guttural noises.

"Hey. We're not going to hurt you." Rayne forestalled Kaelyn, stepping closer. At least she had enough sense to keep her fusionblade ready. "We're just passing by, all right?" She sounded kind and soothing, and Kaelyn figured this was how she reassured a frightened patient. "Are you injured?"

"Careful," Kaelyn said under her breath.

"Ng…ng-y…" The four people, all wrapped in tattered fabrics, with their eyes and mouths covered, now stood in a tight group, arms wrapped around each other.

"What's wrong with them?" Tania whispered from Kaelyn's other side.

"No idea, but we don't have time to figure it out." Trying to usher Rayne to the right, to follow along the right side of the alley, Kaelyn could feel her resist. "We need to move."

"Just wait." Rayne pulled out her small pack of food rations. "Give me yours, Kae."

Knowing it was useless to object, Kae handed over her food.

"Hungry? Is that what you're trying to say?" Rayne held out the packages with her free hand, clutching her weapon with the other. "You can have this, and then we'll be on our way."

The one closest to them slowly raised its wrapped arms, and now Kaelyn realized what else was terribly off. The arms reaching for the food were too short. Where the form's hands were supposed to be were only stumps. Raising her gaze to his or her face, she shuddered at the thought of someone having gouged out the creature's eyes and done something to its mouth. To all of them.

Rayne slowly moved closer and placed the packages on the stumps. Kaelyn heard her swallow hard and knew she had guessed it too.

As it turned out, the wraiths could move fast when required. As soon as they tucked the food away, they whirled in the mist and were gone.

"Shit," Tania whispered.

"Mm-hm." Kaelyn made sure they all refocused and then began leading them down the last alleyway, where they would reach the point of no return. It was pure luck that nobody truly dangerous had approached them yet, and after they turned the next corner, they'd be defenseless.

When they were twenty feet from the corner of the skyscraper next to Rayne's, Kaelyn raised her fist again. Together with Beth, she felt along the wall and found the narrow box that once contained circuit boards but was no longer in use. She used her homemade metal tool and pried it open where it hid snugly along the wall. "I hate this part," she murmured, but we need to leave our weapons here. This needs to be a show of good faith." Kaelyn was certain this was one of the futile parts of their insane plan, but if it helped Wes, it was worth it. "Place your weapons here but keep your blades." She handed a stinger, a short-bladed laser blade, to Rayne once they all had given up their weapons. "I'm leaving mine unlocked except for one magnetic bolt, in case you need to escape without me and can safely reach this point. You won't need a tool to open it. Just tear the hatch off."

"We're not leaving you behind," Beth said quietly. "Just so you know."

"You may have to. If we get separated, get yourself home. That's an order." Kaelyn could see that her barely audible words didn't sit well with her team, not even Rayne. "You take the lead now, Rayne. I have deliberately steered us along alleyways and away from other main entrances, but you'll be able to see our destination clearly. Foster, you will unwrap some of Wes once we get there. Tania, you and Beth look young and innocent enough. Act like it. I'll be in the rear. Let's go."

❖

Rayne straightened her back and refused to let the fatigue that lay draped over her shoulders show. This was her idea, after all. She had to make it work. She walked toward the corner and stopped for a moment to make sure they didn't run headfirst into a team of raiders…soldiers. In the distance, a large, bright rectangle lit up the wider alley. She had never entered one of the main entrances, as various types of aircraft had picked her up on one of the flight decks around the 1900th floor when her expertise had been needed at sea. The mist wasn't as thick here but still gave the entrance a magical glow.

Just as she began moving toward it, something made the fine hairs on her arms stand up. She felt for her fusionblade but remembered she was unarmed, except for the blade. She gripped Foster's arm and shook it. "Do you hear that?" she whispered, frantic.

Foster stood still and then whipped his head around, looking behind them. "Fuck. We have to run." He wasn't trying to keep his voice from carrying to anyone within earshot. Rayne saw Kaelyn pull her knife, motioning for them to move faster.

"Come on." Rayne didn't know what was behind them, as they barely made a sound, but they were fast. She slipped on something, and her right leg folded and nearly sent her headlong into the wall. Foster gripped her arm and yanked her closer. "Keep going. We can make it."

Running without daring to look back, Rayne heard the others breathe heavily as they rushed toward the main entrance. She made out two guards, tall and imposing, but what was behind them frightened her much more than the two sentries.

Then she recognized the sound coming from the ones chasing them. *Wraiths*. Apparently, they thought the team had more food to share. Her stomach felt as if someone had filled it with ice cubes. Rayne doubled down and forced her fatigued thigh muscles to pump faster, propelling her to a place of potential safety.

When they closed in on the entrance, it was obvious that the sentries had heard them and probably the moaning wraiths behind them.

"Please! My sec code is *Garcia 2428001-med*. We have an injured child. We're under attack!" She didn't let their raised weapons deter her but kept running, repeating her security code. "We have an injured child. He needs medical attention. I'm Doctor Rayne Garcia. My parents are Madelon and Rocque Garcia." She rattled off her parents' security codes.

Coming to a halt only feet from the sentries, she tore her knitted hat off and let her hair tumble down onto her shoulders. "We're being chased by wraiths, by non-communicative people wrapped in rags. We're in danger. You have to let us in."

The closest guard, a tall, muscular man that looked like he could be related to Foster, eyed them cautiously. Rayne had no idea why he hadn't fired upon them, but perhaps her security codes had had the desired effect.

"Hey, that's the doc!" a female voice said, and the other sentry approached. She was almost as tall and imposing as her colleague but studied at Rayne with marginally less suspicion. "From the Soldiers' Clinic, remember?"

"You sure—what the fuck's that?" Redirecting his weapons, the male guard aimed at the approaching wraiths.

"It's the damn mummies," the female guard said, firing her rifle in the air, singing in the remnants of the mist. "No idea how they dare to come this close. They never do."

Rayne knew it was her fault. Her bleeding heart had had to offer some of them food.

"Get them inside," the woman ordered the other guard and kept firing low-energy bursts in the air. "I'll hold them off. I don't want to shoot the mummies, but I will if I have to."

With his rifle directed at Foster's head, which made sense from the guard's point of view, as Foster was a massive guy, he let them inside the fortified transparent doors. There, four more guards stood with their weapons trained on them, yet clearly not about to make a move until they received any orders.

Just inside the doors, in a shallow niche, Rayne recognized one of the large identifiers, a computer console that would scan the ID chip every Celestial citizen was outfitted with at birth. She used a small version housed in a wand at the hospital, but it only identified the individual on a basic level. The large computers held everyone's record and family history for centuries back. Hoping to avoid being scanned, as she was no doubt either wanted or reported missing, she held up her hands, palms forward in supplication.

"Please use your comm unit to reach unit 000008. That's my parents' quarters. I mean, apartment. If they're not in, they always have their signals redirected to my father's comm unit." Rayne pressed her right hand to her heart. "My father is influential and will look favorably at the person who helps his daughter return home."

"Identify yourself." The guard motioned at the computer.

Outside, the female sentry was backing up toward the door, as the wraiths—or mummies—pressed on, their humming, guttural voices rising.

"She needs help." Kae moved quickly and opened the door, holding it ready for the woman to back up toward it. "Get inside. Just a few more steps."

As soon as the guard was inside, Kae and Beth threw themselves against it as the wraiths stormed the entrance. "Lock it. Lock it now!" Beth called out, pressing her back against the door. Her boots slipped against the smooth floor. To Rayne's dismay, the sentries keeping them at gunpoint seemed more interested in restraining them than helping with the door.

The female guard tore off her glove and tapped in a command to her wrist unit. Thick rods protruded at the top, but not at the bottom of the door, as it wasn't entirely closed.

"Press harder!" Kae shouted the words as she pressed her shoulder against the door.

Rayne and Tania responded as one, running forward and throwing themselves against the door next to Beth. Slowly, they managed to get it closer to the slots where the rods were meant to go. Only when the male guard joined them, adding his considerable weight to theirs, did the door snap into place. He turned to look at the gang of four drone-like guards that stood as if cast in a toy-soldier mold and snarled at them. "I know your unit is new, but fuck you. Are you stupid? Why didn't you help us?"

"You never gave the order," the one on the far left said, his lips pressed into a fine line. He glared over at the female guard. "And I will have to do my duty and report you, our commanding officer, to the colonel, as you blatantly broke rule 142.3-1 by letting cavers in—" He quieted at her scalding stare, but his main objective in this situation was obvious.

Turning to study the wraiths, Rayne couldn't tear her gaze off their dark eyes, where the nearly black irises seemed to have bled into the white around them. Maybe thirty-some individuals clustered outside, all pressing against the safety doors. Their sounds were thankfully muffled by the thick material in the door, but she still knew she would hear the 'ng's reverberating against the surface in her nightmares.

"They can't get in," the female guard said, sounding out of breath. "Damn, that was close. Never knew them to be that fast, or that numerous. Usually, we can see two or three of them in the distance. That's all."

Rayne wondered how she could have lived almost fifty years and never have heard of any mummies, or wraiths. She cleared her throat and repeated her plea from before. "Please. Place a call to my parents' unit."

"You need to identify yourself first." The male guard was adamant. "It's the law." He studied them all closely. "I'm no idiot. These are cavers, and for all I know, you can have stolen Doctor Garcia's codes." He apparently wasn't as grateful for their assistance as his colleague was.

"Stop. I recognize the Doc. She volunteers every week at the clinic upstairs. She saved Morrow and Case just a few months ago. We sat at their bedside for weeks, but they made it—thanks to her." The woman met Rayne's eyes. "I'm Niner. Give me the info again, and I'll place a call on the screen over here." She pointed at another computer opposite the identifier. "Let's don't be stupid though. Keep an eye on the cavers." She eyed the pale vision of Wes in Foster's arms. "We'll pat them down after the Garcias identify their daughter."

The male guard kept his weapon trained on the others as Rayne moved to face the computer. "Thank you." Praying that her parents would respond, Rayne gripped the small handles on either side of the shelf.

Niner put in Rayne's parents' codes and apartment number. The computer pinged three times before the screen changed into the familiar face of her mother, Madelon Garcia. Her long, dark brown hair hung loose around her shoulders, and her face, pale and void of makeup, stared back at Rayne as if she indeed were one of the wraiths.

"Rayne?" Madelon gasped. "Rayne. Oh, lord our creator. Rocque! Rocque! It's her!" She turned to someone not within view. "She's on the comm unit."

Rayne's father appeared, and if his wife looked unusually unkempt, he looked impeccable, unless you discounted the dark circles under his green eyes, so like hers.

"Daughter," he said, his voice stark. "You're alive."

"I am," Rayne said, shoving tears of relief to see her parents to the back of her mind. "I am pressed for time, though. I have a severely injured child with full-blown sepsis. I need to take him up to my hospital right away, or he'll die. His name is Wes."

"Wait? An injured child? Whose child?" Madelon reappeared, frowning now. "And who are those people behind you? I see the guards have them secured."

"Mother. Please. I need to save the child, and then I will answer all your questions. Please. He's just ten years old, and we've gotten him this far. I can't lose him now."

Rocque appeared to consider her words for a few moments, and Rayne could see out of the corner of her eyes how the male guard gripped his rifle firmer.

"I'm sending a code that tells the guard to bring you up via the rapid lift," her father said. "Just so you know, a fully armed unit will meet you at the hospital floor, and the lift will not make any other stops." He looked firmly at her, clearly his usual hard-nosed self, despite his sleepless nights. There was no other reason for his dark circles and the tension around his eyes. "Understood?"

"Yes. Understood. Please hurry." Rayne turned away from the computer and walked over to Foster, not bothering with the raised weapons. She held up the med kit and opened it for Niner to peruse. "I need to check on him." Rayne placed the temp gauge against Wes's pale temple and couldn't help flinching when she saw how cold he suddenly had become. "Have you received the code yet?" she asked Niner, who had returned to the computer.

"Working it in now." Niner gave verbal commands. "The one to the far right." She pointed at a gold-colored door. "It'll take you up in minutes. The additional message here says your parents will meet you there as well."

Rayne hoped they had minutes. She looked for Kae and saw something resembling brewing panic in the depth of her dark eyes. Rayne prayed Kae would hold it together and not draw too much attention to herself until they were in the protective presence of her parents. It wasn't hard to figure out there was something of a prize on Kae's head as leader of the resistance movement. After all, most Celestials regarded her as a terrorist boss.

While they waited for the rapid lift, Niner patted them down and removed the blades from all of them. With only a raised eyebrow as a reaction, she placed them under the countertop. "I'll just hold on to these for a while, along with your packs. You might just get them back."

"Probably not," Beth muttered. "Glad I didn't bring the book I'm reading. I'd never have known how it ends."

Kae shook her head but looked at her disappearing bag with a dark expression to match her surname.

The rapid-lift door opened, and they entered it without hesitation. Tania stood pressed against Foster, whispering what sounded like prayers to Wes's still body. Niner and her colleague remained at their duty station, and the last thing Rayne heard before the door closed was how they asked for reinforcements, as the wraiths were still pressing against the doors and growing in numbers.

"I've never seen any of them before, and now they're flocking like rats," Kae said as the rapid lift shot up, making Tania and Beth both gasp and hold onto Foster's harness. "Where the hell do they live, and who did that to them? Or, hell, is that a mutation we've never heard about?"

"If it is," Rayne said where she stood with two fingertips against Wes's carotid, "I haven't heard about it either, yet the guards at the entrance knew. Well, the two older ones. The four idiots seemed even more clueless than I felt at the time." She checked the console showing how far they had traveled. They'd just passed the 845th floor. Not long now.

Just after the 911th floor, the rapid lift slowed and then halted at the 924th floor, or so Rayne thought as the numbers kept rolling on the console as if the lift was still going.

"What the hell?" Kae stepped in front, along with Beth, pulling another blade from inside the sole of her boots. She extended the blade that glimmered faintly green and gave a quiet hum.

"It's still counting up the number," Tania said, her voice shrill. "What's going on?"

A metallic sound from the lift door made Kae raise her blade, and Foster half turned his body to protect Wes. A narrow, metal, compound strip came through the small crack where the door met the side panel. After a few moments of wiggling, the door slid up halfway, and Rayne found herself looking at a familiar face. Kae took a defensive position, holding her blade in a way that couldn't be misunderstood.

"Wait. Stop." Rayne pushed forward and placed a hand on Kae's arm, pressing it down. "It's all right." She hoped she was correct at the sight of the scowling man staring back at Kae and her blade. "This is Rocque Garcia. My father."

Chapter Sixteen

Kaelyn studied the man before her. Tall, with shoulder-length, salt-and-pepper hair, slender and wiry, almost too thin, Rocque Garcia looked gaunt, and perhaps some of his haggard appearance had something to do with his daughter's disappearance. It was hard to judge his age, but she guessed he was in his mid-to-late seventies.

"Father..." Rayne blinked quickly. "What's going on? The rapid lift..."

"If you don't get out right away, they units waiting for you on the hospital floor will be able to find out where it actually stopped." Rayne's father motioned for them to step off the lift with an impatient gesture.

"Do as he says," Kaelyn said, mainly because she didn't like the idea of military units getting their hands on all of them. As soon as they were through the half-open door, Rayne's father dislodged the metal strip, and the lift took off with a moaning sound.

From a distance, the cadence of approaching heels made them all turn their heads in the direction of the sound. A woman that could only be Rayne's mother was walking toward them, with four people pulling a hover gurney behind them. At the sight of Rayne, she lengthened her stride and pulled her into a firm embrace. Rayne's startled expression suggested that demonstrative affection didn't occur every day in the Garcia family.

• 155 •

"The child?" Madelon Garcia asked, looking over at Foster. "Ah. Unstrap him and place him on the gurney." It was clearly an order.

"Mother, where are we?" Rayne looked around them, and for the first time, Kaelyn took time to examine the floor where the Garcias had taken them. It was a quiet place, with very few people nearby. Even more odd, only two lifts were available here, though she had counted four doors at the entrance level.

"You need to follow them back to the clinic. You will find everything you might need." Madelon studied them all closely. "You look very young. Are you related to this child? A sibling, perhaps?" she asked Tania.

"Yeah. And you can't take him out of my sight. Or the doc's." Tania took a step closer to Madelon and showed her teeth in a way that Kaelyn had seen only too many times before. It usually didn't end well.

"Tania, go with Rayne and help tend to Wes. We'll be along in a bit. Isn't that so, Mrs. Garcia?" Kaelyn asked pointedly.

"But of course." Madelon motioned in the opposite direction from where Rayne and Tania accompanied Wes and the four medics. "Let's talk about what's happened to my daughter and where we'll go from here." She guided them to a door that opened to an apartment like none Kaelyn had ever seen. Neither had Beth nor Foster, which was obvious from their huge eyes and Beth's loud whistle.

White and gold, with red accents, it was a beautiful, soothing living space. Still, it was clear that nobody actually lived there. Kae saw no personal items in the rooms and no pictures of loved ones.

"A guest apartment that we use for unforeseen events," Rocque said after closing the door behind them. A man in civilian clothes remained just inside the door, and Kaelyn understood that he was just another kind of sentry.

"What's this place? This floor?" Foster asked as he eyed the gold couches with obvious suspicion. "Not even Rayne knows about this, or what you do here, does she?"

"Our daughter is very much part of the establishment, and for her own safety we have kept it that way, or, rather, that's what we've tried to do until she jumped into a laundry chute to save a child." Madelon smiled wryly. "That's the story I know to be true among all the different takes on Rayne's disappearance from the Soldiers' Clinic. She's no traitor. She's true to her calling. We had to keep up the front of being somewhat disappointed in her chosen profession, even to her. It was to keep her, and us, safe." She motioned to the couch. "Please, have a seat. There's sustenance in the food-prep area if you're hungry."

"I'd rather just keep talking," Kaelyn said, even if her stomach was about to start to digest itself.

"I'll make something," Foster said and walked into what looked more like an old film spaceship than a kitchen area. "You all keep talking."

"How about an introduction? You know our names and who we are." Madelon tilted her head in a way that reminded Kaelyn so much of Rayne, she shuddered.

"My name is Kaelyn Dark. You can call me Kae."

"Beth." Beth hadn't stopped fingering the soft fabric of the couch.

"Just the one name?" Rocque asked.

"Yes. Just Beth. For now." Only Beth's innate charm kept her words from sounding standoffish.

"I'm Foster. Just Foster." The deep voice from the kitchen area didn't encourage more questions about his identity. Kaelyn hoped her name would take the focus from her team members. She was certain she was infamous enough in the skyscrapers.

"Kae Dark. Now that's the name of someone I've hoped to meet for a long time." Madelon nodded and looked oddly pleased, which made absolutely no sense.

"Why would your disappointment in Rayne's career help keep her safer?" Kae asked and sat down cautiously on the couch. She could care less about the fancy furniture, but she didn't want Rocque and Madelon to stop explaining. Beth chose one of the single-seaters. "And where, exactly, is Rayne now?"

"The last question first, I think." Madelon sat down with such a graceful movement, it was as if she had been poured onto one of the other single-seaters.

Rocque walked over to a cabinet that appeared to have glass doors. It opened automatically as he came closer and contained a multitude of different-colored bottles. They looked like glass too. He poured himself an amber beverage in a small glass and then looked over his shoulder at Beth and Kaelyn. "Scotch? It's manufactured here in the building. Not the real thing, obviously."

"Is that like wine?" Beth asked.

"In a way, but stronger." Rocque poured a small amount into two additional glasses and handed over one each to Kaylyn and Beth. "Cheers to bringing my daughter home."

"But is she, though? Home, I mean?" Kaelyn studied Rayne's parents over the rim of the tall, slim little glass. It felt frail to her fingers, and she knew she'd end up snapping it in two if she didn't pay attention.

"No. Not really." Madelon had accepted a small glass too, but her beverage was colorless. She sipped it and then pushed her fingers through her hair, disheveling the perfect, dark-blond waves. It was obvious that Rayne had her father's eyes and her mother's hair and bone structure. "This floor, for lack of a better description, doesn't exist."

"Excuse me?" Kaelyn had just sipped and swallowed a bit of the strong, fragrant alcoholic beverage. "Run that by us again."

Madelon took a deep breath. "When this building was being partially remodeled, Rocque and I had just gotten married. We're both what our leaders like to call 'old stock,' as in rich and from influential families. That gave us the chance to put our plans in motion. We used our family's credits, everything we could get our hands on, and bribed the architects, the construction workers, and some officials who, politically speaking, were on the same page as us, to make this floor disappear. The lifts don't stop here unless you program them off the books, so to speak."

"But how? What if someone takes the stairs?" Beth looked intrigued.

"Take the stairs? In the skyscrapers? I doubt it. People go to gyms, but utilizing the emergency-evac stairs? Not so much. Yet you're not wrong. It could happen, but thanks to some engineering and cleverly placed doors, if you want to join us on this floor, you have to know where the secret magnetic doors are in the stairwell. The numbered doors all align to their proper floors with all their amenities, apartments, and facilities intact. If you've always been able to go from floor 923 to 924 without a problem, then why would you ever consider there to be a floor 924.5?" Madelon smiled, but fatigue showed in her eyes. "We have access to everything we need here to eventually carry out our long-term plans. If not for us, then for our children and grandchildren. You know. Generations to come."

"And why are you so openly sharing this information with us? I mean, it's sensitive, and you don't know us." Foster asked as he returned with something that looked like a strip of meat across a bed of vegetables. He placed it in the center of the table, along with smaller bowls and forks to eat with.

Madelon and Rocque looked taken aback that he had put together food enough for them as well. "Oh. Thank you."

"It's synthetic meat, but I have heard it resembles real bacon from the time we still had access to farms," Rocque said. Perhaps he had seen Beth's widening eyes. Beth wasn't much for the rodent-based meat back home.

Kaelyn carefully bit into the "bacon" and nearly moaned. No matter how they put spices in what they ate in the tunnels, nothing had ever tasted like this. "Regarding Foster's question, I think I can answer that." Despite having been under the spell of bacon for a moment, Kaelyn allowed her voice to harden, which didn't go unnoticed by anyone. Beth lowered her fork, and Foster had begun to sit down but remained on his feet.

"Do share." Madelon speared an innocent vegetable and placed it in her mouth, chewing it slowly. Kaelyn noticed something definitely intimidating about that move as well. It told her never to turn her back on this woman—and definitely never underestimate her.

"You're not about to let us leave anytime soon." Kaelyn didn't take her eyes off Madelon, who appeared to be the one calling the shots in this supposed domestic resistance movement.

"True in part." Madelon finished her bowl and wiped her mouth on one of the napkins that sat in a holder on the table.

"The hell?" Beth was about to get up, and only Kaelyn's furtive gesture made her stay seated.

"Listen. Our daughter's action has put her under the microscope of the Eastern Seaboard City authorities." It was Rocque's time to talk. "All the years we kept her safe by alienating her to a degree, she never spent enough time with us to notice our networking and planning. I would imagine that living up here in luxury must appear like a dream for those of you who starve and suffer below-ground."

"Appear? It's a no-brainer," Beth said, her eyes contrasting black against her blond hair. "The food on the table right now, after we finish eating, would keep a family of four happy for several days."

"We are aware," Rocque said, looking pained. "But the cost of this luxury is higher than you think. Just because we have access to the finer things in life doesn't mean we're free. If we step out of line, and I mean even the smallest infraction, the penalty is severe. There's no bacon substitute in the world that can comfort a parent whose child is put into service in the military or law enforcement against their will. The number of body bags over the last decade is staggering. Madelon and I knew we would have to bring Rayne into our secret, as she was starting to ask questions about the death rates after she began volunteering at the Soldiers' Clinic."

Foster finally sat down in a double-seater and leaned forward, his elbows on his knees. "Let me get this straight. There is an organized resistance in the skyscrapers?"

"We are in contact with four others, and two more are about to join this eclectic, clandestine movement. If anyone is caught… well, treason holds a death penalty." Rocque shrugged. "Our young call it death-by-balcony."

"What does that mean?" Kaelyn asked, even if she had a sickening feeling that she could guess.

"For treason, the authorities, after you are found guilty following a summary trial, the punishment is to be taken to the 1500th floor, where, ironically, our most beautiful park is located, and placed in a glass box on the outside. Just before your core temperature goes below the level to render you unconscious, the floor swings open, and you fall to several floors below ground level. I will spare you the gory details." Rayne's father leaned back but didn't avert his gaze. "You can't blame us for wanting Rayne to be safe from that type of death for as long as possible. In the meantime, Madelon and I have played the roles of socialites with amazing careers in business, etcetera. Sticking to that script for decades takes a toll, but it's worth it."

Kaelyn nodded slowly, trying to digest all this information. "In part. That's what you said." She turned to Madelon.

"Yes. We'll need to detain you for a time while we adjust our plans, as everything was thrown into disarray when our daughter proved to be every bit as filled with civil disobedience as her father." Madelon smoothed down her hair and managed to look entirely serene. "I imagine you must be full of follow-up questions, but now that you know you are safe for the time being, you might want to go over to the medical wing and see how the young boy is doing. Wes, was it?"

"Yes." Kaelyn hesitated. "Thank you." She stood and noticed that the man inside the door readied himself and would most likely accompany them. Since they didn't know their way around the secret floor, it was a good idea.

The man turned out to be most discreet as he walked ten feet ahead of them past the lift doors and then stopped by what looked like a small cart. It had no tracks, but Kaelyn surmised its wheels could run on the floor. The man stopped and opened the door, motioning for them to get in. "It will save time."

They entered the vehicle, and to Kaelyn's astonishment, the man sat down sideways next to them and simply asked it to take them to Medical 1. "It is our emergency clinic." This was his only explanation. The vehicle began rolling and soon maneuvered through corridors and squares, until they reached a tall door where the sign suggested they had arrived.

After hurrying off in this apparently self-guiding piece of technology, Kaelyn, Foster, and Beth made their way through the door, anxious to hear about Wes.

Chapter Seventeen

When Rayne saw the familiar hovering gurney behind the nurses and medics, complete with life-sustaining technology, she could have wept with relief. It took only a few moments to strap Wes onto the mattress filled with temperature-regulating, fluidic beads. They moved under him and settled into every part of his body that encountered the mattress. They gave off a soft hum as they began to monitor, and correct, his temperature.

"What's that sound?" Tania asked as they began walking.

"It's the beads. They're helping him." Rayne knew she had to focus on Tania, who might cause a lot of trouble if her temperament got the better of her. "And now the nurse is placing a special sheet over him. See? That's getting a more accurate read of how far the sepsis has progressed. The sheet was changing colors in an alarming way. Whereas the one covering Wes's hands and feet was still a light green, the area around his wound—his upper torso and neck—became a distinct orange. If it turned red, she might not be able to save him after all.

"We can't waste any time," the nurse, a tall, thin woman that seemed to be in charge, barked. She waved to a cart to pull closer. Without hesitation, she hooked the hover gurney onto its back and motioned for Tania to take a seat inside it.

"Doctor Garcia, you need to ride on the stands. He might need intervention before we reach the clinic." The nurse pointed to the extendable footrests that appeared at the edges of the gurney and lowered themselves.

Familiar with the technology, Rayne strapped herself into a belt and stepped onto the footrests. She tightened the lock around the belt and pulled herself close to Wes. He was pale, the corners of his mouth bluish. His organs were shutting down.

"Let's go," Rayne said and was now fully into her comfortable role as a physician on her home turf, even if this might be a less-well-equipped rogue clinic.

The driver of the cart utilized maximum speed and rushed them to the clinic, located in the opposite corner, which Rayne found counterproductive. Why not have it straight off the lifts? She shook the thought away and clung to the gurney as the medics unstrapped it at the entrance. Jumping off the footrests, she got rid of the belt and hurried after the medical team as they entered the clinic. Tania didn't miss a step. She was right behind Rayne.

To Rayne's complete surprise, this clinic might be rogue, but it was in every way as well equipped as her luxurious hospital much farther up in the skyscraper. How had these people, whoever they were, managed to get the latest technology out from under the noses of the authorities and into whatever floor they were on?

Again, Rayne shook the interfering questions from her mind and focused on Wes. A medic pulled up a stool for Tania, who then could observe what they did with her brother but not get in the way.

The more in-depth scans showed that the sepsis was burning its way through him with an alarming speed. Rayne pulled at the cart that sat readily available at her right and began placing patches on every major pulse point on the small, thin boy before her. The medics had cut every stitch of clothing from his body, and, apart from a privacy towel, Wes was now on full display.

"He's so thin." One of the medics shook his head. "I knew they were suffering a food shortage down there, but—" He had a sad-mixed-with-anger expression but kept working, anticipating what Rayne needed before she had a chance to voice it. He had obviously been trained in one of the big hospitals in a skyscraper.

Four mixed antisepsis medications now entered Wes's system, through patches in his armpits and his groin. Over his jugular veins sat larger patches that provided the fluids and nourishment he required.

"Take it easy with the jugular patches. This child isn't used to being fully sated with vitamins and minerals. Set the cells to push them through at forty percent." Rayne watched a nurse wash Wes's inflamed wound with a special micellar solution containing antiviral and anti-bacterial agents. Once she was done, she ran a wand over it, to explore the depth.

"It's not as deep as I feared, Doctor Garcia," she said and smiled behind her transparent mask. "It was very dirty though, despite the Subterraneans' best efforts to keep it clean. I would imagine it's virtually impossible—"

"Don't you dare blame us or Doc for his wound. One of you lot inflicted it, and it can hardly be a secret that we have no fancy medical equipment with fucking hovering gurneys in the tunnels!" Tania had hopped off her stool and stood just outside the markings on the floor that informed observers of the sterile field. "Damn condescending bit—"

"Tania. It's all right. Just take a seat again. The nurse is too busy trying to save Wes right now. Okay?" She smiled reassuringly at Tania. "Trust me. Wes is getting the best care right now, and look. His temperature's already decreasing. Once we can keep him stable at a normal level, you'll soon be able to talk to your brother again. In the meantime, remember that the people here are not your enemy."

Tania remained where she was for a few moments but then climbed onto the stool again. She shook her head, making the beaded braids near the front of her head whip her in the face "So you say. You have no more idea what these people are about and what their agenda is than I do."

Rayne had to give Tania that one. Just because her parents were involved, and everyone seemed benevolent, really didn't prove anything. Once Wes was truly out of danger, Madelon and Rocque Garcia would have to answer all her questions.

Almost an hour after they stepped off the lift with a half-dead child strapped to Foster, Wes's eyelids began to flutter. They had already turned off the sterile-field screens, and now Rayne waved Tania over. "He's about to wake up. I want your face to be the first thing he sees," Rayne said. "Here. Let me get a footstool for you." She pulled out another set of footstools up beside the head of the table. "There."

Tania looked hesitatingly at them and then stepped up, leaning over Wes.

"Just watch out for his patches, all right?" Rayne had to smile at how the siblings were almost nose to nose when Wes opened his drowsy blue eyes and looked slightly cross-eyed at his sister.

"Tania?" Wes said, barely a husky whisper escaping his lips. "Why are you crying?"

"I'm not crying, you little idiot. It's just the rain." Tania smiled through the tears. "Thanks for not dying, by the way."

Rayne wanted to groan out loud but understood that this might be a normal repartee between siblings.

"D-don't mention it," Wes said and coughed.

Tania pulled back and turned around to Rayne, and nearly fell off the footstool.

"Doc?" Tania's eyes were huge.

"Hey, Wes. Remember me?" Rayne stepped up next to Tania. Taller than the girl, she could stay on the floor when the gurney was stationary. "I'm Doctor Garcia."

"Maybe?" Wes coughed again. "I don't feel so good."

"I understand that. Trust me, you've made a good recovery already, but it'll be a few more days before you can run around causing Tania trouble again." Rayne helped him up into a sitting position by pressing a sensor on the gurney. She placed a hand on Tania's shoulder. "Wes is going to cough a bit, as his lungs were affected earlier. That's normal, and good for him. Helps him ventilate and keeps him away from an oxygen infuser."

"Thank the Creators of everything," a dark, male voice said behind them.

"Foster!" Wes beamed and then coughed again. "Don't worry. Coughing's good among the cloudheads."

Rayne chuckled but then grew serious as she turned to search for Kae. To her relief, the rest of the team was there, all looking somber but unharmed. Her parents stood together, Madelon's expression undecipherable when she looked at Wes, and then at Rayne.

"How is he?" Kae asked and came up to Rayne, looking down at her with eyes filled with fatigue and concern.

"He's doing well. He's young, and we got him here in time. If he has a setback, I'm not too worried, as long as he's in this facility. If he continues to improve in the next two or three days, he'll be discharged." Rayne thought of something and turned to Madelon. "Mother, as I just treated this child in this emergency facility, do I have privileges to practice here? Wherever here is?" Not that she really cared about where she had privileges or not, which was a big change from the Rayne she'd been before she jumped into the laundry chute.

"Of course you do, darling." Madelon shocked Rayne when she walked up to her and hugged her close. "I'm so relieved you made it here. It was such a gamble, everything you've done these last two days. We've already briefed Kaelyn Dark and her team about some of it, and you'll be brought up to speed as soon as possible."

Rayne tried to remember when Madelon had last embraced her like this. A cool kiss on the cheek, yes, but a firm embrace as if Rayne truly were the missing daughter returning from the depths? She barely recognized her mother. Rayne studied Rocque over her mother's shoulder. An unreadable expression in his eyes made her uneasy, but then she realized it was unshed tears. Her father, feared by some and respected by all, looked at her with tears forming in the corners of his eyes. She had inherited her long, thick eyelashes from him, and now his formed spikes because of the tears.

"Father?" Rayne mouthed and stepped back from Madelon, who made her way to Wes and Tania. "Are you all right?"

"I am. Now." Clenching his jaw, as if grinding down on his molars would help, he quickly wiped at his eyes. "Never mind me. I'm just being an old fool."

"Please. You're seventy-eight. That's middle age." Rayne tried humor, as it unnerved her to see her father emotional. It was as alien to her as her mother's warm embrace.

"Of course. As I said. Foolish." Rocque's tears appeared to dry up instantly. "I'm glad you were successful with the boy. He looked—" He stopped short of saying the word dead, but it was obviously his sentiment.

"With these resources, I can safely say I was just doing my job." Rayne held her chin up, as she always did when facing her parents, but then a quick vision of her father's tears made her relent somewhat. "And yet, saving Wes…he's more than just a patient. That made it personal. Perhaps not a good thing, but there it is."

"Perhaps not. But not a bad thing either." Rocque walked over to Madelon, who was talking to Tania and Wes.

Kae joined Rayne, her expression not giving anything away. "You did it again. For the third time. How can we ever repay you?"

Rayne cringed. "I don't need thanks or praise. Making sure Wes has the chance to grow up is what counts, as it should be. For Tania—and for you." She smiled tightly. "I'm still trying to figure out how my parents have access to a floor that apparently doesn't exist. How long has this been going on? And why? And…" She sighed and rolled her shoulders. "Damn. I'm too exhausted to wrap my brain around anything at all." She moved to the wall and pressed her back against it. "I could fall asleep standing up."

"It's been a lot." Kae shrugged. "I feel it too, and I'm used to this. Well, not this exactly, but a less orderly existence."

Rayne had to smile. "Is this you trying to be polite about me being delicate?"

Kae blinked and then returned the smile that, as clichéd as it sounded, changed her entire face. The stark features seemed to be lit from the inside, and her dark eyes sparkled despite her fatigue.

"As I understood it, they have guest quarters here, and we're welcome to bunk up, for now. Foster is pretty out of it, in fact, ready to fall asleep on his feet, though he'd never admit it. Beth is, for some unfathomable reason, barely affected at all."

"Because I'm half your age, Kae. I bounce back fast." Beth approached, and even if she did look a lot less worse off, her eyes were red around the rims. "But we all need to rest."

"Let me ask Mother where these quarters are. There's another matter that I need to raise with her. Join me?" She waved them along. "Mother. I need to run something by you. It's urgent."

"Of course. Does it have something to do with your chip?" Madelon stroked Wes's hair and walked over to them. "I should have explained sooner. When you exited the lift, a wrap-around sensor shut off your chip. Whether you keep it, or have us outfit you with a new identity, the sensor in the lift will keep turning it off when you get here and turning it back on next time you pass. This is the only way we can keep this floor a secret from the authorities while we work on our plans." She pushed a few stray strands of hair out of Rayne's face. "After you've rested, we'll brief you about as much as we can, though even your father and I don't know everything." Madelon looked more like the haughty woman she'd been used to dealing with all her life, as her mother let her eyes run up and down Rayne. "And cleaned up and had a change of clothes." She flicked her fingers in the air. "We don't have unlimited time. Rocque and I are attending a fund-raising dinner this evening."

A dinner. Rayne pressed her lips together. "We won't keep you from your social calendar."

Something resembling pain came and went so fast in her mother's eyes, Rayne wasn't sure it had actually been there. "Trust me. If your father and I stood up these people tonight, our endeavor to save the Celestians, and the Subterraneans as well, could be in danger. We have cultivated people like our hosts tonight for decades. If we're missing in action without a good excuse, it might just arouse enough, well, curiosity, rather than suspicion.

We never know what will be the spark that lights the fuse under all our plans."

Rayne's thoughts whirled as she tried to piece together Madelon's impossible words. The phrase "we have cultivated people like our hosts tonight for decades" lingered, and a sickening feeling that she might not know her parents at all made bile simmer just below Rayne's throat. "Will you be back tomorrow? Remember, I don't know anything about this setup with the secret floor. I...I refuse to be kept in the dark any longer."

Madelon's stark expression softened into something so rare for her, Rayne barely recognized what looked like a mix of pain and love on her mother's face. "Let Kae, Foster, and Beth fill you in with what they know. Your father will be busy during the upcoming days, but I'll be here tomorrow morning. Officially, I'll be doing my meditation routine for hours tomorrow, and that way I know nobody would dare to disturb me." Madelon ran a finger along Rayne's cheek. "I'll answer everything as best as I can then. All right?"

Rayne nodded, not trusting her voice. Her mother kissed her cheek, and then she found herself wrapped in Roque's arms. She feared that a bear hug from her father would be what broke her, as this had never happened, not after she became an adult.

"You look shell-shocked." Kae placed a hand at the small of Rayne's back. "Beth has a key to an overnight apartment. Tania's going to stay on a cot next to Wes, but the rest of us should follow your mother's advice. Clean up. Eat. Sleep." She pushed her fingers through her hair and then grimaced. "Yeah. Clean is number one, that's for sure."

"It'll take you about one minute to get rid of all the grime we accumulated," Rayne said, "unless you want an aqua shower, of course."

"Normally, I would. It's just that I'm hungry again, and age must be getting to me. I'm exhausted." Kae smiled as she shrugged.

"Ha. How old are you? Thirty-something? Try climbing all those stairs when you're almost fifty and clearly just imagining that you're in great shape." Crinkling her nose, Rayne turned to find Beth. "Beth. You're the key master. Take us to the apartment before Kae falls asleep standing up."

"Sure thing, Doc." Beth held up a long, silver-glass strip. "We're lucky they had a vacancy in the guest wing, or we'd have had to curl up in a corridor somewhere. "Apartment 443-epsilon."

"I appreciate that more than I can say," Kae said as she waved Foster over. "Come on, big guy. You look worse than the rest of us."

"Compliments will get you nowhere," Foster said and yawned. He removed his knitted hat and scratched his head. "I could do with more food."

"The woman who gave me the key told me they keep their food storage filled. We won't starve." Beth smiled, but then the broad grin waned. "But we have to keep thinking of those we know back home who do."

"Absolutely." Rayne lengthened her stride to catch up with Beth and slid her arm around her waist. "I know I was there for only a few days, but I'll never forget what I witnessed. I only scraped the surface of everything your people go through, but it made it impossible for me to resume the naïveté I lived with before."

Beth mimicked Rayne's motion and wrapped her arm around her waist. She moved them over to Kae and did the same with her. "All right. We're in a skyscraper. Wes is truly on the mend. Tania hasn't killed anyone. There seems to be some sort of uprising or plan to overthrow something, and as long as it's not our people, we should be able to allow ourselves a good meal and a decent night's sleep." Beth clicked with her tongue. "And before you say I'm not in charge here, to hell with that. I'm still right."

Kae chuckled, her voice raspier than normal. "You're often right. Come on. I hope it's not far. She leaned back and glanced at Rayne, who felt her cheeks go warm, which was obviously ridiculous. "And while we eat, we can update Rayne before she implodes from pure curiosity."

Rayne managed to give a tired smile. Everything was, yet again, catching up with her, but she refused to relax until she had a couch or bed under her sore body. Leaning a little more than she should against Beth, she followed along as they walked out of the clinic. Food. Rest. Everything else had to wait.

Chapter Eighteen

Kaelyn had been impressed with the quarters she, Foster, and Beth had been to with Rayne's parents earlier, but she had paid little attention to details, as so many other things were more important. Now she stood inside the door as it hissed shut behind the four of them. Rayne walked over to a panel to the left of the door. "Computer. Privacy lock at this location until further notice."

"Affirmative." A disembodied voice holding a metal undertone spoke calmly. "Information available. Shall I continue?"

"By all means. Yes." Rayne toed off her boots. "Make yourselves at home. Nobody will bother us."

Cautiously, Kaelyn removed her empty harness and dropped it on a shelf. Following Rayne's example, she took off her footwear and jacket. She scrutinized her dirty clothes, comparing them to the impossibly white furniture in the guest quarters. Everything was high gloss and sparkling chrome. In the center of the main room was a seating arrangement consisting of three couches and a low glass table supported by thin, black legs that looked as if they might break if you put your feet up.

"Before anything, I'm going to use the instant-cleaning tube." Rayne looked around and pointed first to the left and then to the right. "Two-bedroom facilities, as far as I can see. Pretty basic setup. I'll be in that ensuite."

"That what?" Beth hadn't taken her boots off yet and suddenly looked as if she was about to bolt. "What the hell's an ensuite?"

Rayne colored faintly. "A bathroom attached to a bedroom."

Beth shook her head. "Got it. I think. Before you disappear, can you just show me how I use the other one. I have to pee."

Rayne smiled and waved at all of them to follow her. "A quick and easy demonstration," she said as she walked through the bedroom and pressed a sensor to yet another door.

Kaelyn peered inside. Everything was white, gold, and glass, or a glass composite, judging from the pattern between the panes. "Fancy," she muttered. Very few, if any, Subterraneans had ever seen anything like this, which made her simultaneously sad and angry.

"Waste facility here. Just sit down, do your thing. Press this sensor, and it will cleanse you before you get up again." Rayne spoke matter-of-factly. "Clean your hands by tucking them into this." She pointed to a glass oval and demonstrated by pushing her hands inside. The piece of technology hummed, and a light-blue sheen came and went. Rayne removed her hands. "All done." She walked over to a round, metal-and-glass-striped tube, at least five feet in diameter and eight feet tall. A small computer platform sat to the side of it.

"This is a tad more complicated, but once you've tried the settings, you'll find what you prefer. You can choose between aqua, waves, and instant. Aqua is for those who like the old-fashioned way of scrubbing oneself clean. Obviously, it takes the longest."

"Obviously," Foster muttered from where he stood leaning against the doorframe.

Rayne nodded as if she hadn't noticed his acerbic tone. "Waves send special airwaves that contain a blend of harmless chemicals, mixed with vibrations through the air. It's not my favorite, but some claim it provides a massage." Rayne shrugged. "And then there's the one I almost always use, the instant. The name says it all. It takes about thirty seconds and uses a magnetic burst that removes every foreign material, dead skin cells, anything you may have encountered. In my case, bodily fluids of all kinds. I use the aqua shower only as a treat. It truly is a luxurious feeling."

"That's the one for me. Show me the button, and I'll use the other bathroom." Beth pushed past Kaelyn, who didn't intend to get in the way of her youngest teammate's desire to rid herself of the grime of the last day.

Rayne showed them all how to program the shower and how they could clean their clothes in the slot sitting above one of the cabinets. "Just push them in here, and they'll be done in a few minutes. Same method as the wave-cleansing cycle."

Now that was a method Kaelyn could get behind. Cleaning just about anything in the tunnels was always tricky. Given their water shortage, detergent or soap shortage, and, having washed your clothes so many times after keeping them around for years, even decades, they were falling apart, staying clean was time consuming. Having some enigmatic waves launder them in minutes seemed like an impossible magic trick, but she trusted Rayne to not exaggerate.

Foster pushed off the doorframe. "I'm going to see if I can find a beer while Beth takes a fucking bath." He looked somber, but his voice was gentler than before.

"I'll join you." Kaelyn nodded at Rayne. "Let me know when you're done. I feel filthy enough to ruin all the damn whiteness here. The sooner I clean up, the better."

"Oh, I'll be quick. I'm hungry, and I could sleep for a week." Rayne rolled her shoulders. "You should find some clothes in the dressers if you need to replace something."

Hardly. Kaelyn closed the door to the bathroom and then walked out to the common area, where she found Foster looking upset. "What's up?"

"I wish we'd asked Doc how to open the cooling cabinet." Foster felt along the nearly impossible lines that appeared to show where the doors began and ended. "I've even hit one of them."

"That's not going to get you any beer." Kaelyn snorted. "Let me see." She ran her finger along one of the lines, and when she reached the right, lower corner, a faint pop sounded, and the door swung open in a controlled way. "Hey, look at that. It's not the refrigerator, but we'll have something to drink out of." Twelve tall glasses sat on a shelf. Kaelyn pulled out two of them and, considering they could hold more than beer, two more for Beth and Rayne. "Left or right, lower corner on the top cabinets. I think."

After opening four more cabinets, Foster gave a deep cheer.

"Fantastic. Beer. It's kept in dark bags for some unfathomable reason, but the bags say 'dark lager,' which is a posh word for a brew. He took two bags and walked over to Kaelyn. "You open them. If I try, I'll just spill something on the fancy-ass white floor."

Smiling again, Kaelyn examined the bags and found a button at one of the corners. She pressed it after making sure she held the corner over a glass. Frothing, ice-cold, dark-golden beer poured into the glass. "Go ahead." She pointed at the glass, delighted to see Foster's facial expression when he took the first gulp.

"Damn! If that's not the coldest, most beautiful beer I've ever had." He seemed in awe. "I admit I harbor a healthy suspicion toward the Celestials, but this beer goes a long way toward their redemption."

"And here I thought having me in the trenches with you would do the trick," Rayne said from behind them.

Kaelyn had just poured beer for herself and now turned in surprise. For a few moments, she gaped at the sight of Rayne dressed in loose pants, a sleeveless shirt, and something that looked like sandals, all of them white.

"Guest clothes." Rayne shrugged.

"I didn't mean you, Doc," Foster said. Looking embarrassed, which was a completely new expression for Kaelyn's old friend, he pointed at the refrigerator. "Beer? Or something else? That thing's full of stuff to drink."

"Thanks, Foster. I can get it. And I know you have every reason to be suspicious of the Celestials. I'm glad I've managed to show that you can trust me."

Foster shifted his glass back and forth between his hands. "I was half kidding."

Rayne walked over and opened the refrigerator, then pulled out water and some other, suspiciously pink, beverage. "So was I, Foster." She passed him and went over to one of the couches, where she curled up in the corner and opened the water bottle. "Rehydrate with water, not just beer. It has the opposite effect. Doctor's order."

"After my instant shower," Kaelyn said and left Foster to fend for himself when it came to Rayne, who looked like some angelic creature where she sat on the couch with her long hair cradling her shoulders.

Five minutes later, Kaelyn stared at herself in the full-body mirror in the bedroom. Her clothes were clean, but she had opted for the complimentary clothes in the drawers. Like Rayne's, they were all white enough to sting her eyes. Not comfortable with wearing a sleeveless shirt, she chose a short-sleeved variety. The sandals claimed to be one-size, judging from the sole, but looked far too small. As it turned out, they easily stretched to fit her feet. Kaelyn studied her face. Clean, yes, but the instant shower wasn't designed to mask her old scars and new bruises. Normally her marks didn't bother her at all, but being this clean, they looked highlighted. Perhaps she would ask to borrow a derma-closing wand.

Going back to the main area, she saw Beth half asleep on one of the couches, while Rayne sat with her legs pulled up, much like Kaelyn had left her, leaning her head into her hand while she read from a tablet.

"She looks even younger like that," Kaelyn said after pulling a blanket over Beth.

"She is young. And you look young in white too, apparently." Rayne tipped her head back. Her hair billowed along the top of the cushion behind her. "You said you were starving earlier."

"Not drastically. I can wait for Foster to return. He's the one who can cook." Kaelyn tore her gaze from Rayne's beautiful eyes and looked around the room. Four computer consoles sat ready to be used at the far wall. A dining table with eight chairs glimmered in a muted silvery tone. Above it sat a flat, wide lamp of sorts. It had its own little panel and no doubt a multitude of settings. The luxury that she remembered Rayne calling "basic" was mind-boggling.

"What you must've thought of my dwelling," Kaelyn murmured as she sat down next to Rayne.

"What?" Rayne glanced from the tablet to Kaelyn instantly. "What do you mean?"

"This. This is what you're used to. White. Silver, gold, glass. Clean. Beverages at the ready. Food waiting to be devoured. Bathrooms that you can use whenever you like it, for free. Clothes that are—well, white." Kaelyn wasn't angry, just taken aback at how different their worlds were, which she should have known.

"I'm used to luxury. Yes. But I'm also used to diseases, injuries, trauma, blood, vomit, fear, pain, addictions, mental-health issues, and so on. I was born into a social bracket that most other Celestials consider upper-echelon. This is true." Rayne put her left hand on Kaelyn's knee. Its warmth sent tremors along the inside of her thigh. "As it turns out, that's not the whole truth. While we wait for Foster to get back and cook for us—although the guy looked as beat as the rest of us, so I suggest we inflate a FlatPak—why don't you fill me in on what my parents told you. It feels strange that you know more about them than I do." Rayne's smile wobbled somewhat. "Besides...I found nothing wrong with your dwelling. I felt safe there, in your home."

Kaelyn didn't know what to say to the last part. "Ahem. All right." She stalled for a moment, trying to gather her thoughts. "Inflate a FlatPak? Sounds like a mechanical maneuver rather than something to do with food."

"Funny. Meals are dehydrated and flattened. We can store tons of them for emergencies, and for convenience. You place one in the ReHyde, and it inflates and rehydrates in moments. I bet there's a cabinet full of them."

"All right. Sounds like a good, but scary, idea tonight." Kaelyn, who had eaten a lot worse in her lifetime, was ready to eat the box the stuff came in. Clearing her voice gently, she began reiterating what Madelon and Rocque had shared earlier. The longer she spoke, the more Rayne appeared to withdraw mentally. When Kaelyn finished talking, Beth had woken up, and Foster stood behind her couch, looking at Rayne with no expression.

"They're…they are like strangers," Rayne whispered, her gaze locked on Kaelyn. "We were never close, but this? They didn't trust me. They feared I might let the authorities know. Or maybe I'm looking at this all wrong. Perhaps I'm the stranger. Clearly, they never knew *me*."

Kaelyn wanted to take Rayne's hand, but obviously that wouldn't go over well. Rayne sat with her back straight, her gaze unwavering, and the tension around her eyes and lips suggested she was in some sort of damage-control mode. She had the expression she wore when performing surgery, times ten. Yet Kaelyn feared that if she did offer a kind word, or a touch, Rayne might shatter. Annoyed at her own unusual dramatic thoughts, Kaelyn tried to relax, but it was hard when Rayne looked equal parts disappointed, shocked, and defeated.

"You will find out more directly from your parents," Kaelyn said softly. "And you'll be able to ask some follow-up questions." She knew her attempts to reassure Rayne were feeble at best. She sensed some of the dynamic between Rayne and her parents, but just as Rayne could never know what it was like to grow up in tunnels and caves, Kaelyn would never fully grasp what it was like to be the child of the formidable couple she had met today.

"I know." Rayne drew a deep breath and covered her face with her hands. She rubbed vigorously. "How about some of the FlatPaks? I'll fix them, and you can watch." Standing up, she seemed unsteady for a moment, but then she pulled her shoulders back. Motioning for them to follow her to the kitchen area, Rayne didn't check to make sure they did. She had obviously slipped back into doctor mode and treated them as she would any intern. Kaelyn already admired Rayne's resilience, and this was yet another proof of her strength.

Beth nudged Kaelyn's arm as she passed her. "She's something," she whispered.

Kaelyn nodded. Rayne was more than something. As she rounded the counter and watched Rayne look through several cabinets, pulling out plates and utensils, the oddly domestic ambiance nearly staggered her. An alien sensation surged from the center of her abdomen and up to her face, and she knew she must be blushing. Busying herself by helping explore the rest of the cabinets, she was grateful that nobody expected her to talk, as her throat was locked to keep from choking on all the emotions flooding her.

"Here. Watch me." Rayne was still somber and methodical. She had pulled out a stack of flat boxes, about an eighth-of-an-inch thick. "Choose your meal. There are starter dishes, entrées, and desserts."

"What the fuck is an entrée?" Foster frowned as he browsed the stacks. "I've never had the majority of these meals."

"An entrée is the main course during dinner. Want me to pick something this first time?" A faint smile appeared on Rayne's lips, giving Kaeylyn hope that she was bouncing back—again.

"Hell, yeah. I like meat. The real kind." Foster leaned his hip against the counter. "And dessert you said? I like pie."

"Apple pie okay?" Rayne searched through the packs. "And here's some venison. Let's go for that. For starters…Calamari?"

"Why not?" Foster sent Kaelyn a glance that made it clear he had no idea what calamari was either.

Rayne opened a black glass door in the middle of one of the tall cabinets. She placed the starter-dish FlatPak into a slot and closed the door again. "Just press this sensor twice, and it will scan the contents and inflate it accordingly." Rayne tapped the sensor, and the piece of technology gave a low hum. Fifteen seconds later, a soft ping sounded, and using a strange glove, Rayne pulled out a tray where golden-brown rings sat in the middle, surrounded by vegetables. Next to it, a small container held a red liquid. Sauce perhaps.

"Why don't you go over to the dining room and start with this, and we'll inflate our starters." Rayne seemed more like her usual self. "Then, after you finish one course, you can all come back and continue with your choices."

"This is like magic," Beth said. After choosing her starter dish, she inflated it, and its scent made Kaelyn's mouth water. She shrugged as Rayne turned to her.

"I trust you to pick something for me," Kaelyn said, pretending to study the FlatPaks to avoid her gaze.

"All right. Salmon rolls is a favorite of mine. Sound good?"

Real fish? "I have no idea, but sure." After inflating her meal, Kaelyn sat down next to Foster, trying to wrap her mind around her unsettling feelings. She tried to focus on the image of Foster dressed in all white, making him look like some paintings she had seen of the Creator, the God that, according to the Believers, had given them all life. No matter how she attempted to steer her thoughts away from her confusion, as soon as Rayne sat down next to her at the table, her stomach clenched.

"How the hell am I going to be able to ever eat rodent meat again?" Foster asked as he popped another of the golden rings into his mouth after dipping it in the red sauce. "You've ruined me, Doc."

Rayne gave a wan smile. "I can only say the same. Not for the food, but for this..." She motioned with her free hand around the table, ending up with it on Kaelyn's shoulder. "Belonging to this team. Fighting for what is right. How can I ever go back to my affluent hospital and treat patients that any of my peers could deal with without a problem? When it comes to the people in the tunnels, who lost their doctor—their lifeline, if you will—how can I forget about them when all I can think of is returning to provide the health care they need?"

The impossible words nearly broke Kaelyn. She could chalk it up to Rayne being caught in the moment and speaking from her heart and not her head. Yet she didn't believe that for a second. Rayne wasn't some starry-eyed young girl with a save-the-world complex. She was a seasoned physician who had been subjected to how the other half lived—and died.

Afraid that her insides were truly melting, Kaelyn took a bite of the fish on her plate, and the explosion of taste made her almost choke as she forgot to chew.

"Kae?" Rayne held Kaelyn's chin and turned her face toward her. "You all right?"

"Mm-hm. Not used to this kind of food." It was true, yet also an evasion.

"I know we're all hungry, but none of you are used to our spices. Be careful." Rayne picked at her own food but then gripped her fork and began to eat.

They sat around the table in silence, only occasionally murmuring as their food awoke taste buds in a way only Rayne was familiar with. When Kaelyn knew she couldn't manage another bite, she placed her plate, utensils, and the FlatPak into the recycling slot. An initial grinding noise concerned her, but Rayne waved dismissively with her free hand.

"It's not a new unit, which is obvious. It's fine." Rayne resumed eating.

"I'm off to bed for a few hours," Kaelyn said. She didn't wait for a response either but entered the bedroom she shared with Rayne. This was yet another thing she had to come to terms with. She had spent the night with Rayne before, but that had been in wildly different circumstances. Now they had to share a bed, which normally wouldn't faze Kaelyn. She had slept tightly wrapped up with every member of her team, mainly to stay hidden and warm. But never once had she felt like this.

The bedroom was serene. Another first. Nothing was ever serene in the tunnels—apart from the bathhouses when she reclined with just her mouth and nose above the water. Kaelyn pulled back the thick bedcover and crawled into bed. The soft mattress hugged her, and she clung to the side of the bed, pulling one of the four pillows with her. She closed her eyes, trying to will herself to sleep, and she must have done something right, as it took only a few moments.

Chapter Nineteen

Standing at the foot of the bed, Rayne studied the woman curled up at the far edge of it. It was amazing to watch how different Kae appeared when fully relaxed: younger, more vulnerable, and devastatingly beautiful. Whereas her sharp focus normally formed rigid planes and angles, sleep revealed the woman she could have been if she hadn't lived her entire life in the resistance movement. This Kae evidently existed inside the warrior, hiding, biding her time. Perhaps someday they could all truly be themselves.

Exhausted, Rayne climbed into bed and pulled one of the pillows into her arms, much like she used to do when she was a child. Living on the top floors of the skyscraper meant being subjected to storms and fearing breaches of the windows and ventilation ducts. Having heard stories among her friends of other skyscrapers where the terrorists had placed bombs in the ducts, creating holes big enough for a young child to be sucked out, she feared the elements. As she grew older, she realized that most of the stories were false, that the malfunctions were rare and almost never led to severe injuries.

Yet, when she was an intern, she had a patient who had become stuck to her window when a micro-fissure had appeared. It had sliced her open and begun pulling at her tissues. Only because her family members had jerked the woman off the window and slapped patches on both the window and her, did she survive. She had required organ repair and replacements, and not even the top plastic surgeons had been able to fully erase her scars.

Not sure why this experience filled her mind tonight, Rayne wrapped her arms around the pillow to silence a whimper. Perhaps her conflicting emotions regarding her parents made her susceptible to memories she normally preferred to block. This thought gave her pause, as she so far hadn't quite realized that she needed to push things to the back of her mind at all. Earlier, before Kae had showed up with the injured Wes, she had considered herself living a charmed life. And sure, she was privileged. She had never seen hardship, until now. Yet, here she was, with parents she barely recognized, wondering if everything in her life had been a lie. If Madelon and Rocque truly were part of some underground movement, why hadn't they told her, shared this fact with her? Didn't they trust their only child? Had they considered her such a liability—like a potential traitor?

Chastising herself for letting her thoughts run away with her and creating scenarios that might or might not be true, Rayne curled up and squeezed her eyes shut. She was exhausted and normally would fall asleep instantly, but now her body was taut with pain, her mind shattered with questions.

Behind her, Kae lay motionless, fast asleep for all Rayne knew. In a strange way, Kae's presence helped ground her. She tried to remember when she had last shared a bed with anyone. Occasional sex partners were few and seldom, as Rayne admittedly lived for her profession. She still worked shifts at the hospital and volunteered at the Soldiers' Clinic, which left very little room for any relationships. Her friends were all in the medical field. They saw each other at work and sometimes met for a meal after their duty shifts. When they had their days off, they usually hibernated and decompressed. Sometimes, Rayne would go to the theater, or the opera, but mainly, she read or watched old-fashioned movies and documentaries. The younger generations among the Celestials preferred interactive holographic films, where they could be part of one, alone, or with friends. Rayne preferred to lean back and just watch. She had enough drama in her work.

Feeling drowsy now, Rayne let go of the pillow and rolled over onto her back. The bed was soft in all the right places and firm where she required it, as it adjusted to her body type. Slowly, she managed to relax and rid herself of the tension in her uncooperative muscles.

A hand landed on her belly, making Rayne jump. She muffled a cry, stemming from surprise rather than fear, and turned her head. Kae had rolled over and now faced Rayne's direction. She moved her arm and was close enough to let it circle Rayne's waist. Kae was obviously asleep, and judging from the movements of her eyes behind her eyelids, she was caught up in a dream.

Rayne stayed still where she lay on her back, uncertain where to place her own arms. Eventually, she folded them over her chest, which wasn't comfortable. As soon as she attempted to relax, her arms began to slide down her sides, which would mean touching Kae and potentially waking her.

Kae murmured something unintelligible and tugged Rayne closer. Rayne could barely breathe at the sensation of Kae's strong arm around her. Sinewy and muscular, it held Rayne in a way that made her feel protected and cared for. Had she ever felt like that? As frightening and upsetting as her life had been since she jumped into that laundry chute, Rayne couldn't remember ever feeling this safe. Heat rose from her thighs and spread throughout her abdomen. Trembling now, Rayne tried to gently move Kae's arm off her but found herself in a firmer grip. Kae pulled her closer, which made Rayne roll over onto her side, facing Kae. There was barely an inch between them, and as Kae was the taller of them, her cheek pressed against Rayne's temple.

Rayne bit back a groan. How the hell was she supposed to breathe with all her senses filled with Kae's scent, her smooth skin, and her gentle embrace? Shifting slightly, trying to put a little more distance between them, Rayne wasn't surprised when Kae moved her hand in slow circles on Rayne's back.

"Just relax," Kae murmured, and it was impossible to determine if she was talking in her sleep or was awake now.

Giving in to her overwhelming fatigue, Rayne allowed herself to melt into Kae's arms. Just for a moment, a magical, unexpected second, she felt as if she was right where she belonged—a sense of security she had never experienced. She closed her eyes and pressed her face lightly against Kae's warm throat. No matter what the next day, or moment, might bring, she would never forget how she felt during this fleeting moment.

❖

Kaelyn shifted and attempted to roll over to her right, but it was impossible. Trying to move her arms, she found that she held the soft, fragrant Rayne Garcia. She drew in a deep breath between clenched teeth and tried to pull her arms back, but she stopped after a few moments as Rayne murmured something against Kaelyn's neck. Rayne's breath was warm and created shivers and goose bumps on Kae's skin, and she became motionless again as she contemplated her options. She could wake Rayne and hope the other woman didn't accuse her of taking advantage of her. Feeling ridiculous, Kaelyn attempted to reel in her suddenly paranoid thoughts. They were both grown women, tossed together by circumstance and, to be truthful, because of her own recklessness and Rayne's courage and compassion.

"You all right?" Rayne murmured and moved closer.

Kaelyn had to swallow the lump in her throat that prevented her from making a single sound before she spoke. "I'm fine." Damn if she was going to apologize for holding Rayne.

"Mm. Good." Rayne grew heavier against her.

"Fuck," Kaelyn mouthed into the darkness of the room as tremors reverberated through her. She slid her right hand up along Rayne's back, following the gentle curve of her spine, until she reached the back of her head, where she slid her fingers into the masses of Rayne's gloriously rich hair.

"Mm?" Rayne tipped her head back, into the touch. She lifted her hand and ran gentle fingertips along Kaelyn's cheek.

Turning her head into the barely there touch, Kaelyn pressed her lips against Rayne's fingertips. "Shh. Go back to sleep," she whispered, praying that Rayne would.

At first, Kaelyn thought Rayne's stillness meant she had done just that. She relaxed slowly and kept her hands where they were, holding Rayne close. This was a once-in-a-lifetime moment; of this she was certain. They knew little about their futures, but this was now, and if she never felt this way again, at least she would have the memory of Rayne's body against hers.

Rayne shifted and pulled her head back a little, and from the faint light in the room, she saw the reflection in Kae's slitted glance. "Kae?" she whispered huskily.

Her heart hammering against her ribs, all Kaelyn could do was to hold Rayne closer. She pressed her lips to her forehead, mainly to keep herself from rolling Rayne onto her back and kissing her fully on the lips like she wanted to.

Gentle yet strong arms wrapped around Kae's neck, and then Rayne pulled her into a firm embrace. "Oh, Kae."

Kaelyn nearly gave in to her arousal, but she fought to keep their embrace not chaste, exactly, but gentle. Reassuring. She felt an entirely new agony, but she could live with it if it helped her keep this woman, and everyone else she was responsible for, safe. Kaelyn kissed her way down Rayne's cheek and ended it with the softest of kisses on her lips.

Rayne's whimper damn near stoked Kaelyn's fire again, but she forced herself to settle down against the mattress. She kept Rayne in her arms, and after a while, she sank farther into Kaelyn, and her breathing slowed and grew even.

It took Kaelyn another fifteen minutes before she dared relax enough to remain where she was and allow sleep to claim her. The last thing she sensed was the gentle caress of Rayne's breath against her neck.

Chapter Twenty

Rayne watched the group her parents brought to the guest quarters with concern. Two of them, two men, married with children, she had known all her life, as they were friends of her parents; a tall woman she had seen only on-screen, as she was famous for something or other; and two others were complete strangers.

Madelon stood to Rayne's right, looking her usual somber self. The way she fidgeted with her belt buckle that cinched her long, cream dress to her waist was the only sign she might feel uneasy.

Rocque had taken up his position to Rayne's left, just behind her shoulder. He wore his blinding smile, but Rayne knew from experience how quickly that grin could be extinguished, and thunder take its place.

Kae and her team stood on Madelon's other side. Kae was flanked by Beth and Foster, and even if they weren't wearing any weapons, it should be obvious to anyone just how lethal they could be if cornered. Oddly enough, the Subterraneans in the room didn't look the least concerned.

Madelon introduced the people she'd brought, and Rayne did her best to memorize the names of the people she didn't already know. The woman she recognized from screen, LaSierra Delmonte, radiated power and confidence. It didn't take Rayne long to realize she was the leader of this particular group, perhaps of the entire movement her parents appeared to belong to.

"Why don't we all find chairs and sit down?" Rocque said amicably. "I know both camps here have questions."

Rayne and Beth pulled out extra chairs from behind the kitchen counters, and soon they sat in an uneven circle. Kae had moved and was now next to Rayne, which elicited a surprised look from Madelon.

"So, this is Kaelyn Dark." LaSierra Delmonte crossed her legs slowly. "Your reputation precedes you."

"Ms. Delmonte." Kae nodded calmly. "I have to confess that I'd never heard of you, or anyone else in this room, before I got to know Rayne."

"Not even on-screen?" Delmonte raised her expertly sculpted eyebrows.

"I'm not sure where you get your intel, Ms. Delmonte, but we don't have screens in the tunnels." Kae gave a crooked smile. "We have lots of old radios though."

Delmonte blinked. "Radios?"

"Audio-only devices from centuries ago." Beth grinned. "You can wear some of them directly on your ears, which is helpful when you're working at the same time."

Rayne hid a smile. Trust Beth to be her true self no matter what. But as interesting as comparisons between Celestials and Subterraneans could be, they couldn't sit here and chitchat. Rayne directed her attention to Madelon. "Mother. I heard some of your explanation from Kae and the others, but I think you owe me more than that. I hadn't counted on us having guests, but I don't really care. I need the truth about what's going on—what has gone on— right now." Rayne couldn't remember ever speaking to any of her parents like that before.

Madelon exchanged a quick glance with Rocque but then nodded. "Your father and I were part of a group of dissidents even before we moved into what became your childhood home in this skyscraper. It was obvious which way the political winds were blowing, and your father and I, both of us coming from the inlands before the sandstorms wrecked our respective home areas, couldn't just sit idly by. We met in college, that much is true, but we also belonged to a growing underground movement that has worked tirelessly to create a world where everyone is welcome, and everyone is entitled to a decent living standard."

Beth rolled her eyes, obviously not impressed with the Garcias' progress.

"Yet you never thought to bring me into your world?" Rayne could hear the steel in her own voice. "You let me continue to work in a hospital for the rich and famous, trying to please you, make you proud of me—and feeling utterly alone. How am I supposed to trust anything you say now?"

"Because we can finally tell you the truth," Rocque said. "It's been hard to keep this from you. We debated it a long time when you were a little girl, but then we decided to let you live your life, become who you wanted to be, and if opportunity knocked, as it has now, we would bring you in, if you wanted to join us. It was never about lack of faith in you. It was for your protection. And to be honest, you helped with our cover, once you became a well-respected surgeon. We are rich. You are famous in your field. Nobody would have a reason to suspect what your mother and I, and our friends here, have been working toward all these years."

Rayne did her best to reel in her sense of betrayal, as this wasn't about her. It was so much bigger than any little family drama, but hell, it still hurt, and it would do so for a while. She looked at her parents, and though she didn't doubt that they loved her in their own way, she also felt as if she were in the presence of strangers.

"All right," Rayne said, and met Kae's eyes. "That's hardly important anymore. What is important is what your people can do to help the Subterraneans."

"I'm sure they have an inkling about some of that already," Foster said, his deep voice barely masking the scorn. "Your people have spies in the tunnels. There's no way you can be doing all that shit you're claiming to without having eyes and ears below."

To Rayne's surprise, Delmonte smiled and nodded. "Of course we do. And no, we're not about to blow anyone's cover. Also, if you think about it, we're not so much interested in spying on you, as in the spies sent by the Celestial authorities. We have proof of sleeper cells ready to be activated immediately if the authorities command it."

"Spies? We counted on those. But sleeper cells?" Kae's lips lost their color as she pressed them into a thin line. "Have you identified any of them?"

Delmonte didn't respond right away. She straightened her sleeves meticulously, perhaps unaware of how that action came across as stalling. "Perhaps. We have indication of groups, even families. Knowing their Celestial identities wouldn't help you at all, obviously."

"A photo might." Beth's easygoing nature had vanished at the mention of sleeper cells.

"We'll see what can be arranged. Handling this type of situation is risky. You may just want to lynch these people, and perhaps rightfully so, but the political play, the intelligence branch among the dissidents—"

"We're not idiots, Delmonte." Kae accentuated the words, and it was obvious she was done with the niceties. "We're here, not because we had any idea about your arrangements, but because a child's life was in danger."

Rayne didn't let on about their second agenda, as this was a moot point. They had hoped to convince her parents to get them in touch with people living close to the Inner Border. What could they possibly hope to gain from Rayne's influential parents now?

"You risked several members of your unit to save a child?" Delmonte pursed her lips for a moment but then relaxed them. Maybe she didn't want to let her annoyance show.

"I'm sure you would do the same," Kae responded silkily. "Or do you find it difficult to think anyone would risk anything for a caver child?" Kae's wrath was obvious. She was not about to play games, and Rayne knew she had to intervene.

"We've received a lot of information today. I'm grateful that I could use your facility here to save young Wes yesterday. Now that I'm back, I realize that I'm a liability, as the authorities must suspect me of aiding terrorists down at the Soldiers' Clinic."

"No. That's been dealt with," Delmonte said, waving her hand dismissively. "Once your parents explained the situation, and your heroic return, I used my sources to go into the computer system and change your status. Your record is impeccable again, which means that you can return to your life, if that's what you desire."

Rayne nearly blurted out "Are you kidding?" but settled for an emphatic, "Absolutely not. I'm going to use my expertise where it's needed."

"What do you mean?" Madelon asked, her eyes narrowing.

"Once Wes is able to be transported out of here, I'm going with him, and the others. The Subterranean lost one of their very few physicians. I plan to return to continue his work. It's that, or they'll have nobody."

"That's…you can't do that. Granted, I'm glad you're not going back to the hospital, but we need you in our organization." Rocque looked appalled, bordering on outraged. He shoved his hand through his thick, salt-and-pepper hair.

"Father. I'm forty-eight. The time you could make decisions for me, or even manipulate me, ended decades ago." Rayne turned her focus on Kae, which made her stumble on her words for a second. Kae's eyes, normally so dark, now glittered, but her eyebrows were knitted into a familiar scowl. They had tiptoed around each other after waking up earlier, but at least they had exchanged a few smiles.

"This might just work out anyway," the man to Delmonte's right said. He had been quiet for the entire time, much like Madelon and Rocque's friends on the couch, but now he looked up and scratched his shaggy hair. He appeared to be in his mid-twenties, and his pallor showed he spent very little time in the sunrooms, or the courtyards. Rayne tried to remember his name but drew a blank. "Just as a reminder, I'm Benny Vance. I work for Ms. Delmonte as her aide-de-camp and general advisor. If you'll allow me, I'll explain what I mean." He glanced around the room as if checking the others for permission.

"Go ahead, Benny." Delmonte leaned back in her chair, gazing from Rayne to Kae before she returned her attention to Benny.

"I suggest we start by issuing identity chips and creating a personal history for the two children in the clinic, and the three, uhm, freedom fighters present in this room. Doctor Garcia is already in the clear. If Kaelyn Dark, Mr. Foster, and—Beth, was it?—could move unhindered throughout the Eastern Seaboard City, that could be very useful. With Doctor Garcia's reputation for excellence, and the tactical prowess of our guests, we could make great use of the situation."

"And while we were gallivanting around doing your bidding, who would care for the Subterranean people?" Kae's voice was lethally smooth again.

"Oh, I didn't mean for my plan to sound like a one-sided thing." Benny colored faintly, probably facilitated by his transparent white complexion. "We would have to offer something in return, naturally." He pushed his thin tablet over to Delmonte. "Like this, ma'am?"

Delmonte browsed his notes. "This is a very daring plan, but if it works, it can propel our mission and bring us further ahead than we have come in the last decade."

Rayne turned to Kae. "No matter what they want you to do, or me, for that matter, your people need medical care. I can't be in two places at once."

"I know." Kae leaned closer. "But that said, we should hear this guy out. He seems ready to actually do something other than just talk."

This was true, but Rayne didn't trust the way Delmonte looked like a sated cat. Redirecting her gaze to her mother instead, she noticed something she hadn't expected. Concern. Worry, even. Just as Rayne was about to speak, she saw Madelon raise her hand a fraction of an inch off her lap and move it from side to side in a way that Rayne recognized.

Be careful.

Chapter Twenty-one

Kaelyn paced back and forth in the living area of the guest quarters. Their guests had left, and she knew they didn't appreciate how she had interrogated them and questioned their motives. The only one eager to share was the young man, Benny. He seemed almost giddy with his idea about sending her team and Rayne into harm's way with false identities.

She wasn't sure about LaSierra Delmonte's motives to let her assistant, or whatever Benny's true title was, run the show. Delmonte seemed content to let him take over and outline a plan about how the Celestial resistance would reach their goal—to overthrow the government of the Eastern Seaboard City.

Stretching from the old border to Canada to what used to be Florida, the Skyscrapers appeared to reach for the stars. As a child, Kaelyn had heard from older Subterraneans how the structures consisted of thousands of stories, inhabited by millions of people, right above them. This information had intrigued, and frightened, Kaelyn. She had looked up at the ceiling of the dwelling she'd shared with her mother, wondering if those tall buildings would make it cave in and crush them. Her mother had laughed and reassured her this wouldn't happen. As an adult, Kaelyn realized her childhood fears weren't as farfetched as her mother thought. Over the years, on several places along the coast, some skyscrapers had settled farther into the ground, flattening the tunnels below and killing thousands of Subterraneans.

"Tell me what you're thinking. Please, Kae." Rigid, Rayne stood perfectly still.

"What I think?" Kaelyn stopped in front of Rayne, using every one of her additional four inches to tower over her. "I think your parents are torn between their cushy life and their political agenda. And then there's this Delmonte woman. She's sketchy as fuck, and that's just scratching the surface with her. I think your parents have complex political motives, but Delmonte—she's on a whole different level. Her guy there, Benny, seems at least to be truthful with his ideas."

Rayne nodded slowly. "To be honest, I'm not sure I know my parents at all, but you're not wrong about their ambitious nature. I just never knew their plans included treason."

"Your authorities, from the commander-in-chief down to the local authorities, are gullible at best, and corrupt at worst." Foster joined them, leaning with his palm against the wall. "Don't look so shocked, Doc. Just because we have to learn mainly in an analogue way in the tunnels doesn't mean we're not provided with some basic knowledge. Having been subjected to the result of the indoctrination by your authorities firsthand, we're clear when it comes to the state of things topside." His words contained a slow-burning fury, but his expression wasn't unkind when he looked at Rayne.

"This plan," Beth said from the kitchen area, where she was busy eating again, this time an inflated piece of chocolate cake. "Benny's plan. He's not wrong. If we can get the information required and then just go poof, we'll have something to bargain with. That could persuade Doc's parents to give us what we need to get some of our people out of the tunnels, at least."

Kaelyn had listened to Foster and Beth, and she didn't disagree, on principle. But something in Rayne's eyes, a hesitation paired with hurt and anger, made her hesitate. "And you're not convinced." She stepped closer, knowing she was well into Rayne's personal space.

"I fear they might see the three of you as expendable. Hell, perhaps me too. I worry they think we're a loss they can live with.

Sort of, if it works, fine, but if it doesn't, well, then they tried." Rayne ran an unsteady hand across her forehead. She looked exhausted, and Kaelyn realized the meeting had to have taken a toll on Rayne on so many levels.

"Hey. That's kind of how we live our lives anyway," Beth said and licked a chocolate-covered thumb. And just so you know, this has totally ruined my tastebuds. How can I possibly eat anything that doesn't taste like chocolate from now on?" She winked and cut another slice for herself. Kaelyn noticed that Beth didn't offer anyone else a piece.

Rayne snorted, a sound filled with mixed emotions. "You're amazing, Beth. You really are." Placing a hand on Foster's muscular arm that he still rested against the wall, she smiled sadly. "And so are you two." She looked at Kaelyn with darkening eyes. "That's why I feel I should protect you against these people, including my parents, and get you out of here as soon as possible."

"But then there's Wes." Kaelyn gently gripped Rayne's hand and steered her toward the couches. "Have a seat. We need to hash this out."

"But..." Rayne sat down and looked ready to repeat her objections.

Foster took a place across from them, and Beth joined him, keeping her plate a safe distance from them.

"Listen," Kaelyn said firmly. "Wes is nowhere near ready to be released, right?"

"True." Rayne raised her chin. "That doesn't mean—"

"Just hear me out, and then you can tear into my arguments, all right?" Kaelyn managed a smile, which wasn't easy, since Rayne's pained facial expression made her ache. "We have a window of opportunity here. Remember what we came here to do after we knew Wes would be safe? We weren't even sure we'd be able to take him home with us. Now he's here, safe on this secret floor, and he has his sister with him. So far, that's a much better outcome than we ever could have conjured up." Kaelyn poured a glass of crystal-clear water from a jug on the low table in the center. She sipped it while she began to sort the arguments in her brain. "They want Foster, Beth, and me to assume new Celestial identities. Apparently, this is an easy task for that prodigy kid, Benny. I won't even pretend I understood half of what he said. One of my demands, and there will be more, is that we get to choose our own names and backstories. Second, that the four of us, possibly including your parents, come up with the plan once we know more details about the objective."

"I guess we have to involve them, as they're the ones with the connections," Rayne muttered. She seemed less rigid, but her eyes appeared to be a harsher green than before.

"This information they want us to obtain. Did I understand it right that the person we're supposed to approach is the daughter of the former commander-in-chief?" Kaelyn kept her gaze on Rayne, who nodded.

"How old is she?" Beth wiped at her mouth with a napkin and tossed it into the ReCyc with a practiced move. Kaelyn had seen her toss Molotov cocktails with exactly the same gesture many times.

"Eh, let me see." Rayne looked up at the ceiling. "A little older than Beth, I think. She's a lawyer, which makes it trickier. Her name is Amy Lindberg."

Kaelyn frowned. "Sounds like you know her?"

"Only professionally. She was my patient just after she passed the bar. I haven't talked to her since, but I remember her well." Rayne shifted where she sat and tucked a small pillow behind her lower back. "Up-front, no-nonsense, and outspoken."

"Sounds like someone else we know," Beth said from where she had curled up. "But that means we have an in. Why doesn't Rayne approach her with a legal issue concerning one of us? Or is that too risky, since this woman isn't your regular Celestial softy?" Beth gestured with both palms toward Rayne. "Present company excluded, of course."

Rayne managed a smile. "If we're going to fool one of our top young lawyers, we have to be clever. To start with, why would I take you, virtual strangers, to her for legal advice?"

"Of course, you remember her fondly from when you fixed her." Wracking her brain, Kaelyn tried to come up with a decent plan why Rayne would contact an old patient for legal advice. "Damn it. I don't even know what legal field she's in. Subterranean arbiters work with every kind of dispute or criminal case, but topside, we know that things are done differently."

"Amy Lindberg is in family law. She sometimes works pro bono for the lower floors." Rayne raised both hands, palms up. "If that helps?"

"At least it's not criminal law. I'd rather not play the part of someone suspected of a crime the first thing I do as a faux-Celestial." Kaelyn snorted. "Family law. And it has to include you, or why would you be involved with strangers?"

"What do you mean?" Rayne asked.

"Correct me if I'm wrong, but it can be difficult to get permission to move from a less-affluent skyscraper to one like this, right?" Kaelyn spoke slowly. "Let's say someone living in this skyscraper that is one of the first ever built and has a prestigious address wants to marry someone from a skyscraper that's not as tall, a lot less luxurious, and not even close when it comes to amenities or opportunities. That has to be a lengthy process."

"Kae? What are you suggesting?" Rayne sat up straight.

Kaelyn smiled broadly, if nothing else than to calm a sudden onset of nerves. "If Benny can create an identity for me to come from such a skyscraper, we will need the assistance of your former patient to be allowed to get married. Especially since we want to live here." Kaelyn's heart thudded painfully against her ribs as she studied the series of expressions on Rayne's classic features.

"Married." Rayne didn't even make the single word a question.

"Brilliant!" Beth said, pumping her fist into Foster's bicep. "Right?"

"Only if Doc thinks so," Foster said in a somber tone.

Rayne covered her eyes with her left hand and groaned. "I think it's insane."

The sting Rayne's words created diminished Kaelyn's plastered-on smile. Of course. How could she ever think Rayne would go for a ruse like that? Rayne lived in this world, enjoyed every privilege that no Subterranean person even knew existed. Kaelyn was about to ask for other ideas, when Rayne lowered her hand and studied her closely. To Kaelyn's astonishment, Rayne appeared vaguely amused.

"I think it's crazy, but to be honest, it is a great idea in its simplicity." Rayne slid closer and took Kaelyn's hand, apparently not caring that Beth and Foster watched with rapt attention. "It means a lot more than you probably realize. The backstory must be impeccable. Nobody can recognize you as Kaelyn Dark. We have to appear completely in love, because why would someone who's been happily single for her entire life, and lived only for her work, marry if not for love? Especially since she's marrying beneath her, which is what everyone in the upper echelons of the skyscraper hierarchy will think." Rayne squeezed Kaelyn's hand. "Can you pretend to love me well enough to fool a shrewd family lawyer?"

Damn her. Kaelyn wanted to pull her hand free and put some distance between herself and Rayne, as she could barely breathe when she looked into her beautiful, inquisitive eyes. "It wouldn't take much," Kaelyn managed to say, fighting to keep her tone light. "You're quite the catch." She regretted her flippant tone as soon as she finished talking.

Rayne stopped squeezing Kaelyn's hand and started clinging to it instead. The skin around her eyes tensed. "If that's how you intend to play it, we might as well surrender to the authorities right away." She tried to free her hand, but Kaelyn knew if she let go now, they truly might fail.

"I'm just nervous," Kaelyn said. She couldn't tell Rayne straight out that she did mean what she said before. It wouldn't take much to love Rayne Garcia, pretend or not. Who in their right mind could resist this woman?

Rayne relaxed her hand in Kaelyn's. "Me too. But if we can just act reasonably affectionate, we can pull it off enough to get close to her—and hopefully close to her father, Eric Lindberg. He's the one who will have a copy of the information we're after."

They sat together on the couches for another hour, chiseling out a rough draft of the deception they planned. They would meet with Benny Vance later in the evening, to get their new identities. The young man had claimed it would take him less than an hour per person, and Kaelyn hoped he wasn't being overly confident to impress his boss.

The door chime rang, and Beth bounced up. "I'll get it."

Kaelyn turned her head toward the door leading out from the apartment. "Check the pad next to the door," she said as a reminder.

"Sure." Beth placed a finger on a sensor. "It's Doc's parents, and Tania."

"Wes?" Rayne stood and was clearly ready to bolt to Wes's side if necessary.

"Hang on. They would have used the communication system if they needed you." Kaelyn hoped she was right. She had no idea about the routines on this floor.

Madelon and Rocque came through the door with Tania, the latter looking tired, something Kaelyn didn't think was possible.

"Wes?" Rayne said, looking at her mother.

"Resting comfortably. Tania needs a few hours' sleep in a decent bed. Until we have a new identity for her, we can't take her to our apartment."

"She can have my bed. I can sleep on the couch." Foster pointed to the room he shared with Beth.

"Come here." Beth put her arm around Tania's shoulders. "We'll tuck you in, and then when you wake up, I'll introduce you to chocolate."

"I'm glad you're here," Rayne said to her parents, but Kaelyn could tell she had put up a wall as soon as her parents stepped inside. "We've come up with a scenario that might work, if Benny is the genius he claims to be."

"And, knowing you, you'd barely consider any suggestion we might have?" Madelon asked, sounding exasperated.

"Please. Take a seat. We have a good plan. If your suggestions will work with ours, we'll hear you out." Kaelyn thought she better head up this discussion, or they would get bogged down with family issues. "This is what we had in mind to get close to your former commander in chief. He's on the list of people that Delmonte gave us as potential marks." Kaelyn provided the information in a few sentences. When she mentioned applying for a marriage license, Madelon began to get up, but Rocque pulled her down again.

"It's pro forma, darling," he muttered. "Kae Dark will be using a false identity. Nothing will be legally binding."

Madelon grimaced but remained sitting by his side. "Very well."

"What was your suggestion?" Foster asked, his low-register voice having the calming effect he was known for. "Does it fit in with any of this?"

Rocque appeared to wordlessly confer with his wife. "In a way, it does. If we create the right sorts of identities for young Wes and Tania." He rubbed his chin, looking oddly uneasy.

"What have you and Mother cooked up?" Rayne murmured. She didn't take her eyes off her parents, and her obvious concern worried Kaelyn more than anything. After all, even if they'd lived a lie for so long, Rayne knew her parents better than anyone else.

"Kaelyn, we have to make you Wes and Tania's legal guardian," Madelon said. She had her hands clasped on her lap. "Once that is established, you will allow us to adopt them."

Chapter Twenty-two

Rayne stood, hands on her hips. "You've got to be joking. Where the hell did that idea come from? And what would that accomplish?"

"From truly wanting to help," Madelon said quietly. "We have things to sort out between us, you and I especially, Rayne, but there's no time for that yet. Before your decision to jump into that laundry chute, we had the leisure of figuring out the next step of our long-term goals, but once you put our family right under the searchlight of the authorities, we suddenly have none at all."

"You're blaming me, when you were the ones leading a life I knew nothing about?" Rayne shook her hands as if to rid herself of something foul.

"I don't blame you for anything. I'm just explaining." Madelon raised her hands in a familiar gesture of exasperation. "Your father and I are not the leaders of the dissidents, but we're pivotal when it comes to planning and executing what we intend to do. Now we can't use our social position the way we could have only days ago. We've already been interrogated twice about your actions. But we can help an innocent child back to life, as he'll need a lot of rehabilitation after his ordeal. As Tania refuses to move an inch away from Wes, she's part of the package. If Rocque and I adopt these children, we can withdraw from public life in an entirely believable way."

"So, you're using Wes and Tania as shields, of sorts," Rayne said, so angry she was trembling.

"I don't disagree that this plan offers benefits for us, but it also helps keep them safe." Rocque walked over to Rayne and gently grasped her shoulders. "You four will be going on this mission to get the information we need to topple the illegal government that has run the skyscraper nation for almost a century. That leaves Wes and Tania vulnerable. If they remain here, on this floor, they'll be protected, but also alone in a world they know nothing about. If we attempt to return them to the tunnels, they might get killed or be under suspicion of collaborating with us up here, and Wes won't receive the aftercare we can give him."

Rayne freed herself from Rocque's hands, hating how logical her father sounded. Their situation was complex, and no matter how she looked at it, she couldn't come up with something better.

"Tania will never go for it," Beth said darkly.

"I already did." A tired voice from the bedroom door made everyone turn their head. Tania leaned against the doorframe, her eyes red and bleary. She was dressed in the same soft, white outfit Rayne had slept in last night. "Can you all quit yelling at each other? I'd just fallen asleep."

Beth gaped. "Really? You agree to have perfect strangers take you and Wes and—"

"They're Doc's parents. They're ready to risk everything to get Wes what he needs. They've spent hours with us in the clinic. They're no more strangers than Doc is. And as Kae won't be able to watch out for us in quite a while, I can use the support." Tania let her tired gaze fall on each face in the room. Rayne could tell she'd made up her mind. "Figure it out, all of you. Preferably quietly. I'm going back to bed." She slipped into the bedroom again and closed the door behind her.

"When in the scheme of things is this adoption going to take place?" Kaelyn asked, her voice husky as she turned to Madelon.

"We're getting you, your team, and the children documentation, plus Benny's latest version of the chips, later today. We'll have a mission briefing tonight, and you'll be set to leave tomorrow morning." Rocque rubbed the back of his head as he sat down again on the couch. "We'll provide the documents for you to sign before you leave and register them immediately via Benny."

Kae seemed withdrawn, as if distancing herself from what everything about Madelon and Rocque's plan would mean in the long run. "And you're sure Benny can deliver?"

"Very sure." Madelon didn't blink when she met Kae's gaze. "I understand that you have helped raise Wes and Tania. That puts us on an even keel. I'll take care of your children, and you will make sure mine is returned to me."

Rayne never would have expected such statements from her mother. Still angry at her parents for shutting her out, she reminded herself that she'd never doubted their love for her, even if they'd publicly lived the life of ambitious jetsetters. Now, Rayne could only hope that she'd be able to truly get to know them at some point.

Kae and Madelon kept talking, but Rayne had to do something about the persistent headache she'd developed during the last hour. She walked over to the kitchen area and searched for a pharmaceutical dispenser.

Beth joined her and ran more water into a tall bottle. "You look kind of pale," she said.

"Headache." It was more than that, Rayne realized as nausea stirred below her breastbone. She found what she was looking for and ordered a medium anti-pain strip. A transparent, green-tinted square slid out at the bottom of the dispenser, and Rayne placed it at the roof of her mouth. It dissolved instantly, and she knew it would take effect within a few minutes.

"That bad, huh?" Beth sipped her water. "I saw you pretty banged up back home, and you never once asked for anything for the pain."

"I couldn't take any of your precious few medications. I know some were given to me anyway, but I just couldn't ask for them." Rayne shrugged and immediately regretted it as more pain shot through the back of her neck. "Damn."

"Does the stuff you took work fast?" Beth frowned and put down her bottle. "You turned ashen. Don't faint on me."

"I won't." Rayne managed a smile. She could imagine the drama that would ensue, especially with her parents present.

Just as the pain began to subside, making her feel almost giddy, her parents came over, her mother scrutinizing her. "For a moment there, you looked far too pale. Glad you took a strip to mitigate whatever's wrong." She touched Rayne's cheeks so quickly, she barely registered the sensation. "Your father and I am going to another meeting, and then we'll be with Wes until Tania's awake. You can reach us via the communication system after the meeting. If there's an emergency, ping Delmonte's admin. Anyone here can give you the code." Madelon checked the time. "You can rest for an hour before Benny's due with the documents. Someone will accompany him with everything else you need."

"All right. See you later this evening, then?" Rayne walked her parents to the door, hoping to be out of earshot from the others. She leaned in as if to kiss her father's cheek and spoke quickly. "I know you put a lot of faith in Delmonte and her people, but I don't know them. Hell, at this point, I'm not sure I know my own parents. I just want to tell you if Kae signs the adoption papers, and you're still not able to keep Wes and Tania safe and together, you won't have anywhere to hide."

"We're well aware that Kaelyn Dark is a forced to be reckoned with," Madelon said, her mouth a thin line.

"She is. But I wasn't talking about her. If something happens to Tania and Wes, something you could have prevented but didn't, you'll have to answer to *me*. I've saved that boy twice. Risked my life for him—twice. I'm not an idiot. I know we have a lot to thank you for—for bringing us all here, making it possible for me to save him. But still, since I'm not clear about your motives, you need to know that I'll come for you long before Kae does if I find you were careless."

When she closed the door behind her stunned-looking parents, Rayne drew a deep breath and pushed her loose hair behind her ears. She returned to the sitting area, barely able to meet Kae's eyes. "I'm going to take advantage of that hour my mother mentioned and rest."

"What was the whispered conversation about?" Foster asked, sounding far too casual where he sat on one of the couches, holding a glass of water.

"I needed to set the record straight regarding how I truly feel about their subterfuge. I mean, I have no idea if I'll ever get the chance to do it once we head out on our mission."

"I see." Foster tilted his head, and Rayne wasn't sure she was fooling anyone.

As she pulled a blanket over her rigid body and tried to relax her taut muscles, Rayne wondered if Kae would join her—and she wished both that she would and that she wouldn't. So much was up in the air, everything turbulent, that she had no room for anything remotely personal. Last night had been caused by fatigue and stress. It was hardly surprising that they had succumbed to a need for some closeness, or even comfort.

When Rayne heard the door to the bedroom hiss open, she forced herself to breathe calmly and evenly, hoping Kae would assume she was asleep.

Chapter Twenty-three

Late that same evening, Kaelyn stood inside the door to Rayne's apartment on the 2823rd floor. Already deciding she would never go anywhere near any windows, she took in the enormous living area. She had thought the guest quarters on the secret floor was luxurious, but now she began to understand that Rayne's place totally outshone it.

Gold and red fabrics framed the eerily large windows. A pale beige carpet made her new, but not too new, shoes sink an inch into its texture. White couches also reminded her of the previous quarters, but these were larger, looked plusher, and framed a gold-and-glass low table. Computer tablets, thin and shiny, lay on the table near some adornment that looked like golden fruit.

To the left Kaelyn saw a kitchen area, twice as big as the one they'd just left. Glossy, green cabinet doors matched the dark-wooden countertops. Four barstools lined one part of the counter, suggesting that Rayne sat down to eat here.

Or perhaps not. Farther into the living area sat another table, looking like metal on very thin legs, surrounded by eight chairs in a similar style. Was this where Rayne ate? Or was it for company?

"Damn. You think you can live among us below ground when you're used to this?" Foster turned a full circle, taking it all in. "This is like one of those palaces in some of your books." He smoothed down the black jacket he wore on top of a blinding-white shirt again. Kae knew he felt as awkward in his new clothes as she did. His gray trousers fit him well, which was only thanks to the features on the ReCyc technology that could adjust sizes within fifteen minutes. It worked only with clothes created by the same manufacturer. With their old clothes, it simply cleaned them before they tucked them into storage.

Beth wore a tight-fitting turquoise dress that reached halfway down her calves. A navy-blue waist-long jacket completed her outfit, together with black shoes with adjustable heels. Kaelyn looked down at herself, still not sure about what Rayne had chosen for her. She had reminded Kaelyn that she was supposed to come from less-opulent circumstances, but the maroon trousers and white, long-sleeve top still felt too fancy. Only the fact that she wore a well-used black jacket over it and shoes that resembled something that could come from the tunnels made the transformation bearable.

Rayne gave Foster a weak smile. "Not a palace, but it's nice. I used to be happy here."

"When did that change?" Beth asked and stepped toward the kitchen before she caught herself and looked back at Rayne. "May I?"

"You can have anything you want from the kitchen, or from my wardrobe." Rayne looked as uncomfortable and out of place as Kaelyn felt. "As for your question…I'd say it changed when we worked to save Wes the second time. I saw the need, the people, hell, the unfairness, and when I thought of my home, which I loved, I realized I just couldn't feel the same about it. Some of the items I've purchased over the years, meaningless things I collect, could have bought months of food, medication, and other supplies for one person in the tunnels. It's not right, no matter how you look at it."

Kaelyn reluctantly agreed, knowing a lot of Celestials wouldn't mind living in luxury no matter whether they knew the truth or not. She found dreaming to be a dangerous pastime. Right now, it hurt her chest to witness Rayne's agony regarding her ignorance, but the truth was, Rayne had spent a lot of her spare time at the Soldiers' Clinic and done so while being kept in the dark by her parents about the dissident movement. Kaelyn could still remember the moans and cries from injured soldiers around them when Rayne had first worked to save Wes. They had been young teenagers—little more than children. She had been totally focused on Wes's survival then, but now it dawned on her that a lot of young kids were intended as cannon fodder for the Celestial authorities and had suffered injuries, which was entirely comparable to how young people didn't fare well in the tunnels. If she was truly honest with herself, Kaelyn had never understood that they were already fighting for all those young people, Celestials and Subterraneans alike.

"Why don't you sit down while I gather my documents?" Rayne asked. "Benny insisted that I use my authentic data unless it's insufficient. I'll have to get my drive from the safe." She didn't wait for an answer before heading out of the living area and into an adjacent room to their right.

Kaelyn was too on edge to sit down after the journey up in the massive public lift, carrying a counterfeit, subcutaneous chip in her left lower arm containing fake documentation. The same went for Beth and Foster, but even if they didn't let their guard down, they seemed less uneasy. Perhaps her own onset of nerves had something to do with signing over Wes and Tania's future to Rayne's parents. Wes had mostly seemed confused when they discussed the pro-forma act to him, but Tania had regarded the digital signing of the documents with deadly seriousness.

"It hit you right in the gut, didn't it?" Foster said, making her jump, since he had closed in on her while she was lost in thought. "The way Wes promised you that he'd be a good boy when you were gone."

Tears burned behind Kaelyn's eyelids, something she normally refused to let happen. "Yeah." Foster was right. Wes had clung to Kaelyn, speaking the heartbreaking words with such sincerity, his little voice husky. "I know the Garcias and our team have each other over a barrel, but the power balance can change quickly. They will take care of Wes and Tania, and we'll get the information they require from the former commander in chief. By then, they've promised to give us the information we need to move as many of our people as possible out of the tunnels unharmed. It's a quid pro quo, but it's fragile. We put a lot of trust in Rayne's parents. They in turn will be in trouble with Delmonte if we fail our mission. Delmonte is at the top of the food chain among the dissidents, but I also have a feeling she has enough backup plans to see her through if things go awry."

"My thoughts exactly." Foster rubbed the back of his head, where a robot barber had cut his dark hair fashionably short. "It'll take a while to get used to this," he said, obviously noticing her glance. "They changed your hair even more."

"I know. Don't remind me." Kaelyn had chosen to block out how strange it had felt to have an artificial individual close in on her with laser scissors. Now she sported high, soft waves and a close-shaven neck. And, strangest of all, it was blue. Not that chemically created color-variations didn't exist among the Subterraneans, but she was normally happy just keeping her hair short and clean. Having a blue, fashion-forward hairdo was perhaps necessary, but it felt *weird*.

"I know you're both cowards, but you have to come look at this." Beth interrupted Kaelyn's musings and made a tapping sound. Glancing around, she softly gasped when she saw Beth standing near the massive window.

"Are you crazy? Nothing out there's worth being so close." Kaelyn folded her arms and remained where she stood.

"You're supposed to be the gutsiest among us, Kae. Come on now." Beth tapped the window again. "This has a label in the corner stating that it's not glass. It's some composite, whatever that means, and unbreakable."

Foster walked closer to the window, not looking as flippant about it as Beth was, but not afraid either. "What are those lights?" He lengthened his stride and stood behind Beth. "They're moving through thin air."

"Thin being the operative word," Rayne said as she reentered the living area. "Those are sky craft. Mostly you travel between the skyscrapers via an air-tunnel system, but law-enforcement, medical, and fire personnel all have access to their own craft. And some, like my parents and those even wealthier, have their own slotted in next to their apartments."

"But not you?" Kaelyn asked and inched toward the window, reluctantly curious.

"Hardly. I've traveled in them many times, but there's no need for regular people to waste credits on sky craft. If we want to travel farther than a skyscraper or two, we can go to the craftportals on the roof and use the shuttle crafts. Much less of a hassle."

"Roof," Kaelyn said weakly. "You go out on the roof?" She stopped about six feet from the window.

"Not *out* on the roof, of course." Rayne gave her first genuine smile since they'd left the secret floor. "There are hangars where you enter the shuttles. All perfectly safe."

"There's barely any oxygen at this level or higher up, isn't there?" Beth whispered, sounding in awe. "It's hard to imagine."

"That, and it's cold." Rayne walked up to Kaelyn and placed a hand on the small of her back. "Come on. It truly is something to see. I promise you it's safe."

Kaelyn couldn't move at first but eventually took a few more steps until she was able to look out the window. Directly in front of her, farther away than she would have thought, she saw a multitude of lit-up, sparkling windows. Of course, the skyscrapers were built to become increasingly narrow toward the top. That said, they were still massive. Where the width of the bases was around 2600 feet, intel suggested they were only two-thirds of that at the top. That meant the next skyscraper could be more than 2000 feet away.

"If you look down, you can see that the closest walk-only tunnels create webs between the structures. This network is possible only up to this level. The very top floors move too much," Rayne said and pointed to the floor.

Look down? Was Rayne out of her mind? But when Kaelyn saw Foster and Beth press their faces against the window, she knew she had to show she wasn't a complete coward. That said, she refused to be responsible if she threw up on the carpet—or fainted.

Once she stood near the window, she reluctantly looked down. The system of tunnels did look like a web spun by a drunk spider. The nearest one was so close she could make out small moving dots, which of course were people going about their day, the majority of them having no clue that they were being observed by people they considered dangerous terrorists.

"We have to go down to the 2780th and cross the tunnel to the skyscraper south of us. It's the twin of this one, and that's where the Lindberg family famously resides. Amy works there, and her father is well-known for his work with different charitable organizations."

"I still don't like that Delmonte insisted we would be able to access the intel we require only after we reach the hotel." Foster grumbled as he pushed away from the window with obvious reluctance. "It's too short a time."

"And if we had carried hard copies, or activated digital copies, after a random search, they wouldn't have even bothered with a trial." Rayne pulled the strap of a small bag Kaelyn hadn't seen before over her shoulder. "I'm carrying my emergency medical-equipment bag, which helps us with our alibi, should we need it. We can't open any files until we reach the hotel because the random checks mostly happen in transit. As my mother explained."

"I know," Foster said and sighed. "It's just this level of technology. It irks me."

"I kind of like it." Beth slapped Foster on the back. "Just imagine not having to take clothes and stuff when you travel. All you need are lists of what you already own that are sitting in the ReCyc buffer, and how may credits you're good for, and then use that information wherever you're going."

"It's convenient." Rayne "I was glad my father wasn't stingy with either."

"He was ready to give us access to so much more until your mother reminded him that we're from the lower decks, so to speak. The whole premise of our backstory." Kaelyn ran her thumb over the area on her arm where the already healed incision holding her chip was located.

"I have what I need. Time to go. Just stay close to me and do what I do. We'll be fine." Rayne opened her front door and let them out. Kaelyn walked past her last and couldn't help but notice how absolutely stunning this version of Rayne was. Her hair looked like gold under the lights where it fell over her shoulders. She wore a white trouser suit over a bloodred shirt and had elevated the heels of her shoes to max, making them nearly the same height.

As they made their way over to the lifts again, Kaelyn placed her arm around Rayne's shoulders and slipped into the role of her lover. Rayne immediately wrapped her arm around Kaelyn's waist and held her close as they matched their steps.

Kaelyn found the closeness reassuring, which was a surprise. Who could have guessed that playing the part of Rayne's lover would come easy to her?

Chapter Twenty-four

Rayne hadn't expected to feel so alien walking among the throngs of fellow Celestials as they made their way through the tunnel system. Around them, well-dressed people talked on their communicators, or to the person next to them, about what they'd been up to lately, or where they were going on vacation, or they complained about their staff or boss. It was almost midnight, but although the inhabitants of the lower floors were already in bed so they could get a good night's sleep before tomorrow's workday, up here, the wealthy didn't go to work, or if they did, they had very favorable hours.

Next to her, Kae gripped her hand so firmly, Rayne was starting to lose sensation in it. Obviously Kae wasn't fond of being this high up, no matter how Rayne had tried to reassure her. That, and being surrounded by the enemy, had to be almost as hard on Kae as the densely populated tunnels underground had been on Rayne.

"We're almost at the hotel." Rayne smiled in what she hoped was a relaxed way. "I look forward to some more sleep." It was true. They had managed to catch only a few hours here and there, which was starting to take a toll even on a doctor who was used to being on call.

"Doctor Garcia!" A male voice called our, sounding either surprised or shocked. Rayne wasn't sure which. She turned her head and saw one of her colleagues from the large hospital on the 2810rd floor walk toward them.

"Damn," Rayne muttered, but then she let the smile she had been practicing reappear on her face. "Doctor Tagger. How nice to see you." She bowed, which was the common way of greeting, even if some older Celestials preferred the old-fashioned handshake.

"I heard the ghastliest rumors about what went on down at that clinic last week." Tagger, a tall, thin man in his late sixties, shook his head. "I refused to believe the especially sordid nature of the gossip, naturally. I told everyone at the neurological clinic that if they thought the daughter of Madelon and Rocque Garcia would lend herself to running the errands of—"

"Glad to hear it," Rayne said, only happy to interrupt the tedious man. "I don't believe you've met my fiancée. May I introduce Kae Drake." Out of the corners of her eyes, Rayne saw Foster and Beth slow down but keep walking. They had decided to not go as a group until they reached the hotel. "Kae, this is a colleague of mine. Doctor Tagger."

"Your fiancée?" Tagger gaped. "Now that's a twist I never saw coming!" It was clear that he realized how unflattering his words might be interpreted and spoke even faster as he tried to salvage the situation. "Nice to meet you, Ms. Drake. I hope you find our little corner of the Eastern Coastal City to your liking."

Rayne regarded Tagger with contempt. Regardless of his shallow nature, she had never been impressed with him, as a person or a doctor.

"I enjoy it very much, sir." Kae spoke politely. "I've never seen credits so well spent in my whole life."

Rayne had to swallow a choked sound.

"I can only imagine," Tagger said and smiled broadly. "It's almost an injustice that this part of our city doesn't lend itself to the masses. I think it would simply lose its charm and character if we did."

"I'm sure it would." Kae's polite smile tensed at the corners of her mouth.

"Ha-ha. Yes. Well. Having new contacts in high places sure makes you a lucky woman." Tagger looked frighteningly close to elbowing Rayne as a "don't we know just what she's been missing" gesture. Instead, he settled for winking at Kae instead.

"We won't take up more of your precious time," Rayne said quickly. "It was nice running into you. Give my best to your wife. Good night." She let go of Kae's hand, wrapped her arm around her waist, and ushered her along before Kae planted her fist in Tagger's face.

"You can work with people like that without killing them?" Kae snarled as they moved toward the end of the glass tunnel.

"I don't work with him, per se, but we're on the same consulting unit when we need to go elsewhere on the coast. I only run into him once every other month or so. He's a skilled neurologist, but he's so successful because most of his patients are under full anesthesia."

Kae was silent for a second before she started to laugh. "Now that I can believe."

Realizing she'd never heard Kae laugh before, or at least not like that, freely and without holding back, Rayne joined in just as they approached Foster and Beth, who were waiting right inside the gates, where they had passed another checkpoint.

Rayne couldn't help tensing up when they walked through the arch, but as it didn't make a sound or turn any of the dreaded colors, she allowed her smile to remain on her lips.

"You look happy. Who was that?" Beth asked as they commenced their walk toward the hotel.

"A colleague. Horrible man, but he'll solidify our story as soon as he gets home. He'll tell his wife, and tomorrow, they will both tell friends and colleagues. It's what the wealthy do here. They gossip." Rayne shrugged. "Never thought I'd be glad for the grapevine."

"Not sure what that means, but you're right." Kae put her arm around Rayne's shoulders. "The more our engagement is stitched into people's minds, the better."

The crowd going through the glass tunnel now dispersed in different directions on their routes to their destination. Rayne distracted herself by looking at the tall screens showing everything from the latest fashion, food, and entertainment to real estate.

"What the fuck is that?" Foster asked and came to a halt. Behind him a group of women circled him, several of them giving him wide-eyed stares. Rayne knew they weren't used to this type of man in all his raw masculinity.

She pivoted to see what had caught Foster's attention and had to smile. A living-video was running a preview, and she had to admit that the cave that opened into the wall was realistic. On the damp, dripping walls a startling number of spiders crawled and appeared to be heading toward them. Music mimicked the rattling of their legs.

"Oh, shit!" Clearly alarmed, Beth took several steps back and hid her face in her hands. "I hate those fuckers. What the hell's going on?"

"Calm down," Rayne said, letting go of Kae and hugging Beth to her. "They're not real. It's a living-video. A participation feature. The previews like these don't have their solidifier activated."

Beth drew a trembling breath. "Why the hell would anyone find that to be their favorite pastime? Spiders invaded my dwelling, and my bed, when I was little."

Rayne saw several people stop and frown at the panic in Beth's voice. She thought fast. "Sweetie, your therapist showed you how to deal with your arachnophobia. Do your breathing exercises, and remind yourself that living-vid spiders are just a projection of lights."

Beth caught on and drew a deep, shaking breath. "All right, all right."

"Poor thing," an elder woman said kindly as she passed. "I feel your pain. I think those terrible vids shouldn't be allowed to run previews in public. They should keep them within the facilities for those who enjoy such things."

"Thank you, madam," Rayne said and smiled. "I couldn't agree more." She nodded to the woman and nudged Beth away from the "cave." "Come on, sweetie."

Foster put his arm around Beth as they kept walking. "I thought I was hallucinating," he murmured.

"I didn't think to warn you." Rayne took Kae's hand. "You all right?"

"I'm fine. I'm not afraid of spiders, but I agree with Beth. What a strange, frivolous way to spend your time, attending an event with spiders." She shook her head.

"Uh." Beth shuddered. "Distract me, please. How many people live on a floor at this level? It seems even bigger on the inside."

"Sure," Rayne said. "This is a mainly commercial floor, but residential areas are available to the owners of the different establishments. A residential floor this size at this level contains somewhere between 80,000 and 100,000 individuals, depending on family configuration."

"Damn." Beth snorted. "It sounds like a lot, but if you think of the space difference compared to back home…it's insane. How many in the structure over all?"

"The last census showed about fifty-five million residents. That's not counting visitors, employees who live in other buildings, etc." It was interesting to watch even Kae do a double take at the numbers. "The skyscrapers were built over a very short period, which is remarkable, considering their size. Remember they had to swallow every citizen of what used to be the United States of America." She grimaced. "Well. Clearly not all."

"We've learned some of this from our elders, but opinions about how it actually happened vary widely," Kae said. "It's interesting to hear the story from this end. Perhaps the truth lies somewhere in between."

"Perhaps." Raine had never questioned the history of the Celestials until now. She wanted to learn the truth but dreaded having her world turned upside down again. It seemed to happen on a regular basis. She was relieved to see the large gold-and-white, petal-shaped portal to the hotel come into view. "There's the Flos Ignis. Mother is very good friends with the owner. We'll be in one of the suites."

"Flos Ignis? What does that mean?" Kae asked.

"It's Latin for Gold Flower." Rayne suddenly found the name a bit pretentious. In the tunnels, they used practical terms that clearly described the item or place. Up here, everything was a competition—outsmarting other people, or being the wealthiest, most successful, or part of a prominent family. If you could claim some, or all, of that, you were indeed golden in the world of the wealthy Celestials. She sighed as they entered through the glass doors and found themselves just inside the security doors a few yards in.

"We need to scan the chips," Rayne murmured. "This is a high-security hotel, catering to politicians and other professionals that could be potential targets." They had scanned their chips on several occasions already, and she wasn't nervous about the process any longer.

The metal doors swung open, and they stepped inside. Suddenly, Rayne heard Kae give a muted gasp, followed by a whispered "Fuck."

Chapter Twenty-five

No matter what Kaelyn had witnessed in her life up till this point, nothing had prepared her for the place she had just stepped into. She had been single-mindedly focused on the mission and anticipating the information they would unlock once they were safely in their hotel suite. Now she stared at the enormous area where people dressed the same way as Rayne's parents milled about, even it if was after midnight.

The floor shimmered in a way her beloved books described as iridescent. Ranging from semitransparent white with gold flecks to completely clear, it looked like someone had dipped their hands into it and created swirls that went on forever. The floor's seeming depth made it hard to get a feeling for which level the glossy surface was. She slowly lifted her foot, which was clad in some dainty boot that wouldn't last ten minutes in the tunnels, and placed it slowly in front of her.

"Fuck is the word." Foster looked ill at ease. "There's no way this will hold my weight. Is anything underneath it, or will we just go straight through?"

"It's entirely safe." Rayne walked ahead of them. "Let me check with one of the night clerks. Unlike most hotels, they don't have any robotic staff here. It's all run by people."

Kae didn't like that Rayne stepped away by herself but understood that her own ignorance when it came to places like this could raise too many eyebrows. "Come on. Let's pretend this doesn't feel like walking on frozen puddles in the alleys. We're simple people compared to the other patrons, which means they won't think it's strange that we're gaping. But that doesn't mean we can look like idiots, all right?"

"Look up." Beth had walked over to a seating area, and now she tipped her head back and did indeed gape.

Finding that the area had a large, thick rug, Kaelyn hurried over, quickly followed by Foster. She followed Beth's gaze and understood her reaction. "Now that's something."

From the ceiling, which she estimated was at least three stories tall, more glass, gold, and wispy white hung in organic forms, lit from inside. This substance created patterns on the walls and the floor, adding to its deceptively frail-looking surface.

Rayne returned. "That's impressive," she said and examined the ceiling. "Makes me dizzy though. I've set up our access to the suite. All you have to do is scan your chip again when you pass the desk. We're on the third floor, facing the courtyard. In other words, we can watch the lobby from above."

Kae followed Rayne past the desk, scanned her chip, and then entered yet another lift. Her head spun from all the new impressions, but it was nothing compared to what their mission did to her brain. She hadn't told Foster or Beth how many doubts she harbored when thinking about their success rate. So much could go wrong, and it was all on her and Rayne to create a believable backstory and keep it going until they got their hands on what Delmonte wanted.

Their suite resembled the guest quarters on the secret floor, but the luxury level was on a different plane, even compared to Rayne's apartment. Unlike the gold and white that dominated the lobby, the suite held softly muted tones of green and orange. The furniture was created from something made to look like pale wood.

"Door is secure. We can speak freely." Rayne pulled off her jacket and kicked off her shoes. "I'm going to have a glass of wine. What can I get you?" She looked at the others while she pressed a sensor at a narrow counter on the left side of the living area. A cabinet opened and showed a set of eight round containers that looked like the prisms down in the lobby. Holding different beverages, they shifted in color from bloodred to gold and silver.

"Why not?" Kaelyn removed her jacket and kicked off her boots. Her feet sank into the plush carpet, and she was secretly relieved their windows overlooked the courtyard rather than the nothingness she had been subjected to in Rayne's apartment. "I'll try some of what you're having."

Foster asked for a beer, and so did Beth. After placing their glasses on the round dining table, Rayne used the control console and lowered a glimmering shade inside the windows.

"Privacy shades. You never know who's watching." After fetching her bag, she sat down next to Kae. "All right. We're here." Taking out a small, flat item from her bag, she slid her arm over it, scanning her chip. She nodded at Kae. "Now you."

One by one they let the small item scan them. Kaelyn wasn't sure what she'd expected, but the small piece of technology didn't make a sound. Instead, it created a blue-tinted screen out of thin air. When Kaelyn watched Rayne move objects on the screen by pushing at literally nothing with her fingers, she could barely take it in. The few pieces of technology available in the tunnels were more than a century old. The auto-didact people in charge of them had managed to start them and use them for registers and mapping. Here, Rayne's fingers fluttered as she browsed through the enigmatic symbols.

"Here we go." Rayne slid her finger along a long, narrow rectangle. New boxes of text and what looked like blueprints appeared. "You can scroll down using this," she said and showed them how to slide the objects and zoom in on the maps and blueprints using only their fingers.

"Ah. I see." Kaelyn tried to ignore her clumsiness as she began reading, pointing in the air and pushing at nothing.

"Amy Lindberg works out of the same office where her father runs his foundation." Kaelyn murmured as she read. "The offices are spread out over four floors and employ ten attorneys, eight paralegals, and four assistants. They lease a cleaning service from another building. Eric Lindberg works on the fourth floor, employing his own attorneys and assistants. He uses the same cleaning service though."

"Can that be an in for Beth and me during off business hours?" Foster asked.

"We can easily change our chips to the mode that Benny showed us," Rayne said. "That way the computer system conveniently erase any trace of us as soon as we log out. It's crucial that you remain undetected when you're inside. There will be surveillance scanners, but we have technology that can help with that problem—to a degree."

"Just like magic." Kaelyn leaned in and pointed to a folder to open it. "This is it. What they want us to find out." She met everyone's gaze, one by one. "This can be the true start of our plans, or it can be what gets us killed. When we open this folder, we can't turn back. Do you understand?"

The other three nodded solemnly.

"Of course." Kaelyn snapped at the folder with her fingers like she'd seen Rayne do, and it sparkled ice-blue before it opened, displaying documents and detailed blueprints. This was all the information they had, and whether it was enough remained to be seen. From now on they could only push forward. Kaelyn suddenly thought of Wes and Tania, and before she managed to shove the image of the two siblings to the back of her mind, her heartache made her lose her breath. If things went badly, if she didn't make it back from this mission, at least Rayne's parents had somewhat legally adopted them. No matter how it had come about, the papers were legally binding in the Eastern Coastal City. That thought, combined with an instinctual feeling that Madelon and Rocque truly cared for the ragtag caver kids, to a degree that Madelon seemed quite taken aback by her own devotion, was a relief. Rocque appeared to find it easier to show his warmth, if Kaelyn read him right, but Madelon seemed to keep herself in complete control, perhaps because she'd had to keep her own daughter at arm's length for so long.

"Kae?" Rayne touched her shoulder.

"Sorry." Chastising herself for allowing her emotions to take over, Kaelyn pushed the thoughts even farther back in her mind. "I must truly be tired. Can you repeat what you just said?"

"Don't apologize. We all feel it. I'll call Amy's office tomorrow, and if she's not available, I'll try to find out where she might be if she's not in the office. I'm fortunate that my name opens doors that normally would be slammed in our faces." Rayne waited until Kaelyn approved the initial step of their plan. Then, damn it, she talked to the computer, which documented everything.

"It's damn eerie," Foster said and yawned. "Speaking to a fucking machine."

"Just wait until you have to talk to one of the robotic individuals that hold a multitude of positions around the city. They can certainly be lifelike in a spooky way. When it comes to some of the expensive brands, it can be hard to tell if they're human or not." Rayne chuckled. "They're programmed to be very safe, obviously."

"Obviously," Foster muttered. "With my luck, I'll run into a malfunctioning son of a bitch, or one programmed by a fucking sociopath."

Rayne's chuckle turned into a full belly laugh. She tossed her head back, and the beautiful sound of her mirth made Kaelyn think of small bells falling down a wooden staircase. Soon Beth joined in, and then they were all wiping at tears from laughing so hard.

After everyone calmed down, Kaelyn found she had relaxed enough to clear her mind. "Let's find out what's so important." Kaelyn motioned for Rayne to open the last subfolder.

Rayne tapped it, and Kaelyn, Beth, and Foster pushed back from the table, Foster so quickly that his chair toppled over. A three-dimensional topographic map of sorts lowered itself slowly onto the table, exceeding its size by at least ten inches. Rayne pushed her chair back, but of course the image didn't touch her. It merely looked like it pierced her torso.

"Creator, help me," Beth whispered. "What is that?"

Rayne's paling face worried Kaelyn. "It's a very detailed map of a place that's not supposed to exist." Rayne blinked, but small tears formed along her lashes. "If you look closer, or we can zoom in, you'll see how specific this is." She motioned for them to move even farther back.

Kaelyn took the chance to move over to Rayne's side. "What's wrong?"

"Just look." Rayne's lips were tense around the words. She pressed her hand against the hills and valleys that appeared too precise and symmetrical to be a natural occurrence and pulled at the image. The map grew yet another couple of feet, until it covered half the living area. Beth and Foster joined Kaelyn and Rayne and stared at the vision before them.

"This...this looks like a transparent city, or something." Beth bent and squinted at the details. "I don't get it. What is it?"

Kaelyn had raised her gaze to the screen above the map. She read aloud. "Document 55beta87gamma. Beta version of the satellite mapping from Aeroton 6. Unsigned document." She looked at the map again and thought she must be more exhausted than she realized as it seemed to vibrate.

Rayne pulled up another folder. "And here are Delmonte's notes." She expanded it. "Document 55beta87gamma is an unsigned living map from the satellite Aeroton 6. It will not be accepted as proof in a court of law as it is a beta version. Only two people have access to the signed and classified map: Eric Lindberg and our current commander in chief, Felicia van Bry. For our movement to reach its goal, we need to prove to the authorities, and the Celestial people, that this place truly exists. Before we have the signed and approved document, we can't risk moving forward. Benny has outfitted you with all the technological tools available for you to carry out this mission. Good luck."

"I know we've all had the same thought. Why us? Why tunnel scavengers? They must have highly skilled agents to send?" Beth shook her head. "That just doesn't make sense."

"Unless you consider that we sort of forced their hand by showing up like we did," Kaelyn said slowly. "Combined with the fact that Rayne's parents took her, and thus all of us, to the secret floor and exposed their whole setup, it placed Delmonte in a bit of a fix."

"Yes." Rayne rubbed the back of her neck. "That's the only reason she showed up in person. I bet she's furious with my parents, but she's too seasoned and ambitious to let on. Either they had to kill you guys or find another way to keep you quiet."

"The kids." Foster's expression darkened. "They promised to take care of Wes and Tania. Their wellbeing was the only reason Kaelyn would have agreed to go on this mission. Of course, they dangled the carrot of helping the subterraneans reach the Inner Border. They played us well."

"Don't sell us short," Kaelyn said. She bent next to Beth, who was still studying the map. "They needed someone who could find a way into the Lindberg office space, and very few people have the same way in as Rayne. Wait. Hell! We have to magnify this some more. May I?" She motioned at the map and looked up at Rayne.

"Go ahead. Don't mind if it goes beyond you. It won't go through the walls," Rayne said and remained by Kaelyn's side.

The map grew another three feet, and Kaelyn could see she hadn't imagined it. Small dots moved between what looked like structures. "This is either live or a damn recording!" She bent again and studied the small dot. It moved rapidly along what had to be a road, made a perfect ninety-degree turn onto another road, and then stopped. A smaller dot appeared next to it and disappeared into a square that might represent a house.

"I had no idea." Rayne blinked. "Not about this technology. Maps, yes. I've seen several of the city, but this... Whether it's a recording or live, I'd say it must have at least been live at some point."

"What did you mean by this being a place that isn't supposed to exist?" Beth asked, turning to Rayne.

"I know you don't have maps like this, but if you study that outline over there by the couch, surely you recognize it?"

"What do you mean? Kaelyn rounded the table and walked through the map over to the couch. This was the outskirts of the city, as she could see more organic shapes take over. She studied it for several minutes, along with Foster and Beth. And then she saw it. It was as if her brain superimposed it on her old atlas, and she recognized the natural outline of the Lehigh River, the river that had a familiar curve she had studied so many times. "This is Inner Border territory." She rose and minimized the map back to table size. "What the hell's this place, Rayne?"

"Like a lot of other people, I've only heard rumors of a city somewhere inland. The authorities have always denied it and been able to provide aerial images of the desolate areas. Only a few structures for the guest workers that sow and harvest crops, that's it. I can understand now why the rumors refused to die down. There's clearly a huge settlement out there." She gripped Kaelyn's arm. "I had no reason to think there was any truth to this rumor. There's never been any evidence."

Beth looked up, appearing somber. "But there is. It's in this Lindberg dude's office, and we're the ones who have to fetch it."

Kaelyn nodded. "And damn it, we will. This city—that's the best option for our people, Beth. I can feel it. We thought we'd have to break new ground if we ever got out, but this discovery puts everything in a whole new light. I wish we could let our inner circle back home know."

Rayne removed her hand. "That's not possible," she said, her eyes suddenly opaque. "You can't jeopardize this new information by doing something foolhardy."

"I won't. Just wishful thinking. But when we've completed the mission, we won't hand over the map until we have assurances that Delmonte won't go back on her word." No way was she letting this bombshell news out of her hands until she'd squeezed all the bargaining power possible out of it. Kaelyn studied the ground surrounding the city. She saw many options, but as amazing as this map was, it was impossible to make an educated guess where her people's future home might be.

"Fair enough." Rayne ran a hand along her face. "Why don't we go over everything tomorrow morning? I need to get some sleep, or I'll end up making a mistake."

"Good point." Kaelyn looked around the suite. "Two bedrooms. Guess we share again, Rayne. After all, we're engaged."

"Yes." Rayne didn't look flustered or awkward, but something existed between them that hadn't been there only moments before. A tiny wedge, and Kaelyn didn't understand where it came from.

"I'm going to get something to eat," Beth said, "and *water.*" She snickered. "Of all the delicacies here, I'm still most in awe of chocolate and water."

"I'd never have guessed," Foster said, bumping her shoulder with his fist. "I'll join you. I can imagine having one of their sandwiches with that fake meat."

"Too tired." Rayne closed the map and screen, and then she said good night and disappeared into the bedroom to the right.

Wanting to give her space to get ready for bed, Kaelyn took her glass of wine and walked over to the couch and sat down. She sipped the smooth wine and hoped she wouldn't get used to how good everything here tasted. Once she was in the tunnels again, it was back to mushroom-based food, and Mama Doe's herbs and hydroponics vegetables.

Only when she lost cohesion in her neck the second time did she relent. It was time for bed. She placed the glass on the counter, uncertain if it went into the ReCyc or not, and walked toward the bedroom. Inside, she found Rayne curled up on her side at the very edge of the bed. Her even breathing suggested she was fast asleep, but it was possible she just didn't want to acknowledge Kaelyn's presence. That possibility created a hollow feeling in her chest. They had gotten closer until just recently, or had she imagined it all?

Not about to question every word or interaction, Kaelyn used the bathroom, which of course was a marvel of technology and design. Thankfully all she had to do was stand under the perforated ceiling tile for water to come. She needed an aqua cleansing. Nothing could soothe her like a bath or hot shower, and now she closed her eyes where she stood inside the semi-transparent shell that surrounded her and sprayed her body from all directions.

"I can't sleep."

Rayne's voice from the doorway made Kaelyn jump and nearly slip on the wet floor. "Damn. Are you trying to kill me?" She blinked against the water and saw Rayne leaning against the doorframe, her arms folded over her chest. She wore a sheer camisole and shorts of the same thin fabric. Her eyes normally shone with intelligence and intensity, but they now radiated only fatigue. The tense skin around them made Rayne look older and weary.

"I see," Kaelyn said, making sure she put no emphasis on her words.

"You worried me. Earlier." Rayne drew trembling fingertips across her eyes, and only then did Kaelyn notice that her cheeks were damp from tears. "We have to talk about it, or we'll fail tomorrow."

"All right. I'll just get ready for bed." She watched Rayne push off the doorframe and return to the bedroom.

She took her time, although it irked her to admit she was uncomfortable. Nervous even. Growling under her breath, she used her chip to conjure one of the white night clothes that seemed to be the popular choice. She stopped by the mirror, also a novelty, as the only mirror she used back home was less than four by six inches. Here, it showed her entire body, and seeing herself like this, in this soft light, made her feel she was observing a stranger. An unknown person with dark, brooding eyes, lean and wiry arms and legs, and very pale skin compared to everyone else they'd run into while making their way to the hotel.

Kaelyn entered the bedroom, prepared to defend herself from whatever Rayne perceived she had done wrong. Rayne sat on the bed, propped up against two fat pillows that seemed to cushion her perfectly.

"All right," Kaelyn said quietly. "What about me worried you earlier?"

"Come to bed. I can't talk to you when you're standing over there shivering." It was as if Rayne had stepped into her stern doctor persona, but at least she noticed that Kaelyn was ill at ease and, yes, cold in the climate-controlled room.

"All right." Dreading the conversation, and really too tired to rehash everything, Kaelyn crawled into bed, half sitting with one pillow behind her and one between her and Rayne. It was ridiculous, of course, but she truly felt she needed a shield.

Chapter Twenty-six

Rayne could barely breathe when Kae sat down next to her in bed and pulled the covers over her. She held a pillow in her arms and returned her gaze under her short, blue hair. It was obvious she was bracing for impact, and that wasn't what Rayne wanted at all.

"You seemed to forget certain aspects of the plan, and what we all stand to risk, if you try to push Delmonte into a corner. That woman hasn't backed off in her entire life, trust me, and if you give her an ultimatum once we hopefully get our hands on the signed and official map of the area east of the Lehigh River, it will end in disaster. Maybe, with my parents as a buffer, the kids would be all right, but you wouldn't, nor Beth or Foster. And you would jeopardize the future for those among the Subterraneans who want to leave the tunnels." Out of breath and worrying she had alienated Kae by being too blunt, Rayne pulled her knees up and wrapped her arms around them.

"And you got all that from a remark that I told you was mostly wishful thinking?" Kae spoke without obvious emotion, but something stirred in her eyes.

"Yes. You said it was wishful thinking, but then you outlined very clearly how you wouldn't hold up your end of the plan." It was hard to keep her tone cordial. She wanted to shake Kae, force her to promise she'd stick to the plan and be careful.

Kae looked down and appeared to study her hands for the longest time. After a while, she raised her gaze, and now Rayne detected no opaqueness. Instead, a fire seemed to roar in the center of her pupils. "I realize we haven't known each other very long, but we've been through more together than most people do in a lifetime. I've done my best to keep you and the rest of the team safe, correct?"

Unless Rayne brought up how Kae had dragged her through the alleys blindfolded, how she'd nearly pulled Rayne's arm out of its socket when Rayne saved her from falling, how she'd dangled from a wire high above the massive mob that could easily have killed her if they'd identified her as a Celestial.

"I won't tally up the score of who did what for whom. It's counterproductive." Rayne wanted to pierce Kae's aura of defensiveness. She got up on her knees and moved closer. "If you and I can't trust each other, especially each other's motives, we don't stand a chance of pulling this off. We have to find a way to get into Lindberg's office and put our hands on the files, and we have to do it fast. If we fail, my parents will become Tania's and Wes's adoptive parents for good. How well do you think Tania will handle that situation in the long run? Right now, she's content that Wes is safe and recuperating. Soon, she'll begin to feel like the alien she is in this world, and she'll have nobody around her that knows her like you do. Like Foster and Beth do." Gripping Kae's shoulders, Rayne could feel the wiry muscles under her fingers. "If I'm caught a second time, Delmonte won't be able to save me, no matter how many strings my parents pull. Please, Kae..." Rayne didn't blink as she tried to read what Kae was thinking.

"I won't let anyone get caught." Dark and raspy, Kae's voice was barely audible. "I would never risk you or the others."

"But you could sacrifice yourself if you thought it was the only way." Frowning, Rayne hoped she was wrong. "It's as if you carry your surname like a badge. Kaelyn Dark. There is a darkness about you sometimes, and I realize we don't know a lot about each other, but remember, we *do* know a lot. We've seen sides of each other that we haven't shown anyone else. I know that's true for me, and don't ask me how, but that's true for you as well."

It took a few more moments, but just as Rayne thought Kae would deny what she'd just said, she lowered her head and sighed.

"You're not wrong. And yes, I do tend to slip into my role as team leader. I'm used to being in charge and responsible for a lot of people. Being herded around by strangers in a world I know nothing about is…a lot. I did speak without thinking how it sounded to you." Kae lifted her hands and stroked Rayne's cheeks with her thumbs. Only then did Rayne realize her tears had begun to run down her face again.

"You're tired," Kae said, with something new in her voice, a hint of tenderness that made Rayne tremble. She wanted nothing but to melt into Kae's arms and feel safe, if only for a moment.

"So are you. Let's try for some of that sleep." Turning, Rayne climbed back under the covers and pulled them up to her chin, still shivering.

"Come here." Kae adjusted the pillows and created a nest for the two of them before pulling Rayne onto her shoulder. "I'm cold too."

This was like the previous time they'd lain in the same bed, though different. Kae's arms were gentler, her voice soothing, and the way she pressed her lips to the top of Rayne's head was heartbreaking.

"Tell me something about you I don't know." Kae stroked along Rayne's back.

"Oh." Rayne wasn't sure what Kae was after. Deeply personal things, or something more superficial? She knew the answer as soon as she asked herself the question. Why would Kae want to talk about shallow things the night before they truly began their mission? "Uh. I haven't been in a relationship with anyone for several years. Not even on a casual basis. I've been all about my work."

"Why?"

"I think…working hard gave me very little time to wonder about past circumstances that hurt me. Like my parents' emotional distance. At least I understand that a bit better now. A little."

"Couldn't you have confided in a lover when it came to your feelings?" Kae murmured the words against Rayne's temple.

"I wanted to use my pent-up energy to help the kids in the Soldiers' Clinic." Rayne held her breath for a moment. It was Kae and her teams that oftentimes put the teenage soldiers in the clinic in the first place.

"That sounds just like you. Doing things for others rather than yourself. That's why you jumped into the chute." Kae was quiet for a while.

"And you? Tell me something about you." Rayne tipped her head back and studied what she could see of Kae's features in the faint light from the curtain-covered windows.

Kae nodded slowly. "For a lot of years I used sex as a shield, to such a degree that it became an addiction. A lot of drugs are around in the tunnels, as you saw. Dangerous stuff. My own 'poison' wasn't dangerous per se, but it was damaging anyway—to those I took to bed, especially if I let them stay a while, and to me. When Wes's and Tania's mother died, I knew I had to make a change. I did."

"Was it hard?" Rayne pressed her face into Kae's neck.

"It was. Until it wasn't. I'm not sure how it happened, but I suppose when you're trying to bring up kids and set a good example, you can't subject them to nameless sexual partners on a regular basis."

"Has there been anyone since then?"

"No. Not really. I have seen some women, but mostly on a friend basis." Kae's speech was beginning to slur, and Rayne's eyelids felt impossible to keep open.

"Thanks for sharing that with me." Rayne knew it must have been hard for Kae to show her vulnerable side this way. "Go to sleep. I set the console to wake us up in the morning. Well, in five hours."

"Mm. Good." Kae grew heavier against Rayne's body, and it was such a great feeling. Rayne hoped the headway they'd made just now would linger and solidify in the morning. After all, they were supposed to convince everyone they were fighting for the right to get married.

Chapter Twenty-seven

Amy Lindberg turned out to be a diminutive woman in her forties, with delicate features, white-blond hair, and gray, guarded eyes. She was dressed in a white trouser suit, and the only pop of color was her bright-green shirt.

"Thank you so much for seeing us, Amy," Rayne said and made the Celestial gesture of polite greeting, pressing the palm of the right hand to one's chest and bowing discreetly, something that Kaelyn had begun to recognize. "This is my fiancée, Kae Drake. We need legal advice, as we understand that there are certain limitations when it comes to marrying and, thus, bringing someone new into my building. Surely in this day and age, this is an archaic way of looking at things." Rayne raised her shoulders and smiled.

"You would think so, but when these two skyscrapers were erected, these laws were put in place for a reason. It was a way to differentiate between the ones in power and the ones who were not." Speaking with precise enunciation, Amy primly laced her fingers on top of her desk. She wasn't smiling, and she radiated something Kaelyn couldn't put her finger on. Perhaps it was entitlement.

"That will only lead to a risk of people being inbred," Kaelyn said amicably.

"Hm. Ha-ha. That said, I know others have challenged these laws in court, and that's why we need your advice." Rayne gave Kaelyn a warning glance. "I remembered that you're an accomplished family lawyer."

"I have been known to successfully argue cases such as yours, and when the daughter of the esteemed Garcias asks me for a favor…and having once saved my life, then who am I to turn her down." Amy tilted her head in a way that Kaelyn found odd as she studied her. "Kae Drake. I took the liberty of checking your background. You work in law enforcement at your building, I understand."

Kaelyn was grateful she had at least gotten those five hours of sleep the previous night and was able to remember her backstory. "That's right. I imagine it's a low-level position compared to the precincts at these famous towers. Still, we have our hands full."

"I imagine so. I'm sure your skills when it comes to petty crimes are admirable."

The thin, condescending smile on Amy's lips gave Kaelyn the urge to plant her fist there, but she merely nodded. "They sure are petty,"

Amy blinked slowly, as everything about the entire woman moved in slow motion. Returning her focus to Rayne, she said, "My assistant has pulled the initial documents you and Ms. Drake must fill in before my office can file them with the court. It is quite the process, and the sooner we begin, the better. "

"That sounds fantastic," Rayne said, beaming. "Don't you think so, Kae?"

"I do." Kae leaned closer to Rayne and pressed her lips to her temple. "I can't wait to make everything official." She watched Rayne's pupils dilate and her full lips turn into an "o." Kae wanted to kiss her properly, but the way Amy looked at them—as if she feared Kae would clear her desk and have sex with Rayne right in front of her—made her restrain herself. "Let's hope it all goes smoothly."

Amy hurried to push a small octagonal disc toward them. "Everything you need to know at this point in the process is on this disc. If you have any questions, contact my second assistant. He'll be able to guide you through the document. I will handle things personally once we're ready for court."

So, Amy was a performer, the type that didn't like to share the limelight.

A knock on the door made Amy frown, the tiniest wrinkle. "Excuse me. I did ask that we weren't to be disturbed. It must be important. Enter!"

The door slid open without making a sound, a plus that Kaelyn was pleased to notice.

A tall man with an elongated face and silver hair, and wearing a long green coat over his charcoal suit, entered. "I apologize for interrupting, my dear, but I heard that the woman I owe my happiness and heritage to was in the office. I had to stop by and say hello."

"Of course, Father. You obviously remember Dr. Rayne Garcia, and this is her fiancée, Kae Drake." Amy had gotten out of her chair, and so had Rayne. Kaelyn stood, realizing that this was indeed the former commander in chief, Eric Lindberg.

"Sir. It's an honor to meet again." Rayne bowed, deeper this time. Kaelyn did the same, and to her surprise, it didn't irritate her as much this time. Perhaps because Erik Lindberg didn't annoy her like his daughter did.

Commander Lindberg kissed Rayne on both cheeks and then turned to greet Kaelyn. "You're a lucky woman, Ms. Drake. Dr. Garcia is one of the most skilled physicians in this part of the city. I know my daughter will work day and night until you are able to legalize your union before the Creator."

Kaelyn blinked. She hadn't heard the Creator mentioned more than once or twice by anyone since she came topside and entered the skyscraper. This man, the former commander, appeared to speak very easily about the deity that was held in such esteem, and many times the only source of strength and comfort for the Subterraneans.

"I can't wait to celebrate our love in that manner." Kaelyn couldn't help but return Lindberg's smile. "It's an honor to meet you. I never thought I would."

Lindberg placed a warm hand on Kaelyn's arm and squeezed gently. "The honor is mine. Dr. Garcia would never choose a life partner who wasn't as upstanding and amazing as she herself is." He winked at Rayne, who colored faintly.

"I believe that Dr. Garcia and Ms. Drake were just leaving," Amy said, her face pinched. "And my next appointment is waiting."

So, not about to share the spotlight in her father's presence either. Kaelyn found it interesting, and the insight into Amy's persona could come in handy one day.

"May I show you around the offices before you go, or are you truly in a hurry?" Lindberg asked jovially. Amy's eyes widened at her father's offer, but of course, she couldn't join them as she'd just stated how busy she was.

Kaelyn could barely believe their luck. Now they wouldn't have to feign using the restroom or try to map the office building in a much more unsafe way. A quick glance in Rayne's direction showed Kaelyn, her "fiancée," had caught on as well.

Lindberg's office suite breathed opulence but was smaller than his daughter's, as his staff wasn't as extensive. He chatted happily with Rayne and made an effort to bring Kaelyn into the subjects, which made her reluctantly like him even more. She hadn't paid attention to who governed the Celestials over the past years, but how could a friendly, amicable guy like Lindberg continue the attacks on her people? Surely, he had shared all the knowledge, been briefed about the so-called terrorist attacks, and was ultimately responsible for the retaliation against innocent people in the tunnels?

"I run several non-profit organizations and foundations from here, but that's not all." Lindberg walked toward what looked like a very old wooden door, and it opened as soundlessly as all the others. As they followed Lindberg into the space behind it, Kaelyn heard Rayne gasp.

Kaelyn simply stared. Of all the many items and spaces among the Celestials that she'd never seen before, this had to be the most unexpected.

"Isn't this magical?" Lindberg beamed proudly and threw his arms out as if he were trying to embrace the room. "The staff is in a meeting, which is why we have it to ourselves right now."

Like the door they'd just walked through, bookshelves made from similar wood, or wood-like material, covered the walls. Eight large desks, four of them holding impressive computer consoles, formed a circle around what looked like a tree. Having seen trees only in her old books, Kaelyn had to swallow the burning sensation in the back of her throat. She wanted to push her way past everyone and touch the lifelike replica, because surely that was what it was? She craned her neck back and regarded the vast crown reaching the full height of the high ceiling, at least thirty feet.

"Isn't that impressive? It's so fitting that we managed to grow a horse-chestnut tree in an office area. Normally you need the features available only in the park areas. Still, when my tenure as commander was over, they asked what customary gift I would like—and it was no contest. I wanted a tree."

"It's impressive, Mr. Lindberg," Rayne said, appearing confused. "And what do you do in this particular office since you've decorated it so differently? It has a quite remarkable ambiance."

"Here's where we store the documents that describe the history of the human experience over almost eight centuries. The oldest records are from the mid-1700s, and even if some of what we have access to after that is incomplete to a degree, we can safely say that our collection is the most comprehensive in existence. Especially from the early 2000s and onward. That's where we can calibrate our computers to read the saved digital records." Lindberg's expression grew somber. "It is sometimes bleak to study our history, as we haven't always lived to our full potential. The late 2000s especially, when mankind nearly became extinct..." Clearly affected by his knowledge of history, Lindberg shook his head mournfully. "The climate changes were to blame for most of it, and we were responsible for the overheating of our planet." He shrugged and smiled sadly. "How we as humans managed to turn it around and begin again, almost from scratch, in the 2150s, well, I'm in awe. They had lost so much knowledge, so much of their history, and only the fact that different groups of people, not even knowing about each other as they lived on different continents, began their quest to regain the old knowledge is amazing."

Kaelyn listened with rapt attention. As she stemmed from marginalized people who were never considered worthy of being part of the regeneration of humankind, she knew very little of this, if anything. She glanced quickly at Rayne and saw that she didn't look surprised. Perhaps Celestial children learned about this part of their history in school.

"I think the miracle was how they managed to assemble people from the scattered settlements along the coast and begin to reconstruct a functioning society," Rayne said, confirming Kaelyn's theory. "Not to mention when they made contact with what used to be northern Europe."

"Isn't that just amazing to consider?" Lindberg ran his fingertips along some book spines. "They sacrificed a lot when they drew up the new borders that eventually grew into Eastern Seaboard City, which in turn has become a hub of sorts when it comes to travel and serving as a liaison between other nations. We take pride in being a model society, even if we aren't a hundred present successful." Lindberg patted Rayne's right arm. "As you yourself must be aware of after the incursion at the Soldiers' Clinic."

"That was different." Rayne raised her chin. "It entailed an injured child, and we as Celestials take great pride in our humane treatment of others, especially those of us who are medical professionals." Her expression was still polite, but her tone grew firmer, to a degree that Kaelyn worried Lindberg might become suspicious.

"That is the type of attitude that sets you apart from a lot of your peers. You look to the person, whether it be someone like Amy, the daughter of a former commander, or a caver child. Most admirable, my dear." Lindberg ended his praise and led them by the bookshelves until they reached a computer desk. It was vacant, and Kaelyn caught Rayne's glance. She wanted to give it more than a fleeting look, which meant Kaelyn had to create a distraction.

"Commander Lindberg," Kaelyn said and hoped she'd managed a pleading tone. "May I ask a favor? I have never seen such a magnificent tree as this." She gestured at the chestnut tree. "Would it be possible for me to touch it? Where I come from, there's nothing like this." That was the truth, but Kaelyn hoped the former commander would assume that the parks in the building where she had lived were not very impressive.

"Ms. Drake," Lindberg said, a broad smile returning to his face. "It would be my pleasure to escort you. And for goodness sake, call me Eric. I'm no longer in office." He chuckled and offered his arm.

At a loss what he wanted her to do with it, Kaelyn felt a moment of panic until she saw Rayne making a motion like placing her hand on something. Ah. Kaelyn did so and gave Lindberg's lower arm a squeeze, mindful not to press too hard. The way his eyes widened suggested she might have been too forceful anyway.

Kaelyn tried to fathom that she was walking on the arm of the former Celestial commander to feel up a tree. The surreal nature of it all made her come dangerously close to laughing aloud, but she bit the inside of her cheek to remain in character. As she stood closer to the tree, its trunk at least three feet in diameter, she momentarily forgot about the man next to her. She let go of his arm and cautiously pressed her palms against the surface. The bark tickled her fingertips, and the scent was so new and indescribable, and not at all like the small trees Mama Doe had managed to grow in her hydroponic units. Kaelyn tried to imagine a forest of trees like these, but it was too much. She just couldn't.

"Fantastic, isn't it?" Lindberg watched her closely. "I hope this tree will produce enough nuts for it to be the mother of many more trees like it. Even in your parks up north." Lindberg patted the tree reverently, which Kaelyn found oddly endearing until she remembered his role in the oppression of her people. How could this man be this amicable, yet responsible for maintaining the war machine against the Subterraneans?

As they turned around to rejoin Rayne, Kaelyn made a sign behind her back, hoping she would see it. Rayne was using a scanner small enough to fit into one of her earrings. She only had to pretend to fiddle with it to turn it on and off. When Lindberg and Kaelyn turned around to make their way between two of the desks, Rayne was standing by the bookshelves, perusing the spines with great interest. She met them halfway and wrapped an arm around Kaelyn's waist. "Thank you so much, Comm—"

"As I told Kae, call me Eric, please. We'll meet again soon, as you'll be visiting my daughter in her capacity as your attorney. We can't keep spouting off the titles—it gets tiresome. May I call you Rayne?"

"Of course. Thank you, Eric." Rayne fired off a blinding smile. "I look forward to getting everything taken care of." She winked up at Kaelyn. "Right, darling?"

The sudden twitch somewhere deep in Kaelyn's chest nearly made her lose all her words. Instead, she bent and kissed Rayne gently on the lips. "Right."

"I'm very happy for the two of you. I met your parents in passing a while ago, and your father was worried about your working too hard." Lindberg shook his head. "I had to politely disagree. If you hadn't worked as hard as you do, my daughter might not have made it. Your diligence helped save her life."

"It was my honor, sir. And to be frank, I was merely doing my job." Rayne pressed closer to Kaelyn, who could feel fine tremors reverberate over to her. Whether it was the tension, or fatigue, it was obvious that Rayne was starting to have enough of this part of the mission. Time to go.

"We have taken up enough of your time, Eric," Kaelyn said and let go of Rayne long enough to bow to Lindberg. "Thank you for taking the time to show us around. I will never forget your kindness." Or his part in the atrocities.

Lindberg insisted on walking them to the main lobby, and once they said good-bye and he left with his security entourage, Kaelyn had to draw a deep breath.

"That went well," Rayne murmured when they entered the lift that would take them to the floor where Beth and Foster waited. "I got more than enough."

"Our friends will be pleased." Kaelyn leaned against the wall. She barely got the words out, before Rayne pushed up against her and kissed her on the lips.

"Mm?" Kaelyn tried to speak, but the far-too-sweet pressure of Rayne's mouth on hers made it impossible, mainly because arousal surged up Kaelyn's spine so fast, she could only hold on.

Rayne pulled back a fraction of an inch. "Surveillance in all the lifts," she whispered.

Ah. Of course. She expected Rayne to pull back after her demonstration for the scanners, but she didn't. Instead, she cupped Kaelyn's cheeks and rose on her toes to kiss her again. This time, there was no force behind it, just tenderness in the soft brushing of lips.

"Touch me," Rayne said, obviously not caring if anyone overheard that remark.

Kaelyn pulled her close and slid her lips down Rayne's neck. Rayne moaned and wrapped her arms around Kaelyn's neck, tipping her head back.

Only when the lift stopped, and the door gave the muted hiss that had become familiar by now, did they break apart. Turning her head to check which floor they were on, Kaelyn found herself looking at Beth and Foster, both sporting broad grins.

"No wonder you were gone so long. How many times have you ridden the full 3,000 floors in this thing?" Beth folded her arms and bumped Foster with her hip. "Didn't I tell you?"

"You did." Foster was still smiling, but his gaze probed Kaelyn's, and only when she gave the shortest of nods did his smile reach his eyes.

"Time to get something to eat. We want to tell you our news. We now have representation, which means our chance of getting married just grew exponentially." Rayne enunciated a little too loud, clearly for the surveillance behind them in the lift. "And food sounds great."

As they made their way through the Celestials who buzzed around them, leading their innocent, busy lives, Kaelyn's mind was elsewhere. Considering everything they had learned and experienced in the Lindberg office building, one thing stood out more than anything. When Rayne had kissed her in the lift, and they held each other tight, she could suddenly picture a forest of trees, reaching as far as the horizon.

Chapter Twenty-eight

The package from the Garcias had been waiting for them when they got back to the hotel. Transported in a secure tube system to the personal-safety compartment in Rayne's and Kaelyn's bedroom, it consisted of four small parcels, shaped like tubes. Rayne opened it at the dining table, surrounded by the others.

The four tubes were marked with the initial of each other's first name. After handing them out, Rayne opened hers, frowning at the thin filament threads attached to a transparent sheet. The tube also included a small tag for her computer system.

"What the hell's this? Weren't they supposed to send us what we needed to get into the office?" Kae ran a finger along the mesh.

"I think this is it." Rayne held up the tag. "I'll plug it in, and we'll know."

She placed the small rectangular device they'd used last night back on the table and inserted the tag. Immediately, an image appeared and slowly turned before them. It was easy to recognize the filament mesh attached to the sheet. Another image appeared to the left of the first, and Benny's face appeared.

"Hi there. This is what you need to wear when you enter the Lindberg offices. That is, of course, if you've managed to scan their systems at all. If you haven't, this won't do you any good." He shrugged and then shoved both hands through his thick mop of dark hair. "Anyway, wear any clothes you want, but once you're dressed, place the two sheets all over you. You'll need to help each other and make sure the mesh is connected around you. No gaps. If you need to cut it in places, that's fine, but make sure the endings find each other. If there's a loose end somewhere, it won't work." Benny pointed to the area where the mesh glimmered above the dining table. "See the highlighted area here? That's your on-and-off switch. You have to switch that to blue before you enter the offices. And when you're done, you have to switch it back to orange before you step out among people. It will screw up the sensors if you don't. Just imagine if a sentry appears and gives you a routine scan—and sees that you are there, but you don't register." He raised an index finger. "Another thing, equally important, do *not* forget to also block your subcutaneous chips before you enter the offices, or wearing the mesh will be useless." Benny paused, and it seemed as if he were hesitating, but then he smiled briefly and said, "Good luck."

After Benny's lecture, Rayne could tell that Kae and the others weren't convinced. "I know this sounds like a bit much, even to me, who takes a lot of the technology available in the towers for granted. Still, Benny's come through for us so far. The chips have worked without any glitches. Our backstories are firmly locked in place."

Kae drummed her fingers against the tabletop. "And it's not like we have something that'll work better. It's this or aborting the mission. I just wish we could do a dry run first."

"He must've done that." Rayne didn't have a lot to back up her statement. She hoped Benny was a consistent genius and not the intermittent variety. She had run into colleagues over the years who shone at the tested-and-true procedures, but who fell short when it came to improvising. If any one of them had ended up in the tunnels like she had, they wouldn't have known what to do when robbed of the technology they depended on. Hopefully Benny had the expanding mind that thrived on challenges.

"I suppose." Kae unfolded the sheet with her mesh. "What powers this device?"

Rayne opened her mouth to state what she had thought should be obvious, but then she closed it again. After a few moments, she gestured around them. "I'm so sorry for not explaining the basics. I do take things for granted more than I realized. So does everyone else, since nobody has informed you. Everything needing power to function runs on wireless electricity. The source of this is, of course, the sun."

Kae looked around the room and then back at Rayne. She didn't appear convinced. "Excuse me? Wireless electricity that originates from the sun?"

"In a manner of speaking. Solar power has been around for a very long time, centuries, even," Rayne said, hoping she didn't come off as condescending.

"I know that. I've read about it," Kae said. She sounded more astonished than anything else.

"I haven't. I don't have your affinity for curling up with a moldy old book." Beth grinned but then turned serious. "Is it safe? I mean, to have electricity floating around?"

"It's not floating, per se, and yes, it's quite safe. It's not a new technology, and it has been perfected throughout the last five or six decades. It was revolutionary when it came, my father tells me. The only cables we need now go vertically throughout the center of the buildings. They connect to the emitters, and that's it. Now, there are exceptions. If we were to go somewhere there's no steady access to the sun, such as on the surface." Rayne looked down at her hands, only now realizing how tightly she'd laced them together. "And, of course, that's always the case for you."

"And that's why we need to borrow from those cables of yours." Beth rounded the table and put a hand on Rayne's shoulder. "Our engineers, and, yes, we do have a few self-taught ones, have become geniuses at charging batteries and rerouting cables."

"Yet most people cook over an open fire, read to their kids in the light from the lamps run on tallow, and wash in cold water." Foster looked grim. "The more I learn, the more the injustice and atrocities committed by your people—"

"Foster." Kae's voice was low and not unkind, but it was clear what she meant when she went over to stand well within his personal space. "Don't go down that rabbit hole tonight. We don't have time for it. I know we need to address the subject later, but not now. And besides, Rayne isn't to blame for the politics of her government."

Rayne wasn't so sure. She had lived in ignorant bliss so long, and only when she began volunteering at the Soldiers' Clinic did she begin to question certain things. But even then, she had no idea what the conditions for the Subterraneans were like. She had bought into the "volatile terrorist" indoctrination like most other people did. Even her parents, who were part of a union of dissidents, didn't know very much about life in the tunnels. It was impossible to imagine Madelon and Rocque moving among the dense crowds below-ground, sitting on a train cart, eating real meat from a questionable origin, and bathing in public bath facilities.

"How long do we have before we need to suit up?" Foster asked, his voice having lost some of its wrath.

Rayne checked the time on the floating screen. "I'd say, you and Beth, as part of the maintenance crew, half an hour before closing time. That's three and a half hours. Kae and I will enter half an hour after closing."

"We'll be able to scout for stragglers," Beth said. "But we won't have long to warn you."

"I'm sure people will still be in the building." Rayne placed one hand on the table and flicked through information on the screen with the other. "A busy paralegal, for instance. There are bound to be night guards and security, as it is the office of the former commander. Wouldn't look good if the entire building was compromised."

"Which is why we can't leave a trace, not one, digital or physical." Kae nodded. "I think we all know what our respective roles are. Apart from that, we need to be quiet."

"You are all trained in how you move without making a sound. I've seen it." Rayne sighed and sat down at the table. "I'm used to being on my feet for hours on end, but quiet—there's never been much of a demand for stealth in my line of work."

"You'll do fine. Just don't wear those extendable heels," Beth said, making even Foster laugh.

Beth stretched and made Rayne wince at the sound of her vertebrae popping. "I'm off to get some rack time. I'll need to be at my very sharpest tonight, and right now I feel like a slug high on mushrooms."

"I need to rest as well," Rayne said, but she was so tired, she couldn't get up. They had played tourists and gone sightseeing to act their parts, and after a while, she had half forgotten that it was all a ruse. She had enjoyed showing the others the beautiful parts of this skyscraper, which was the twin of the one where she lived. Perhaps it was the obvious difference between what Foster had seen today and his home that had set him on edge.

Foster said good night and surprised Rayne by stopping behind her and patting her on the back. "No hard feelings, Doc."

"None. Never." Rayne looked up at the burly man who had become such an unlikely friend. "Remember what I promised, okay."

Foster stood there, motionless, for a few moments. He quickly caressed her cheek with the back of her hand and then left the room to join Beth in their bedroom.

"What promise did you mean exactly?" Kae approached slowly.

"I did say that I would return to the tunnels and keep working as a replacement for Doctor Boro. I meant it then, and I still do."

Kae's eyes darkened, yet her face relaxed. "I believe you." She extended a hand and pulled Rayne from the chair. "You look ready to fall asleep on the table. Why don't you switch off that witchcraft of a computer, and we'll go get some sleep?"

Rayne clicked her fingers to the screen, and it switched off instantly. "There." As she walked ahead of Kae toward their bedroom, she found herself wishing that this part, when they were alone, could have been more authentic. To sleep in Kae's arms had been a wonderful feeling that she had hoped to return to, but the pace they kept getting their mission underway didn't allow for personal dreams. In the lift, when she had meant to kiss Kae to stop her from revealing anything to the surveillance technology, it had quickly turned real for Rayne. She wasn't ashamed to admit that she had forgotten everything else but how the kisses made her feel. As if that hadn't been enough, Kae's response had indicated that she too was similarly affected. Rayne couldn't remember ever losing track of her surroundings like that, and when the lift reached their destination, she had been entirely taken aback at the sight of their two companions standing there.

Kae closed the door behind them, and then Rayne found herself with her back against it. "I hate what bad timing this is. We're going to stick our heads into a wild animal's cave later, and we should be focusing, or even visualizing, as Beth calls it. Instead, all I can think is how much I want to kiss you again. And that's totally detrimental to our mission. I can't be thinking about you like this when I need to focus on the ways to save my people. And yes, I know, to aid the dissident movement here." Kae leaned in, keeping her lips a fraction of an inch from Rayne's.

"Oh..." Rayne couldn't think of anything to say. All she could do was nod.

"Am I the only one?" Emotions seemed to run fast just under Kae's skin. "Did I misread everything?"

"No. You...you didn't misread." Rayne wanted to share exactly how she felt, but Kae was right. This wasn't the time.

And yet—Kae didn't move. And Rayne didn't push her away.

"Oh, this is dangerous." Muttering, Kae placed her palms against the door, on either side of Rayne's head. "You just have to look at me that way, and I feel—something I shouldn't."

"There's a lot we shouldn't." Her blood must have changed color from red to burning orange, the way it seared through her veins. Rayne didn't move, hardly dared to breathe, because if she did, she would lose control and take that step from where there was no return. She could think of nothing else she wanted more than to unite with Kae in all the ways that mattered. But here they were, on the cusp of the mission that would give Kae's people the help they needed to carry out their plans to leave the tunnels.

"What are you saying? That this thing between us is imaginary, temporary, or just one more thing we need to ignore long enough for it to go away? A hazard that we just have to duck?" Kae stepped close enough for Rayne to feel the heat radiating off her.

"You know me better than that. I don't know how you couldn't. We've been dealt a crash course into each other's personalities and lives. Even when we were still enemies, we fought for the same thing. Saving people. Getting justice. Rescuing loved ones, which entails the entire Subterranean population for you. And it will for me too, even if they most likely want to string me up."

"They won't want that. Not when they know who you truly are, what you'll sacrifice to be their doctor. They'll end up loving you." The tenderness behind the words sounded so impossible, but it was there, in Kae's voice and in her eyes.

"Even so, we can't let our guard down—even toward each other." Rayne hoped Kae would understand. "Before we complete the mission, and a lot can still go wrong, it has to be our only focus."

"You're not wrong, but you're not entirely right either." Kae pressed her lips to Rayne's forehead. "I know I can't ask more of you than this right now. I know that." She murmured the words against Rayne's skin. "But the way I feel will sharpen my senses. Working toward fulfilling the mission so we can carry out the rest of it, saving my people, together, will make me better at what I do."

"That's reassuring…and it's a little heartbreaking." Rayne tried to will the hot tears in the corners of her eyes to return into their ducts, but they insisted on flowing down her cheeks. "I have no experience in going on missions, other than what you've taken me on this past week. I think I have my nerves under control, but I can't swear to it."

Kae took Rayne in her arms and held her tight. "You can't see it, can you? The way you took charge when we went through

Benny's files. I've often been told that I'm a born leader. I think it's true." Lifting her head, Kae looked down at Rayne. "But so are you. If you think back on your role as a physician, has there ever been a doubt who is in charge in the operating room, or on your wards?"

Rayne considered Kae's words. Perhaps she had a point, at least to a degree. "That's my arena. The operating theater. The emergency clinic, and so on. That's what I know. This mission? I'm not sure."

"You think fast on your feet. You have great instincts. Remember, we're doing this as a team. You're not alone." She ran her index finger along Rayne's lower lip. "When we get back with the information Delmonte needs, we'll revisit this subject, if you want to."

Rayne had never been closer to tearing off another person's clothes. She would have given a good part of her soul to be able to kiss Kae like she'd done in the lift. "I do," she said, barely audible.

Kae gave one of her rare, broad smiles. "I'll hold you to that."

Rayne promised herself that she would do the same. No matter what, they would return successful and alive, and once they had, she intended to take Kae Dark to bed as if she truly were her fiancée.

Chapter Twenty-nine

Kaelyn adjusted the narrow harness that secured the strange weapon at the small of her back. The four items with their respective sets of ammunition had arrived as they prepared to deploy Beth and Foster. They quickly logged in with the added chip and listened to Benny summarize the manual for the use and technology of the ShadowPulse and its bolts.

Running on the energy that powered most things in the skyscraper, the ShadowPulse contained tiny dots, barely visible to the naked eye and fastened to a thin magazine. The small square's cold surface was chilled through the strap that hooked it to the back of Kaelyn's trousers. It was a simple weapon, from a Celestial point of view. All you had to do was palm it and watch it turn into the shape of an *s*, which attached to the wristband magnet that came with it. The trigger sat comfortably when you bent your middle finger.

Non-lethal, it sedated the target in less than a second or two, depending on where you aimed. It was not advisable to shoot someone in the face or neck. Though it wouldn't kill the person, they might end up in a coma for a few weeks.

"I feel ridiculous using a weapon smaller than a deck of cards." Foster pulled the ShadowPulse a few times before he was satisfied. "I think I'll hang on to this one. Could be good the next time I have a bout of insomnia."

Foster and Beth left first, and Kaelyn found herself sitting across the dining table from Rayne, merely focusing on her breathing. She had begun doing this after Wes and Tania's mother died, if she had time before going on patrol. When she calmed herself, listened to her own heartbeat and the rush of air in her lungs, her focus sharpened exponentially. Now she could only stare at Rayne, who seemed to have a similar technique. Perhaps she was used to doing something like this before a major surgery.

The thought of Wes and Tania lingered. She wished they had been able to communicate with them, but apart from Benny's tube packages and encrypted messages, radio silence was in effect.

After an hour, Rayne stood, adjusting her clothes while checking her reflection in the full-body mirror by the door. "Nobody can see the mesh. I rolled the hood in under my collar. Do I look okay?" She turned toward Kaelyn.

"You look fine." Kaelyn stood and made Rayne turn away from her. No filaments poked out anywhere in the back. "Check my clothes." She turned slowly before Rayne, who apparently didn't trust her eyes to be enough, but patted Kaelyn down like she was a shroomer under arrest.

"You're fine too." Rayne smiled gently. "Time to go."

Kaelyn pulled Rayne close and kissed the top of her head. "Yeah. Time to go."

❖

They made their way to the beverage stand across the broad aisle in front of the Lindberg Building. Most of the windows were dark, or if a light on were on, it was muted to ten percent. On the level where Amy had her office, the light was on in three windows. Rayne tried to figure out exactly which offices were behind them. She didn't doubt that Amy worked her assistants and paralegals until the small hours, even around the clock, if it suited her.

"Lindberg's bottom floors are all semi-dark," Kae said and sipped the hot tea she had bought as a cover for them sitting at the cart's counter.

Rayne checked the time. "Another ten minutes and we're on." She tried not to tremble. So much depended on their timing. If they missed by so much as a few seconds, they would set off alarms and risk getting caught red-handed, or worse.

Rayne and Kaelyn pretended to be deep in an amusing conversation, occasionally engaging the barista. They both wore makeup in a way they'd never do otherwise. Kaelyn had painted a blue-black wide strip across her face from temple to temple. Her lips were covered by a light, neutral color that was currently popular. Surprised at Kaelyn's fashion-forward appearance, she finally realized Beth had advised Kaelyn in this area. She had perused one of the many fashion and beauty channels on the screen at the hotel, which was a brilliant move.

In contrast, Rayne had painted her lashes and brows white and used a metallic-green lip dye on her mouth. Together with a set of crystals glued in a harlequin pattern on her forehead, and her long hair in a wet, tight ponytail, she was virtually unrecognizable.

"All right. It's time." Kaelyn gave the barista a wave, and they began walking to the office doors.

Glancing back, Rayne noticed that, fortunately, four apparently inebriated men, who took the four stools and started shouting out orders while laughing raucously, were keeping the barista suitably busy. Nobody else seemed to be nearby.

Kaelyn stuck her hand under her collar and pulled the filament hoodie up over her head and face. Rayne did the same, grateful that her hands were as steady as usual. Now they could only hope that Beth and Foster had done their job. The doors wouldn't open automatically like earlier in the day, but they should be able to push them apart enough to slip through.

As it turned out, the doors were lighter than expected, gliding open a little more than a foot, which made it possible to wiggle through. Rayne helped Kaelyn shove them closed.

"What the hell's this?" Kaelyn hissed and pressed her fingers against two green-tinted flat rounds attached to the filament hood. "Were they there before?"

"No. Mine showed up too." Rayne peered through them and saw clearly everything that the muted light masked. "Night vision."

"What?" Glowering at Rayne, Kaelyn nearly went cross-eyed trying to look through her dangling lenses.

"Push them against your eyes. Hurry!" Rayne heard a repetitive sound, a faint hum and even thumps, which came from the other side of the empty desk area where the receptionist normally sat.

Kaelyn gave a muted yelp when the lenses locked into place, and Rayne placed a hand over her mouth. "I think one of the lifts is moving. We need to do the same."

Kaelyn nodded and, walking heel to toe in a rolling fashion, keeping her knees bent, she made her way to the inner first-floor offices. Rayne thought of the blueprints—and grabbed Kaelyn's right arm with both hands when said blueprints became visible in a soft, muted, transparent manner.

"What the fuck?" Kaelyn whispered. "What's wrong?"

"Think of the blueprint."

"I don't have to," Kaelyn said. "I've memorized what we need to—shit!" She stopped so fast, Rayne nearly walked into her. "You damn Celestial show-offs." Kaelyn raised her hand to the lenses, but Rayne stopped her.

"You'll get used to it. Come on. This'll help us find our way easier. Four sets of stairs. Come on!"

They pushed another unlocked door open, and at the same time, the lift pinged, and its door hissed open. Heavy footfalls could be heard through the door, which proved it wasn't Beth or Foster. They would never make that much noise.

Neither did Kaelyn. Like a shadow, she made sure her outline melted into the walls as they soundlessly ran up the stairs.

❖

Rayne was right behind Kae, grateful for her basic fitness that made it possible for her to keep up. At least for now. She wasn't combat-ready when it came to hand-to-hand fighting.

Kae stopped and raised her hand. "We're here. This door leads to the outer lobby, according to the glasses. Ugh. They're making it hard for me to see."

"Hang tight." Rayne drew a finger along the top of her glasses, and the highlighted blueprints appeared. She immediately identified the floor they were on and what to expect behind the door. "They should have a proximity scanner," she whispered to herself.

"If you say so," Kae muttered.

Fiddling with the settings, and nearly giving up as screens came and went so rapidly, Rayne began to feel motion sick. Then the blueprint screen appeared again, and when she slid her fingers against the bottom edge, four dots became visible. Blurry at the edges, two of them were moving away from the door.

"This is our chance." Rayne flipped the images away. "Can you get the door open?"

Unceremoniously, Kae pressed a slim metal-alloy tool into the crack in the center of the door. After a short buzz, followed by a dark-gray smoke that rose toward the ceiling, the doors opened a couple of inches, and it was easy enough to pull them apart. "Remind me we have to repair this breach when we leave if we're want to remain stealthy."

"Will do."

They slipped through the half-open door, and Kae pushed the halves together behind them. The office area utilized only a five-percent illumination, but it was enough for them to not have to use the night-vision setting. Instead, they relied on only the proximity scanner.

"Pull your ShadowPulse," Kae said and held up her own. "Two individuals up ahead. It could be Beth and Foster, but we don't know."

"I wish we could be sure." Reaching back, Rayne allowed her magnetized bracelet to make contact behind her back. As soon as she pulled her hand forward again, the small rectangular device turned into a form-fitted, *s*-shape blade. "Done."

Moving toward the library part of the former commander's office, Rayne kept looking around her, even if the proximity scanner should alert them of anyone approaching. The technology was new to her, even if she seemed to deal with it a bit easier than Kae did.

A scent of citrus became increasingly apparent the closer they got to the library. Clearly a cleaning crew had just passed through. Rayne doubted the dots she saw on the transparent screen were Beth and Foster.

When they reached the reception area just outside Eric Lindberg's office, Kae raised her fist. Rayne stopped instantly. She listened intently and refreshed her scanner. The dots had moved and were now just around the corner, only a few feet away. She tapped Kae's shoulder, gesturing emphatically to the left. Kae nodded and put a finger against her lips. She raised her ShadowPulse and waited until Rayne had done the same. Her heart raced, and she struggled to swallow, her throat dry. This weapon merely incapacitated any person she fired upon. This knowledge was reassuring but also intimidating, for the individual would regain consciousness in half an hour or so.

On Kae's signal, they rounded the corner and found themselves eye to eye with Foster, who stood ready to shoot, with Beth right behind him.

"Fuck!" Kae lowered her weapon toward the floor. "Where are the guards?"

"Believe it or not, it seems it's someone's birthday. They're having pastries one floor down." Beth harnessed her ShadowPulse and then moved to the door behind the reception desk. She ran a blade like Rayne's along the crack, and the door clicked open in only a few moments.

According to their plan, Foster pulled the door almost closed and remained just inside while peering through the narrow opening. Rayne was already on her way to the computer she had scanned during their visit earlier in the day. It sat on standby, and when she ran her hand along the sensor, it came to life. Unlike the one with the AirScreen they'd used at the hotel, this had a glass screen infused with imagizer crystals.

"How long till the transfer's done?" Kae murmured.

"Depends on how deeply they've buried the information. It can be difficult to find, but my initial scan shows me what section it's not in, at least." Rayne ran her fingers over the two satellite screens under the larger one. An image of the library shelves came up next to a list of all the digital folders that contained classified information.

"Of course it would be easier to know what we were looking for if they named their files accordingly." Beth grimaced. "'Strikes Against the Cavers 2501,' for instance."

"Not helping, Beth," Rayne said softly. "But you're still onto something. Can you read the spines of the books kept behind locked doors? Something about them must make them precious or valuable."

"I'll help with that." Kae moved over to the transparent shelves.

Rayne glanced at Foster, but he still looked relatively relaxed. Returning her focus to the computer, she began using the creative search methods she had constructed for herself when she went to medical school. She'd written several algorithms to help her find information for her final thesis about trauma surgery. It would help weed out redundant information.

Fifteen minutes later, Kae and Beth had pulled three books from one of the cabinets. Rayne was down to four main folders when Foster quickly shifted position and raised his ShadowPulse toward the crack in the door. Everyone grew rigid, but Rayne kept sliding her fingers, frantically looking for the information they needed. One by one, she eliminated the files, until suddenly she found one called "Territorial Expansions." Clenching her teeth to stymie an excited gasp, she opened it, but it was further protected. Cursing inwardly, she decided to download it to the computer she'd brought from the hotel. As she pulled it from her pocket, her heart nearly stopped when it got tangled in the mesh, threatening to expose her presence in the library.

Foster waved at them and held up two fingers, then pointed toward the door. Two people approaching. It could be a cleaning crew or two of the in-house guards. Rayne didn't think it was the cleaning crew, as they had obviously already been there this evening. This had to be the guards, unless the staff, or even Lindberg himself, had forgotten something.

Raising his hands as if he were holding a rifle, Foster confirmed Rayne's thoughts. She checked the download time. It was fast, but the folder was huge. The moving, shimmering circle indicated that it would take four and a half minutes longer. Rayne held up five fingers, hoping the others would understand.

Kae rolled her eyes and came to stand by Rayne's side. Their objective was clear. Remain out of sight and undetected until every other method was exhausted.

The minutes went by slower than usual, so Rayne decided to read the names of the remaining folder. "Registers of naturalized minors." Was any air left in the library? There couldn't be, as Rayne's diaphragm worked hard to draw new breath.

"What's wrong?" Kae whispered directly into Rayne's ear.

Rayne pointe to the screen with a trembling finger.

Kae remained still by her side. Then her hand landed firmly on Rayne's shoulder, squeezing her painfully hard. "Get it," she snarled.

"Shh." Beth stared at them with huge eyes.

Rayne's fingers moved as of their own volition, flying across the satellite screens, pulling the last, much-smaller, folder into her personal computer. Just as it gave a faint buzz, Foster took a few steps back and aimed toward the door.

Rayne shoved the computer into her secure pocket again, but this time she more than snagged the mesh. One filament detached, which meant her presence had been compromised. Thanks to the modified chip, she couldn't be identified, but if any surveillance cameras had managed to capture her at the computer, she was screwed. The others would still be invisible, but only while their suits were intact.

Fumbling, Rayne pushed the mesh back in contact with its tiny slot. It took two attempts, but then she could feel it come to life.

"Damn. Did it break?" Kae bent to examine Rayne's mesh.

"It came loose. I fixed it."

"Come on. We need to be out of here fast. Keep close to me." The intensely whispered words made Kae sound furious. Perhaps she was.

They moved until Beth and Kae flanked Foster, Rayne right behind him.

Calm voices reached them. Two men were discussing a sporting event in an amicable way. They seemed to move around the outer office, once laughing raucously, but after a few moments later, they went dead silent.

Foster placed his legs farther apart and steadied his aim. Kae and Beth did the same.

"Something in there registered movement, though for just a second," one of the men outside hissed. "My wrist unit is brand new. It has the upgraded sensor attachment."

"You sure?" The other man didn't sound convinced. "The door's closed—wait a minute. Is it though? That doesn't look right."

"Should I call for backup?" The first man sounded closer, and Rayne could hear the jostling of clothes. "But whoever stirred in there didn't give off an ID tag."

"That's fucking weird. Call for backup. I'm going in."

"Foster gestured with his hand for them all to move forward. Rayne gripped her ShadowPulse, careful not to press the trigger sensor prematurely. She wasn't a bad shot, but she wasn't used to this type of scenario. It hadn't escaped her that the glitch the guards had picked up on was her filament coming loose.

They moved fast, heel to toe, and just as one of the men pushed open one side of the door, Foster pushed his way through, firing at the man's hand that was clutching a much-bigger pulse weapon.

Kae tackled the man out of the way, using her shoulder, and he fell to the floor, seemingly unharmed. Rayne had to violate every part of her oath as a medical professional not to crouch by his side to make sure. She couldn't afford the risk, and neither could all those they might be able to help.

Beth had fired on the second man in the meantime. "Damn it. He had time to alert his colleagues!" She rolled him onto his side, while Kae did the same with the first man. "Not sure if backup is in the building, or if it's otherwise close by. We need to get out of here now. Did we get *anything*?"

"We did," Kae said, and to Rayne, her words sounding surer than she herself felt. Yes. She had downloaded two folders with a multitude of files in the first one, but was it what they came for, or had she failed? Shivering now, she realized her adrenaline levels were spiking.

"Come on. We need to find a way out. Now that they've sounded the alarm, we can rely on them closing all exits instantly. They're going to find the unlocked door where we came in. They're going to find these guys. Cat's out of the bag. All we can hope is that they don't realize what we've downloaded."

Chapter Thirty

Kaelyn took the lead as they made their way down the corridor. Used to ducking through moldy tunnels and not having anything but her gleamer and sharpened senses, she felt out of sorts as she tried to disregard the humming ventilation, the shiny surfaces, lack of smells, and general feeling of being out of her element. Behind her, Rayne, Beth, and Foster followed her seamlessly. How the four of them had managed to become this well-functioning team in such a short time amazed her.

Rayne, especially, moved as if Kaelyn had trained her for years. She had to be a genius mimic, but Rayne was obviously rather accomplished at everything she attempted.

Beth, who had the youngest set of eardrums among them, picked up on the distant voice first. "At least three people," she whispered. "We're running out of options."

They had stopped in an area of the corridor where the closest illumination came from an angle that put them in the shadows. "We could circle them if we cross over to the parallel corridor here and hit the staircase." Foster pointed.

"More of them will be waiting when we get downstairs," Kaelyn said.

"What if we go up instead? They won't be able to scan for us if we're quiet enough." Rayne looked hesitant. "If we run out of options on the stairs, we can shoot those bolts at them."

"They might have full-cover suits on," Kaelyn said slowly. "We'd have to fire at their faces or necks. I doubt they'd have visors."

"If we're doing that, it'll have to be now. They're gaining on us." Foster motioned for them to continue, and Kaelyn checked the corridor briefly before she waved them over to the other side of the office. "Stairs are four doors down to the left. Go!" She took up the rear, hearing the voices behind them now. The guards hadn't spotted them, but no doubt they had found their unconscious colleagues. Taking time to engage her proximity viewer, Kaelyn saw four dots gathering around two still ones.

"They're in the library. So far, no new contacts on this floor. Beth, check the staircase when you're closer."

"I can't get the door open," Beth whispered back. "Doc?"

"On it," Rayne said, then moved up to half-run next to Beth. The two of them moved at the same pace, and Kaelyn could focus on keeping them safe from the rear, along with Foster.

They reached the door leading to the staircase.

"Well?" Kaelyn asked, still not taking her eyes off the corridor behind them.

"Two contacts that appear to be at the door on the ground floor of the office space. Two more at the staircase door," Rayne said. "As far as I can tell, they're just meandering for now."

"That won't last. Judging from the loud voice I just heard, our new friends have found the old ones we gave a nap in the library. We need to move before they spot us."

Foster nodded. "Let's go." He held the door open as Kaelyn hurried through it, securing the landing. When they were all through, she pulled out the device she had used to open the door and managed to lock it from the outside. Hopefully that barrier could delay the guards enough to confuse them.

"Good thinking," Rayne said and peered up between the hand railings that rested on some thin metal alloy. "I think this staircase moves on up past the next ten levels."

"Then start climbing," Beth said with new urgency. "The ones in the library are heading this way. Fast."

Her heart hammering at the idea of the corrupt Celestial authorities catching them, Kaelyn felt her scalp prickle, a sure sign of her rising stress level.

If they intended to be fast enough, they couldn't worry much about being quiet. As long as no guards were in the stairwell, Kaelyn didn't think anyone could hear them, and they needed to reach as high as possible. Sure, it was unlikely that the guards possessed a technology that allowed them to scan for her and the others, but she didn't have enough knowledge about Celestial technology to know whether her fear was valid.

"Come on. Just one more flight of stairs and we'll be able to blend in with the night crowd," Rayne said from above. "I think we're close to where the festivities take place at these hours of the night."

"Remember to disconnect the mesh as soon as we're outside the door." Kaelyn was right behind the others when they reached the door two floors above the one they'd just left. "Hurry. Open it!"

"Give me a second," Beth said and pulled out her device. She pushed it against the crack like Kaelyn had done earlier, but nothing happened. Beth positioned the thin instrument at all angles, moved it up and down along the door, cursing under her breath.

Below them, steps kept moving upward. Kaelyn hoped the guards would assume the invaders they sought had used the door they'd just locked behind them and entered the Lindberg offices that way. If they were thorough and well trained, they would send at least one, maybe more, farther up the stairs.

"Let me try," Rayne said and held out her hand for the tool.

"Go for it." Beath stood and assumed a defensive stance next to Foster and Kae, ready to shoot their bolts at whoever might approach them from below. Kaelyn didn't know anything about the technology behind the ShadowPulse weapon, but one thing was clear. The bolts didn't penetrate clothes. Would backup guards be wearing more protective gear than the ones on-site? Perhaps.

"Kae? Help me." Rayne pressed against the door. She had managed to get her gloved fingers inside the two halves and grimaced in pain. Kaelyn slipped her weapon back in the belt and shoved her fingers in above Rayne's.

"All right. You push, I pull." Kaelyn dragged the reluctant door toward her. "How the hell can it be so hard?"

"The tool isn't truly unlocking it, but I managed to press it between the magnetizing parts. That was enough to pry my fingers in." Rayne looked up. "Foster? We need you."

"On it." Foster put his weapon away as well and took over Rayne's grip. "Let me at it." He placed a foot at the opposite doorframe and dug in his finger deeper than Kaelyn was able to. Slowly he pulled his half of the door open. Two inches. Three.

"Be ready to deploy your weapon, Doc," Beth whispered curtly behind Kaelyn. "Let them worry about the door. I think we're about to have company. Yeah. Like that. Good."

Kaelyn had her weapon out too before Beth finished talking. She moved around the other two women and peered into the void created between the railings. She saw flickering shadows rather than individuals moving in a billowing pattern up the stairs.

"You two, keep going up," a gruff female voice barked below them, making even Kaelyn flinch. "The Lindbergs are a prime target for terrorists."

"On this floor?" a younger, male voice asked.

"Just go. Do not terminate anyone. Capture and incapacitate."

"Affirmative."

Kae saw the shadows begin to move up from two landings below. She directed her weapon in an awkward angle. Depending on the guards' gear, she might have to go for their necks.

"Foster?" she whispered, hoping the guard's loud footfalls would drown out her words.

"A…few…more…moments…" Gasping each word, Foster groaned, and then Kae heard a too-loud squeaking sound.

The guards' steps increased to double-time. They'd heard him.

"You ready?" Beth glanced at Rayne.

"Ready," Rayne answered, sounding entirely calm. She steadied her hands on the railing, her feet planted one foot apart.

Just as Kaelyn glimpsed the top of a white helmet, Foster shifted behind them.

"Come on. Squeeze through now!" he hissed.

"Go ahead. I'll be right behind you," Kaelyn mouthed more than whispered and saw Beth obey immediately. It took Rayne a few moments, but when Kaelyn quickly motioned in Foster's direction with her chin, she harnessed her weapon and moved away.

"Now you," Foster said, the snarl showing how stressed he was. "Come on, Kae."

Kaelyn yanked herself back before the guards below looked up and threw herself through the narrow opening Foster had managed to create. Only when she was on the other side did she realize he would never be able to pass through it. Knowing it was futile, she still pivoted and gripped the edge of the door. "Foster!"

"Just go. Save the documents. I'll be fine. Just go!" Foster let go of the door, and it slid shut with an infuriating little click.

Chapter Thirty-one

As soon as she was through the door, Rayne realized where they had ended up. This skyscraper was indeed the twin of hers, and this was part of the main food court in the commercial area that catered to the extremely wealthy ones. Around them, people ate and talked, even if it was the middle of the night. Nobody had paid any attention to her and Beth as they rushed out the door in the corner, as it was half covered with greenery growing in metal pots.

"Quick. The mesh," Beth said. She tugged at hers with frantic hands.

Rayne switched hers off and removed the hood and glasses. Reaching out for Beth, she pushed Beth's trembling hands away and helped her do the same. Just as they moved aside, Kae pressed her way through the opening that looked smaller again. Then it slid shut, and Kae slumped back against the wall, covering her face.

Thinking only about their safety now, even if her heart had stopped for Foster, Rayne switched off Kae's mesh and pushed the hood and glasses from her face. Making sure nobody was looking their way, she hooked her arms around Beth's and Kae's waists and pulled them toward an empty table about ten yards away from the door. The waiters hadn't cleared it from the last guest, and judging by how busy the food court seemed, it would take a while.

"Pretend we just finished our meal. It'll already be paid for. We can sit a while and see what happens." Rayne wasn't sure how she managed to keep her head and take charge, but someone had to. Beth and Kae seemed to only be able to stare at each other in stricken disbelief.

"I know it's a lot to ask, but you have to pretend to smile and make small talk." Rayne shook their knees under the table. "The door will open any time. You have to seem like you've been sitting here for the last hour, just finishing a midnight meal."

Beth sniffled but then managed to plaster a heartbreaking smile on her face. Kae seemed to look at something that didn't exist. Rayne took her hand. "Just say anything. Count or recite the alphabet. Anything."

"A-B-C-D..." Kae's eyes grew shinier with each letter. "A-B-C..." she repeated, and that's when the door opened with a strange, piercing sound.

The patrons closest to it turned their heads and then looked back at their dinner companions under raised eyebrows when two security guards in full gear showed up.

"Heavenly Creator," Beth whispered, and her rigid smile made the prayer more eerie.

"Where is he?" Rayne murmured. "They should have him in custody, right? But they're here, looking for, well, us. Did he have time to keep going up? Or—"

"Stop it." Kae placed her gloved hand on Rayne's arm and squeezed, the coldness seeping through two layers of fabric. She laughed, but her eyes were nearly black with suppressed emotions. Rayne took her hand in a firm grip and managed a smile of her own.

"Something's going on, girls," Rayne said, louder than before. "Always fun with a little bit excitement in the middle of the night. I wonder who they're chasing. Someone might have cleared out the new line of Miss Golga's latest outfits. I hear they're quite the rage." She cackled in the way she had heard some of her mother's more annoying friends do.

"Now wouldn't that be something to tell everyone back home," Kae said.

The guards moved among the tables but seemed more interested in the people going about their business outside the food court. They were probably certain that anyone getting away would keep running.

"Time to go," Kae said and slowly rose, making sure to straighten her clothes. The mesh looked like an adornment rather than a potent piece of digital stealth equipment. Rayne followed, but Beth seemed rooted in her chair.

"Come on," Kae said, her voice softening.

"No. We can't just leave him," Beth murmured.

"We're not. We're going to discover what happened, and we'll find him." Rayne bent to kiss Beth's cold cheek. "For now, we need to continue with our plan. All right?"

Beth looked over at the closed door with a longing expression, but then she stood and followed Rayne and Kae out of the food court. The guards had apparently made their rounds, as they passed only a few feet away, heading back to the door. They didn't so much as glance at the three of them. Rayne cheered inwardly. For all the guards knew, they were just some rich bitches having had a lavish meal among their peers.

When they left the feasting people behind, it became easier to breathe. Enough people were still out that they could blend into the crowd.

It took them more than an hour to get back to the hotel. Rayne refused to be rushed. She forced Beth and Kae to browse the shop windows and pretend to enjoy themselves. Only when they were in the lift going up to their floor at the hotel and had reached relative safety did the mask fall off all of them.

"Fuck!" Beth grabbed the nearest object, a composite vase holding artificial flowers, and threw it across the room. "Fucking hell!" She stormed into hers and Foster's bedroom but returned right away, now suddenly looking slapped around and defeated.

"He's not there."

"He might be on his way. We'll use this time to work on the data we collected. We owe it to him and the Subterranean people to fulfill our mission." Rayne motioned for the couches. "Go sit, both of you. I'm bringing something to drink."

"Pure alcohol would be preferable," Kae sad as she took a seat. She pushed off her boots.

"I'm sure it would be, but let's start with something that restores our electrolytes." Rayne realized she too was trembling now that they were here. She programmed the beverages and brought them over on a small tray. "Now drink. Doctor's orders."

Beth took the mug without objecting and downed its contents in a few gulps, which made her wince. "Uh. Not my favorite taste. And it's orange."

"Based on carrots," Rayne said automatically. She sat down next to Kae and pulled her computer from her pocket. "Let's not waste time." Feeling somewhat restored by the drink, Rayne started up the small rectangle and placed it on the low table between the couches. As she knelt next to it, she felt a hand on her shoulder. Looking back, she saw Kae leaning against her from where she sat. Kae placed one leg of each side of Rayne, which felt like true support in more ways than one.

The folder containing the two files Rayne had uploaded to her small device opened without a glitch, but the files were still encrypted.

"We need to contact Benny. He's the only one I can think of who can help us see what it says," Rayne said.

Kae squeezed Rayne's shoulders gently. "If we contact him, they'll know we managed to carry out this part of the mission. They'll send someone to retrieve the files, and we won't see them again. They'll use them for their agenda, if it's possible, and our people might see justice done, or they might not. We need to read the information before they get their hands on it."

Rayne studied the files. Kae had made a chilling point. She wanted to fully trust her parents, and she had begun to, almost reluctantly. But she didn't have any faith in Delmonte, as the woman's political ambitions most likely outweighed the lives and safety of masses of people, below *and* aboveground. "I could try to contact my parents without alerting Delmonte and her people. That's our only chance. We have no equipment here. It must be delicately handled by someone who knows what they're doing. They might be able to reach Benny, and we could rendezvous with him on neutral ground."

"Neutral ground. There's no such thing up here. This is all Celestial."

"True, but not all Celestials are under the thumb of the authorities," Rayne said softly and turned around where she sat between Kae's legs. "I know I have nothing to back up my hunch, but Benny seems like a good person. He holds his own power."

"Which is why Delmonte won't want him out of her sight," Beth said. "But maybe he can be persuaded to ditch her and travel here in one of those private fancy vehicles. I'm betting your parents have their own."

"They do." Rayne wanted to groan aloud at herself for not thinking about that possibility. "My father has a license for both indoor and air travel."

Kae cupped Rayne's cheeks and kissed her on the lips. "Call them and make Rocque get Benny over to this building. That park we saw some of yesterday. That's a good spot away from the hotel."

Rayne agreed. The park had lawns and benches that offered the visitors a semblance of privacy. The hotel could be invaded, and they could be taken by surprise if Delmonte or the authorities wanted to spring an attack on them. Delmonte was expecting them to deliver, and she wouldn't be pleased if they circumvented her, using her own man. Rayne couldn't shake the feeling that Delmonte's agenda placed the Subterraneans farthest down on her list of priorities, no matter how she'd sounded when they met her. It was up to the people in this room to make sure the most vulnerable and disenfranchised weren't forgotten.

Using the hotel room's communicator, she called her father's extension. She prayed Madelon wouldn't answer and sighed in relief when Rocque did. She knew he had the confidentiality setting on by default, which made the conversation at least somewhat secure.

"Hello, Father," Rayne said, doing her best to sound cheerful. "I know it's late, but I thought I'd update you on our visit to Amy Lindberg."

"Rayne. No matter. I was up. You know me." Rocque sounded cautious, and she couldn't blame him. Calling him at any time during their mission wasn't part of the plan.

"We've got all the paperwork we needed to get the ball rolling." Rayne hoped her father would catch on. "Unless we run into a snag, things should go smoothly from here."

"That sounds reassuring. Your mother and I are excited about all the plans." Rocque was quiet for a moment. "So, nothing major came up that you think will create a hurdle, legal or otherwise, down the line?"

"We had one setback, but we hope to resolve it. Then there is all the legal text that we need to read thoroughly as soon as possible. Remember our mutual friend that we spent time with yesterday? B? We need him to look it over. Do you think you could bring him over tomorrow? It's rather urgent, as I like to be prepared, as you know." Rayne pinched the skin on the side of her leg, wanting to spell everything out to her father, but she had to be cryptic. If someone was listening in, she couldn't drop names.

"B. Ah, yes. He's such a talented young man. I'm sure he'll translate for you if I ask him." Rocque cleared his throat gently. "And you didn't have time to go over those particular documents today?"

"No time at all. More clients were waiting, and all we could do was leave and hope to address things later. We did get all the legal documents we were there for, though. How about you take the glider and meet us at Ryan's Park tomorrow around oh-nine-hundred hours, if that's good for you? If you can't reach B, or he can't make it, call me half an hour before then, please."

"I'll do that, my darling." Rocque sounded strange, as if choking on something. "I'm sure B and I will arrive on time."

"Thank you." So grateful she could cry, Rayne bid her father good night and ended the call. Kae and Beth were still on the couches, waiting for her to return. "He's going to bring him. I'm starting to think my father has a better connection with Benny than Delmonte has. He seemed so confident when it came to being able to bring only him."

"Sounds good." Kae was pale and sat slumped to the side.

"How about we catch a few hours' sleep?" Rayne asked. "Beth?"

"If I can fall asleep after tonight, then yes. We need to rest." Beth stood but stopped when she faced the door to the room she shared with Foster. "I'll nap on the couch, I think."

"All right. Just wake us if you need…well, anything." Kae stood and gave Beth a quick hug. "Try to get some sleep. Tomorrow we'll find more answers, and we'll look for Foster."

"Damn straight, we will." Beth managed a pale smile.

Suddenly exhausted, Rayne fell onto her side of the bed. The mattress was obviously set to ultra soft and hugged her gently, which made it impossible for her to muster any strength to sit up and get rid of her clothes.

"Let me help you with the boots at least," Kae said and flipped open the fastenings that kept them a perfect fit around Rayne's feet. They seemed to lose cohesion and then disappear. "Roll to the center and let me free the blanket for you."

Moaning, Rayne rolled over and felt a short tug when Kae pulled the blanket free and then spread it over her. Closing her eyes, Rayne was almost asleep when she remembered to set the alarm. "Computer. Wake me up at oh-seven-hundred hours." She slurred her words, but the computer must've been programmed to understand even the most inebriated of hotel guests, as it confirmed the request immediately.

Kae lay down on her side of the bed and pulled another blanket over herself, still dressed. "I would have given anything for a bath, but I probably would've drowned," she said and turned to face Rayne.

"Doubtful. Hotel baths have anti-accident features. You could leave a toddler alone without worrying." Rayne yawned and pressed her forehead into Kae's shoulder.

"Comparing me to a toddler. Great." Kae managed to move her arm underneath Rayne's neck and pull her closer. "I need to hold you," she murmured quietly as she nuzzled Rayne's hair.

"Mm. Good." Rayne drew a deep breath. So much had happened this late evening, it was insane. Ending up in Kae's arms made her feel safe, even if an insistent part of her brain tortured her about Foster's fate.

"Just go to sleep. We'll take care of the rest tomorrow." Kae pressed her lips against Rayne's temple, and that was her last sensation before sleep overtook her.

Chapter Thirty-two

The park had seemed soothing and generally tranquil the day before, but now Kaelyn couldn't relax her sore muscles no matter how she tried. She regarded other people in the park, most of them running or carrying out some strange slow-motion gymnastics on the lawn. Tall trees of different types lined the walkways, and part of them seemed designated for small bikes or boards sporting wheels of different kinds.

"They're not that late," Rayne said, sounding mostly as if she was trying to reassure herself. "Five minutes is nothing. They could have been held up in the hangar facility."

"All right," Kaelyn said. She was so tense, even her jaw wouldn't loosen up.

They had left Beth in the hotel lobby with the hope that Foster would make his way back. They had all packed their small bags and carried them. Neither of them would return to the hotel room. It just didn't feel safe. Beth had two backup locations if she felt unsafe in the lobby. Both were on their pre-selected list, and Foster would know to check these places as well, if it was impossible to remain at the hotel.

"Thank the Creator. There they are." Rayne raised her hand and waved to her father and the thin young man next to him. Benny didn't look his age, and compared to his peers in the tunnels, he resembled a child. "Father!" Rayne rose and kissed Rocque's cheek, and Kaelyn knew she should do the same, as she was posing as the man's future daughter-in-law.

"Kae." Rocque kept his arms around her and Rayne's shoulders for several moments. "Let's sit down. Benny brought some of his ridiculously miniscule pieces of technology. They shouldn't be detectable unless someone comes right up to us."

They sat on one of the double benches that framed a narrow table. Rayne gave her small computer to Benny and didn't take her eyes off him. She was as prepared as Kaelyn to grab him if he tried to run off with it. But as it turned out, he merely nodded at them and attached a few flat objects to its side, then inserted everything into a ten-inch screen. Unlike the bright, see-through variety they had worked on last night, this one was opaque from behind, which meant they all had to move to the same side of the table to be able to see.

"Ah. Standard Celestial authority algorithm protection. Hm. With a bit of a twist, but I know this code, mainly because I wrote the base for it." Benny slid his fingers across mini versions of the satellite screens Rayne had used last night. "And there we go. Just one more...what the hell? What's this?"

They all leaned closer to see better, and Kaelyn felt Rayne's hand on her thigh. The gentle touch made some of her muscles finally relax. She studied the long list of flickering letters on the screen, trying to make them out. Little by little, the fuzzy signs became clear, and she realized they were names. Some were just first names, but some also included surnames. The next column held numbers, and it took Kaelyn a nauseating moment to understand they were the person's age. They went from zero to eighteen. She remembered the name of the folder. This was the list of naturalized minors. From what she could deduce, these were lists of children that the Celestial authorities had taken over time. How far back this list went was anyone's guess, but she would find out. And more than that, she would find out what happened to them.

"Shh. You're growling," Rayne said and pressed closer to Kaelyn. "We'll figure everything out. I promise."

Kaelyn knew it was perhaps a futile promise, but the obvious truth in Rayne's voice did help her calm somewhat.

Benny had opened the other, much larger, file. Now he was running the same decoder on its security setting and smiled triumphantly when they watched a clear part of a high-resolution image. Whereas the other map had been more like a blueprint version, this was as if someone were watching the real place from the sky in real time. Kaelyn wanted to bring up this image on the bigger AirScreen and peruse every part of it, but now she had to settle for watching what Benny had time to show them out in public.

"Here. More long buildings. What are those? Barracks?" Rocque sounded as puzzled as Kaelyn felt. "What could they possibly store in those?"

Nothing moved in the streets other than occasional vehicles and people. If they had access to a bigger screen, which they might if they got back to the secret floor, Kaelyn truly wanted to explore everything, but currently other things mattered just as much. They had to locate Foster, and she wanted to see Wes and Tania.

"Whoever built this town is expanding it." Benny pointed out what looked like construction sites at the north part of the area. "Unless I'm mistaken, that looks like more barrack-like structures." He showed them the parallel, half-ready buildings. A lot of machinery moved about, but Kaelyn couldn't spot any people.

"This gives me an eerie feeling," Rayne said. "We were hoping to find a place for the Subterraneans who want to leave the tunnels to have a new future. This seems like a place being run by someone with a set plan. The expansion seems to happen all along the border, not just the north. Are these truly farmers?"

A memory stirred in the back of Kaelyn's mind. Something flickered there, a picture she'd seen. She couldn't put her finger on what made her associate what they were looking at with something she'd seen a long time ago. She had lived her entire life in the tunnels, yet something about the images on the screen poked and prodded at her brain, trying to surface.

"I have no idea, Rayne," Rocque said slowly. "I'm as uneasy about this as you are, and for good reason. After you came back from the tunnels, Delmonte has been putting things into motion, and she shares very little, even with your mother and me. I'm not saying she knows exactly what's happening at this place." He pointed at the screen. "But I suspect she knows more than she deigns to share with us. I'm not impressed with how quick she was to endanger my only child, taking advantage of your vulnerable situation. Your mother would have come too, but we've promised each other that one of us should always remain at the clinic with the children."

"Wes?" Kaelyn sat up straight. "Is he…?"

"Wes is doing very well. You'll be pleased when you see him. No. We just want to be sure no one gets the less-than-bright idea to use him and Tania as pawns as well. That was the whole reason for adopting them. They truly are innocent in all of this, like so many Celestials and Subterraneans. If we can't protect these kids, how can we hope to work together to create a just society for everyone else?"

Kaelyn slumped into Rayne, who placed a hand against her back, moving it in small circles. "Thank you, Rocque," Kaelyn said quietly. "I know you lead busy lives."

"We do, but we're also privileged enough to create our own schedule."

They studied the images on the small computer for a few more minutes, until Rocque got up and announced that he and Benny had to get back. Benny had made a copy of the deciphered files and placed it on Rayne's computer. They planned to deliver the original little drive to Delmonte and her closest associates when they got back.

"What if you get in trouble for dropping off the map, so to speak?" Rayne asked, looking worriedly at her father.

"As I said. Privileged." Rocque held her tight for a moment and then kissed Kaelyn's cheek. She had yet to get used to all this cheek-kissing business but understood that the man tried to show he appreciated her help.

Benny merely bowed in their direction before he and Rocque began to walk back to wherever they'd stashed their, what was it called, glider?

Rayne's eyes glimmered with tears as she turned to Kaelyn. "I just had the strangest feeling." She drew a trembling breath. "When Father hugged me. I felt like it was for the last time. That's just me being ridiculous, right?"

"Of course you'll see him again. And soon." Kaelyn tried to find words of encouragement. Back home in the tunnels, this fear was an everyday occurrence. But she wanted Rayne's to be unfounded. "We'll get Beth, locate Foster, and then return to the secret floor."

"All right. Sorry." Smiling tensely, Rayne stood and rolled her shoulders. "We better hurry. Beth's bound to be ripping at the seams."

They walked among the clueless Celestials on their return to the hotel, but when they got there, they couldn't find Beth. Kaelyn checked with the desk to see if she had left a message, but she hadn't. Even paler now, Rayne pulled Kaelyn's arm and began heading toward the first of their other two rendezvous locations. At the other side of this floor was a small coffee house, where the people who worked in the office areas apparently indulged in breakfasts or lunches. It was easy to find, and Rayne had picked it for that reason, and because Beth had fallen in love with the small toy section that sold tiny plush animals.

It was a reasonably safe bet that they'd find Beth there, but still Kaelyn's heart began skipping beats as they approached it. Well-dressed people sitting on tall stools around glass tables drank their coffee and chatted about their work and lives in general, she imagined, but no matter how many times she scanned the small shop, she didn't see Beth.

"Where the hell is she?"

"That's what I want to know too," a blissfully familiar voice said behind them.

Kaelyn swiveled and stared at Foster, although it was a version of him she'd never seen before. He was immaculately dressed in a black suit over a red shirt. His shoes were new and shiny as well. He carried a flat bag in his free hand and had wrapped the other around Rayne's shoulders. And if she wasn't losing her mind, it looked like his long, black ponytail had been treated with something glossy and trimmed.

"Foster." Kaelyn shoved her fist into his solar plexus. "Where the hell—"

"Not here." He didn't even flinch. "Where's Beth? I went to the hotel, but all of you were gone and had checked out. I came here, and neither of you was here either. The second location was a bust as well."

"She wasn't at the fashion store either?"

"No. Or she could be there now, of course. I left it half an hour ago and decided to wait here." Foster glanced down at Rayne, who seemed unusually quiet. "You all right, Doc?"

"We're fine." Kaelyn rubbed the back of her head. "When we left Beth to go meet Rocque and Benny in the park, she was waiting for you at the hotel in case you managed to get back."

"I was there an hour ago. She wasn't in the lobby then." Foster's eyes had a familiar, flat expression. He was worried, and so was she.

"We were gone for only about ninety minutes." Rayne wrapped her arms around herself as if she were freezing. "Either she must've felt in danger right away, or…" She swallowed visibly. "Someone took her."

Kaelyn didn't think she'd been filled with rage this fast since Wes and Tania's mother died, due to a lack of resources. At that point, anything the Subterraneans managed to scavenge had been systematically depleted. If the Celestial authorities had apprehended Beth, how the hell would they get her back?

"Let's go to the fashion store." Rayne had obviously harnessed her fear and anger enough to take charge. "While we're on our way there, you have to tell us why you look like a banker on his way to buy half the skyscraper."

Foster smiled bleakly. "As it turned out, the chip in my arm entailed quite a few credits, and I used them at a tailor's shop. When the guards were almost on me in the stairwell, I ran up the last two flights and found an unlocked door. I knew blending in wouldn't be easy, looking the way I do. As it turned out, I was in the back of a men's fashion store. When I emerged from one of the fitting booths, one of the assistants mistook me for a customer." Foster walked between Rayne and Kaelyn, and it was as if telling his story now helped him keep his worry at bay. "She offered her assistance, and I immediately realized that I needed to change my appearance completely. Not so much to alter my complete look, but to look like I belonged and then some."

"I find the result fascinating." Kaelyn did her best to sound calm.

"You have no idea. They stuck me in a strange sort of scanner, dressed in only my briefs. It took them less than an hour to create a suit, cut my hair, and, I know I'll never hear the end of this, give me something called a facial."

Rayne started laughing, and Kaelyn had to join in, despite her onset of nerves. The mental picture of Foster being slathered by some ointments and attacked by strange instruments made her step out of her fear-induced panic.

"I knew it." Foster shrugged.

"Here we are." Rayne stopped outside a fashion store that displayed clothes for young people who enjoyed fluorescent primary colors. Lined with glowing seams and cords, the window dressing looked like what a young person in the tunnels would draw on the walls using straws and brushes. Apparently, the kids in both societies might not be so different after all.

"I'll go in," Rayne said. "Wait here." She held Kaelyn's gaze until she answered.

"We'll be here." Kaelyn could understand that Rayne was afraid to let them out of her sight.

After ten minutes, Rayne came out, and even if she looked disappointed, she had a new spring in her step.

"She's been here," Rayne said and ushered them over to a water dispenser. Grabbing a disposable bottle, she filled it while speaking quietly. "The salespeople remembered Beth and estimated that she was there for about ten minutes, browsing the clothes. They noticed she kept staring out the windows as if looking for someone. At first, I thought she must've been on the lookout for any of us, but when one of the assistants said that Beth seemed concerned and appeared to be hiding behind racks of clothes, I figured she was running from someone else."

"It had to be someone she either recognized or overheard saying something suspicious." Foster clenched his hands into massive fists, making the handle of his fancy bag creak.

"Do you think the Lindgrens are suspicious already?" Rayne asked, leaning against the wall and sipping her water.

"It could be that, and if so, then we're dealing with the Celestial authorities. That's a dangerous scenario." Needing something to do with her hands, Kaelyn took a bottle and filled it. "Or we have someone in the dissident movement that resents the way we do things, or the power the Garcias hold even if they're not officially in charge. This would actually be even worse."

"Because then it would mean that everything and everyone on the secret floor are in danger." Foster ran a hand over his broad face.

"There's one scenario that's an even bigger nightmare," Rayne said and tossed her empty bottle into a small ReCyc unit. "Both scenarios may be at play."

Chapter Thirty-three

Rayne didn't know what else to suggest as their next move. They had scanned the entire floor, as well as the one above and the one below, for Beth but didn't find her. After they gave up their futile attempt of a grid search, Rayne risked contacting her father a second time, but he was in a meeting. Holding her breath, she used a public communicator to reach Madelon. When her mother answered, Rayne had to clear her voice twice.

"Mother. It's me."

"Rayne? What's..." Madelon stopped talking, and Rayne could hear the sound of high heels against high-gloss flooring. "What's wrong?" Madelon said again, this time in a low, urgent voice.

"There's a situation. We're on our way back to our skyscraper, but I'm not sure if we should return to my place. We've lost contact with Beth. We don't know who's behind her disappearance, or if she's still on the run."

"Do not go back to your apartment." Madelon spoke harshly. "Go to the children. Take the same lift as last time. We'll be monitoring. I can't keep talking, as sooner or later they'll find this uncertified communication. Get yourselves there and we'll investigate." Madelon disconnected, and Rayne didn't know how to relay her mother's orders, because that's what they sounded like.

"What did she say? Does she know anything?" Kae kept walking. "Rayne?"

"We need to return to the kids. Right now, without stopping anywhere." Rayne lengthened her stride to keep up with Kae and Foster. Flashbacks from the surface, when she had been blindfolded, and later in the tunnel, when she had forced her cold, aching body to keep up, flickered through her mind. "She sounded rattled. My mother's never rattled. She must have talked to my father or even seen some of the files."

"Did she know anything at all about Beth?" Foster asked.

"No. Or not that she shared over an unsafe communication channel. She disconnected pretty fast." Rayne noticed that they were approaching the checkpoint leading to the glass tunnel bridge ahead of them. "Here we go. Make sure your meshes are off. Just keep walking."

Rayne was the first to go through, and the scanner pinged and showed a green light on the console. The checkpoint master nodded and waved Kae forward. The scanner kept blinking all the different colors, over and over. Rayne pressed her fingertips to her lips, wondering if this was the moment everything ended.

The green light stabilized, and Kae casually strolled through. She gave Rayne a cocky smile, clearly for the benefit of the checkpoint master.

Foster stepped into the booth, and his colors began flickering as well. Rayne knew it had taken Kae only moments to get through, even if it had felt like minutes. Then the lights changed, and only two colors changed back and forth in rapid succession. Yellow and red, over and over, until they looked orange. Rayne moaned and found Foster's gaze. He was not staring at the lights anymore, but at the two of them. His enormous body filled up the booth to a degree it looked as if he was wedged in.

Then the light landed on red.

"No." Kae moaned the single, pained word and began taking a few steps toward him. "Foster…"

He put up a hand toward her, as if warding her off. Rayne held Kae's arm, trying to pull her back. From her vantage point, she could see how his arms seemed to swell when he engaged his muscles in a way she had never witnessed before. Foster was absolutely the largest man she had ever seen, but his steady red light meant security guards were only steps away.

Not sure what made her react the way she did, Rayne returned to the booth, where doors kept Foster trapped. When she entered the narrow walkway leading to the door toward the bridge, she saw, more than heard, the door's locking mechanism click half open.

"Foster. Run! Fight your way out and run!" Rayne saw his face change expression from sorrow and defeat to determination. Not able to kick the door open, as there was no room to take aim, Foster used his upper body strength and shoved at the door multiple times. Eventually, after what indeed felt like long minutes, but was merely seconds, one of the doors hung off its hinges. This was enough for Foster, who pushed through and began running toward them.

"Time to go!" Kae yelled and took off down the bridge. "Arm yourselves!"

Rayne pulled out her ShadowPulse, and it took the shape of her palm. Kae was right. No way would the checkpoints on the other side of the bridge let either of them through.

"No being squeamish now," Kae called out as they ran. "Anyone gets in your way, you aim for the neck or face. They'll live."

Rayne shuddered but knew Kae was right.

When they were twenty meters from the other end of the bridge, it was obvious the officials were prepared for them. Six men and women in uniform stood with raised weapons, ready to shoot. Rayne guessed their ammunition took a bigger bite out of you than the ShadowPulse did.

"Halt." Kae raised her hand. "Let's not make it any easier on them." She took her, by now, familiar stance, and so did Foster. Rayne acted without thinking, raising her weapon as she stood between them.

It was obvious that the guards at the checkpoints weren't prepared for either of them to be armed. If intel about them had been released, it hadn't reached these guards. Kae fired first and hit two of the ones to the left. Foster's bolts found the three on the right, and Rayne took out the remaining one in the middle, but not before he fired against them with his lethal weapon.

Rayne was glad he missed. She had seen what damage those weapons could do. Just look at poor Wes.

"We have to run!" Rayne called out the words and couldn't understand why her legs wouldn't move. "Let's go before their reinforcements arrive."

Only when Foster threw her over his shoulder did she realize someone had been hit by the stream from the guard's weapon after all. She was down.

After this, it was all a blur. The world seemed to consist of jumping, flashing lights and the pain from where Foster's shoulder dug into her hip that was on fire.

"This one," she heard Kae call out. They were standing still until Kae yelled, "Returning fire. Keep her safe!"

"Kae…" Rayne tried to talk.

"She's coming, Doc. Don't you die on me now."

The flickering light was now a steady glow, and in one way Rayne felt as if they were moving, and on the other hand, it seemed they were obviously stationary.

New light poured in, and then it began swaying and flickering again. Foster put her down on a bed, or…no, a gurney. It floated above the ground, and she should have felt safe that she might be seeing a doctor for her injury, but all she could think about was Kae.

"Kae!" She called out her name over and over, but the face that came into view was Madelon's.

"Darling. You're going to be fine. I promise you." Her mother's face was wet from tears, but that couldn't be right. Surely something else was going on.

"Kae!" Was she not with them? What was happening? And why did they press her head down every time she tried to look for Kae?

"I'm here." Kae's voice rolled over her like a soothing aqua shower. "Your mother's right. You'll be fine."

Looking up, Rayne finally saw Kae's face, but to her horror, the woman she cared so much about was drenched with blood.

"No, no, no," Rayne whimpered. "What about you? They have to help you first. If they let me up, I can assist. I can—"

"Shh. It's not mine. It's not my blood." Kae took her hand. "Foster and I are all right. We're on the secret floor. You're on your way to the clinic." Pressing her lips to Rayne's, Kae smiled gently. "I'll be with Wes and Tania while they patch you up, all right? Foster too."

"All right." Rayne relaxed marginally, but then she remembered her mother's wet cheeks. "Mother?"

"I'm here, darling. I'm going with you to the exam room." Madelon stroked Rayne's hair from her face. "You can't keep scaring me like this."

"S-sorry." Shivering now as adrenaline traveled through her system, Rayne kept holding onto her mother's hand. "Father?"

"He's in Delmonte's office on this floor. He's been there for two hours. Ever since he got back together with Benny." Madelon had to let go of Rayne's hand when they entered the exam room, but then she took it again. "He might be in trouble. I don't know."

"Shouldn't you be in there with him?" Rayne asked huskily.

"I should, but there's something more pressing out here." She pressed her lips to Rayne's hand. "My daughter needs me."

This comment broke Rayne, and she began to cry like she hadn't done since she was a little girl. Always the strong and competent one, she had never let herself go like this, but now, while being held by her mother, she wept until the sedation took hold and darkness engulfed her.

Chapter Thirty-four

Kaelyn stood next to Rayne, who refused to remain in the hospital bed, but instead sat in a chair with tall back support and padded armrests. She had no idea how anyone could manage to look elegant and professional when they had just woken up after surgery two hours ago.

"He said he'd join us in a few minutes," Madelon said and tugged at her fingers. "He's never late to anything, and he won't be now." She was clearly trying to convince herself as well as Kaelyn, Rayne, and Foster. The latter had changed into his old clothes that the ReCyc technology had managed to mend and clean until they looked brand new.

"There he is." Madelon stood by the door and peered through the glass. "He has some people with him, and oh, damn…LaSierra Delmonte too. And Benny." Madelon opened the door as the entourage around Delmonte and Rocque approached. Kaelyn studied the group and didn't know what to think when Madelon suddenly covered her mouth with her hand. "Sweet heavens."

"What's wrong, Mother?" Rayne made a motion to get up, though Foster placed one of his gigantic hands on her shoulder.

"Nothing, darling. It's just…I see Beth." Madelon returned to Rayne and sat down on one of her armrests. "Somehow Beth's here."

Kaelyn rushed toward the door, but the group of people was already there. Beth pushed Delmonte unceremoniously aside and threw her arms around Kaelyn's neck. She squeezed hard and then did the same to Foster. It seemed to be a day for tears, as he also wiped at his eyes.

"What happened?" Rayne said when Beth gently hugged her and kissed her cheek.

"We'll tell you, Doctor Garcia," Delmonte said regally, "but all in good time." She closed the door after Benny stepped through. The other people of her entourage were guards, and they placed themselves along the glass, effectively functioning as a privacy screen as well.

Delmonte took the last remaining seat and motioned for Rocque to talk.

"Ms. Delmonte, Benny, and I have scrutinized the three-dimensional map and video image you retrieved from the Lindberg office. We spent the better part of two hours going over as much of it as possible. I'll put together a report for the members of our own council, but it will be a difficult path to undertake, no matter how we choose to do it."

Benny drummed his fingers against one of the metal carts and then looked over at Beth. "One of our agents saw how this woman was being followed and later almost abducted. He works on the floor where your hotel is located, and it was his job to make sure we knew if someone was on the prowl for you." He shrugged. "When Mr. Garcia and I came for the files, we didn't notice anything untoward, but our agent, who was back keeping an eye on Beth, saw several teams of different constellations circle the hotel. Clearly, Beth is also aware of her surroundings, and soon it became a matter of Beth running from some people, while others tried to neutralize them to save her. Eventually, they did. They took her on a detour to lose the individuals in question and returned her directly to Ms. Delmonte's office."

"I tried calling you." Rayne looked at her father.

"I was already in the meeting with Ms. Delmonte and didn't know what was going on until your mother managed to get word to me. By then Beth was safely in there with us."

"This is really touching, but we're not sure what this operation has cost us. If there's the slightest risk we might be compromised on a higher level, then we're all in danger." Delmonte's voice was harsh and her gray eyes entirely opaque. "We could draw some quite horrifying conclusions regarding the map. Not only are Lindberg's and two of his predecessors' signatures on it, but also the current commander in chief's. This runs far back and appears fully anchored into the future."

"What are you talking about…ma'am?" Foster asked, folding his arms over his chest.

"You must've realized that this town is not like any of the small farmland villages we anticipated seeing." Delmonte suddenly sounded tired. "And the fact that it is designated Inner Border—Division Three, suggests that there are at least two more places like this."

Kaelyn had been quiet for a while, trying to take in all the information. She had kept looking at Beth to see if she already knew what Delmonte was referring to, but Beth appeared tired and tense, much like the rest of them. Then Kaelyn's memory seemed to fire up. The old books she had read when talking about Earth history with Tania appeared in her mind, accompanied by old photos, horrible pictures, of other atrocities, some even worse than those committed against her people. "Work camps," Kaelyn said. "Those aren't towns or farmland villages. Not even close. No matter what they're doing down there, those are work camps."

The stunned silence around her showed Kaelyn that Delmonte, Rocque, Benny, and Beth had reached the same conclusion, but her deduction, coming from another source, had still managed to shock them.

"Exactly," Delmonte said darkly. "And that means, no matter what level of compromise might have occurred last night, and only hours ago—"

A loud, blaring sound interrupted Delmonte, who bounced up from her chair. A piercing, pulsating sound was interspersed with a metallic voice stating, "Emergency evacuation in effect! Emergency evacuation in effect! Use SkyBirds or escape tubes."

"There's the answer," Delmonte barked. "Everyone to their designated SkyBirds."

Kae had gotten up with everyone else but now looked over at Rayne, who struggled to stand. "Help her." Foster moved at the same time as she uttered the words. "We have to get the kids." Kae looked at the Garcias and saw that Rocque was already out the door, followed by Beth.

"We'll rendezvous at our Bird," Madelon called out after them. Rocque merely waved over his head.

"Now is a good time to tell me what's going on," Kaelyn said to Benny as they hurried out and were immediately caught up in the throngs of dissidents. She ran behind Foster, who appeared an effective icebreaker as he parted the crowd in front of them.

"We've reached critical mass when it comes to being compromised. It can't just be your mission—it must be more than that. We have to get to our escape vehicles that are kept in the floor beneath us. Once we deploy them, there's no turning back. The entire floor will be uninhabitable. We have thirty minutes to get everyone off it, and those who don't want to leave the skyscraper have the option to try the tubes. They will emerge in hidden locations a few floors under us. It's a gamble, but some have families or other reasons for wanting to stay." Benny gasped for breath as he ran with his computer pressed to his chest.

"I don't know how to operate such a vessel." Kaelyn didn't take her eyes off Foster but still made sure that Madelon wasn't lost in the shuffle. She was running next to Delmonte, who was surrounded by her guards. Kaelyn wanted to look for Tania and Wes behind her, but it would have been a disastrous move among the many people rushing around her.

"You don't have to. We all belong to Delmonte's detail—well, you, Foster, and Beth, sort of by default—and our SkyBirds will follow hers."

Delmonte's entourage took a sharp left toward a large area where people were raising floorboards up toward the ceiling, row after row, facing a corresponding window.

"This first one is Ms. Delmonte's." Benny halted, and soon they were within the guarded circle consisting of Delmonte's people.

Kaelyn regarded the long line of sleek vessels, resembling large beads on a necklace, disappearing into the floor. As soon as one floorboard was raised, the others followed automatically, until the entire row of little ships was revealed.

"Ten of them in each row. Each able to hold eight people. Delmonte and her people will be in the first one, and then the rest of us. All in all, there's room for 3,000 people and emergency equipment on 450 Birds. Good thing that the Garcias have their own, with room to spare." Benny waved at Kaelyn and walked over to the third in the row of Birds.

A loud bang set the vessels in motion. Kaelyn had just turned around to look for Beth and the children but quickly snapped her head back and placed protective hands around Rayne, who lay in Foster's arms, her eyes closed. The SkyBirds rose from their hiding place on narrow rails until they clicked into place.

"Rayne?" Kaelyn pressed her lips to Rayne's temple. "Are you all right?"

"Just so tired. Had surgery, remember?" Rayne opened her eyes. "Children?"

"Not here yet, but they're on their way." Watching the people fill the areas next to the rows of SkyBirds, with still no sign of Rocque, Beth, or the kids, made her stomach burn.

"If we're riding in this one, we should get Rayne inside." Foster stepped closer to the hatch on the side of it. It slid open, and he stepped inside, nearly doubled over to fit through it.

"I'll help you." Madelon had managed to tear herself away from Delmonte and now ducked into the vessel behind Foster and Rayne. "Put her over here. This seat should recline more than the other ones."

Kaelyn left them to get Rayne comfortable. She couldn't see over all the people around her and looked for something to stand on. When she couldn't find anything, she felt with her foot on the side of the SkyBird. It appeared rock hard, and she carefully climbed on top of it and stood up. Now she could see how many were flocking around the small ships, and it seemed like everyone was taking the repetitive alarm klaxons seriously.

Suddenly she noticed movement to the far right of the crowd. Next, she heard Rocque bellow, "Make way! Make way!" He was pulling the first of a long line of injured or sick patients on hover gurneys from the clinic. Beth was pushing yet another one, and Tania was right next to her.

Jumping off the SkyBird, Kaelyn called into it. "I see them. They need help."

"On my way." Foster climbed out, and they began ushering people out of the way, creating free passage for the gurneys from their end. When Kaelyn finally stood by Wes's gurney, the boy looked up at her with huge eyes and promptly burst into tears. "Kae!"

"I'm here, kid. We're all leaving together." She pulled Tania into a quick hug and then helped pull the gurney toward the Garcias' SkyBird.

"Shit." Tania's eyes grew wide at the sight of the small ships, and Wes forgot about his tears.

"We don't have long. Another ten minutes and they start the countdown. If the hatch isn't locked by then, we'll have missed our chance." Rocque began unstrapping Wes, with Tania's help.

"The other patients?" Kaelyn felt herself go cold.

"Look." Rocque nodded farther up the rows of SkyBirds. There, the gurneys were pulled along and then pushed into slots and lifted. The process went so fast, it was impossible to watch it without becoming dizzy. "Damn."

They made sure Wes was secure in a reclining seat next to Rayne, who took his hand.

"All seats are filled here," Rocque said to someone outside. "Please try the next one. Everyone should fit. Most of the birds have redundant seats."

"Thank you, sir," a woman said, and then Rocque climbed inside and secured the hatch.

Kaelyn had chosen the seat just in front of Rayne, and Tania the one in front of Wes. Madelon sat in front with Rocque, and behind them Foster and Beth.

The countdown began for the hatches to be closed. No one but those sitting up front could look outside, but Kaelyn didn't want to know if any last-minute stragglers had been left.

Underneath them, everything began to hum, and now it was impossible not to try to see what was going on. Kaelyn looked at the faces around her. Old combat buddies, the kids, the woman she had come to care for far too deeply, and her parents. They were so important to her, and she hoped they all survived this insanity. Throwing themselves out the window from just above the 924th floor, what could go wrong?

"Blasting off will commence in five seconds. Four. Three. Two. One."

The large window before them imploded rather than exploded outwardly. The sound the shards made against the fuselage was unnerving, and Kaelyn reached behind her and gripped Rayne's right foot. The warmth against her hand anchored her, and that was all she had time to think before Delmonte's SkyBird shot through the window frame and pulled them along. The Garcias' escape vessel hurled through the opening and fell. Kaelyn squeezed her eyes closed, thinking she might throw up, but then the hum that had been barely audible rose to a whining pitch, and the SkyBird raised its nose and flew in a semicircle as it rounded the skyscraper.

Certain there was no room for any vessels in the alleys between the enormous structures, she remembered that the buildings tapered off as they ascended. As she sat up and dared to truly look forward out at the sky, she could tell they were climbing. She didn't know where they were going, just that they were all alive right now and, with luck, would end up somewhere they could work to find everyone a future.

Epilogue

Everything was pitch black. It was impossible to make out anything around her, and she hurt all over. The harness had dug into her shoulders and hips, and even if she tried to unbuckle it, she couldn't move her fingers on her left hand, which made it impossible.

"Uh." A male voice in front of her moaned. Who was it?

"Give me your name," she managed to say, hoping he wouldn't ask for hers, as that information seemed to simmer somewhere in the very back of her mind.

"Carson." It seemed to be the only thing the man could muster.

"Carson. Did we crash?" Why was she out flying in the middle of the night?

"S-sorry. Don't know."

Perhaps she wasn't the only one who struggled to grasp the situation.

A clonking sound made her flinch and then moan as her hand and arm erupted in pain. Bright light flooded the vessel she was in, and she realized it had to be one of the SkyBirds. She had been evacuated.

"Hey, are you okay?" a female voice said. A blond woman climbed inside and pressed her fingertips against her throat. "Heart racing. At least it's working. Let me see if I can get you out of here, and then we can help your guys."

"Where am I? Who are you? Damn it, who am *I*?" She needed the answers, or she would go crazy.

"I'm not sure I'm the right person to ask about our location, but my name's Beth. You are LaSierra Delmonte and, from this moment on, I suppose, the leader of the free world."

About the Author

Gun Brooke, author of thirty novels, writes her stories surrounded by a loving family and two affectionate dogs. When she isn't writing her novels, she works on her art, and crafts, whenever possible—certain that practice pays off. She loves being creative, whether using conventional materials or digital art software.

Web site:http://www.gbrooke-fiction.com

Books Available from Bold Strokes Books

Can't Buy Me Love by Georgia Beers. London and Kayla are perfect for one another, but if London reveals she's in a fake relationship with Kayla's ex, she risks not only the opportunity of her career, but Kayla's trust as well. (978-1-63679-665-9)

Chance Encounter by Renee Roman. Little did Sky Roberts know when she bought the raffle ticket for charity that she would also be taking a chance on love with the egotistical Drew Mitchell. (978-1-63679-619-2)

Comes in Waves by Ana Hartnett. For Tanya Brees, love in small-town Coral Bay comes in waves, but can she make it stay for good this time? (978-1-63679-597-3)

Dancing With Dahlia by Julia Underwood. How is Piper Fernley supposed to survive six weeks with the most controlling, uptight boss on earth? Because sometimes when you stop looking, your heart finds exactly what it needs. (978-1-63679-663-5)

Skyscraper by Gun Brooke. Attempting to save the life of an injured boy brings Rayne and Kaelyn together. As they strive for justice against corrupt Celestial authorities, they're unable to foresee how intertwined their fates will become. (978-1-63679-657-4)

The Curse by Alexandra Riley. Can Diana Dillon and her daughter, Ryder, survive the cursed farm with the help of Deputy Mel Defoe? Or will the land choose them to be to the next victims? (978-1-63679-611-6)

The Heart Wants by Krystina Rivers. Fifteen years after they first meet, Army Major Reagan Jennings realizes she has one last chance to win the heart of the woman she's always loved. If only she can make Sydney see she's worth risking everything for. (978-1-63679-595-9)

Untethered by Shelley Thrasher. Helen Rogers, in her eighties, meets much-younger Grace on a lengthy cruise to Bali, and their intense relationship yields surprising insights and unexpected growth. (978-1-63679-636-9)

You Can't Go Home Again by Jeanette Bears. After their military career ends abruptly, Raegan Holcolm is forced back to their hometown to confront their past and discover where the road to recovery will lead them, or if it already led them home. (978-1-636790644-4)

A Wolf in Stone by Jane Fletcher. Though Cassilania is an experienced player in the dirty, dangerous game of imperial Kavillian politics, even she is caught out when a murderer raises the stakes. (978-1-63679-640-6)

New Horizons by Shia Woods. When Quinn Collins meets Alex Anders, Horizon Theater's enigmatic managing director, a passionate connection ignites, but amidst the complex backdrop of theater politics, their budding romance faces a formidable challenge. (978-1-63679-683-3)

One Last Summer by Kristin Keppler. Emerson Fields didn't think anything could keep her from her dream of interning at Bardot Design Studio in Paris, until an unexpected choice at a North Carolina beach has her questioning what it is she really wants. (978-1-63679-638-3)

StreamLine by Lauren Melissa Ellzey. When Lune crosses paths with the legendary girl gamer Nocht, she may have found the key that will boost her to the upper echelon of streamers and unravel all Lune thought she knew about gaming, friendship, and love. (978-1-63679-655-0)

The Devil You Know by Ali Vali. As threats come at the Casey family from both the feds and enemies set to destroy them, Cain Casey does whatever is necessary with Emma at her side to bury every single one. (978-1-63679-471-6)

The Meaning of Liberty by Sage Donnell. When TJ and Bailey get caught in the political crossfire of the ultraconservative Crusade of the Redeemer Church, escape is the only plan. On the run and fighting for their lives is not the time to be falling for each other. (978-1-63679-624-6)

Undercurrent by Patricia Evans. Can Tala and Wilder catch a serial killer in Salem before another body washes up on the shore? (978-1-636790669-7)

And Then There Was One by Michele Castleman. Plagued by strange memories and drowning in the guilt she tried to leave behind, Lyla Smith escapes her small Ohio town to work as a nanny and becomes trapped with an unknown killer. (978-1-63679-688-8)

Digging for Destiny by Jenna Jarvis. The war between nations forces Litz to make a choice. Her country, career, and family, or the chance of making a better world with the woman she can't forget. (978-1-63679-575-1)

Hot Hires by Nan Campbell, Alaina Erdell, Jesse J. Thoma. In these three romance novellas, when business turns to pleasure, romance ignites. (978-1-63679-651-2)

McCall by Patricia Evans. Sam and Sara found love on the water, but can they build a future amid the ghosts of the past that surround them on dry land? (978-1-63679-769-4)

One and Done by Fredrick Smith. One day can lead to a night of passion…and possibly a chance at love. (978-1-63679-564-5)

Promises to Protect by Jo Hemmingwood. Park ranger Maxine Ward's commitment to protect Tree City is put to the test when social worker Skylar Austen takes a special interest in the commune and in Max. (978-1-63679-626-0)

Sacred Ground by Missouri Vaun. Jordan Price, a conflicted demon hunter, falls for Grace Jameson who has no idea she's been bitten by a vampire. (978-1-63679-485-3)

The Land of Death and Devil's Club by Bailey Bridgewater. Special Liaison to the FBI Louisa Linebach may have defied all odds by identifying the bodies of three missing men in the Kenai Peninsula, but she won't be satisfied until the man she's sure is responsible for their murders is behind bars. (978-1-63679-659-8)

When You Smile by Melissa Brayden. Taryn Ross never thought the babysitter she once crushed on would show up as a grad student at the same university she attends. (978-1-63679-671-0)

A Heart Divided by Angie Williams. Emma is the most beautiful woman Jackson has ever seen, but being a veteran of the Confederate army that killed her husband isn't the only thing keeping them apart. (978-1-63679-537-9)

Adrift by Sam Ledel. Two women whose lives are anchored by guilt and obligation find romance amidst the tumultuous Prohibition movement in 1920s California. (978-1-63679-577-5)

Cabin Fever by Tagan Shepard. The longer Morgan and Shelby are stranded together, the more their feelings grow, but is it real, or just cabin fever? (978-1-63679-632-1)

Clean Kill by Anne Laughlin. When someone starts killing people she knows in the recovery world, former detective Nicky Sullivan must race to stop the killer and keep herself from being arrested for the crimes. (978-1-63679-634-5)

Only a Bridesmaid by Haley Donnell. A fake bridesmaid, a socially anxious bride, and an unexpected love—what could go wrong? (978-1-63679-642-0)

Primal Hunt by L.L. Raand. Anya, a young wolf warrior, finds herself paired with Rafe, one of the most powerful Vampires in the Americas, in an erotic union of blood and sex. (978-1-63679-561-4)

Puzzles Can Be Deadly by David S. Pederson. Skip loves a good puzzle. Little does he know that a simple phone call will lead him and his boyfriend Henry to the deadliest puzzle he's ever encountered. (978-1-63679-615-4)

Snake Charming by Genevieve McCluer. Playgirl vampire Freddie is on the run and a chance encounter with lamia Phoebe makes them both realize that they may have found the love they'd given up on. (978-1-63679-628-4)

Spirits and Sirens by Kelly and Tana Fireside. When rumored ghost whisperer Elena Murphy and very skeptical assistant fire chief Allison Jones have to work together to solve a 70-year-old mystery, sparks fly—will it be enough to melt the ice between them and let love ignite? (978-1-63679-607-9)

BOLDSTROKESBOOKS.COM

Looking for your next great read?

Visit BOLDSTROKESBOOKS.COM
to browse our entire catalog of paperbacks, ebooks,
and audiobooks.

Want the first word on what's new?
Visit our website for event info,
author interviews, and blogs.

Subscribe to our free newsletter for sneak peeks,
new releases, plus first notice of promos
and daily bargains.

SIGN UP AT
BOLDSTROKESBOOKS.COM/signup

Bold Strokes Books
Quality and Diversity in LGBTQ Literature

Bold Strokes Books is an award-winning publisher committed to quality and diversity in LGBTQ fiction.

Milton Keynes UK
Ingram Content Group UK Ltd.
UKHW031113080824
446563UK00001B/100

9 781636 796574